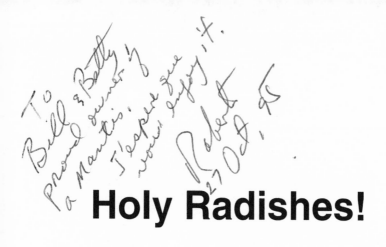

To Bill & Betty,
Proud owners of
a Mantis. I hope you
would enjoy it.
Robert
27 Oct. 95

Holy Radishes!

Roberto G. Fernández

Arte Público Press
Houston, Texas
1995

This volume is made possible through grants from the National Endowment for the Arts (a federal agency) and the Andrew W. Mellon Foundation. The writing of this book was made possible through a fellowship from the Florida Arts Council and a sabbatical from the Florida State University.

Acknowledgments:

I wish to express my gratitude to James Rhea and Silvia Novo-Pena, la décima musa, who read this book to make it look right. Thanks to Hinsel Scott III for his help in choosing the title.

"Nellie" appeared in *The Apalachee Quarterly* and *Iguana Dreams*; "Radishes" in the *Michigan Quarterly*; "Milkmaid" in *Manoa*; "Dans L'Apres Midi" in *Latin American Literature and Arts*; "Et tu, Delfina" in *Trafika*; "Silence" and "The Last Supper" in *The Americas Review*.

Recovering the past, creating the future

Arte Público Press
University of Houston
Houston, Texas 77204-2090

Cover illustration and design by Gladys Ramirez
Photo: Phil Pollock

Fernández, Roberto G.
    Holy radishes / by Roberto Fernández.
       p.   cm.
    ISBN 1-55885-075-9 (clothbound). —
    ISBN 1-55885-076-7 (paper)
    1. Cuban Americans—Florida—Fiction. I. Title.
PS3556.E7243H64   1995
813'.54—dc20   95-9767
                                  CIP

For Elena Reyes Uceira,
source of so many emotions.

Holy Radishes!

Nellie

Nellie was glad she hadn't burned herself this time. She unplugged the sizzling iron, put the starch underneath the kitchen sink, and began folding the freshly ironed clothes. She began placing the garments in two worn suitcases which rested open-mouthed at the foot of the bed. The luggage was spotted with faded stickers, echoes of long-ago sojourns—a faceless bullfighter battling half a bull, a Tower of Pisa which no longer leaned, and a Beefeater beheaded by time. First she packed the underwear, then her blouses, followed by skirts, shirts and slacks. On top, she carefully placed her favorite and only remaining evening gown, a royal-blue dress with brocades, pearls, and sequins. Though the dress had not felt the warmth of her flesh or heard the music and laughter of a ballroom for some time, Nellie brought it out to look at it for a moment when she ironed each day. She covered the clothes with moth balls, impregnating the house with the stench of time. Then, with a suddenness born out of her small hope, she slammed the suitcase shut and with a series of vigorous kicks made the luggage disappear underneath the bed.

She licked her index finger and flicked the iron, making sure it could be stored inside the closet without risking a fire. Delfina had warned her when she was a child to be careful of fire. At the time, Delfina had been trying to light a blaze under a kettle of water to boil Nellie's father's soiled shirts while Nellie, contentedly sucking on a mango, and always the observant child, watched her.

"See the fire, little girl?" Delfina asked. "In your path there is something charred by flames. Beware of anything that burns!"

Though the two years her family had spent in the bungalow seemed like twenty, Nellie could not bring herself to unpack their bags. Her daily routine of ironing and repacking helped to keep her faith from being snuffed out altogether. She hoped that this was not lasting, not permanent.

It was hot for January. Nellie took the cardboard fan she had found on her doorstep and escaped to the porch, where it was cooler. The front of the fan depicted a Scandinavian Christ resting by a riverbank shaded by tall beech trees, and holding a black sheep in his lap. On the back, a holy message was written in incipient Spanish: *PESCADOR ARRE PIENTA DIOS ENOHADO CON USTED VEN Y TIEMPLO PRIMERO VIVO LLAMAR REVEREND Y AMIGO AUGUSTUS B. FENDER. OLE! SE HABLA PEQUENO ESPANOL.* (FISHERMAN, REPENT! GOD MAD WITH YOU. COME AND I SCREW FIRST LIVING. CALL REVEREND AND FRIEND AUGUSTUS B. FENDER. OLE! A SMALL SPANISH IS SPOKEN.) Nellie wiped the rocking chair with a rag that hung from her left pocket and smelled of garlic, then sat down. She started to fan and rock herself in perfect synchrony. Her gaze was lost in the cane fields that surrounded the house and stretched beyond the horizon. Her eyes became cloudy remembering Rigoletto, attiréd in a light red sweater. His memory grew smaller and smaller until it became a tiny glowing speck on the edge of her mind.

Nellie remained on the porch with her eyes fixed on the fields until she heard the clanking and whirring of old bicycles approaching. School was out for the day and her children, happy to be free, were coming home. She hurried to supervise the cola-fueling operation and lament her fate to the children. After Nelson Jr. and María-Chiara had left, burping with satisfaction, she turned on the television, an old RCA whose picture faded in and out every five minutes, and began watching *Donna Reed*, her favorite show. The set did its best to produce a vision of family life, but the fuzzy picture soon became a downpour of tiny gray dots. It forced Nellie to rely on her ears to follow the plot. As best as she could tell, Donna and Dr. Stone were planning a trip to Europe. Donna wanted to go to Paris and her husband to London. In the last scenes the couple was in the midst of an argument. They suddenly hushed because Jeff and Mary had come home from school. Donna dried her tears with her apron and Dr. Alex Stone welcomed the kids with a big smile.

The theme music signaled that the show was over for today and that her husband, Nelson, would arrive in an hour. He worked as a stocker for Rosser and Dunlap Trucks and Rigs. It was the first real job he had found after arriving from Xawa; he held on to it, happily stagnant despite having once been the head of his father's vast business empire. For Nelson, his new environment was a labyrinth from which he didn't want to escape. He was frozen like a pre-Cambrian bug in a drop of amber.

Nellie, wearing her flaps, padded into the kitchen to prepare dinner. She walked in as if facing a firing squad. A note from Nelson was held in place on the refrigerator door by a magnet in the shape of an angry green worm holding an M-19 on its right shoulder and a tricolor flag with a lone star in its left. The note suggested: "After placing the pots, pans, and skillets on the burners, make sure to turn the burners on." Nellie usually forgot that final detail. She opened her cookbook and began reading the instructions:

SAUTEES—Sautee a la Criolla: cup olive oil, one diced pimento, one chopped bell pepper, one teaspoon sugar, one teaspoon oregano, one-half teaspoon cumin, one chicken-broth cube, 1½ cup thinly chopped onions, 5 garlic cloves, one can tomato sauce, 1½ teaspoon salt and one teaspoon vinegar. Nellie was overwhelmed by so much chopping, so many teaspoons, so much slicing. She closed her eyes and wished her fairy godmother would come to her rescue and turn the bell pepper into Delfina, the onion into Tomasa, and the garlic clove into Agripina. She closed her eyes again, but this time much tighter. Her godmother was obviously vacationing somewhere. Resigning herself to her fate, she opened the kitchen closet and took out a can of Kirby's Black Beans and opened it. She poured the contents of the can in the pot and turned the burner on low heat. She rinsed her hands, and her eyes examined the large scar which marred her pale forearm, reminding her of the battles she had fought with the house. Nellie rubbed the iron-burned flesh, thinking that the imitation tortoise shell bracelet which she had seen at W. T. Grant might camouflage the burn. She dried her hands with the garlicky rag and went to her room.

She pulled the suitcase with the bullfighter sticker from under the bed and dug around the clothes searching for her photo album. Nellie was reconstructing her old life with pictures Delfina sent in exchange for Gillette razor blades and flints which she could sell on the black market. Nellie enclosed them in each letter, padded with toilet paper to avoid the letter censor back home. The photos came from the old albums Delfina has found under a pile of trash by the curb a few days after Don Andrés' mansion was confiscated. Seated in front of her dresser, Nellie began combing her hair 100 times, a ritual she followed ever since she battled tinea when she was almost ten. With her free hand she flipped through her album.

On the first page was her favorite picture: "1940 Yacht Club Dance—The Odalisques' Conga." The note on the back of the photo read, "I also danced in the Ladies' Tennis club, the Air Club, and the Doctors' Club." Then "Xawa-on-Deep River." And in much fresher ink: "To remember is to live again, but I feel like dying when I remember. Belle Glade, Florida, 1963. (Still in exile)." The Odalisques' Conga displayed eight delightful damsels, society's best. They all wore red transparent linen veils, velvet cassocks embroidered with silver thread and gold coins of different sizes to cover their convulsing navels. In the midst of the make-believe harem sat a sultan called Mario. He was a tall, dark gentleman with hairy arms which brought about nightmares, insomnia, and premature ovulations in the unsuspecting harem. Nellie never realized that her attraction to *The Donna Reed Show* had its basis in the similar secondary characteristics shared by the sultan and Carl Betz. But, why tell her? It would only cause her anxiety to know that she was unfaithful to Nelson every Monday through Friday from two to three in the afternoon.

The days of the Big Band era were rolling. It was the time of American actors, of smoking Lucky Strikes and dreaming yourself blonde, pale, and freckle-faced. From left to right, forming a bouquet enveloping Mario: Pituca, María Rosa, Loly, Cuquín, Helen, Ignacia, and Nellie, though, among themselves, they went by Joan, Ginger, Hedy, Betty, Debbie, Lana, and Irene.

The aroma of a nearby Kentucky Fried Chicken made Nellie recall Lana's premature death in '42. It was attributed to the chicken with which she slept. His name was Curly, and he was a gift from one of Irene's father's young farmhands who had fallen in love with Lana. The biped arrived in a shoe box with a note which said: "For Miss Ignacia. Now, you'll never be lonely. Truly, Juan Benson." This was the only way the poor farmhand could have gotten close to his beloved. In a few months Curly grew from a fuzzy yellow ball into a robust specimen with shiny feathers, fastly developing spurs, and firm comb. The bird accompanied Lana to every rehearsal of the conga ensemble and perched in the first seat of the second row patiently awaiting for the odalisques to finish their act. At night, Lana would dress the rooster in flannel pajamas and cover its comb with a diminutive cotton hat. But Curly was very demanding. Many were the parties Lana couldn't attend because of the unyielding biped. It loved to go to bed early— seven at the latest—and wouldn't sleep unless Lana was there. Irene (Nellie) secretly envied Lana and wished Curly could be hers. She became so sad that Don Andrés gave her a little pet of her own. Irene named it Rigoletto. One night after Curly was sound asleep, Lana left silently for a New Year's Eve party at the Yacht Club. When she returned the following year, Curly was nowhere to be found. The rooster had flown through an open bedroom window to the chicken coop where he joined all sorts of low-life hens. Lana found the bird three days later almost featherless and with a bleeding comb damaged by violent pecking. In its frenzy Curly had made amorous advances toward a peahen without realizing that her peacock was perched directly above.

It was that night that Curly was contaminated with lice carrying a deadly microbe. A week later, Lana woke up with a bleeding scalp from her nocturnal scratching. Irene had come to visit her to show her the new silk veils for the ball. Lana had greeted her with a big smile and a blonde wig that her father had bought for her on a trip to Key West. Three days after Irene's visit, Lana was found dead, a pool of dried blood under her wig, her brains exposed. A few days later when Juan Benson found out about his lady love, in despair he cut off the pinkie and ring fingers on his right hand with his machete.

Facing Lana in an exotic Middle Eastern pose and with the biggest coin in her navel was Hedy. Hedy and Irene played the piano every afternoon at Fabre's Academy of Music. Hedy wanted to be a concert pianist and play with the national symphony. She was jovial and always wore shorts, a legacy of her days at Mobile's Finishing School and a scandal for her hometown. It was while in Alabama that she met her boyfriend Rudy Jones. He was attending Springhill College. Rudy died during the Normandy landing, but not before he had given Hedy the only passionate night she was ever to experience. One afternoon, when Irene was accompanying Hedy in her personal rendition of "Claire de Lune," Elvirita, the instructor, tried to imprison her hands, using the lesson as pretext. Hedy and Irene escaped screaming from the ambush that Elvirita was launching from the island of Lesbos. Thus, Hedy abandoned a piano career that undoubtedly would have led her to Carnegie Hall. When Hedy was forty and still a spinster raising her younger siblings, she decided to stop mourning for Rudy. She married Senator Zubizarreta, the owner of La Campana Hardware Store. The husband forbade her to use shorts, forcing her to wear long, heavy black stockings to the beach. Finally exile gave her enough courage to have her marriage annulled.

Though she saw them often at Pepe's Grocery, Nellie didn't care for the remaining four odalisques. And the sultan? He was born, grew up, and died in the same old town. He never married because the responsibility of the annual odalisques conga line didn't leave him with much time for love. He had hardly finished one year's conga when he immediately started laboring on the variations for the next—more veils, more tambourines, less gold. His choreographies propelled him into national limelight. But he didn't allow fame to cloud his world vision, never accepting the many bribes that were offered by politicians and capitalists to have their daughters join his seraglio. Mario continued selecting his girls from Xawa's cream. He never suspected the many moments of secret joy he had given generations of dancing maidens, young girls whose fingers, in the midst of the night and the intimacy of their alcoves, went wild sinking uncontrollably beneath their panties as they dreamed of the hirsute sultan. When Mario died in a train accident, the Legion of Mary took a collection to build a monument to perpetuate his memory. The statue was sculpted from a single piece of Carrara marble by Gianni Galli. It bore the name, "The Surrendering of the Odalisques." The inscription read: "To you who filled our free time with the greatest of joys. We will not forget you, The Legion of Mary and the Ladies' Tennis Club."

She turned the page once more and time elapsed swiftly. Skipping the sleepless night when she felt the vacuum of her mother's absence, her coming-out party, her first cigarette, Nelson's first kiss through the living room window, she stopped at Nelson's graduation ceremony. It was 1944 and the allies were bombing Dresden. This time Nellie was in the center of the photo, elegantly dressed in a black silk gown, embroidered by her own hands. She had taken up embroidery to occupy her time while Nelson was away finishing his degree. They had been engaged for nine long years. Nellie sewed sixty-two blouses, knitted twenty-five sweaters for Rigoletto, embroidered thirty-two table cloths, and made all the Lent covers for all the saints of all the churches, monasteries, and convents in her diocese during those years. When she completed these tasks, she still had two more years before Nelson's return. To fill her time Nellie began the composition of five-hundred and four sonnets. All the poems were recorded in the Italian manner as prescribed by Marco F. Pietralunga (Pietrarca) in his *Viaggio All' Amore: The Muses Within Your Reach.*

The tenth sonnet of the one-hundred-four rhymed like this:

> Your divine eyes, Nelson
> are not what submitted me to love's yoke';
> nor your swollen lips, the blind cupid's sweet nest,
> where nectar springs,
> nor your olive cheeks,
> nor your hair darker than a chestnut;
> nor your hands, which have conquered so many;
> nor your voice, which seems more than human.
> It was your soul, visible in your deeds,
> which was able to subject mine,
> so its captivity would last beyond death.
> Thus, everything that has been mentioned can be
> reduced simply to the power of your soul,
> for by its commission each member performed its
> ministry.

Pressed against the paper on both sides of the tenth sonnet were a pair of seductive, purplish marks.

As Nelson's commencement godmother, Nellie wore her hair loose in a cascade that started from her forehead and ran down her neck, finally coming to an end one half inch from her shoulders. Nellie, who still thought of herself as Irene Dunn's twin, had blossomed. Her physical attributes could have been listed in terms of apples—two in front and half of one in the rear. She had used heavy make-up around her eyes to accentuate their almond shape. Nelson, with golden spectacles and sporting a cap and gown, held a diploma in his right hand, trying to assume an air of sagacity. His business administration degree had cost him more than sweat, and given him a nervous stomach. Nelson's fear of having to head his father's businesses after graduation was the source of the stomach spasms which caused him to shower his peers with pineapple chunks, black beans, and salami before each exam. He became known as Black Vomit. That night, after the prescribed picture-taking beneath the loving arms of the Alma Mater, the radiant couple danced at the Montmartre. Rene Touzet's orchestra played "You Don't Need To Know," while Nelson held Nellie very tight against his chest. He murmured the lyrics in Nellie's ear while thinking of The Squirrel's roomy hips. Like any other Saturday, The Squirrel would surely be waiting for him until three o'clock in the morning, when the night was still young and her older clients were headed home to their suspecting wives. Nelson always left her a generous tip and a few pieces of bubble gum.

Nellie was about to flip the page when unexpectedly someone knocked at the door. She immediately thought it was the roving reverend bringing a new cardboard fan. But she was amazed to see a woman dressed in tight pants and a sleeveless blouse. Nellie strained her eyes to observe the woman better through the peephole, recognizing the lady who had diligently ordered around the Mayflower movers. She was obviously one of the people that had moved to the corner house, the one that had been vacant for years. Since no one answered, the tightly clad lady peeked through the window of the Florida room, shouting: "Hello, hello. Any one home?"

"My husband is not here," answered Nellie uneasily.

"My name is Mrs. James B. Olsen," she said, raising her voice.

"My husband is not here. He is working," Nellie answered.

"I ain't here to see your husband," a slightly irritated Mrs. James B. responded with a musical rhythm. "I'm your new neighbor. My name is Mrs. James B. Olsen II. May I come in?"

"Well, yes, of course. Excuse me, I am even losing my manners. Please, come in," Nellie said, opening the door.

"We've just moved to the white house. The one with the picket fence. We hail from Tallahassee. You know where that is? Where you from?"

"Oh, yes! The corner house. Do you have any children? We have a boy and a girl. The oldest is Nelson, Jr. and the youngest is the little María-Chiara. The boy goes to the junior high school." Nellie was feeling nervous and started scratching her head.

"Yeah! We've got ourselves a little couple, too. The boy's name is James B. Olsen III, and we call the little belle Missy, but she's really named after me. They're both in boarding school in Mississippi. James B. III goes to a military academy and Missy to pre-finishing school. You just can't send kids to public school no more, too many negroes." She had lowered her voice to utter the last three words.

"That is very bad because the children could have played together. Maybe in the summer. May I offer to you anything to drink?"

"Yes, coffee. But no cream, please. I like it black. Where are you from?" Mrs. James B. raised her voice for the last question and carefully enunciated each syllable.

"Please make yourself at home. I am from Xawa, but I was meant to be born in Mondovi."

"Oh, is that so! Oh! A picture album. I love albums! A picture is worth one-thousand words." Mrs. James B. started flipping through the album without first asking if she could.

"You can open it if you want," said Nellie after the fact.

"I could bring mine tomorrow. I have lovely family pictures. Actually, they aren't pictures but photographs. And there's a difference! Photographs of my great-great-grandma's plantation, Fairview. It had a beautiful wrought iron fence. The Yankees sacked it and burned it to the ground. My great-great grandma died trying to save the family heirlooms. But please, don't come to my house. If my husband knew I was here he would kill me. I've always been ahead of my time. Do you realize I was Leon High School's homecoming queen? There were lots of people that came to my crowning, even though it was the same weekend as the county fair. I had to compete with the Ubangi Woman, the Alligator Lady, the Bearded Lady, and the Quarter Man. I remember it as if it was today. I was crowned inside a giant redwood log. Boy, did I cry that day! I felt special and fearful of the great responsibility I was about to assume. My ladies in waiting—those are the girls that tended to my every wish—were throwing rose petals at my feet. I was crowned by the football team captain, Captain James B. Olsen II. His jersey was number 24, and it was retired. In the school year book he was chosen most likely to succeed, most athletic, best personality, and best all-around during his sophomore, junior and senior years—something really unique in American history. He was really dying to place that shining crown on my head. It was the week before we played the Marianna Bulldogs. We made this huge bonfire and burned a bulldog in effigy. An effigy is something like a big dummy, except you can be really nasty to it. Before we threw it in the fire, the big dummy was just mauled by the sharp teeth of our fighting Lions. Mr. James B. took the biggest bite and ripped off a flank. Do you want to know what

we did next? We began pelting the smoking bulldog with
marshmallows, and we shouted that he was no bulldog but a
chihuahua, which is a small scrawny South American dog
from Mexico. Then the Captain slowly climbed the steps to the
podium and told my future subjects, 'It's surely nice for you to
show up. Let me tell you that team made the trip here for
nothing. Y'all gonna be eating hot dogs for breakfast tomorrow
morning. We wanna have our best game and we're gonna try
our hardest to do it.' The Lions went wild and the band started pumping them up even higher by playing 'You Ain't Nothing But A Hound Dog.' And right when I was gonna lead them
into an uproar of GOOOOOOOOOOOOO BIGGGGGGGGGG-
GGG REEEEEEEEEEEEEEEEED BEAAAAAAAAAAAAA-
AAAAT BULLDAWWWWWWWWWWWWWWWWGS, a tiny
figure made her way through the pack. It was Mrs. Cornelia
Williamson, James B.'s grandma, who grabbed the microphone. She was wearing a red sweatshirt with the words MY
GRANDSON and the number 24. Then everybody heard her
yell, 'Who's gonna win tonight?' The crowd didn't wait to
answer her cracking voice. It roared L-E-O-N L-I-O-N-S. I
never forgave her. It was the most important moment of my
cheerleading career, and she ruined it for me. Her grandson
carried her on his shoulders while the band played, 'When The
Saints Go Marching In.' But let me tell you about James B. II.
He fell for me all the way back in the seventh grade. Do you
know what he wrote in my eighth-grade yearbook? He wrote:
'I wish I was a mosquito so I could bite you. But please don't
squash me. Lots of love, JB II.' All those years he was longing
for me and I only gave him tiny, little bits of hope. Like when
he invited me to go to the pig races in Georgia and I made him
wait for an answer the whole month! Actually, I really wanted
to go 'cause they're a lot of fun, and Sugar, Uncle Blue's sow,
was one of the contestants. James B. arrived early, driving his
father's brand new pickup. He had just gotten his restricted
license. I made him wait for forty-five minutes even though I
had been ready for over two hours. James B. had used Bryl-

creem for the first time and had brushed his teeth at least fifteen times. He smelled of fluoride toothpaste and breath mint. He didn't dare to even hold my hand, and at the end of our date, he didn't know how to say goodbye. He leaned forward and said in a deep voice, 'I had a ball!' I'm lots of fun! Oh, something smells. Are you killing roaches or something? What is it?"

"Please, please make yourself comfortable. I will be right back with the coffee."

"And who are all these people?"

"Myself and a group of friends at a party," said Nellie from the kitchen.

"I just love your dresses. Ain't them adorable? Do you always dress like that in your country or just on Sundays? And who's the man wearing the turban? Are y'all his girlfriends?"

Nellie couldn't quite hear her since the water for the coffee was boiling, so she nodded from afar.

"I couldn't have shared my Mr. James B. Olsen with no one. Did I tell you he was chosen most athletic? He's always been my cup of tea. I was the captain of the cheerleading squad," she added while she wet her index finger to flip the page.

"The one with the toga is Nelson, my husband. That was the day he graduated from the university. And the man to his left is my father. He was the owner of many factories, including the one that made the best rum, and of the national railroad.

"I hate trains. They always wake me up in the morning with that awful whistle. I was thinking maybe you would like to come with me to W. T. Grant. They're having a clearance sale. On the way, we could stop at the Dairy Queen for some ice cream. Have you ever had ice cream?"

"Well, thank you very much. I wanted to buy a bracelet, and the ice cream is okay, too."

"What about tomorrow before Mr. James B. returns from baseball practice? If he catches you near our place, he'll hunt you down like a wild deer. He ain't very broad-minded."

"It will be a pleasure, Mrs. Olsen."

"Well, I'd better go back to prepare Mr. James B.'s supper. I'm going to perfume myself. I'm his horse doovers; it's French for snack. When he sees me, I drive him wild. He chases me all over the house, and when he finally catches me, he kisses me savagely while I scream, 'Go, go, go, go, big red.' Before I forget, did you ever meet Talihu Medina?"

"No."

"How about that. She being Filipino and all that. Anyway, I'm sure you'd have loved her, too. Many of my friends thought she was my maid. Can you imagine! When we went shopping, I managed to always go a few steps ahead of her. You know how short their legs are. As I told you, all of my friends thought she was my servant. I never told them so, but I didn't deny it either. I just smiled. She left when her husband, Sergeant Bahama Joe, was transferred to Eglin. Don't you forget, I'll come fetch you tomorrow morning. Well, like y'all say, 'sayonara.'"

Nellie was happy to have made a new friend. She went to the mailbox and found a letter from Delfina. They always came with the same stamp, a white dove surrounded by the word "peace" in many languages. She opened the envelope and saw her wedding picture. She took it out and put it on top of the night stand so she could show it to Mrs. James B. first thing in the morning. She walked to the kitchen whistling *The Donna Reed Show* theme song and opened her recipe book. She looked under "desserts" and started getting the ingredients to make her new friend a coconut custard. While measuring out the wrong amount of sugar, she realized she had forgotten to tell her that her name was Nellie.

Milkmaid

Don Andrés sat in his study, the shutters tightly closed to keep out the sun, and cleaned out his desk. He placed the deeds, stock certificates, legal receipts and love letters to one side and discarded those yellowed documents whose importance had long since escaped him. He was distracted momentarily by a shouting quartet of baritones coming up the street. He glanced at his watch, determined they were on time, then returned to his sorting. As usual, the foursome arrived in a camouflaged jeep and backed it up to the mansion's main gate, the gears whining all the way from the main road, and began their daily harangue. The ensemble had become so predictable that Don Andrés had started timing his afternoon bath with their finale.

The show was led by Rulfo, a self-proclaimed hero of the people whose largesse with the belongings of others was overshadowed only by his belly. Rulfo's scornful vibratos could have garnered him acclaim at La Scala.

"What do we want for the lackeys?" Rulfo boomed out.

"The firing squad, the firing squad," the group responded in unison.

"Louder!" he screamed, his carotid veins ready to burst.

"The firing squad!"

"What do we want for the vampire that sucked our blood?"

"Red coals, red coals."

"Where?"

"Up his ass, up his ass."

"What do we want for the exploiter?" the chorus inquired, changing roles.

"Hang him, hang him, by the balls, by his tiny, little balls," Rulfo blared with such gusto that he fell back into the driver's seat, his fat body wedging against the wheel and making the horn blare.

Don Andrés opened the shuttered door to the balcony overlooking the gates. He held a lonely hand in their direction. Then, slowly and deliberately, he closed his hand into a fist, with his middle finger sticking out in solitude, like a lightning rod defying the masses and driving them into a deeper frenzy. This ritual had become perfectly synchronized during the past four months. It had come to resemble a scene from a decadent tropical operetta.

"Papá, Papáaaaaa! Close that door immediately! Why must you incite them? Don't you see that's exactly what they want? I can't believe you're letting them entice you into their low-class ways! Please, Papá, you know I can't get upset!"

"Bah! Next time I'm going to open the gate and set the dogs on those bastards!" He paused, then continued as his face broke into a devious smile. "Besides, they entertain me. It breaks the mid-afternoon ennui." Don Andrés remained on the balcony with his chin arrogantly high and his finger still sticking out in its defiant solo.

"I will cover my ears if you insist on saying bad words."

"Oh, Nellie, I'm sorry, my little edelweiss."

"Benson is taking you to Gilda's Studio for your picture. Delfina says we can trust him. He offered to give you a ride on his bicycle."

"I have a travel document."

"It has to be renewed, Papá. And Dr. Cabrera will be expecting you at six. It's for the smallpox shot. You need that, too. Remember to wear long sleeves so no one can see your shot. If they see it, they'll figure out what we're trying to do and keep us from leaving this godforsaken place. I should have been born in Mondovi where I could go digging for fresh truffles with my pig Rigoletto. I know you promised Mamá I was going to be different, that I wasn't going to be born here...."

"We tried to have you in Mondovi," Don Andrés shouted to his daughter over his shoulder, his arm still outstretched like Moses. "But you came two months earlier than expected. I remember we bought the trans-Atlantic tickets in advance, but we had to cancel the trip. It would have been a terrific cruise on the *Ile de France*.

"Now I am going back to my desk. I have work to do," said Don Andrés, satisfied that he had stood his ground.

"Don't forget your appointment!"

As Don Andrés retrieved his hand, the choir began its wailing finale, the lyrics had become ominous.

> From limb to limb, from head to toes,
> we're going to dismember you in the slaughterhouse
> and feed your guts to the vulcons.
> We're going to tear you from limb to limb, old man!

"Okay, Rulfo," said one of the chorus, "don't get carried away. It's time to go back to headquarters."

Don Andrés, still quite calm, sat down in his overstuffed leather chair, a souvenir from his last trip to Mondovi in 1955, and began placing the deeds to his eighteen houses, the rum factory and the rice mills in three plastic envelopes. He secured the envelopes and placed them inside a much bigger envelope which he sealed with paraffin. He planned to bury the package near the poinciana tree by the courtyard fountain as soon as it was dark enough to evade any curious eyes. While rummaging through his desk for ink to fill the well, he found the first picture his wife had ever sent him. It read: To my Andrés, when you are far from me listen to the birds and the wind and they will tell you that my love is true. Forever yours, Angelina, XI-XI-MCMX. She held a rose with her right hand, and her long black hair fell over her shoulders onto a dress of white lace. Don Andrés looked into her green eyes and remembered that she had always smelled of vetiver-scented baths. He felt the heat inside him as he recalled how she had titillated him, but kept him at bay during the day, only to remove the lace barriers to her body at night behind a folding screen. She would signal with her hand to turn out the lights as he covered the mirror over her vanity table so the moonlight would not filter through the curtains and reflect her image. Don Andrés was beginning to sink into a mist of nostalgia when he encountered in the same drawer, submerged in a crevice, an old letter from Rosa, one of his mistresses. In her anger, she expressed her hopes that Andrés' daughter would die of consumption. The letter was dated 1923. His daughter, Edilia, had died in 1926, while Don Andrés was away negotiating the settlement of a strike in his rum factory. On his way home, he stopped by Rosa's, not knowing that her curse had taken effect.

He placed the letter on top of Angelina's picture, intending to place it somewhere else when time allowed, and carefully began to draw a map. He sketched a poinciana tree, a fountain topped by a statue of Ceres with a broken nose, and a faded peplum. Twenty-five tiny footprints led from the fountain to the tree. Next to the toe of the last footprint he placed a giant childlike "X". A directional star pointing north crowned the diagram. He blew on the chart to dry up a stray rivulet of ink, then put it inside an airmail envelope. It was addressed to a Sergio Bruno, in faraway Mondovi. Don Andrés wanted to make sure he could reclaim his confiscated properties once the flood was over and the waters had receded. "Nothing lasts forever," he murmured as he licked the rancid glue on the envelope, hoping the time would come to reclaim what was his.

Don Andrés whistled in anticipation as he heard the clanking sound of Delfina making her way upstairs with a bucket of water she had heated for his bath. She knocked five times, then the door swung open slowly, seemingly by itself. A smiling Don Andrés was hiding behind it. Delfina went straight to the tub, without bothering to look for the invisible bather, poured out the hot water, and opened the faucet to mix it with the cold. The water heater had been broken for four years. The parts to fix it still could not be found. A similar fate had befallen the refrigerator which, reverting back to a previous stage of evolution, now functioned as an icebox. Delfina worried that the water pump would soon join the other appliances. This would mean she would have to cart the cold water upstairs as well.

"Maybe we should all have been born in Mondovi, near the Alps, like Nellie says," Don Andrés muttered to himself as he tested the water temperature. "It has become unbearable," he said aloud, to conclude his thought. Delfina started to disrobe Don Andrés while he lamented the absence of the Turkish oils, the English lavender petals, and the multi-shaped imported sponges that Delfina—and then the others— had so skillfully used in his daily ablution. Don Andrés' only consolation was that pumice was still plentiful; that Delfina kept on grinding it, scenting it with guava juice, and using it as talc to dust his genitals after drying him. She had been his faithful chambermaid for over thirty years.

"It's a little bit too cold, Delfina! Would you mind going downstairs to heat some more water? Remind Tomasa to come up. It's time to read me a story."

Tomasa was the last and the youngest in a series of chambermaids that had left because of Don Andrés' bathing practices. Only Delfina had remained faithful through the years. She was a novice, a young country girl, when she first began preparing his bath. Angelina was still in her prime and Nellie was barely a toddler. It was hunger, then love, then hope, and finally devotion that kept Delfina rubbing Don Andrés' back, oiling his chest, and powdering his testicles.

Tomasa was already on her way up when she met Delfina halfway downstairs. Delfina spat on the floor and stepped on the spittle with her left foot, muttering "bitch" between her teeth. She knew Tomasa wasn't going to be reading any story.

Tomasa would do the same thing that Felicia, Fidelia, Teresa, Rita, and Agripina had done before her. But Delfina knew Tomasa didn't do it for love as she herself had done it. This thought comforted her somewhat. She knew that Tomasa did it for the can of condensed milk Don Andrés gave her from the cache he kept in the cellar. In a place where bread was rationed, that can of milk was a luxury, as much a status symbol as an emerald or a pearl would have been in the old days. Don Andrés had filled the cellar with cans of condensed milk, foie gras, artichokes, bamboo shoots, dandelion greens, caviar, and capers long before their disappearance from his favorite delicatessen in the capital. However, his supplies were dwindling.

"C'mon in. Don't be shy."

"Miss Nellie said to tell you she isn't feeling well. Being pregnant and all that, and then last night there was the biggest full moon…I think it could be any time now."

"I'll take care of that matter later on. Don't you worry about it. Shall we begin?"

"Yes, sir. But could you please give me my can first?"

"No, no, no. First we play, then you get your reward."

"But sir, you didn't give me my can yesterday."

"You know that the rate is 29 days to a can. Last month had only 28 days. This is not a leap year so you'll get your reward today. Do you have any demerits?"

"No, sir."

"Are you sure? Don't lie to me."

"No, sir. I have no demerits. You always say that I have been the hardest to give demerits to."

"Then let's not lose any time!"

Don Andrés began by hiding a small bar of olive soap under his armpit for Tomasa to find. Eventually, the bar would work itself down to his buttocks, and Don Andrés, like a nesting capon defending its eggs, would peck Tomasa with his deflated pecker as she attempted to rescue the soap. After his first game was concluded, they would proceed to the "Doggie

Game." Now Tomasa would crouch on top of the tub's rim facing away from Don Andrés. The grand finale was the "Submarine Game." This time Don Andrés would submerge under the waves of foam, with only his periscope visible. Tomasa was supposed to grab the periscope and push it under the water. If Don Andrés managed to keep the periscope above the water Tomasa would lose the game and receive demerits that would postpone her receiving the monthly prize.

"Papá, Papá," Nellie screamed from the pantry.

"Yes, precious. I'm still shaving."

Everyone knew Papá wasn't exactly shaving, but it was a time when words changed their meanings to keep the world righteous.

"Could you hurry up? I think you might have to get the midwife."

"I'll be out in a minute. I'm trimming my chin."

"Sir, may I have my can?"

"Of course, here you are." Don Andrés reached under the tub for the prize. "It's a good brand, Milkmaid, and it has a great jingle: 'Though it might be hot or cold, condensed milk Milkmaid never tastes old.' Think of me when you're savoring it. And make sure Delfina doesn't see you with it. It might upset her. I think all that pumice dust makes her oversensitive."

After the ritual was over, Don Andrés pulled the cord that rang the kitchen bell signaling Delfina to come upstairs to dress him in his impeccable Irish-linen suit. Years before he simply had to press a button to summon her. It was Delfina who had come up with the ingenious idea when there were no more batteries to energize the bell.

When he was groomed to meet his high standards, Don Andrés left on foot for the Peñas' house. Mrs. Peña could surely drive him to the midwife. She was the only neighbor with a viable car. Don Andrés' Eldorado Brougham had become a museum piece when the motor sprang a mortal oil leak. Before crossing the street to the Peñas', he grabbed his solid

silver cane for protection. Engraved on the handle was: "To
Andrés P.: 30 years of membership in the Galician Club."

On the way to the Peñas' he noticed the local fauna busy
gathering their morning sustenance. As he walked, he kept an
eye on a hummingbird that couldn't quite position his beak
inside its favorite flower. Don Andrés was so taken by the
determined bird that for a few seconds he failed to notice that
his knuckles were clattering against the corrugated surface of
the official government seal which was pasted on the front
door. The house must have been confiscated by the authorities
over the weekend. The Peñas had either fled the country or
had all been arrested. He peeked through the bay windows
and saw that all the elegant furnishings were still in their
places—the Bohemian chandelier, the Sévres porcelain collection, Macuqui's watercolors, the gilded door leading to the ele-
vator, the Delft pots harboring hybrid cherimoyas, and Emile
Van Der Xawa's gigantic portrait of an enigmatic Mrs. Peña
gazing at a bridge flanked by two angels and spanning the
way to heaven—the bridge her philanthropy had proffered
upon her hometown.

As he turned around, thinking how much fun it would be
to have an angel involved in his bathing ritual, an official car
drove into the garage. The three uniformed men that climbed
were coming to inventory the Peñas' property, as was obvious
by the pads of yellow paper they carried. Don Andrés tried his
best to hide behind the wall surrounding the porch.

"Hey, fossil. Yours is next!"

"Yeah," replied the other man. "That old fart has a big
mahogany table that will be great for ping-pong."

Don Andrés did not reply in turn with his traditional
hand signal. Instead, he hurried out of the yard and walked
briskly to the midwife's home. He repeated to himself: "Not
the table. Not my grandmother's table. Not anything."

At two o'clock in the morning, Nellie gave birth to an
eight-pound baby girl. She named her María-Chiara after her
great-great-grandmother. As a present, María-Chiara's grand-

father, Don Andrés, gave the baby one of his most valuable possessions: a bottle of Tuscan extra-virgin olive oil which he had secured from a friend at a stiff price.

"María-Chiara, María-Chiara," he said as he touched her forehead with a thumb wet with oil, "at this rate this might be your only dowry, so take good care of it."

Don Andrés was finishing his admonition when the jeep of revolutionaries rattled up the driveway to begin a nocturnal shift. Fat Rulfo was preparing to deliver his aria when a tiny woman, her head covered with a scarf, made her way toward the jeep. She held in her hands a small plastic Santa Claus light which had been used to crown the Pardos' Christmas tree when Christmas was still permitted. The figurine had become a bit dull with age—the bright red suit had faded to rose and the long beard had yellowed—but the woman held the relic before her as if it still possessed its former powers. As she neared the jeep, a veil of clouds that covered the moon behind her parted, casting light upon her and upon the plastic saint. The shadow of the American idol fell over Rulfo's face, startling his company. Rulfo stopped the maneuver before it had a chance to start, threw the jeep into first gear, and screeched out of the driveway. A victorious Delfina saluted Don Andrés, who was peeking from behind the door to the balcony. Delfina shouted, "Rulfo's always been afraid of the supernatural." Don Andrés nodded in appreciation and disappeared. Delfina watched the light that poured out through the louvers be swallowed by the night. Then everything became very still. Inside, little María-Chiara listened to a colloquy of frogs and crickets, trying to focus on the bottle of oil on the night stand next to her crib. Women picking fruit in an olive grove were depicted on the label. In the background a dark green liquid gushed from a giant press. Across town, in a shack by the river, Tomasa hid under her bed covers and scraped with her index finger the last sweet drops of liquid from the bottom of her can of Milkmaid.

The southwesterly monsoon had given way to the north-
easterly winds of the dry season. Cool breezes rushed through
the open window as a chubbier María-Chiara slept soundly.
Don Andrés was "shaving" while Nellie, who was busy packing the four suitcases the government allowed her to take,
hummed her favorite song: "*chi le confida/ mal cuato il core!/
Pur mai non sentesi/ felice appieno/ chi su quel seno/ non liba
amore!*" After months of prayer and intercession, Nellie's
dream of escape seemed finally to be coming true. The family
had been granted permission to emigrate. At first, she had
elevated her supplications to God in the cathedral, but when
its doors were shut after the expulsion of the priests, she
began beseeching Him in the sewing room. She had turned
the chamber into a chapel, decorating it with religious statues
she and Delfina were able to rescue from the deadly blows of
atheistic hammers. Presiding over the celestial corps was the
Holy Infant of Prague, who sat on top of the cabinet for the old
Singer, surrounded by three virgins: Lourdes, Fatima and
Guadalupe. But it was Venus, not the Infant, who had
answered Nellie's prayers. Dina, the dean of the mistresses of
Colonel J. L. Sanchez, thrice a hero of the revolution, had
arranged the Pardos' departure. Dina Ferro had been coveting
the mansion's accoutrements for as long as she had been coveting the colonel.

Nellie hummed louder as she thought she would finally
see her husband after eight months of separation. Nelson was
nervously awaiting his family's departure. Under suspicion of
illegally transferring millions to the main branch of The Royal
Bank of Canada in Montreal prior to its nationalization by the
Revolution, Nelson had been continuously under surveillance.
But he had managed to take refuge in the British Embassy
until safe passage had been arranged for him to leave the
country.

Nellie carefully positioned her royal-blue evening gown, an amalgamation of taffeta, pearls and Val Saint Lambert beads, in the leather case. While playing hide and seek with Rigoletto, she had received a telegram informing her that their exit visas had been approved by the Ministry of Interior. She immediately had abandoned the game and her pet hog and rushed inside to pack. She was sacrificing one whole suitcase to carry her prized heirloom. The Pardo family was to take the eight-o'clock train to the capital and to present themselves at the airport on the third of July for departure. They would catch a KLM flight to Montreal.

It was long past midnight when the tack-tack sounds of a hungry axe and breaking glass awakened Nellie. As she walked down the hall to the staircase, she noticed that the porcelain bathtub had been rendered useless, its surface pitted and slashed like a mobster's face. Frightened, Nellie tiptoed downstairs to find an energetic Don Andrés feeding the fireplace, which had only been lit once before in the winter of 1939, with the mutilated components of the French provincial living room furniture, Louis Quinze dining room set, and the chaise lounge. He had also smashed the chandelier and the ornate hall mirrors. Don Andrés Pardo y Abrahantes was giving the coup de grace to his grandmother's mahogany table when Nellie, horrified, screamed for her father to stop.

"PA-PA-AAAAA," her voice reverberated through the living room.

Don Andrés did not appear to hear or see his daughter as he threw the splintered pieces of table into the fire. He continued the rampage, pulling down the Flemish tapestries, and then began to eye the old English desk. By the time his daughter convinced him to give her the axe, a century of heirlooms were gone. Remnants of the pendulum clocks, the music box, the girandoles, the prayer stools, the Lalique bombonniere, the saints' canopies, the Faberge ova, the tortoise shell

decanter collection, the pre-Columbian jade and emerald
masks, and the embalmed parrot fish—a memento from the
fishing-bacchanal extravaganza Don Andrés offered to Gonza-
lo, the visiting Spanish Crown Prince, in 1932—littered the
first floor.

Don Andrés found himself in a small cell, confined for
destroying state property. Rulfo, who had been roaming the
neighborhood that night, was surprised to see smoke spewing
out of the Pardos' chimney and had called state security.
When Dina Ferro, the commanding mistress, discovered what
Don Andrés had done to her furniture, she demanded from
her lover the head of the arsonist on a trash can lid. Then she
performed untamed sex on the colonel, a sensational explosion
of -lingus and -latios. The colonel promised that she would be
avenged, but that it had to be done legally. A trial would be
set with the Provincial Tribunal for September the eighth.
The still bedridden colonel, his pinky in orbit around Dina's
aureola, devised a plan to starve the prisoner before the trial
and blame his death on suicide. The guard was to bring his
meal and, immediately, there would be a change of guard. The
second guard would remove the food before the inmate had a
chance to eat. They could not be accused of starving the prisoner since the first guard would attest that he had personally
delivered the food. Dina smiled when she heard the plan, but
she swore, as she circled her meaty lips with her tongue, that
the colonel would not touch her again until his promise was
fulfilled.

It was raining and the sun was shining. Nellie looked at
the growing pile of dirty diapers accumulating next to the
washboard. After the siege of her house, she had taken refuge
with the children in Delfina's shanty. She lamented that Delfina had been busy all week procuring food from the black mar-

ket and could not do the wash. After all, Delfina had more experience. Nellie covered her nose as she approached the washboard, but her retching drove her back. While she was engrossed in trying to break a branch from a nearby guava tree to transport the diapers to the diaper pail for soaking, a messenger rode up on his official red and blue bicycle.

"Is this the home of Nellie Grace Pardo?"

"Well, no. But she is here."

"Are you she?"

"No. I'm her maid," said Nellie, ashamed to be seen performing such a lowly task.

"Her maid? There are no more maids!"

"What am I saying? Of course not. I meant to say I'm helping her because she just gave birth. I'm breast-feeding her baby because she's sick. I am her wet nurse. We've been friends for years."

"Can you forge her signature? She's supposed to sign it, but I don't want to make another trip."

"I'd be delighted."

It was the official authorization from the Tribunal allowing her visitation rights. She was allowed a ten-minute visit every other day until sentencing day. Nellie, liberated from the distasteful chore she was about to begin, threw the branch away and ran into the house to get dressed. She put on the slip Delfina had sewn for the occasion and then her emerald-green dress. The undergarment had several hidden pockets so she could smuggle a few of her father's favorite morsels that Delfina had retrieved from the cellar: a small flat can of paté, a few dried apricots, and ten stuffed black olives. Before leaving, she fed the baby and left eight-year-old Nelson Jr. in charge since Delfina was still out searching for food.

When Nellie passed the prison's main gate she thought she had fooled the guard who had asked her to leave her purse with him. She was led by a plainclothesman sporting a pencil-thin moustache to what Nellie thought was her father's cell. He opened the door, and Nellie quickly scanned the room for her father's figure. Then the man closed the door and asked her politely to change into the jute sackcloth robe he was offering her. The unforeseen predicament made Nellie freeze, so the guard, using Nellie's own hands, helped her start the process of disrobing. He instructed her to hand him her clothing as soon as she was finished undressing. Regaining her aplomb, she pushed his hands aside and defiantly demanded some other room or closet where she could change, but the escort didn't bother to answer. As he turned around, he matter of factly informed her that she had just three minutes to disrobe, which was just long enough for him to enjoy the final puffs of the cigarette he was holding with his front teeth.

As Nellie handed the garments to the sentinel, her hands showed a slight tremor. The escort pretended not to notice, but when she disappeared behind the door, he jotted it down in a small ruby-colored notebook. Nellie prayed they would not find the bits of ambrosia in her clothes. The escort led her to another cell, opened the iron door, and waved her in.

"Papá. Papá, it's me, Nellie. Where are you, Papá?" she said, her voice overshadowed by the sounds of the door closing behind her.

When her pupils finally adapted to the scarce light, she saw her father's stooped silhouette.

"Papá!"

Don Andrés didn't have the energy to answer.

"Papá! What have they done to you? You haven't cropped in days." She purposefully avoided the word "shave". "I was bringing a few of your favorite delicacies, but the guard made me change into this. I really didn't want you to see me dressed like this, Papá. I knew it would upset you. Look, the fabric must be made from some sort of sackcloth."

As Nellie embraced her father, she failed to notice his scrawny ribs and the sagging flesh of his once plump, rosy face.

"Papá, you have to at least crop your beard! Shame on you, Papá. You must force yourself to look good. We've got some good news from Nelson. We still have some contacts who might be willing to help us."

"Food," Don Andrés managed to whisper.

"Papá. I know you hate this thing they gave me. But I swear to you, Papá, that I came dressed properly with my green dress. I even ironed it since it was already packed."

"Food."

"Time is up!" said the guard.

"I'll be back, in two days. Bless me, Papá!"

"Time is up!"

"But I just got here! Must you be so crass?"

"The first visit is for only five minutes. The next one will be longer. Let's get going, Miss."

"You should clean his cell. The stench is infuriating. People can get sick in these types of conditions."

The heavy metal door closed behind them.

"I need to change back into my dress."

"What dress?" replied a familiar voice from behind them.

"My gown. My green taffeta gown. My mother bought it for me during her last trip to Belgium. It's made from the finest fabric Baron Van Rjckengem's mills had to offer."

"Yeah. It is beautiful, all right. I'm going to give it to my Tomasa. Today it's her birthday. She's going to be so damn happy when she sees it. She might even want to do it more than once tonight." Nellie recognized the tenor voice that had harassed them for months. It was Rulfo. "She looks just fine in silk."

"It isn't silk. Stupid! Where's the other guy?"

Rulfo didn't answer.

"You don't expect me to go out looking like this!"

"You have two choices: either you go as you are or you can go naked. I'd love to see you naked. I'll bet you you have a nice freckle on your right cheek. By the way, the olives were delicious," he added while flossing his teeth with a piece of lace string he had taken from the dress. "Bring some more next time."

Nellie felt the pain of indignation spreading from her stomach in all directions. She walked away, propelled by her anger. Rulfo didn't stop her. Instead, he shouted, his voice echoing through the hallway: "Don't bring that gooey paste next time. I didn't like it. I fed it to my dog and he puked."

"Oh, shut up. Eat *caca*!" shouted Nellie in anger.

She was walking to Delfina's as speedily as possible, her mind producing different scenarios to get even with the uncouth brute. She would make him kneel on corn kernels, sit on a fire ant hill, take the air out of his tires... She had walked for a while when she saw an inviting park bench a few yards from her. She sped up her pace and was about to take a respite when she realized she was wearing the jute sack. Feeling humiliated and embarrassed, she ran to the hedges that enclosed the park to prevent anyone from seeing her. Nellie was in deep agony, facing a great dilemma. How was she to get back to Delfina's and still elude the prying eyes of those who surely would converge on the park for their mid-morning stroll? After moments of anguish and uncertainty, she opted to go back by way of the river. There were plenty of bushes in which to hide in an emergency.

Once by the river, Nellie was more at ease and able to relax a bit. She was slowly recovering her composure, trying to digest the morning's events when the shouting started, followed by a rain of pebbles and mud.

"It's the wicked forest witch!" shouted the leader of the tattered gang of boys.

"Don't get near her! She'll drag you to her cave and eat your brain!"

"I'm not afraid of her," another youth said as he catapulted a mixture of mud and rocks which landed on Nellie's right shoulder.

Nellie howled in pain and started running toward the attacking army.

"She's coming to get us! She's going to turn us into perch and then have us for lunch!"

"Run for your life! She's going to turn us into urchins. Look! She's becoming a giant sea star. She's going to eat us!"

The gang, panicking with each new theory, disbanded in disarray. Even the leader, who had launched the first projectile, was running as fast as he could. Nellie managed to recognize one of the fleeing brats. It was her son, Nelson Jr.

It was past noon before Nellie finally reached Delfina's.

"Miss Nellie! What happened? Where's your dress?"

"Oh, Delfina! They made me change into this thing, stole my green dress, ate the olives, fed the paté to a vomiting canine, and to top it off, you let Nelson Jr. associate with those trashy kids!"

"What are you saying, child? Calm yourself, calm down. Those are our neighbors. He has to play with someone. He was taking care of the baby when I arrived. I let him go out. You just relax and let Delfina get you something decent. I'll get you something that will make you very happy."

"Delfina, the planets want the sun to revolve around them! The world is coming to an end!"

"It isn't the planets! It's the angels. You see, baby, the Lord only made a set number of guardian angels to keep man out of trouble. Way back then, an angel could keep an eye on seven people, but now there're just too many people in the world and the same angel has to keep three-thousand people out of trouble. That's why we're in such a mess! They're overworked. Just too many people, baby, just too many people... Now close your eyes and don't peek. I know you like to peek, so don't try to fool Delfina. That's how you won so many pin-the-tail-on-the-donkey games when you were little. One, two, three, you can open your eyes now!"

Delfina had made Nellie a dress with one of the linen tablecloths she had smuggled out of the mansion. Although it was marked with a few burn spots which gave it a polka-dot effect, it still was somewhat stylish.

"Where did you buy it? It's not my favorite color. Next time get it in light emerald and in a softer material."

"Hush, baby, hush. Put it on. How did you find the master?"

"Papá is rather tired, but he seems to be doing fine. He got so upset when he saw me dressed like this that he didn't say much."

"Oh, baby, baby. I found out something while you were gone. I thought you would find out by yourself during your visit. I didn't want to be the one to tell you. I've cried a lot since. They aren't feeding him. The colonel wants to kill him. His mistress told him Don Andrés tried to touch her."

"Papá wouldn't lower himself to touching trash! Who told you?"

"Lazarus' wife, Magda. Lazarus is one of the guards."

"Isn't she the tall mulatta? Macuqui's nanny?"

"Yes. She used to come in every Saturday when she was a child. She remembers I used to give her the leftovers. That's how I found out."

"It must be a lie. I didn't notice anything. Are you sure those monsters aren't feeding Papá? You know how picky Papá is with his food. Do you remember how he insisted on you taking out the raisins, onions, olives and pimentos from his favorite dish?"

"Of course I remember. He always said he enjoyed the flavor but not the actual ingredients."

"Poor Papá!"

"This is very important, Miss Nellie. You've got to listen to me very carefully. Do you love your Papá?"

"Of course I do."

"You aren't going to feed your baby on Tuesday. Don't worry, I'll give her some molasses with water. Nothing will happen to the baby. That way you'll have enough milk for your father."

"What?"

"That's the only way you can save him. They are frisking you and making you change. There's no way you can smuggle anything for him to eat. You'll have to breast-feed your father. That's the only way to save him."

Nellie couldn't believe Delfina's plan. Actually, she couldn't quite grasp its significance. She didn't say much after that conversation. Her thoughts took her to the forest where she could really become the wicked witch. It wouldn't be such a bad life after all, and she could retreat to her cave whenever things got out of hand. But she also felt like petting Rigoletto. This last thought proved to be most comforting. She went to her room and looked for him under her bed. She could not find him and began looking for him everywhere, not knowing that Rigoletto had become part of her three days ago when she had so voraciously devoured the pork rinds Delfina had served for supper. Nellie accused the pig of being a fair-weather friend, that just because she couldn't get any more imported truffles for him to dig up was no reason to leave her. Many years later, in a letter addressed to Nellie from Xawa, Delfina would reveal the fate of Rigoletto to her. The day Nellie received this confession, she burnt her only picture of Delfina, one she had tacked on the kitchen wall with a rusty thumbtack.

On Wednesday Delfina came to Nellie's room early in the morning. She had filled the baby's milk bottle with beer. "Drink it all. It will make you flow easier," she said to Nellie as she pressed the nipple against her lips. Nellie didn't refuse. Her life seemed to revolve around her absent pet pig. She drank it and started her tirade against the unfaithful Rigoletto. How she used to select the best truffles imported from Mondovi, dig small holes and place the mushrooms by the pig's favorite digging grounds so he could enjoy himself. Now that she really needed him to help her rescue her father, he was nowhere to be found!

"You don't have to be shy, baby. I know this whole thing is making you nervous. I know how proper you have always been. I even remember when you used to take a shower with your training bra on because you thought there were holes in the roof and people could be spying on you. But you can pretend you're his mom. Think of the master again with us! Here with me and you and the grandkids in my house. It's like a dream come true. I mean his getting healthy. Make sure you control your flow so that he doesn't choke. I really wish I could do it myself. I've been wishing that for the longest time." The last phrase she muttered to herself.

It took Delfina most of the morning to braid Nellie's hair in the French style that made her feel so ladylike. When Nellie finally nodded, signaling satisfaction, Delfina brought her the linen dress in whose secret pockets were concealed olives and two petrified truffles. Their inevitable detection was intended to throw the guards off track.

A smiling Rulfo greeted Nellie when she arrived at the prison.

"I like your new dress."

Nellie didn't bother to respond, toying with her braid instead.

"Let's go to the cell where you can change into something decent," Rulfo said sarcastically.

Nellie obediently changed to a brand new jute sackcloth garment after being frisked even in her most intimate parts by one of the female guards that Rulfo had rushed in for the occasion. He then opened the iron gate which led to the cell.

"You have five minutes to see the old fossil," said Rulfo with a certain glee in his voice as the screeching sound brought Nellie back from her thoughts of Rigoletto.

Once inside the cell, she found her father in the corner. The place smelled putrid.

"Papá, papá. It's me, Nellie. Your Alpine meadow! I must have a serious talk with that insolent guard. He must come and clean this place up. Delfina says they aren't feeding you properly. Is that true?"

There was no response as Nellie sat on the floor next to her father. She touched him slightly.

"Oh, Papá, guess what happened? Rigoletto is gone. Can you believe that? I suppose he has a girlfriend, or maybe he's just mad because I left him stranded while we were playing hide and seek. Delfina said he'll come back. She said larders are very temperamental and maybe Rigoletto's jealous of María-Chiara. I told her that it was a lot of nonsense since I love them the same. It was precisely the first thing I told him when the baby was born. I told him, 'Letto, I love you. My heart is big enough for the two of you.' Then I gave him two dried apricots which I stole from your cellar. I know I should have asked for permission, but it was to make someone else happy. After all, Papá, you gave me Rigoletto for my birthday. Then I wrote him this aria since he loves opera so much, and I will sing it to him when he comes back to me. Listen, Papá:"

> My Love, tell me where you've gone?
> My Love, tell me where you are!
> Let me know—where is your new nest?
> Each day I love you more!
> With your sweet love oinks
> a new world was born before me
> and if my lips became so mute
> with my coup d'oeil I answered you.

"What do you think, Papá?"

Don Andrés answered with a hoarse cough.

"Oh, Papá. I guess I have to feed you," she said while releasing her breast from the dress. It shone in the darkness. "Please don't open your eyes. I wish they were feeding you. Maybe they are and it's Delfina's imagination. This will taste just like goat's milk but sweeter. But I don't want to be your mom. Delfina says that I could pretend to be your mom if I got embarrassed, but I'm not embarrassed. I want you to promise me you won't consider me your mom, which means you would become María-Chiara's brother, and Nelson would become your father and Mamá would become my daughter-in-law, and your real mother would become your grandma, and I can't do this, Papá, I just can't do it. I'm too ashamed to do it. I'll come back tomorrow. I have to go and find Rigoletto. He is going to help me get you out of here."

Don Andrés' moribund eyes saw a few drops of milk glistening in the dark as Nellie began to rustle her breast back into its retainer. His swollen tongue started out of his mouth.

"Five minutes are up!"

"Thank you, guard. Thank you so very much," Don Andrés heard her say as she rushed from the cell.

Yoohoo

"Howdyyy...yoohoo...anybody home? Yoohooo, Nellie! Nellie, yoohooooooo!"

Mrs. James B. began knocking on the front door as she sustained the last syllable of her last unhurried yoohoo, providing a rhythmic beat to the undulations of her ululations. She continued rapping, but the house was silent. Mrs. James B. scurried around the house and tapped on the bathroom window.

"You in the john? Are you in there, Nellie? Yoohoooo!"

At first there was no response, but then she heard a faint trickle of water which prompted her to yodel a sharper greeting. Instantly, a glass pane cracked and Nellie, fearing a higher note that could shatter the entire window, anxiously inquired above the turbulent, swirling, gurgling waters of the flushing toilet, "Who is it?"

"It's me!"

"Mrs. James B.?"

"The very same, sweetie. Did I catch you at an intimate moment? I'm sorry, lollipop, but I have to talk to you. Were you reading anything interesting? I love to read the T.V. guide when I'm in the can myself."

Nellie, ashamed at being caught in the performance of a bodily function, immediately denied any connection with such a lowly activity. It was a direct legacy from her childhood. Angelina, her mother, had taught her that of all the functions of life, "Number Two was the most debasing."

"Oh, no, Mrs. James B., it's not what you are thinking. I was doing my nails! I will open the door right away."

Nellie swiftly pulled up her high-waisted cotton panties, sprinkled the entire bathroom with rose water, fumbled through a drawer for her manicure set, applied a quick-dry pink enamel to her nails, threw on her robe, and ran down the short hall to open the front door. Years later, after her disappearance, when Nelson Jr. was asked by his sister, María-Chiara, what her mother's most remarkable quality was, he would assert with conviction, "Mamá never went to the toilet." Nellie always waited for an opportune instant—when the kids were at school or outside playing, or when her husband was at work—to perch herself on the toilet, or, as she preferred to call it, the "inodorous." The weekends were especially strenuous, eventually causing her chronic constipation.

When the door cracked open, Mrs. James B. was welcomed by a soft and polite, "Come in. How do you do?"

"Dadgummit! Do you have a paper towel? It's something like a Kleenex, but sturdier. Look at my arms and face! People might take me for colored and dump me in Brass Ankle. They must be burning the hell out of those cane fields! I swear I musta swept a tater sack full of soot from my porch this morning. I declare, one of these days we're all gonna be buried alive under ten tons of smut like that city in Mexico. But, anyway, I came to tell you something that's life-changing."

"Here is the paper towel. Would you care for some coffee, Mrs. James B.?"

"Is it fresh? Reheated coffee is bad for your complexion! I read it at the dentist's office in the same magazine I read about that Mexican town where every living creature was buried under lava about a million years ago. Did you know you can go there and see the bodies because they were dug out by these people called excavators, and they found people in exactly the same positions they were in when the lava fried them; some were even peeing. I know in exactly what position they would have found me and my Mr. James B. II. I know you're getting a bit confused with the lava, Nellie. It's not just a soap like you think, it's really hot rock which turns into liquid and can burn the hell out of you. I learned that in tenth grade with Mr. Evans. That's the only thing I learned in that class. He wasn't much into teaching back then; he had the hots for Miss Hicks. She started hating me back when I was a freshman, except I'm a woman so I reckon I was a fresh-woman. She sensed I'd be crowned queen in my junior year and that Mr. Evans would fall for me. Do you know something, honey? When I cash in my chips, I want to be buried in my backyard with my homecoming-queen dress, my crown, my cereal bowl, the silverware with our initials J.B. II & Mrs. Them diggers will surely go wild when they find my resting place filled with all those trappings. I must admit, even after I'm gone I'd love to cause a commotion. I'm a sprinkler of ideas! No wonder I was crowned homecoming queen. Eat your heart out, Miss Hicks."

"I will go to the kitchen and make fresh coffee for you," Nellie said, turning to leave the living room. "But tell me what is so important?" Nellie shouted from the kitchen.

"You're a sweetheart! What's so important is that there's a rumor 'round the packing house. They might close by year's end. I overheard that bird turd Jack talking with the owner. He thought I was listening to the radio. He's so doggone bean-headed!"

"How's Mr. Olsen?"

"His usual wild self, a wild bull and I his tender heifer. Last night he was so sweet! He brought me a bag of boiled peanuts and a see-through negligee. He's such a demon, always leading me into temptation..."

"*Amor, che 'ncende il cor d'ardente zelo di gelata paura il pen constretto,*" Nellie said, straining her voice to be heard over the sounds of a clattering fan. "It means, 'Love burns the heart.'"

"You got it right, Nellie. You got it right. Is Nelson a wild horndog like my Mr. James B.?"

"Horndog? What is the meaning of horndog?"

"I mean does he chase you around the house?"

"How are your children doing in school? It must be hard for you to be separated?"

"Personally, I think you should have seduced that sultan in the picture you showed me a while back. He looked like a hot tamale to me. I'd bet you anything he had a good pair of buns."

"Sugar?"

"Yes, sweetie!"

"No, no. Sugar for your coffee?"

"Yes, three. It keeps me finger-licking good. Did you hear me when I told you about the packing house?"

"No. I was making the coffee. Here you are. Stir it a little bit more because the sugar settles fast. What is happening?"

"The packing house might close down, which means we might be out of a job by Christmas, which means we have to think fast, which means I already thought fast. A queen is supposed to do that. I've got the idea that's gonna make us rich, rich enough to buy fur coats, have air conditioners in every room, piss champagne, eat fancy and shit expensive. Are you ready, Nellie?"

"Sure, sure I'm ready," she said, her mind meandering, taking her to Mondovi and the smells of the lilies of the fields, the chirping of the three-note orioles, and herself on a swing hanging from a linden tree, Sergio and Adriano pushing her forward from her hips, the sweet smell of trampled chestnut leaves and warm pasta fresh from the oven, and the air blue, like a bundle of flax.

"Listen to what's gonna make us richer than Rockefeller...a mini-zoo! Actually, I thought first about a chicken farm, but I remember Daddy always said, 'Animals with beaks never make the owner rich.' Nellie, we're gonna build us a South American mini-zoo—right here in the best country on earth, right here in the winter vegetable capital of the good old U.S. of A. No more working in that awful packing house where we ruin our hands so damn yankees can eat radishes and celery in winter when they're freezing their asses off. As far as I'm concerned, if they want greenery they can dig for it under the snow!"

"A zoo?"

"Yes, a zoo! You know, a place where people come to see strange animals and pay money for it. Ain't people strange? People are the only critters that pay to see other critters. Did you know that Reverend Fender swears the Catholics say we're animals, too? But I don't believe them communists. They lie through their teeth. They ain't got no business being here!"

"Who, the Catholics or the communists?"

"It don't matter which—Catholics, communists...they're all the same. The Rev says the only thing they do is follow orders, worship statues, and use the metric system."

"The metric system?"

"Yes! It's a system invented by the Pope to make the whole world pay him money."

"Oh, Mrs. James B., that's not quite right. I know for a fact that my father was not a communist but a Catholic. He used the metric system and never gave the Pope any money."

"Look, Nellie, I ain't got the time to argue nonsense with you. If the reverend says it, it's 'cause it's the truth. God said it, I believe it, and that settles it. So, do you want any say-so in this zoo?"

"But Mrs. James B., where are we going to get the money to buy the animals? They are very expensive. Papá used to keep exotic animals and they were very expensive to feed. They eat a special diet. We will need lions, elephants, tigers, yaks..."

Nellie grew silent as thoughts of the yak catapulted her mind to her youth. She remembered Don Andrés telling Juan Benson, their American gardener from the Isle of Pines, not to be so clumsy and to pay extra attention to the crates. The crates held a lynx, a pair of yaks and a condor. These jewels of the animal kingdom were to be the primary attraction for the festivities marking the visit of the Prince of Spain. Instead, they ended up roaming wild throughout the town. The condor,

was entrusted with delivering to the sovereign the key to the
city. Distracted by a coquette bald vulture during its flight to
the royal tent, the condor dropped the key it carried in its
beak as it began its courtship with the flirtatious female. In
the end the couple set up household in the steeple of the only
Presbyterian Church east of the capital. By 1950, bird watch-
ers from such remote places as Kalamazoo, Michigan, carrying
tripods and binoculars and wearing Hawaiian shirts and
British explorers' hats, flocked to Xawa to witness the majestic Vulcons (as the new breed was called) begin their complicated mating ritual of encircling the town sixteen times. The
entry in *The Great Soviet Encyclopaedia* reads:

> Vulcon (*cathartes auracuntur-sarcorhamphus gry-*
> *phus cubensis*) a very large bird with a useless
> hooked bill, a bare head and feathery neck. It is only
> found in the city of Xawa. Its intricate mating season
> lasts sixteen days. The males fly clockwise and the
> females counter-clockwise. The mating itself takes
> place only atop the steeple of the town's abandoned
> Presbyterian Church. During the mating season the
> Vulcons emit a harsh cry that can be heard for
> approximately 10.3 kilometers. These rare birds feed
> exclusively on the yellow coral-winged cricket, which
> they dig out from their burrows with their strong,
> long claws. Vulcons shed their tails during their mat-
> ing, making their flights adirectional and giving rise
> to major property damage as they crash against
> objects and structures during their erratic soaring.

Nellie floated on the waves of time, the memories of a
gentler era entrancing her. In Nellie's mind the mini-zoo
amounted to a partial rescue of a golden age.

"It won't be expensive at all," she heard Mrs. James B.
shout as she came down from her rapture.

"I guess you're right. I know very little about animals
here."

"Listen, baby, ours are gonna be the most exotic animals
this side of the Mississippi, and that's the biggest river in the

world. That's why it has a lot of letters. We must keep our plan a secret, otherwise Wakulla Springs or Weekee Wachee would surely try to do us in. I mean, who would go to those places after we open our South American Rare Critters from South of the Border? What do you think of the name, by the way?"

"It's fine, but I am afraid. Ever since that afternoon at the confessional...and my father passing away, I haven't been the same. I was more energetic before those events. I was Nellie then."

"When my daddy expired, I became sort of a zombie myself, but you have to snap out of it. After all, sugar, how many years has it been?"

"He passed away two years ago."

"My daddy died from bad moonshine. And yours?"

There was a long pause.

"Mine just died. He was old, and... at the very end, he refused to eat..."

"That happens a lot to old folks. The tug from heaven is so strong it clenches their jaws shut so hard they can't eat."

The soot from the sugar mill was beginning to blow in hard, and with the sultry southerly wind, black particles were being scattered everywhere, sticking to blades of grass, trees, roofs and sidewalks. In a couple of hours Belle Glade looked like a lonely widow wearing her black mourning veil.

"I hate them sugar mills. I knew this was coming this morning when I felt the wind blowing south. I swear, one of these days it's going to start sooting so hard we're all gonna be buried like them people in Mexico."

"Why don't you stay for lunch? It is sooting so hard. You will not be able to find your way home."

"I can't. Mr. James B. is coming for lunch today. Just lend me your sunglasses, a raincoat, rubber boots, and your kitchen gloves, and I'll be all right. I'll be back tomorrow around 7:30, right after breakfast."

"Okay, Mrs. James B. See you later, alligator."

"You learn fast, dumpling! After a while, crocodile."

Nellie kept waving from her blackened porch as Mrs. James B.'s feet, encased in their rubber boots, made the soot screech angrily at every step. Her hooded torso sailed through the upper air like a caravel. Nellie shut the door tight as the particles of soot swarmed against the window panes and darkness enveloped Mrs. James B.'s figure.

The soot had fallen on roofs and porches, trees and gates, and on every single path. They sky had descended on the town, and the flowers, panic-stricken, struggled to gaze at the sun. There were hundreds of sets of tracks leading everywhere, and the surface was trampled and littered. The sidewalks were filled with children with unsharpened pencils and sticks of different sizes drawing geometrical designs on the besmirched cement surface; the more aggressive came with their beach buckets loaded with molasses and were preparing their arsenals: a mixture of soot and gook. A few cries could be heard as the children attacked unsuspecting passersby with sticky soot balls that stuck to the victims like lumps of gritty clay.

Finally it stopped sooting as the winds shifted to the northwest, carrying the clouds of soot toward the Everglades. By then the accumulation was knee-deep, reaching Nellie's threshold. With the additional burden, the house hunched, making the light bulb appear closer to the floor. Mrs. James B. was tempted to stay inside, but her dream of the mini-zoo drove her out to the house of her new friend. When she arrived, leaving behind footsteps of her trail and a big heart with initials on the driveway (J.B.II + Mrs. J.B.II), Nellie was waiting for her on the front porch. This time Mrs. James B. didn't find her in the lowliest of lowliest. Nellie's nails were still in good shape and the excuse of having to do them again would have confirmed the Mrs.' suspicion. Mrs. James B. returned the articles she had borrowed, complained about the soot, and praised her husband's staying power, remarking he had just too much love for one heart to bear. Then she sighed and asked for a cup of freshly brewed coffee.

"I need a jolt, sugar. What about some freshly brewed coffee?"

"My pleasure, Mrs. James B."

"Nellie, I need to borrow your hose. Mine broke. I have to hose down my front yard to get rid of this damn soot. I wish it would melt."

Nellie walked to the kitchen to start her brewing under the watchful eyes of Delfina, who from her photograph observed all her movements. Nellie looked for Nelson's stove instructions posted on the refrigerator door, but couldn't find them. Maybe one of the kids had taken the magnet that held the instructions to the door, Nellie thought. Puzzled, she turned one of the knobs and placed the empty pot on it, but there was no heat. She sat on the stool facing Delfina's picture. It was all a mystery to her.

"Nellie, what's taking so long? Did you sneak out to the john?" Mrs. James B. shouted.

There was no response, and Mrs. James B. marched into the kitchen to find Nellie facing the photo.

"For crying out loud, woman! How can you make coffee sitting on a stool facing the wall? Here, just place the pot on the stove to heat the water, pour it over the filter, and zap, you've got yourself a fresh pot of coffee."

When she finished she poured the coffee into two cups and brought some to the still unmoving Nellie.

"You'll do fine from now on. You just needed a little bit of advice. Three sugars as usual."

"Thank you, Mrs. James B. Would you like some cookies with it?" Nellie said as she winked at Delfina's picture. Nellie was sure her fairy godmother had rescued her.

"No, Baby. I had breakfast already. I just love to drink coffee. Has your sister sent you anymore pictures? I would love to see them while we talk business."

"She's not my sister," Nellie hurried to correct her.

After deliberating on the future of their enterprise, Nellie and Mrs. James B. II commenced the first day of a shopping journey that would take them almost as long as the mating of the vulcons. Mrs. James B. always tried to stay a few paces ahead of Nellie in case her friends were to see them together. On their way to the first targeted store, Red Hodel's Swellings from the Ocean, Mrs. James B. went over the basic concept required for the operation of the zoo. Nellie argued that the enterprise should be called Vertebrate Paradise. Mrs. James B. convinced her that the name wasn't catchy enough, and that if they really wanted to make it big, the original name was the way to go. Nellie pinched her nose as they approached the seafood market.

"Don't do that, Nellie. He might think we don't like his business, and we need his help."

They rang the doorbell, which greeted the customers with the notes of Dixie and alerted the owner of the arrival of prospective shoppers.

"Howdy, Red."

"Good God Almighty. If it isn't Mrs. James B. Howdy!" Red was gutting a large jewfish while swatting the swarming flies, the atmosphere reeking of fish liver and gall. "What can I do for you lovely ladies today? The jumbo shrimp are mighty fresh and the oysters practically walked over here."

"Well, Red. I was wondering if I could go through your trash bin and pick a few things I need for this project of mine?"

"Why surely, Mrs. J.B. Is it some sort of fund raiser for Coach Olsen's baseball team? He's getting those boys ready for a fine season. Go Rams, beat the Devils!"

"You hit that nail right on its head, Red. You sure are smart, catfish."

"You make sure you say 'hi' to Coach Olsen for me. Tell him I might go by the field and teach them boys some men's catching. Well, little lady, you just go round back, and if you see LeRoy, tell him you get first pick today. He's usually inside the bin by around this time. And what's your ladyfriend's name? I haven't seen her round these parts?"

"Her name is Nellie, but she hardly speaks. She's almost deaf and dumb and is doing some cleaning at Reverend Fender's church. He said it was okay if she gave me a hand with the project. You know how much the reverend loves baseball."

"She sure's a pretty thing, though. I might have to start going to church. Wait a jiffy, this will make your job easier. Them beautiful hands shouldn't be spoiled!"

Red dried his bloody hands with his apron and went inside his office, bringing back with him a small shovel. He winked at Nellie as he handed her the spade and tried to press her hand against his. Red's winking eye made her uneasy, and she breathed a slight "*vamos*" to Mrs. J.B. Red, who had heard her, turned to face Mrs. J.B. and said, "Ain't she talking deaf people's language? My great aunt Dorothy was deaf and she used to speak all sorts of gibberish."

"Well, Red, if it sounded like gibberish to you, it's because it was. I appreciate your kindness. C'mon, Nellie." Mrs. J.B. made a left-turn hand signal, pretending it was sign language.

"Mrs. James B.," said Nellie, as they exited the seafood emporium, "why did you tell him I was deaf and that I clean a church? That wasn't very nice. No one has ever cleaned anything in my family. Delfina can swear to that."

"My, oh, my, aren't we touchy today! I told him because that old buzzard wanted to flirt with you and you just don't know how to defend yourself from a beast like that. You're used to your sultan, and he ain't one. People're so ungrateful with those that try to help them!"

"I am sorry, Mrs. James B. Are you still my friend? One of these days when I go back to Mondovi, I'll take you with me."

"Let's run before LeRoy beats us to the prime trash."

"But are you still my friend?"

"I'll be a better friend if we get rich. C'mon, Nellie. Let's run!" Nellie was afraid that Mrs. James B. might leave her behind, so she ran as hard as she could.

As she ran around the building, Mrs. James B. expected to see LeRoy burrowing inside the container. She was anticipating a fight over the garbage, and she had no chewing tobacco to bribe him with. Fortunately, LeRoy was running late, because, as Red Hodel would have said, he was attending some sort of colored-person's rally so that he could drink from the same water fountain as normal people.

Mrs. James B. climbed inside the bin and used the shovel to scoop and lob all the spare parts she needed for the enterprise: assorted fins, flippers, tails, and discarded shells of scallops, oysters, mussels, clams, crabs, lobsters, crayfish, and shrimp. The two women repeated the same procedure with every receptacle they visited. They were everywhere—the slaughterhouse, the barbershops, the beauty parlors, the Pawn Shop, W.T. Grant, and all the budding retail stores in town. And people took them for Mormon missionaries or Jehovah's Witnesses.

Nellie's house became the depot. Her porch was surrounded by paper bags of all sizes, each with a different color ribbon sticking out from the top to color code the contents for prompt and efficient usage once the operation got into full gear. Blue ribbons marked the spoils from the W.T. Grant bin, mostly carpet scraps in various shapes and sizes, broken buttons, burned-out light bulbs; black, old radio antennas, wood chips and shavings, pieces of multicolor plastic, and human hair of all textures and colors; red, the plundering of the slaughterhouse refuse, a hodgepodge of dried-up tails, and assorted ears. Mrs. James B. had taken the time to cure these appendages and entrails in her smokehouse. Mr. James B. II didn't pay much attention to his wife's comings and goings, because she was always smoking mullet or some other trash fish out there.

Not all the store managers the women encountered were as willing as old Red Hodel in granting permission to rummage through their dumpsters. At first, the future zookeepers were greeted with suspicious looks, but the coquettish Mrs. J.B., in her killer outfit—bursting tight shorts, push-up bra, leotard top with false opening in the middle, which she baptized her Mr. James B. Killer Scuttle, and Cuban heels—coupled with a few "sugars" here and a few "honeys" there, always managed to prevail easily upon the most recalcitrant of storekeepers. However, when they wanted to know about her sudden interest in their trash, she answered invariably that she was making a compost pile for her garden, or that those knickknacks were for Reverend Fender's mission to the Seminoles. Nellie, as a rule, remained silent, true to her newly acquired handicap.

The final inventory took place on the anniversary of Mrs. James B. Olsen II's crowning as homecoming queen on an autumnal day in 1957. To commemorate the occasion, and before she opened the inaugural bag adorned with a red ribbon, Mrs. Olsen sadly remembered her reign with a poem:

The bonfire with its leaping flames
Is too a part of the past.
It marked the end of breathtaking games.
And died, oh, much too fast!
Our junior prom—an enchanted dream—
With colors red and white,
Misted our night with a foreign theme
And enchantment at its height.
From dawn to dusk went the crimson sun
Leaving memories of a day,
It left for us the frolic and fun
We spent along the way.
In looking back I plainly see
The challenges and cheers,
And wishing time would set me free
to relive my crowning every year.

"Oh, that's beautiful, Mrs. James B.! I did not know you were also a poet. I wrote poems, too, when Nelson was away at the university."

"Well, thank you, Nellie. I'm glad you like it. I wrote it right after my crowning. It made it onto my yearbook's back cover."

Nellie and her friend went back to their work with light hearts. Mr. James B. was away at a baseball tournament, and Nelson was doing so much overtime lately that he hardly came home. By the time he got in, around 10:30, the two entrepreneurs had put away the scraps from the day's labor.

"Baby doll, we've got to get busy."

"The kids rounded up all the stray dogs and cats they could find. But I am afraid to touch them! Some have bleeding skin and almost no hair!"

"Great! A gift from Heaven! It will make our work much easier. What else did them darling rascals find?"

"Two jackrabbits."

"Good, Nellie. You know what good that spells for us? It spells M-O-N-E-Y." She had enunciated each letter and at the same time did her own deaf gesture for "good," which was an upside-down victory sign. After so many days of telling people Nellie was deaf, she had come to believe it, and in the process, had created her own sign system.

"Mrs. James B., I can hear you perfectly. I am really not deaf. Don't scoff at me."

"Excuse me. I got carried away with the excitement. We're gonna be rich. That's r-i-c-h. Give me an R, give me an I, give me a C, give me an H. What do you spell? What do you spell?... Say it, Nellie!"

"..."

"Goodness gracious, don't you people know how to answer a simple cheer? You're supposed to say the word I am spelling. You might as well be deaf, for all I know."

"I will do better next time."

"And don't keep on speaking gibberish that people ain't gonna understand. If you're gonna be an American, you have to speak like one. None of that 'scoff' stuff."

"It means to make fun. I looked it up in the dictionary. It's what Donna told Dr. Stone in the last episode."

"Listen, Nellie, do you want to be rich or to read the dictionary? Let's get busy now; we've work to do! We have to set traps to catch us a few large birds."

"How do you make a bird trap?"

"Don't you know how to do anything? No wonder you lost it all in wherever it is you come from. Are you sure you ain't from Poland? You simply get a metal box with no lid and put it against the ground upside-down. Then place a stick inside the box; make it look like an open mouth. Next, put some birdseed in it, and bingo, we get us a few birds or other hungry critters."

"But how many do we need?"

"As many as possible."

"But you have to promise me we will not use any pigs."

"Why not? Pigs make excellent critters for our zoo."

"If you use a pig, I am no part of this business." Nellie's voice sounded determined.

"Well, lollipop, if you feel that strong about it. I guess we won't use pigs. In that case, we'll need more dogs. You're making things harder, but I'll respect your pigs."

Within a few days the traps had done their job, and Mrs. James B., in a Noachian mood, started taking a census of all the future residents of the zoo before they underwent metamorphosis: two sea gulls, one opossum, two jackrabbits, five parrots, three owls, eight mongrel dogs, three cats, four sparrows, one bullfrog, one turtle, and one rat.

"Nellie, let's start with the bullfrog. Hand me that purple spray. Let's paint his legs. Then, get me half a lobster shell and fit him inside and then strap it with a rubber band, but not so tight that his guts burst out of his mouth. And paint the rubber band purple."

"Oh, Mrs. James B., it really looks strange. Look how it jumps. I can't catch him."

Mrs. James B. quickly came over and held the frog with her foot while sorting through the black-ribboned bags.

"What shall we name him?"

"You name him. Give him one of those overseas names you seem to like so much."

"The purple armored toad from Iquitos (*Iquitus cornuta*)."

"That's really good, Nell! You are a mess otherwise, but you're a smart one for funny names. I swear, people are gonna go wild in this zoo!"

"What's next?" asked Nellie with a big smile.

"Bring me that hairless dog. I think if we glue pieces of carpet all over his body and then glue tiny feathers to his legs and...cows ears."

"And we can call it the pygmy long-ear short-neck llama from Cochabamba (*Auchenia glama pigmica cochabambensis*)."

"Are you sure that's a place? It sound like one of them deaf-mute words. Anyway, you think of the next animal."

"Okay. What about the old dog with no tail? We can give him three tails; one from a calf, one from a bull, and one from a...I know, one long feather from a peacock. Then we will cover his body with pieces of carpet and glue oyster and mussel shells, and fit him with hooves, and paint his eyes with mascara, and put some rouge on his cheeks, and perfume the carpet with rose water."

"That sounds great, baby. Now you're cooking. But I want to name this one. It's my turn to name one!"

"Okay, name him."

"I'll name him the Two-Tailed One-Feathered Shelled García, and then we can lie and say he flies every full moon, and on Halloween, it develops bat wings. García was a man who used to work for Daddy in the fields, and he used to tell me stories and bring me a bag of boiled peanuts. That's why I'm naming this creature after him. I never forget kindness."

"Where is this animal from?"

"I don't know! I ain't good with places. You tell me a place."

"What about Aracataca?"

"Wacattata?"

"Yes! It even sounds better when you say it. Introducing the Two-Tailed One-Feathered Shelled Flying García from Wacattata."

"But, Nellie, it also needs a weirder name at the end."

"No problem, *astacus gnu avis wacattatensis*," Nellie smiled again.

When the big day came, the village fathers and pillars of the community were to enjoy their first visit to the zoo without the nuisance of the annoying throngs. The crowd was to be admitted after twelve. They would have to pay a 50-cent entrance fee. Mrs. James B. had convinced her husband to provide an honor guard at the main entrance. It was composed of baseball players in full regalia. As an added touch, both the players and the junior high band trumpeters carried Mexican serapes over their shoulders. Cheerleaders were noticeably absent from the event at the request of Mrs. J.B. She had promised to personally provide a solo cheerleading exhibit of the finest quality.

It seemed as though the whole town was going to participate in the grand opening. The week before, the President of Mini-Zoo, Inc. ran an ad in The Belle Glade Herald with a big picture of the Two-Tailed One-Feathered Flying García—its Latin genus and species included—announcing the spectacular opening of the first zoological garden in the Lake Okeechobee area, the only permanent attraction in the region's history.

The zoo had a total of thirty-two cages. On each cage, in glitter, were the scientific nomenclature and home of the fauna. The most visited cages in the first two hours were:

Cage 1—Pygmy Three-Ear Short-Neck Llama from Cochabamba.
Cage 5—Purple Armored Toad from Iquitos.
Cage 22—Two-Tailed One-Feathered Shelled Flying García from Wacattacata.
Cage 9—Three-Pouch Red Miniature Kangaroo from Kamaway.
Cage 17—Siamese Golden Hairy Sparparrot from Tiahualilo.
Cage 14—Leathery Silver Ox-Tailed Mutant Seal from Galápagos.

The entrance to the zoo was a golden arch that stretched 100 feet upward at its zenith. Hanging from the middle of the arch like a pendulum was a picture of Adam and Eve surrounded by some of the zoo's bizarre inhabitants. There was a sign twenty feet above the arch which read:

WELCOME TO THE SOUTH AMERICAN RARE
CREATURES FROM BELOW THE BORDER
WELCOME TO PARADISE

A small ticket booth was located at the head of the path that led to the cages.

The day before the grand opening, Mrs. James B. and Nellie called in sick. The packing house was operating at full capacity, and there were no rumors of an impending closing. Mrs. James B. and Nellie were planning to quit work after the official ceremonies were over and the crowds had started buying their tickets.

"No more, Jack!" shouted Mrs. James B. in her bliss.

The town's elite was eager to shine in such an important event. The mayor cut the inaugural ribbon with a pair of specially-made golden scissors. While the trumpets from the junior high band and the glee club added a majestic note to the occasion, Reverend Fender of the First Living Souls

Church led the visiting dignitaries in a prayer of thanksgiving. The gathering bowed their heads, and the reverend, his voice reaching all the highs and lows of the human register, began:

> Lord, when you made the last animals on the twenty-third hour of the fifth day of creation, it was a joyous juncture. But you were tired, oh Lord! when your hand extended over the Mexican Continent which geographers also refer to as South America. Lord, you gave them the strangest of creatures! Today, we are fortunate, bless the Lord! to see them here with us, and alive after their long journey! For the purpose of these creatures is not only to entertain us, but to bring to our Mexican brethren that dwell where these creatures came from to your true flock and make them cease their idol worshipping. Praise the Lord! Amen, amen, amen, amen, amen, amen, Olé!

Ahs of admiration and awe echoed throughout the zoo, which was located in the old town landfill. The site had been rented to Mini-Zoo, Inc. for the nominal fee of one dollar per year.

The mistress of a local magnate was so taken by the pygmy llama that she didn't want a new emerald necklace for their anniversary, but the diminutive animal itself.

"Lori, I don't think it's for sale," whispered Mr. Rossner.

"You've got the money. You go on and buy it. If you don't, I won't ever let you touch me again."

"Don't get upset, precious. I'll do my best.

Mrs. James B., sporting a beautiful purple orchid, was beaming. And Nellie's mind catapulted her to a previous life when she roamed the foothills of the Alps and dug for truffles with her pig, Rigoletto, who had turned into a handsome prince with black hair and sparkling blue eyes flanked by his two faithful pages, Sergio and Adriano, while a pasta-making Delfina was waving at them from the castle's kitchen at Mondovi. Nellie didn't even notice Red's flashing winks.

Mrs. James B. was anxious for the dignitaries to scatter or leave so the awaiting crowd could enter the zoo. She wasn't

seeing people but walking 50-cent silver eagle pieces. The line
was so large it went around the perimeter of the zoo, stretch-
ing for at least a mile to Reverend Fender's church. The news
of the zoo had spread like wildfire through the glades, and
buses from Pahokee, South Bay, and Canal Point were
extending their services to include a new bus stop at the zoo's
arch. Mrs. James B. envisioned herself on television giving
advice to the President, sleeping on a giant empress-size bed,
but more than anything, she thought of Mr. James B. Olsen
bringing her a single fragrant rose.

There were close to $150 in entrance fees wandering
inside the park when suddenly the north wind that had been
blowing dropped. A warmer breath came from the south and
clouds pregnant with soot hit the town with a vengeance. The
particles were long and nasty, getting into people's orifices.

"Piss! Shit! Nellie, Nellieeee. Where are you, woman?
Stop daydreaming! Get your ass in gear and take those old
paper bags and make hats for the public." Then she looked up
to the clouds and with a clenched fist yelled, "I hate you, damn
soot! Shit, shit, shit!"

Nellie, back form her trance, answered. "Mrs. James B.,
don't say bad words."

"Excuse me! I know it isn't ladylike, but shit again!"

"Papá only said one bad word in his entire life. I remember he was by the balcony when he called Rulfo's gang what
he called them. I remember what it was, but I just can't repeat
it."

"That's fine and dandy, but get busy with the paper hats."

"That I know how to do. Would you prefer bonnets, tri-
corners, or tiaras?"

The clientele didn't seem to care too much about the soot.
They were accustomed to it, but gladly accepted the hats anyway. Instead of thinning, the crowds grew larger and larger,
and Mrs. James B.'s worries seemed to dissipate as she rang
the cash register at the entrance booth and heard its merry
sound. When it finally stopped sooting, the debris almost

reached the cages, making it cumbersome to walk, but people kept on pouring in. Mrs. James B. thought maybe the soot was an omen of prosperity as she wiped the first big three raindrops that landed on her head.

The sky thickened. Low clouds, drooping at the edges like felt, sailed over the zoo, and rain leapt from them, warm, smelling of soil, soot, and sweat, and, like a laundryman with determined fury at a stubborn stain, started to wash away the black armor plating the earth. Most people welcomed the rain with applause. At first the drops were sparse, but with each elapsed second they grew in diameter and multiplied their numbers, gathering intensity to form a torrent of water that started carrying with it the mounds of soot that threatened to clog the town's drainage. The crowds were still coming in when someone noticed that the water was rising to their ankles. There was plenty of room for the water to play. It flung itself down the street and filled every pothole to over-flowing. It streaked through the cane fields, momentarily bog-ging down in the soot that tried to hinder its movement. It ran hissing on level ground or hurtled down and made itself into a torrent. Mrs. James B., sensing the situation, began to gather her animals like a desperate Noah, but the wind was blowing the rain right inside the wire cages, and before the eyes of hundreds of soaked and amazed zoo-goers the famous Flying Garcia was losing its shells one by one, reverting back to the old hairless dog that scavenged the neighborhood trash cans. The Silver Ox-Tail Seal changed back to a plain opossum. And the Armored Toad escaped from its imprisonment inside the lobster shell, its color washing away until it became a familiar grey frog.

News of the zoo hoax spread through the drenched multi-tude, and the chorus of "thief" and "money back, money back" reverberated against the town's water tower. A frightened Nellie opened the cigar boxes with the $150 in 50-cent pieces and patiently began to give back the shining coins to the vocif-erous crowd. In her mind she saw herself dressed as a nurse distributing loaves of bread to the hungry masses from an open cart. The allies had liberated Mondovi. In the meantime, Mrs. James B. was running from cage to cage in a futile attempt to save the creatures from further deterioration. The waters were rising by the minute, but by the time the big entrance sign started floating with the current, she had gathered most of her metamorphized species and placed them on top of the picnic table. The board began drifting with the deluge, the flood that ultimately drowned her American dream.

The doves were flying over the village with pieces of cane leaves in their beaks. The rains were over! A gentle mist was falling and drops of murky water fell from the branches of the trees as Mrs. James B. floated by on her back, and Nellie, who had taken refuge on top of a sturdy oak, waved to her. She was brimming with a vague feeling of happiness; under an overturned boulder she had spotted on higher ground a giant puffed-up truffle.

Review

Viaggio All' Amore, Marco Francesco Pietralunga Ricciardi (Pietrarca). Saluzzo, Italia: The University of Saluzzo Press, 1939, ($50).

Don't think *Viaggio All' Amore* is a silly book replete with the verse of a bard who is mad for mush. This is a wealthy world of words, the revealing of a Piedmontese soul who experienced love and lived. It is precisely the account of what arose from that tritanopic experience, his twoness—two tongues, two homes, two women, two siblings... As for the poetry itself, it is tricked out in the rhymes of the mumble king, the bard of the angstics. *Viaggio All' Amore* definitely holds much wisdom, sound and terse. And for the easily offended by the words muttered by mammals in the heat of ecstasy, one bit of advice: The whitest flour is wont to lie with the darkest grain.

The poetry presented by Pietrarca in Viaggio All' Amore should dispel the myth that contemporary poetry is a sterile wasteland of choked imagination. Pietrarca Ricciardi is a modern St. Augustine before his conversion. His *occhi* were certainly *aperti* when he wrote Viaggio All' Amore; he didn't miss much, and neither, dear reader, will you!

Caterina Myers

Blue Moon

Nellie and Nelson strolled down O'Reilly Avenue under the watchful eye of Delfina, who kept a prudent but determined distance from the couple. Nellie's playful Rigoletto kept tripping the lovers as Nelson tried to draw Nellie closer to him.

"Nelson, you need to go to Miss Olivé to try on your costume for the Yacht Club Dance."

"What Yacht Club Dance?"

"The Odalisque Conga."

"I didn't make any appointment to see Miss Olivé?"

"I did. I wrote you about it a month ago. I guess you don't read my letters. I told you Mario is choreographing the dance and all my friends are in it."

"You know I don't like crowds. Besides, I don't like that guy."

"We're going to wear stylish ensembles. Red transparent linen veils and cassocks. The cassocks are either going to be blue- or gold-velvet."

"I said I don't like that guy. He's too unctuous."

"And I don't like your roommate either. He's too wanton."

"Keep Bernabé out of this. I'm not taking the train all the way from St. Christopher to see you jumping around with that slimy Mario."

"All my friends are going: Joan, Ginger, Hedy, Betty, Debbie, Lana and Vivian."

"Who are those people? I don't know them."

"Oh, you don't know anything. You are so old-fashioned!"

"I don't care who's going or not. You are not!"

"Please, Nelson. I've been practicing already."

"I can't believe you. There I am, studying like mad, and you want to cheat on me with some depraved Moor."

"I have been dreaming about this dance for months!"

"You can't go alone, and I am not coming down for it."

I'll do what Lana does. She's bringing Curly with her."

"Curly who?"

"Her baby."

"I didn't know she had a child."

"It's her precious little poulette. And I'll bring Rigo. I'll be like a lonely widow tending to her child." She stuck out her tongue at Nelson.

Nelson was getting upset and felt like kicking Rigo, who kept encircling the couple. He hated having to compete with the swine and yielded.

"I'll go this time, but I won't wear any silly costume." He tried to sound determined.

"Don't be silly. It's a costume dance."

A street vendor passed by chanting the fruit selection of the day, and a cowed Nelson whistled at the man who turned around and handed Nelson two juicy papaya chunks in exchange for three copper coins. He licked his fingers, dripping of papaya juice, and held the other piece in his free hand. He was about to feed Nellie the tasty seed pod when Rigo began to oink.

"Give my piece to Rigo," Nellie said as she pointed to the hungry animal. "It's past his dinner time."

"I bought it for you. Why do we always have to share with him?" asked a slightly exasperated Nelson.

"Because...because my Mamá would have."

Nelson bent over and placed the fruit near the pig's snout, and the greedy Rigo immediately opened his mouth, swallowing the piece of papaya in a single gulp.

"Nellie, there's something I have to ask you."

"Oh, Nelson! I thought you'd never ask. The answer is yes."

"It isn't that. You know I have to finish school before that. My Daddy would never allow it. I want to know why you wrote me that special-delivery letter. You knew I was busy with school work."

"I wanted to see you. You don't come as often as last year. It was a little white lie. How many poems have I written you? Do you realize how many sweaters I have knitted you since you left for school and how many poems I have written? Fifty-two sweaters and 110 sonnets!"

"A white lie! I had to leave my exam. If I flunk that course, Daddy is going to be upset."

"It was just a white lie," Nellie chuckled.

"Don't you remember what you wrote?"

Nellie shrugged her shoulders as if she had forgotten.

"Let me read it to you." Nelson searched the right pocket of his vest and showed her the wrinkled paper. "Come soon or I'll die without saying goodbye to you. I have been very ill. Dr. Cabrera doesn't want to tell me, but I know I might not recover. Only your presence could make me better. I didn't want to tell you, but I feel weaker by the minute. If you come I'll muster all my energies to be with you. Nelson, dearest, I'm a shadow of my former self, a shadow that longs to embrace you before disappearing forever. In case you can't come because of your studies, I've told Delfina to cut my locks and save them for you."

The letter was signed with a pair of crimson lips.

"Oh," said Nellie shyly. And then added, "You should be so honored that on my death bed my only concern was you."

"Do you realize that I might not pass accounting!" he snapped.

"Yesterday, when I went to my room, the vase was empty! I didn't see one of your orchids. Delfina puts them in the vase as soon as you send them."

"I forgot. I've got too many things in my head. Daddy wants me to become head of the firm. I don't know if I'm ready. I'm too young. I want to do things, like being a captain in the merchant marine." Nelson seemed to be talking to himself.

"You don't bring me flowers anymore! Nellie said, puckering her lips as if she was about to cry. "And now you even want to join the merchant marine." She cried softly on his shoulder.

"Oh, no, Nellie. Don't cry! You know you are always in my heart."

"Even though I'm far away here in Xawa?"

"Yes. I'm the willing prisoner of your love."

"Would you love me always, as Rigo does?"

"Yes! Beyond life, beyond death." He was going to grab her forcefully as he had seen it done at the movies and begin kissing her neck when Delfina cleared her throat as a friendly reminder of what was expected of a gentleman.

"Remember the day you proposed to me?" Nellie sounded moved.

"It was at the Ladies' Tennis Club. There was a full moon. It was the night of the eclipse," Nelson answered matter-of-factly as if he was taking a quiz.

"Yes, it was a beautiful blue moon." Nellie's voice grew tender.

"It seemed blue from all the thundering clouds in the distance."

Somehow Nellie felt saddened by Nelson's remark.

"It's a blue moon because you don't love me and I'm always alone!"

Nelson tried to kiss Nellie to convince her, but this time Delfina didn't have to intervene. She felt edgy inside, and pushed him away. She remembered her mother and how she never had to question her love. She was silent for a few minutes, and Delfina worried she might never speak again. She felt relieved when Nellie spoke.

"If you love me, you would kiss Rigo?"

"What?" said Nelson as he remembered the woman dressed as a squirrel he had kissed so many times at Marina's place.

Taking advantage of Nelson's noticeable confusion, Nellie lifted the animal, held it against her bosom, and kissed Rigo on his partially opened pinkish snout. Then she offered him to Nelson.

"I can't, Nellie," Nelson begged her.

"You don't really love me! First no flowers and now this. Rigo feels rejected just like me." Then she said, addressing the animal, "It's okay, Rigo. I love you. We're going back home."

"That's asking too much," said the still imploring Nelson.

"If you don't do it, I swear I'll never kiss you again. Rigo is the key to my affections."

Nelson closed his eyes while Nellie lifted Rigo so that his snout would be at the level of Nelson's face. His tense lips felt the larder's breath on his own. In an effort to endure this trial, he evoked the squirrel woman hiding bubble gum in the canopy of a fake tree at Marina's. Suddenly, he embraced Rigoletto and kissed him passionately until Nellie's words broke the spell.

"I guess he can walk back with us, Rigo," she said to her pig.

Tulips

Xawa-on-Deep River
"Year of the Defeat of Imperialism"

Nellie Pardo
18 NE Ave Z
Belle Glade, Florida
Estados Unidos

Dearest Baby:

I haven't been able to answer your letter sooner because sometimes it is not easy to find someone who's willing to write it for me. I've learned to read a little bit, but writing is harder. The pencil shakes too much at my age! Magda, Macuqui's old nanny, is writing this letter for me. She got married and has two children, Celia and Raoul. She married Juan Benson's oldest son, Lazarus. Juan sends you his regards. He went blind a year ago this June. He got poison ivy in his eyes. Macuqui lives up North where you live. Maybe you can go and visit her. She's Mrs. Peña's youngest granddaughter. She is María Rosa's daughter. María Rosa is the one who married the heart doctor. He was in prison with Father Santos but was released. They live in a place called Sells, but Magda says they are moving to where you live.

Every three days, I walk to the cemetery to spend a few hours talking to the master. I bring him flowers in your name and keep the bronze shiny. I wish I could bring him tulips, his favorite flowers, but that's impossible now. But don't worry,

I'm sure he's beginning to like the wild daisies. They last longer.

I imagine Bernabé is still living in Belle Glade. I wish he would move some place far away from you. He was always such a bad influence on Nelson. Belinda, Mr. Benigno's mother, hasn't returned to Xawa. Neither has Hilda, your half sister. I think they don't have the courage to face so many memories. Sometimes memories take up form, wrestle and peg you to the ground and you become paralyzed. I remember when Hilda fell in love with Nelson. She had come to visit the master from Fort Matanzas that summer. They met at Key Esquivel Beach...but you were much more beautiful, shining like the sun. You melted Nelson's heart before Hilda even had a chance.

And how are Nelson Jr. and María-Chiara? I kept María-Chiara's olive-oil bottle (the one the master gave her when she was born). I have their pictures under the glass on my night table. I always pray for them and for you. Are you taking care of your skin? Are you having your almond bath to soothe you in the afternoon? Is Nelson washing your hair with avocado oil and sour milk? Make sure he strokes it one-hundred times backward and fifty-one times forward. That's to shape that beautiful crop God blessed you with. Always let your tresses down at night, for a woman's hair is the curtain of love. Men enjoy parting the tresses. Keep in mind love follows a well-groomed head of hair.

Have you found a seamstress for your new dresses? Try not to get upset. I'm sure you'll be able to go back to Mondovi where you really belong.

There's no one left from Oña Heights. It's sad to walk by the houses and see them suffering. Houses are like people. They have souls. The master's Villa Ronda has been turned into an elementary school. The poincianas I helped your mother plant, where you carved your name, are really blooming this year. I used to keep their roots trimmed to keep them from blooming too much. You know the old saying, "Poincianas with too many blooms, babies out of womb." And I don't want any more suffering in the world. The soursop hasn't given a single fruit. It has to be a male tree. Males don't produce anything, just sap the soil and give nothing in return. All men have excuses for what they do. But the worst part is that people can only be happy in pairs. Nature can be so cruel. The vine the master planted when the Spanish prince was here is giving sour grapes. Baby, I guess it is better to be a tree than a person! They stay put, never move anywhere. I wish we all had been born trees and were together.

The Sisters of Charity, the ones that ran the old people's home where I wanted to spend my last days, were expelled last week. The radio called them leeches. Dina Ferro's son died last night. (No one knew exactly who the father was.) It was all a mistake. He was sick with a cold, nothing serious. Death was coming down Clara Barton Street, but she was kind of tipsy that evening. I saw her dressed in her sexy black-silk gown, but she was stumbling and waddling. She fooled a lot of people, but she didn't fool me. There were men whistling at her and giving her the eye treatment. I'm sure she was coming for Waldo Dieste, who was sick with the mumps. Imagine being sick with the mumps at his age. I saw Death entering Dina's house and I wanted to yell: "Hey, Death, wrong house! It's Clara Barton 21 that you want, not 23." But I covered my mouth. I know I shouldn't have, but I thought about you. I got so afraid she might come my way and take me with her. I remember I closed my door. I don't want to go without seeing you again. The hope of taking care of you again keeps me alive. That night when I heard Dina's screams, Waldo Dieste felt much better. I see him every Thursday as he passes by my window on his way to the market. He must be close to ninety-five. When I came to work for the master, he was already an old man. Now that Death missed him, he might live to be older than Methuselah. I feel sorry for Dina Ferro! Her flesh is beginning to sag. She's not even the shadow of her former body, when people called her the chocolate doll. That's why I never hate people when they do something nasty to me or to my loved ones. I leave it up to life to take care of them. Life is the great evener.

Renato's funeral was sadder than most. That was the kid's name. She named him after her father, Renato Ferro. He was a decent man. His only flaws were platinum teeth, a limp in his right leg, and his daughter. Dina sat next to the pine coffin. It was resting on two chairs. She was dressed in a black miniskirt and a scotch-tape-tight broad striped top. She was wearing no underwear, but she was decked in jewelry—two rings on each finger, ten gold chains of different sizes, and enough bracelets to make her left arm completely stiff. These were all gifts from Colonel J.L. Sanchez. According to Consuelo Palomo, she ought to know since she was tutoring Dina's child and went to her house quite frequently.

Well, baby, Dina Ferro sat next to the box, and each time someone came in, she told Renato who she or he was, what he or she said, and how they were dressed for the event. It went something like this:

"Renato, guess who's coming now? Tomasa. She's wearing a nice blue dress and a pearl necklace. She has a silk shawl draped around her shoulders. I wonder where she got it. I like the color. I still have a nicer butt than her. Hers is too low. She says she's sorry you died because you were very young and that someone older should have died instead. She brings you flowers and a piece of bubble gum for me.

"It's Mateo Pietra, the poet's son, your best friend. He's by you now. He's wearing his Pioneer uniform and is carrying his baseball hat. He's telling you how much he hates it without you. He says your baseball team is losing without you on first base.

"Here's Juan Benson. You can't see each other because you are dead and he's blind. But he's here. He's his usual self, tall, lanky with black hair and balding. His eyebrows are still sandy and thick, one higher than the other. Remember how you used to make fun of his brows. There are bits of noodles clinging to his beard. I'm going to give him a piece of toilet paper I keep in my purse and tell him to wipe his beard."

And she went on and on, explaining to Renato who came and who went. Colonel J.L. Sanchez didn't go to the funeral. Consuelo told me he was in One Hundred Fires for a very important army meeting. Talking about dead people, Mr. Conway, the last foreigner in town, also disappeared. You know very well he was allergic to mosquitoes, and lately he was walking around town all wrapped in a mosquito net and talking gibberish. I guess the mosquitoes got him in the end, or maybe he went back to his land. I will try to find out. He was a good friend of Nelson's father.

Baby, I've got something I've been meaning to tell you for a long time. I really wanted to tell you before, but you left and it was all so sudden. It's about your pet, Rigoletto. He didn't run away with a loose sow. He didn't get lost in the forest, either. You see, baby, you were always saying that he would come back and help the master. He did! He died for us, but it wasn't painful. I drugged him with a bottle of nerve pills your mother left before she departed to the unseen kingdom. I fed him the pills mixed with the last truffles he ever ate. Rigoletto fell asleep, then I strapped his mouth so he wouldn't arise the Militant Muliebrity's suspicions with a final oink. His passing happened in complete silence! Remember when I told you Lazarus (he's Magda's husband now) told me what they were planning to do with the master. Well, baby, he told me all right, but I had to bribe him with Rigoletto's lard. His left hind leg I used to barter in the black market and the rest I cured and salted. It kept us alive until the time you left. Don't be too upset, baby! Don't be too harsh on Delfina. It was the only way to keep us chewing when the rest were having to dig for roots.

Write soon! Your letters are the only thing that keep these old rattling bones meaty. Remember not to eat too much chocolate. It'll ruin your beautiful skin. Take care of your hair. Kisses for the children. Talk to them about the master, Villa

Ronda, the lady, your sister Edilia (may she rest in peace), your half sister Hilda, and if there's a little room left, tell them something about Delfina.

I know your tears will turn into dancing. I love you forever,

Delfina

Delfina Rey
Kilometer 5, 5th green house to the left
Road to Isabella, Xawa-on-Deep River

P.S. I'm glad you have found a friend. But be careful with the Americans. I remember they used to get drunk in the park and had no manners, burping all the time.

Rulfo is still mean and fat. He's now district commander. Tomas' teeth are turning yellow!

Mosquito Killers

"Hello. Pardo's residence."

"Mr. Nelson, please," a heavily accented voice requested.

"Who is this?"

"I am a friend of Nelson's, Delfina. It's imperative that I speak to him. It's urgent!" Mr. Conway sputtered, leaving a foamy residue on the mouthpiece.

"Do I know you? Do you know that many people get me confused with Tomasa? I don't know why. She sounds like a peacock. The only thing she has is youth, but youth doesn't last a lifetime."

"Please, Delfina. Get Nelson on the phone!" Mr. Conway said, sounding exasperated.

"Right away, sir. But let me guess. You're either Father Santos asking for alms for the missions or Mr. Valley from the Yacht Club."

"Please, Delfina! If Nelson isn't available, get me Don Andrés!"

"Oh, no. I can't bother the master now. He's busy in his library, sorting papers, and I'm getting ready to heat the water so he can shave properly. I'll get you Mr. Nelson."

"Thank you!"

"Hello?"

"Nelson?"

"Yes, this is he."

"This is Floyd Conway from the Royal Bank. I've something that I'd like to discuss with you personally. It's about the golden canary with the deep black eyes..."

"Something wrong?"

"Oh, no! But I think it's about time we mate him with that female I suggested a few months ago. Ten o'clock tomorrow."

"I'll be there, Mr. Conway."

"Give my best to Don Andrés and his wife."

"Sure. But where do yo want us to meet?"

"At Ariza's. Shall we say at 9:30?"

"I'll be there."

"Please, British time..."

Xawa was inundated with the sounds of insurgent anthems, military marches, the monotonous chanting of the Federation of the Militant Muliebrity, and the chirping of revolutionary slogans by the one-thousand trained talking parrots, especially brought from the southern city of One Hundred Fires by "The Passionary," Mima de Rodríguez, at the request of her friend Dina Ferro, the chocolate doll.

Every other block, loudspeakers hanging from telephone poles like sprinklers, showered the town with the sound of clashing cymbals, the shrill of chanteuses and the clamor of fowl. Hundreds of colorful barges paraded down the Deep River, each one representing a red-letter day in the town's struggle for social justice. On land, camouflaged jeeps crisscrossed the muddy streets, while the rum soaked militiamen smiled at the crowds and fired into the air. Awakened from their morning rest by buzzing bullets, the vulcons were encircling town. Today was another anniversary of the city's uprising. It was April Fools' Day.

Nelson was pedaling fast, riding his bicycle through back streets and alleys, avoiding the plaza, which was the focal point for the celebrations. He didn't want to become a theme

for future canticles. Ariza's Cafe was catercornered to the
main square. As he neared the river on Bayou Street, he
caught a glimpse of the festive barges. The main barge fea-
tured ragged peasants with broken shackles shouting at the
hanging effigies of five men. The dummies were wearing different colored coats and were identified by name tags: Joseph
Fern G., Floyd Conway, Mr. Valley, Andrés Pardo A., Mr. Tito
Guiristain.

Nelson recognized the last two effigies. One was holding a
silvery cane, Don Andrés trademark, and the other had a big
cigar like Nelson's own father. Feeling a knot in his stomach,
he pedaled faster. As he neared downtown, to his relief, he
heard Rulfo directing the chanting throng. Somehow, the
familiarity of his voice put him at ease.

The Militant Muliebrity was aiming its thundering a
capella at the local curia. The avalanche of unsynchronized
voices precipitated the parrots' premature molting, covering
the square with a carpet of green feathers. The crowd's interest focused on the floating feathers rather than on the anti-
pastoral refrain.

> Open that heavy door
> that clumsy church door
> and bring your machine gun
> to make them dance
> to our song.

When a smelly Nelson arrived, Mr. Conway was waiting
for him in one of the cubicles reserved for Ariza's dwindling
select clientele. Mr. Conway was sporting his traditional green
barber-like shirt called a guavavera. This garment had been
especially designed for him by his sister, Mrs. Vera Wood-
small of stormy Aberystwyth. He received the parcel when he
was under a guava tree, wiping the arroyos of sweat that
sprung from his forehead and threatened to drown him. To

remember the momentous occasion, he named it "guavavera": from "guava," a shrub of the myrtle family, and "Vera," his sister's name. From then on Mr. Conway declared the guavavera as the only shirt suited for the tropics.

"Mr. Conway, what a huddle outside!" Nelson said as he took off his panama hat.

"Quite a show, quite a performance. "Sean," he said to the waiter, "two Mosquito Killers, as usual." The waiter's name was Ignacio, but Mr. Conway had the habit of changing people's name to bring Wales a little closer.

"Sorry, Mr. Conway, we're out of Chivas," replied a smiling Ignacio.

"What do you mean we're out of Scotch? That's my only protection against mosquitoes! Thirty years on this moor and not a single bite! Swim the ocean if you have to, but bring me my libation."

"I'm sorry, sir. But there's half a bottle of gin left."

"In that case, two gins, but go easy on the tonic."

"Don't worry, sir, there's no more tonic either."

"Two gins with whatever you can find."

"With pleasure, sir."

"Make yourself comfortable," said a perturbed Mr. Conway. "Let's do some arm wrestling while we talk. C'mon. Sit down and roll up your sleeves." Their hands were locked in combat. "As you well know, things are changing very fast. It was quite different when I arrived here three decades ago. You were then still in swaddling clothes. I contributed personally to the rebel cause to be on the safe side, but…" The final "but" suspended in time.

"Most of us did, Mr. Conway." Nelson was straining his arm, shaking but still holding his place on the center of the table.

"There's no need to cry over spilt milk. To the point, then. Your family has been banking with our institution for more than four decades. We've been given secret orders by our main branch in Montreal to help out certain clients before the government changes the currency and limits its flow outside the country. In other words, we're willing to funnel your assets out of the country at three to one."

"But with all due respect, Mr. Conway, how can you be sure the government is taking that measure?"

"We have ways, Nelson. If you decide to take up our offer, I will personally open the bank vault for you at midnight tomorrow. If you agree, we'll place all of your family's liquid assets in a regular traveling suitcase, which you would bring with you. You would catch the next train to the capital. Once there, you will walk to our embassy, and from there your assets would be transferred in the diplomatic pouch."

"Here you are, sir."

"Thank you, Sean." He stirred his drink with his middle finger. Floyd was convinced that at these latitudes people simply didn't know how to clean properly.

"What if someone follows me?" questioned Nelson, his stomach ready to betray him once again and his hand getting dangerously close to the table's surface.

"No one will, Nelson. No one will. But if you wait a couple of weeks maybe someone will. We still have friends inside the Ministry of the Interior. But I don't think they will be able to hold out for more than a month or maybe three weeks. All of them will be shot."

"How can you be so certain? I mean about them being shot."

"Nelson, in order to divert government attention to buy us some more time to divest and to transfer all of our holdings out of this country, we will have to snitch on them. Business is business, Nelson," Floyd Conway let out a cracking yell and a tempestuous fart as Nelson's arm came crashing down against the table.

"You people are made out of clay," Conway started laughing. "One of these days, I'm going to give you a few pointers."

"Thank you, Mr. Conway. Thank you. You are still the champ! If you would excuse me now, I'll go and talk to Daddy." Nelson shook his hand and held it for a few seconds. Mr. Conway seemed to enjoy the adulatory gesture.

"Don't mention it. Make sure you say hello to Don Andrés and the Mrs. and give my best to your dad."

"I sure will, Mr. Conway. Oh, Mr. Conway, make sure you go around the square. They might get rowdy if they see you."

"I won't be leaving this room any time soon. I have to chat with three other clients. There's no more Chivas, and I'm allergic to mosquitoes. Yesterday I saw my neighbor, Mrs. Palomo, crushing the heads of three newborn kittens with a rusty iron pestle. I tried to stop her, but I arrived too late. She said she had no food to feed them and went on saying that it really didn't matter that much since their eyes were still closed and they hadn't seen the world. I can justify the killing of a human, but not an animal. They cause no harm. It's all downhill from here. To think that I thought that Xawa would always suit me, Nelson. I'm going to miss this town. The first time I saw it, fresh from Aberystwyth, I thought it most charming and curious. I was given a machete when I stepped out of the freighter. The ship was stopping only for a few hours to replenish with coal, and then we would continue our journey. I was on my way to Charleston where my mother's cousin, James Parker Rhea, Esquire, was developing the ballpoint pen which later bore his name. He had sent for me to help him with my marketing and finance expertise. The colonials have never caught on to the practicality of we who live beyond the ocean."

"More gin, Mr. Conway? You might as well finish the bottle."

"Yes, Sean, another round. What about you, Nelson?"

"None for me, Mr. Conway," said Nelson.

"Make it a double then, Sean."

"Yes, sir."

"I was given a machete to cut myself a path to town. The coal station wasn't exactly adjacent. I battled a thick forest of enormous trees, the like of which I had never imagined. Their branches began almost at the ground and were covered thick with orchids, which I mistook for large roosting birds. Each tree was bound to the next by vines like tangled ropes, some drawn as taut as the halyards of a ship. There was a moment when I raised my machete on high, ready to strike, because they were so twisted and wrapped around the branches I though they were boa constrictors ready to drop upon my shoulders. I felt like a knight entering a steamy enchanted wood."

Mr. Conway's face was getting redder, and the ceiling fans of Ariza's Cafe seemed powerless to exorcise the heat that was seeping through the cracks.

"The forest gave way to a grove of manacca palms as delicate as ferns, and then there was Xawa, bright and warm and foreign-looking. It reminded me of the colored prints my sister Vera had in her parlor. The houses at the time were thatched clay huts with gardens around them crowded with banana palms and trees hung with long beans, which broke into masses of crimson flowers. Xawa hypnotized me, and I cabled Cousin James. I remember the exact words: 'Previous business commitments force me to stay here. Will take next steamer to Charleston. Warmest regards, Cousin Floyd.' I guess he has been awaiting my return for thirty years."

"Have a nice day, Mr. Conway. I'll get in touch with you as soon as I can." There was no answer from Mr. Conway. His head was resting on the rim of his glass.

"It must be the gin, Mr. Guiristain. He always drinks Chivas. He isn't used to gin."

"I think you are right, Ignacio. It must be the gin."

When Nelson left Ariza's Cafe, the chanting had waned and the barges were no longer in sight. Nevertheless, Nelson rode around the square as a precaution. He went up Light Street, and from there, he shot straight to Clara Barton. He turned left to the Jesuit School of the Sacred Heart, and then meandered with the river to Oña Heights. Nelson seemed worried. The conversation with Mr. Conway had placed him under stress—the pressure of talking with his father. He passed the cigar factory, and the smells of the twined tobacco leaves made him regurgitate the morning's breakfast. More than the chanting women, the firing militiamen, and the talking parrots, he feared a confrontation with the Old Man.

He saw himself at seventeen, rehearsing talking to the Old Man, explaining why he wanted to become a merchant marine officer, why he loathed economics, business, and accounts payable and receivable. When he finally mustered the courage to knock at the door of his father's library, his part of the dialogue memorized, the Old Man was already waiting for him with an array of business-school brochures. Nelson had simply nodded and signed the application the Old Man judged most appropriate for his son's role as future head of his business empire. Nelson was chosen at birth to be the crown prince of the family's fortune. After all, it was the fate of all firstborns. His whole life had been planned when he innocently floated inside his mother's haven. Nelson left for the university in the Fall of '41, to become a nervous wreck with each accounting exam, each finance presentation. His brother, J.R. (José Rolando) had been luckier. He had left town two weeks previously with a circus that had visited Xawa. He would become its best trapeze artist.

After years of nodding, fate was at last making a confrontation possible. He knew his father wouldn't be pleased with the idea of exchanging his assets three to one. "It would certainly be an uphill battle," Nelson thought aloud.

He entered his parents' house through the back entrance and lightly tapped on the Old Man's office door.

"Daddy, I have something to tell you," Nelson announced after being admitted to the chamber.

"What's on your mind?" he said as he puffed on his cigar.

"I finished talking to Mr. Conway from The Royal. He says the government is getting ready to change the currency. His bank is willing to help us transfer our assets three to one..."

"Three to one! That old, greedy gizzard! I ain't changing my hard-earned cash for peanuts. Tell him to suck my dick!"

"...But that the alternative is risking everything!"

"Don't your raise your voice at me, boy, or I'll smack you."

"But, Daddy, try to understand. Did you see the barges?"

"What barges?"

"There were barges with effigies of Don Andrés, you, and most of your friends. Hanged effigies."

"Bastards! Ingrates! Who brought the sewage and electricity to this town? I did! Who paved Martí Street and Clara Barton? Don't stand there like an asshole, answer me!"

"You did, Daddy."

"I'm going to teach these fuckers a lesson. I'll go ahead with Mr. Conway's plan. I'll paralyze the economy. They'll come crawling on their knees, begging for their lives."

"Really, Daddy?" Nelson was surprised at his answer.

"Yes, really. I'll take some money out. Enough to teach them not to mess with me."

"But, Daddy, the government will probably freeze all accounts, at least temporarily."

"I dump on the government. I'm the government in this town. Tell Mr. Conway we'll exchange one-third of our liquid assets at that bloodsucking rate. We'll leave it in Montreal for a few months, and when all this revolutionary crap has become shit, I want every single penny back and might even start my own bank to teach Mr. Conway that that's no way to treat your friends."

Nelson was dumbfounded. He never expected the Old Man to be so cooperative. Somehow his determination made him tenser. He was so sure his father wasn't going to give in.

"Any news from J.R., your brother?"

"He's still with the circus."

"One day he'll come crawling back. He has always been a stray bullet. I knew it since I saw him in his crib. Each time I placed that pacifier in his mouth, he spat it right out. When I put some strawberry jelly on its tip, he wiped the jelly with his tongue and out it went anyway. He's been with that circus for what...three years now."

"Oh, no, Daddy, it has been now close to eighteen years."

"That shithead will come back crawling like a scared dog with his tail between his legs. Anything else?"

"No, Daddy."

"How's Nellie?"

"She's doing just fine."

"Is she still playing with her pig."

"Yes, Daddy. It's her pet."

"You should have married someone from the capital. That whole family is defective. You better go back to work. One loafer in the family is enough!"

"Should I see Mr. Conway?"

"Didn't I tell you to do it? Do as you're told, young man. I'm going to bring this fucking town to its knees. I'll show them what to do with their barges."

"Yes, sir."

At the stroke of midnight, Mr. Conway opened the vault and placed one-third of their stock certificates, bonds, insurance policies, and stacks of $10,000 bills amounting to 3 million in an inconspicuous looking suitcase.

"Are you certain no one will follow me, Mr. Conway?"

"If you stick to the plan I told you, you shouldn't have any problems. Remember, a man will be at the embassy's gate. You will ask him if his name is Raleigh. He must answer you affirmatively and right away take one step forward and two steps back. Be just a little bit careful, lad, and you will encounter no problems. Trust me!"

Radishes

Mrs. James B. beeped the horn of her 1956 Chevy, threw the shift in park, and turned off the engine. She flipped the radio dial and tuned in to the Mighty Voice of the Glades. The Country Hit Parade was on and she began tapping the wheel with her knuckles and the gas pedal with her foot to the rhythm of "Foolin' Around," sung by Buck Owens and The Buckaroos. She waited for Nellie to appear on the front porch. She turned on the small battery fan that rested on top of the dashboard. The Chevy's windows were rolled all the way up to keep out the legions of nocturnal bugs that had descended on Belle Glade after the big flood. Old timers that had witnessed the hurricane of 1929 said firmly that back then there were lots of bugs but that at least they were local bugs; this time they must have come from some place else because they hadn't seen the likes of them before. The whole town smelled primordially putrid from the vapors given off by the muddy stew of decaying vegetation and carcasses of drowned animals. Thousands of years from this date, with a little heat and pressure, this same spot could be the site of a gigantic oil field.

"Shit, what's taking her so long? I hope she ain't in the john!" Mrs. James B. thought aloud as she turned the radio lever all the way left to the treble position.

The porch lit up and she heard the door slam. Nellie, clad in her work clothes, a yellow raincoat, a towel turban to cover her head, and a pair of her husband's socks to protect her hands, approached slowly.

Mrs. James B. cracked her window for a second and shouted, "Hurry up, woman! We ain't got the whole day!"

As she finished uttering the last word, a squadron of pal-
metto bugs, buzzing in kamikaze formation, hovered, ready to
crash against the Chevy's high beams.

"Good morning, Mrs. James B. Oh, but what happened to
your face? It's swollen."

"A bee got me this morning. But close that door quickly!
Close itttt! I swear, sometimes I think you have a pea for a
brain. What took you so long? Were you in the act?"

"Oh, no. I don't act. But I once played the part of Gene-
vieve de Brabant for the Ladies' Tennis Club Spring Festival
of Plays."

"No kidding!"

"I can still recite all my lines," added a proud Nellie, and
then continued, "I know I took a little bit too long, but I have
been so happy all this week. I am as if floating on pheasants
feathers."

"How can you be so chirpy when we lost our zoo? I swear,
this time it's really beyond me. Do you realize we're going
back to our crappy jobs?"

"Oh, Mrs. James B., but I have great news! I saw a real
live truffle when I took refuge on top of that tree. Do you know
what that means? It means truffles never live alone. If you
discover one, there are many more around. They bring such
joy to me, memories of Rigoletto..." She sighed slightly when
she said his name.

"What in the hell is a truffle?"

"It's a delicacy. They grow in cool, moist soil, under rocks
or underground. My father said the name comes from the
Latin 'trufera' which means tuber. They were so abundant in
Mondovi..."

"It sounds to me like one of them mushrooms. I hate
them. I spend more time pulling them darn things out of my
pizza than eating it. And I mean pulling out 'cause they get
stuck in the cheese, and I swear you need a shovel to dig them
out."

"But, Mrs. James B., a truffle is not a mushroom. There is no comparison!" Nellie sounded politely indignant.

"Listen, Nellie, we better get moving, so leave your mushroom talk for later." Mrs. James B. turned on the ignition as she talked to her friend.

Crrrr, crrrr, crrr, the Chevy shook. Mrs. James B. kept turning the key, but the old heap stood its ground. The high beams flickered, losing power with each crank.

"Gummit! Do you know anything about cars? She corrected herself as soon as she said it. "What a dumb thing to ask. Of course, you don't."

"The air smells of gasoline," Nellie said. "When this happened to father's El Dorado, he used to call Juan Benson, our gardener, so he could open the hood and check inside."

"Is that a fact!" a slightly sarcastic Mrs. James B. responded, and then said aloud, but talking to herself. "I'm gonna let it cool for a while. Maybe the hot weather is making something stick."

"What do we do now?"

"We wait, Nellie. We twiddle our fingers!"

"I could call Nelson, but he doesn't know much about cars either."

"Air, air, air! I need to get out. I'm getting them hot flashes again. I need fresh air," screamed Mrs. James B. as she wiped the large drops of sweat that were breaking out on her forehead.

"But the insects...Mrs. James B., the insects..." Nellie reminded the sweltering driver.

Mrs. James B. opened the door and rushed out, swatting at the flying critters. Once out in the open, she yelled at Nellie.

"C'mon, Nellie. C'mon out. You got your coat. They won't bother you! C'mon out and I'll teach you something to cool us down. I'm gonna teach you a cheer."

"Okay," she said as she gracefully placed her right foot out and propelled herself with her left hand.

The teaching began.

"Repeat the words after me and move when I do. Is that clear? Do you follow me?"

Seeing that Nellie was attentive, she started. "Ready? Let's go: 'Lions, let's get to it, M . OH . VEE . EE. Move it!' You have to shake your butt more when you say 'Move It.' Like this," and she wiggled her buttocks.

"I think I know now Mrs. James B. It's like a standing-still tarantella."

Seeing that Nellie wasn't getting it, she walked behind her and, grabbing her rump, shook it, and said, "M. OH. VEE. EE. Move it, Nellie, move it!"

They practiced five more times, and when Mrs. James B. thought Nellie had it, they coordinated a cheer, shaking their butts in unison. In her cheerfulness, she hadn't noticed her arms covered with creeping things. When she saw them at the end of the last "move it," she screamed, and both women rushed inside the car. Mrs. James B. cranked it twice, and when she was about to yell a louder 'gummit,' the frightened motor turned and roared. She floored it, and they shrieked around the corner. A few seconds later, they were cruising down Main Street. On their way to the packing house, Mrs. James B. yawned a few times and decided to stop at Bertha's Big T truck stop to get a quick cup of coffee. She could have easily stopped at the Dairy Queen, avoiding all those extra turns, but Mrs. James B. loved to see the truckers' heads craned around and feel their fixed stares as she sauntered to the counter.

"Kenny, a cup of coffee. Better make it a corn dawg and a cup of coffee," she ordered.

"For crying out loud, if it ain't Mrs. James B." He was happy to see her.

"The very same one, but make it snappy. I ain't got much time to socialize."

Before she got her order, Mrs. James B. tightened her belt two more notches to accentuate her imprisoned buttocks and further incite the truckers' lusty glances as she walked back to the car, her hips swaying in the night.

"Do it to me, baby!" the teamsters yelled in harmony, their tongues swollen with satyriasis.

Mrs. James B. stopped to smirk at them.

Inside the car, and while drinking her coffee, a beaming Mrs. James B. told Nellie what to say in case their fellow workers harassed them for their zoo fiasco. Mrs. James B. hadn't invited any of them to the ribbon-cutting ceremony. She thought she was about to become somebody, and somebodies don't have to hang around nobodies.

"You leave it up to me, Nellie. You keep quiet and let me handle it. When we get there, you walk nimbly like Jack."

"Jack, the foreman?" asked a puzzled Nellie.

"No, no. The guy I read about when I was five. Didn't they teach you anything! And don't forget this time to please sit between myself and Naomi. I don't like her sitting next to me."

The foreman, Jack Jackson, was standing in front of the main entrance, and they could hear the monotonous sounds of the conveyor belt bringing in the produce. The other workers were already at their stations, their hands moving like a sideways millipede.

"Good afternoon," said a sarcastic Mr. Jackson. "A bit late, aren't we?"

"Beat it, Jack. We had car trouble, and you ain't paying us extra for getting up so early," answered back a sassy Mrs. J.B.

"You're lucky to have a job." Jack laughed balefully and plucked her by the sleeve on his way to answer the ringing phone.

"Good morning, gals," said the late comers as they entered the nave's long corridor, illuminated by dim light to save on electricity. Mr. Jackson pocketed the difference. "That bleach sure smells mean today," Mrs. James B. added when a whiff from the radishes' soaking tank reached her nostrils.

Nellie walked a few paces behind her as was their custom,
Nellie thinking it was a mark of distinction (as did Mrs.
James B.).

There were ten women working in station five, counting
the two new arrivals: Loly Espino, ex-wife of Senator
Zubizarreta; Victoria Rey, wife of the poet laureate Lisander
Pons; Pituca Josende, wife of Chief Justice Josende; Aïda
López, the leading national contralto, Naomi Brown, nobody's
wife anymore; Mirta Vergara, the freedom fighter; Maria Rosa
García-Peña, daughter of the first President of the Ladies'
Tennis Club; and Helen Valdés-Curl, wife of the late Pete
Frey, the inventor of the improved muriatic acid.

The conveyor belt bringing the radishes was going at full
speed, working to capacity as five trucks pulled into the rear
parking lot bringing thousands more radishes to be unloaded,
sorted, and packed. The belt was moving so fast the drier
didn't have a chance to evaporate the moisture from the
radishes after their journey through the bleach-soaking tank
and red-dye tank that had made them redder and more
appealing to consumers.

"I think I am going to faint," said a dizzy, pale Loly.

"Don't look at the conveyor. Keep your eyes up, Loly."

"I can't, Victoria."

"Take your pearls off. I know how you start twisting the
string around and counting the beads. That makes you dizzi-
er. Take a break. I'll give you a hand. I'm fast!"

"Hey, ladies, stop the bantering and get your asses in
gear!" shouted Mr. Jackson from his cubicle.

"It's okay, Vicky. I am feeling much better," answered a
slightly agitated Loly.

"He's so vulgar. He takes advantage of us because there
isn't a man around. If I were to tell Lisander, he would come
and ask him to apologize to us, or else he would ask him to
choose his weapon and meet him at daybreak in the Winn
Dixie parking lot. My husband is a gentleman. But I won't tell
him because that beast might fire me, and we need the money.

Lis is trying to find work, but it's not easy for a man of his caliber to find work suitable to his status. You know he's our poet laureate."

"I know the feeling. I am also a supporting beam in our household and for this reason we have to endure all sorts of rubbish. Before I forget, Vicky, I heard a rumor that if someone in the family isn't working, the government comes and relocates the entire family to Montana. Then they make you work on buffalo farms where the women and the children have to milk the cows and the men have to make the cheese. And let me tell you that that place is as cold as Siberia and that...oh, excuse me!" Loly burped. She seemed bewildered by the prolonged sound that had come out of her mouth. "I am so sorry! I feel so humiliated! I have never burped in my life! Never. Not even as a chid! I am so sorry! I am the first Espino to burp. What's becoming of us in this country! I am so sorry." With the last sorry she began to cry.

Vicky held her hand, trying to console her as she continued sorting out the radishes with the other.

"Don't cry, Loly. It was a very small burp. No one heard it." Vicky smiled.

"Are you sure?" said Loly as she wiped the tears off her cheeks with her string of pearls.

"Yes, I am."

"I am very nervous, Vicky. My brother Cioci and my sister Mely were arrested yesterday. You know how they go to different restaurants when we don't have the proper diet at home and they wait for the waiter to bring the basket with the bread and crackers and the butter squares and they start eating and when the waiter goes in to give their order to the kitchen, they grab what remains in the basket and run out as fast as they can. But yesterday Cioci stumbled on a chair and they were apprehended. They were released on bail. It cost me this month's rent."

"Oh, Loly! Let me cheer you up with one of Lisander's poems. The one he wrote when our son, Julian, was born. It goes like this. Of course, when he recites it, it sounds much better. I don't have his eloquence or his diction.

> A child from deep in his soul
> gave me such a sincere kiss
> that the day I meet my maker
> I will feel that kiss again.

"That's really beautiful," said Aïda, the contralto, who was eavesdropping. "He should set it to music, and I'd love to sing it."

The rest of station five nodded in approval, except for Naomi and Mrs. James B., who didn't understand what was going on, and Nellie, whose mind had flown to Mondovi.

"Whut she say?" asked Naomi to Pituca while wiping off the red dye on her apron.

"Is a poem her husband wrote for their son. Very nice, very nice," Pituca Josende strained her voice, struggling with the guttural sounds.

"Ah had uh hosband once tuh, but he left me wid four mouths tuh feed. He jus' took off one mornin'. He said he wuz goin' tuh de sugar mill tuh see if dey needed help and dat wuz de last time ah seen dat man."

"Losing a husband is nothing! The loss of your motherland is a weight that sinks your soul into the abyss of everlasting depression, forever damned to be a pariah," shouted Mirta, dressed in her camouflaged, tight, army pants. "But we shall return." This time, her voice echoed through the nave. Then, in a lower tone, she added, "This is the struggle between civilization and barbarity. The hour has arrived to dislodge the sanguinary tyranny that has enveloped our beloved island. We must keep the pressure on. We mustn't be soft with the oppressors, for the tigers, scared by gunfire, return at night to their prey. We were that prey. The tigers approached on their velvet paws. We were relaxing, enjoying ourselves, with our guard down, asleep, and when we awoke and realized what had happened, the tigers were already upon us, devouring our flesh. We must go back and hunt the tigers! Why do I constantly incite you to struggle, to fight day and night at Pepe's Grocery, at Pituca's canasta parties, at work? I do it because I have known the pain of prison in my own flesh. It's the hardest of pains. The most destroying of afflictions, that which murders the intelligence and withers the soul. But let me tell you something, women of our land, the absence of the motherland is worse than a prison cell. It's a loneliness that spreads like a cancer and is nourished by every somber sorrow, and finally wanders about, magnified by every scalding tear. If for some of you the concept of motherland is vague, think of your Xawa, especially you, Loly, you, Pituca, you, Nellie…"

Nellie interrupted Mirta's patriotic harangue. "I'm not from there."

Mirta continued, ignoring Nellie's remarks.

"The motherland, Xawa, must be the altar on which we offer our lives, not a pedestal to lift us above. How many of you in this packing house are willing to take up arms, to become the paschal lambs on the altar of freedom?"

There was absolute silence.

"I know it's criminal to promote war when it can be avoided, but for us war is unavoidable. I know at the bottom of my heart that when life weighs less than the infamy in which it crawls, war is the most beautiful and respectable form of human sacrifice. Yes, war is frightening to those mediocre souls incapable of choosing perilous dignity over a useless life under oppression. I would like to ask each one of you if you are the type of women who think more of yourselves than of your neighbors, and detests the procedure of justice that can bring your risks or discomforts. I know you are not! I know you are women who love the certain benefits of a free motherland more than the dubious benefit of a never ending exile, which will be the sole legacy to your children. I know you are ready like I am, willing to expose myself to death in order to enable our country to live. I am working in this place instead of training for the invasion because I am in need of cash to buy a machine gun. Now I want you to start your commitment to freedom by donating any amount, a quarter, a dime, a half dollar to expedite the process of freedom by helping me to buy my weapon. Then you can rest assured that I will join the freedom fighters' training camp by the lake."

Mirta passed her military cap around, but heard no metallic sounds. Her cloth plate returned empty. She said nothing and went back to work.

"Ah don't know nothing 'bout yo' mama or whut yuh wuz sayin' about tigers and war but ah can tell yuh dat life ain't got no better after Johnny took off. Dere's another man goin' round muh place every night. Ah guess muh mama wuz right. She said ah wuz bad news 'cause ah gathered men 'round me lak ants to spilled sugar. Ah think dat man smells ah'm widout auh man and wants an easy piece, but ah ain't messing round wid nobody. Ah might git me uh gun, not uh fancy one lak yo want, but just uh plain old gun. Lawd, mah feet are sho killin' me today. How many chillums yuh have, Mirtha?"

"I have no children. My children are the bullets I will put in my gun to bring freedom to my land!"

"We need a break, fast!"

"We sho do, Mrs. Pituca. De night is losing flesh and blackness, but he ain't gon give us one 'til we finish dis load. Ah know dat man is uh son uh bitch."

"No, no, no, Naomi. No bad words. Wash your mouse wis soap. Is no nice for a lady," Pituca scolded her, and went on, saying, "My stepsister, a communist, says many bad words. I will not talk to her ever in my life again. If she has no food, I will never give her nosin. Never!"

"Yuh have younguns, Pituca?" inquired Naomi.

"Eh?"

"Younguns, chillum, kids," she made a gesture with her free hand, indicating height.

"Jes, I have four."

"Oh, just lak me den," Naomi grinned.

"Change the station for just a second so we can listen to the news," Mirta yelled to Mrs. James B. who was at the other end, rocking her hips to the rhythms of country tunes.

"I can't, Mirtha. It's 'Foolin' Around,' my favorite song. Besides, the news brings bad luck," Mrs. James B. yelled back, and continued to sing along the last refrain with The Buckaroos, "When you are tired of foolin' with two or three, c'mon home and fool around with me."

"Leave her with her music, Mirta," intervened Victoria, "I know that's her favorite song because she's always whistling it. It makes her happy, and you know how much she suffered during the flood."

"I'll be cow-kicked, Mrs. Pons, if you think you can bad-mouth me. I ain't suffering a bit! But I'm ticked off 'cause I have to work with you pig-meats when I was about to piss on ice! I hate this rat hole as much as I hate the rain! So mind your own business or stick it where the sun ain't shining!"

Loly was going to say something to defend Vicky, but the conveyor belt was churning, making its loud monotonous cries which drowned her soft voice. Mr. Jackson, who made his rounds to each station, making sure the socializing was kept to a minimum, turned up at station five. It was their turn. He got real close to some of the women, rubbing his dark regions against the unsuspecting backs, pretending to be checking on their quality control. Soon enough, the women realized what he was up to and warned each other of the impending lecher's attack.

There was silence now, each worker concentrating on the blemished radishes. Only the twinkling sounds of Vicky's and Pituca's bracelets, heavy with charms, broke the silence as they swatted mosquitoes. The bracelets were loaded with big, shiny medals commemorating their coming-out parties, twenty-dollar gold pieces, silvery crucifixes, tiny tennis rackets, diminutive cupids shooting arrows at unseen targets, and small, green figures in the form of babies representing their offspring. Vicky had two. Pituca had four. Neither woman had

had the courage to pawn these treasures. Pituca had walked once to The Pawn Shop, but as she was about to knock on the door, she remembered her godmother who had given her some of the heirlooms, and sighing heavily, she turned around to leave. The following day she ended up at the packing house and at Mr. Jackson's mercy.

The sun was beginning to stir in the sky, its soft vermillion hues nearly blocked by the heavy fog that was rolling in from the Big Lake. It settled so heavily inside the nave, it seemed that floating, bodiless hands were toying with the produce. Then a cry of anguish was heard which awoke the workers from their zombie-like state. It was Loly.

"They are coming to get us! They want my pearls!" Loly's face was red, and drops of perspiration stood out on it like the morning dew. She was looking at her fingers, now swollen, numb, and peeling from the bleach and covered with tiny welts that had begun to bleed.

"Who's tryin' tuh git who?" asked a haggard Naomi.

"They." Loly pointed to the radishes.

"Girl, yuh crazy. Yuh afraid uf dem radishes? Yuh crazy!"

"They're coming. They are coming to take me to Montana!" she said, running toward the next station, looking for a place to hide.

Some of the women rushed after Loly, trying to catch the fleeing Miss Espino and calm her down. Loly was too fast and eluded them, leaping like a frightened antelope. Mrs. James B., who had remained at her station listening to the end of the Country Hit Parade, got up and ran to the right of the soaking tank, sensing Loly's next move. Remembering one of Mr. James B.'s best tackles, she grabbed Loly by the ankles and brought her to the ground. Their collision knocked Loly out. When she came back to her senses, Naomi was wetting her forehead with a damp handkerchief.

Vicky had stayed behind, working and reciting her husband's poems, oblivious to what had transpired.

"Hey, hey, hey, stop the ruckus and get back to work. I have someone new for your station. Maybe it will make you work harder. And you'll have to do that batch again. I swear you're like children. The minute I don't look, you start goofing off. Her name is Dina Ferro."

"There ain't no ruckus here, Jack. She was upset because her hands are falling apart. You promised the new gloves would be here last week," said a sassy Mrs. James B.

"Get back to work! They'll come when they come. I ain't the factory that makes them!" He punctuated his sentence with a threatening gesture of his fist.

"I swear, if you touch me, you sissy, my husband will grind you into fine powder," she yelled back as she swaggered back to the station.

Jack didn't answer her, but showed Dina to her stool.

The fog was beginning to burn off and the conveyor belt had stopped churning. The women, taking advantage of their break, were now sitting on the floor eating honey buns and drinking rusty-tasting coffee from the dilapidated vending machines that sat across from Mr. Jackson's cubicle. Loly, who had borrowed Nellie's socks to protect her swollen hands, was completely calm.

"Ah didn't ketch yo' name," Naomi said. "Demita, right?"

"No, no, my name is Dina. In my country I was university professor of anatomy!" She punctuated her sentence by covering her tongue with the bubble gum she was chewing.

"Aw, is dat so. Ah'm Naomi Brown."

"Loly, are the socks helping any? I'm sorry they are not silk. I used to wrap Rigoletto's in pure Chinese silk," said Nellie as Loly kept gazing at a nail that protruded from the wall by the vending machine. "This would never have happened in Mondovi, never, never, never!"

"Dat where yuh from?" asked an inquisitive Naomi in a nasal-sounding voice. She spent the whole break, or whenever she had a free hand, pressing her nose between her thumb and index finger.

"Practically, yes. I was destined to be born in Mondovi, but navigational problems prevented what was meant to be."

"Are y'all from de same place?"

"Yes and no, but let me tell you about Mondovi. It is paradise on earth where the truffles are as common as wild flowers. I can see it in my mind: my father talking to Sergio and Adriano, and Antonio Roasio shutting the door to his room in Albergo Tre Limoni D'Oro and walking down the Red Bridge della Madonnina and then crossing the Ponte Monumentale, heading for Besio's Clinic where his sister, Franca Milano, lies sick. After the visit, he would stop at the Shrine of Our Lady of Mondovi and light two candles, one for his sick sister and the other one for the soul of his friend Mario Trigari, who died during the Spanish Civil War defending the Crown Prince of Spain, who was my father's personal friend, against the Reds."

"Who's de Reds? De Indians?"

"Oh, no, the communists."

"Yuh sho remember uh whole lot, Nellie. Ah wish ah remember dat much. Ah remember some when ah wuz growin' up in Cordell livin' wid mah grandmama. Mah mama sent me to her when ah waz three, and ah ain't never seen mah papa. Ah remember muh third-grade teacher, Miss Myers. She wuz white. She always made me sit in de front desk uh de second row. She said ah wuz tuh light tuh sit way tuh de back. She said, 'Naomi, yuh very light and if yuh press yo' nose everday yuh gon do fine in dis world.' Ah always made better grades dan de real dark kids dat had tuh sit way in de back," she replied proudly.

"You made me remember a little verse my father wrote on his last visit to my meant-to-be-homeland. Pietrarca, a well-known poet, would probably say it has no literary value, but for me is like my national anthem."

"Say it, girl."

"Do you sincerely want to hear it?" Nellie was moved by the request, her voice quivering.

"Say it, woman."

"It goes like this: '*Comme sei bell a o Mondovi, a chi giunge/ nuovo a 'l tuo seno, e bella a chi ritorna/ spronato dal desio che 'l cor gli punge!*'"

"Whut yuh say?"

"My father used to say that words that are like magic should never be rendered in another language. What I said is beautiful. Believe me."

While the conversation between Nellie and Naomi centered on Mondovi and Naomi's native Cordell, Georgia, her children and her missing husband, on the other side of the room the dialogue between Vicky and Pituca Josende centered on their bracelets and was escalating to a scalding crescendo.

"Oh, Pituca, that's a beautiful jade figurine. Did your husband give it to you?"

"I beg to disagree with you," said Pituca. "This charm was given to me by my godmother on the occasion of the birth of my firstborn, Eurico. It's an authentic Colombian emerald in the form of a child."

"It looks more like jade to me."

"An envious heart makes sightless eyes. Looks are deceiving to the untrained seer. I remember the day when my godmother gave it to me. We were horseback riding on our 40,000 acre recreational ranch. I was on a thoroughbred, and Goddy was riding her Arabian stallion. We were riding side by side, and she told me to close my eyes and open my hands, and she deposited the precious stone in my palm."

"It must have been around the same time Lisander was courting me while we were canoeing in my family's private 150-mile river. He was a wonderful sailor, avoiding the rapids with the skill of a professional paddler. No wonder he represented us in the 1948 Olympic Games."

"A river. What is a river when you control the water sources?" responded Pituca with contempt. "My father, may he rest in peace—and I thank God each and every day of my life until the day I die, for sparing him this diaspora and taking him in his sleep five years ago—controlled the waters. He possessed all springs seen and subterranean, the lakes, the rains, the hurricanes, the cold fronts and any other water phenomena. If he had wanted, he could have transformed your river into a dry bed."

"What is water, Pituca, in comparison to my family who owned all insects, amphibians and birds? We were sole proprietors by a Royal Decree of 1763, when one of my ancestors, Epaminondas Rey, bravely defended the capital against the English pirates. In gratitude for such valor, the King of Spain himself bestowed upon the family for perpetuity all the 'aves,' 'amphibia' and 'insecta.' To put it simpler for you, like my Lisander would say, birds, frogs, and bugs. If we really had wanted, we could have sent wave after wave of mosquitoes, gnats, wasps, bees, yellow jackets, fire ants, spiders, silverfish, aphids, whiteflies, mealybugs, thrips, spider mites and scale crawlers, just to mention a few, and your silly father would have been forced to replenish our river in a hurry with all the water it needed. And I still say that charm is jade and not emerald."

The last words so offended Pituca that she tried to yank Vicky's bracelet from her wrist.

"Help, help! She is trying to steal my bracelet," blared Vicky in distress.

Loly, Helen and María Rosa rushed in but were unable to quench the quarrel, when Mirta stepped in and scolded the pugilists, pushing them aside and lecturing them on their obvious lack of patriotism, especially at a time when the motherland was mortally wounded by the red spear of communism.

"In the memory of my late husband, Pete," Helen's voice quivered as she spoke to the combatants from behind the veil that had shrouded her countenance since her husband's abduction, "I beseech you not to debase yourselves by brawling."

"What's all the fuss?" asked a puzzled Mrs. James B. as she turned her radio down.

"Ah don't know whut dey were saying, but ah think dey fightin' over jewelry," answered Naomi while pinching her nose.

"Nellie, Nellie," screamed Mrs. James B., pretending not to hear Naomi, "What's going on?"

"I didn't hear the whole argument, but I gathered Vicky said Pituca's charm was made out of jade; that it was not a true emerald, and that her family was going to force Pituca's into filling up her river to the brim."

"All that fuss for that! Who gives a horse's patooty if it ain't a jade or not!"

"Mrs. James B.," replied Nellie, "The gem's origin is not really important, but the threat of sending those plagues is, because her family owned that array of insects and could have very well forced the Josendes into replenishing the river, and if things got out of hand, even into serfdom."

"Hey, gals. The break is over. Get your asses back on them stools. You're a bad example to this Johnny-come-late-ly." He grabbed Dina by her left shoulder. She seemed to enjoy that extra attention. "One more thing—Reverend Fender will be talking to you tomorrow as you work. He has asked for my permission, so you make sure you show some respect to the reverend."

There was no need to identify the thundering voice.

"Ah wish her family'd sic all dem bugs on Mr. Jackson," muttered Naomi as she walked back to work.

One Day in 1942

"Hey, Nelson. I'm glad you're sitting down because I've become a believer. Mary Magdalene pray for me. I've been to paradise!"

"Quiet, Bernabé! Can't you see I'm studying? In case you've forgotten, I'm not going to let you cheat off me anymore if you don't make an effort to study. Did you go by the post office box like I told you?"

"How could I if I was in paradise!"

"Cut the crap. I'm having problems with this page and you're bothering me."

"That's what I like about you, Nelson. You're a solid citizen, a credit to our community, a friend, a pal, a confidante, a man for all seasons. Can you lend me $10 for a good cause?" Bernabé rested his arm on Nelson's shoulder and made a begging gesture with his free hand.

"Who do you think I am, City Bank? Is this so you can go to 43 Crespo Street? If it's for that, you know damn well they only charge a dollar and you don't last ten times."

"How would you know how much they charge?"

"You still owe me a dollar from last week," Nelson avoided the issue.

"Fourty-three Crespo Street! What a child you are!" Bernabé, with his arm still resting on Nelson's shoulder, cleared his throat for his exposé. "I graduated from that elementary institution eons ago, and you're still in kindergarten. I've discovered the meaning of love, my dear, stingy, rich friend. I've discovered Marina's, the last frontier of bliss."

"So that's why you didn't go by the post office? You can't be trusted to do anything right!"

"What's a silly letter from your girlfriend relating her most recent adventure with her decrepit swine? Besides, didn't she say in her latest she didn't want to see you anymore because you wouldn't kiss the pig? This is your golden opportunity to break the chains of chastity!"

"Leave my girlfriend out of this!" Nelson sounded offended.

"Okay, pal, I believe you, but could you lend me your ears for a few seconds while I preach the good news to the unbelievers?"

"My shoulder is getting tired, so grab a chair."

"Bernabé grabbed one of the folding chairs and sat facing Nelson. Bernabé could smell Nelson's cauliflower breath; he thought it was a small price to pay for his conversion.

"I was walking down the street by the monument to the Maine, on my way to the post office, when I saw a score of chauffeurs parked on both sides of the street. Obviously they were waiting for their bosses and, *voilá*, I saw a pink-marble mansion with Corinthian columns and emerald shutters. Right away my keen senses confirmed this place was heavenly, Gomorrah descending."

"How do you know they were Corinthian and not Doric columns?"

"Nelson, who gives a damn what type of columns they were? I called them Corinthians because it's the only name that stuck in my mind when we took that shitty art-history course with that pansy English guy."

"Okay, speed it up. I've got to study." Nelson stopped reading his notes and raised his eyes.

"When I saw Mayor Sánchez waving at a woman dressed in a giraffe costume and heard the animal giggling while he threw kisses at her—which she pretended landed on her ass—I knew that I, the Sir Alexander Fleming of lust, had made a great discovery. I approached one of the chauffeurs and had what must have been the same feeling Columbus had when he approached Queen Isabella. I asked him to let me borrow his hat and coat so I could enter the mansion under the pretense I was looking for my boss. Of course, the infidel said no. But I waved in front of his greedy eyes a crisp ten-dollar bill which Mom had sent me for the month's groceries.

"How inconsiderate! That poor widow must have sewn like mad to send you that money."

"No footnotes, please! The chauffeur took my bait, and I went straight to the mansion pretending I was looking for a Mr. Febles, my boss, who was really the chauffeur's boss.

"What a place! I was in paradise! The golden age in which animals and humans lived in total communion with nature and with each other! No wonder so many Arabs are willing to die in a holy war. Then I had my first vision. There was this sparkling fountain in the shape of a waterfall surrounded by women dressed as animals—rabbits, giraffes, deer, poodles, doves, goldfish, koalas, beavers, butterflies, kittens, squirrels, and even a pony. I was in ecstasy contemplating the bare, chested fauna when I was tapped on my shoulder by Marina herself. To me she was like an angel with the most succulent breasts mortal eyes have ever seen—and I have seen hundreds. I was so taken by her radiance I knelt by her feet in an act of worship. She knew right away I was not a chauffeur but a trespasser. I thought she was going to call one of the bouncers to kick me out, but she was so moved by my adoration, she let me stay for a few minutes. I begged her to let me enjoy the tactile pleasures of paradise. I even offered to feed the animals so they wouldn't have to move from their peaceful rest by the fountain. 'I don't think you carry the type of food those animals eat,' she said with a grin. I implored her to let me caress one of the beavers."

"Why a beaver?"

"Because there were more beavers than any other type of animal."

I thought she was about to acquiesce when she said, 'You're cute, but business is business. You're out of your range here. Unless you cough up ten big ones, you can't hunt here.'

"Ten big ones!" I said as vibrations of despair ran though my vocal cords. That angel denied me permission to remain in Eden."

"And then what?"

"Ten dollars," her unwavering voice echoed against the paper-mache hills which encircled the perimeter of the hall. I had to think fast. I took my chain off and offered her my gold medal of Our Lady of Charity. She bit the medal, smelled it, lifted her robe, placed it inside her sex, waited three agonizing minutes, and declared that it was real gold since it didn't tarnish. Then the angel said I had to limit myself to hoofed animals and to be out in six minutes."

"But you wanted the beaver, right?" Nelson's privates were far beyond the point of arousal, and the perceptive listener could have heard the rhythmic taps against the bottom of the table.

"Right, but I had to decide between the giraffe and the pony. I chose the pony. Marina then whistled and the pony came to where we were. She gave me the reins to Furia, that was the girl's name.

"It was glorious! The pony took me to a room fixed like a stable and filled with hay."

"And then what?"

"Aren't we getting interested now? I knew you would because you're a lecher at heart. Well, while we were naked and rolling in the hay, she asked me to ride her. I did, and she shouted she was not a pony but a wild Italian mare. She started kicking in the air and twisting her neck to bite me, yelling loudly in Italian: 'Volgio essere scopata da un cavallo bianco. Mettimelo dentro, cowboy. Lo voglio di dietro, John Wayne!'"

"What does it mean?"

"I don't know, but I imagine it was something really dirty, which made me even hornier."

"Keep going. Don't stop now!"

"Furia was trying to unseat me, but I had a good grip of her buttocks. I rode her like a real cowboy. Those six minutes seemed more like an hour, but I tamed that wild Italian mare."

"How do you know you tamed her?"

"She neighed and collapsed in the hay."

"Bernabé, I give up. It's impossible to study with you distracting me. Take me to paradise!"

"You slimy jerk-off! Only if you let me cheat from your paper, pay half of the groceries, and lend me ten dollars."

"Okay, Bernabé. Do you think I have time for a quick shower?"

"Why? Do you want to smell pretty for the beasts?"

Nelson put his books and notes aside and went straight to the shower. A few minutes later, Bernabé heard the sounds of gargling and the tiny cries of thousands of foul-smelling microbes being destroyed by Dr. Lister's love potion. When Nelson came out, he smelled of Castile soap. His hair was parted in the middle instead of to the right, and he was holding a piece of paper which he promptly tucked inside his pocket.

"Could you step up your pace, Bernabé? We're going to be late. Maybe they have already closed?"

"It never ceases to amaze me how little you know about life, Nelson Guiristain. It seems your mind has atrophied from studying too much. They are not closed. This is not, I repeat, this is not 43 Crespo Street. These are the big leagues, my friend. Hard ball, do you understand? Hard slides. Fast pitches. Aggressive base running. Squeeze bunts. Four baggers. A place for sluggers like me."

"I have something to tell you if you promise not to laugh."

"Spit it out."

"When I was in the bathroom, I wrote Nellie a small letter. I was feeling kind of guilty about going to his new place. I want you to read it since you know so much about women."

"When it comes to women, I'm the Bible. Hand me that piece of papyrus...." Bernabé scanned the letter.

"Are you through, Berna? What do you think?"

"It is really lacking. Your introduction is passable, but the body is weak, real weak. You might know a lot about accounts payable, but you don't know shit about what's really important. I guess you study about life; I live life. Give me a pen."

"Here, Berna."

"What's her favorite flower?"

"Gee, I don't know, but her father's is the tulip. I know since he always wears one on his lapel."

"She probably takes after her father; most women do." Bernabé proceeded to read his composition out loud. "The pink tulip that I gave you on the day that I first met you, it wasn't a tulip, baby, but a dart to pierce your heart. Yes, Nellie, you're the sunshine of my life, my irresistible bag of potato chips... I can't eat just one! Just sign your name, and we'll mail it right after we finish our business."

"Thank you, Berna. She's always sending me these complicated poems, and I can't think like that. Thanks, pal!"

"Maybe with your generous help I might be able to pursue the elusive beaver."

"Do you think I'll be able to get the squirrel?"

"I'll see what I can do for you once we get there. I have connections with the guardian angel of Eden."

They knocked on the heavy bronze door, and Marina's face appeared on the threshold of the misty gate flanked by two immense Nubians. They were ready to frisk the newcomers when the angel recognized her ardent, young worshipper.

"It's okay, boys," Marina said, turning her face to the Nubians. And then, looking Bernabé straight in the crotch, she said, "I'm not accepting any more medals."

"That won't be a problem, ma'am. This is my third cousin and good friend, Nelson G-G-Guiristain," he said, stuttering.

"I'm not interested in introductions. Do you two have cash? Not monopoly money, real bills."

Nelson was experiencing heavy stomach cramps which were usually followed by the emptying of his guts. Embarrassed for what might happen and to relieve his fear, he opened his wallet and took out a twenty which he kept in the secret compartment for emergencies. He placed it in Marina's hands. She put it against the light and judged it to be legal tender.

"C'mon, boys. Make yourselves at home."

The hybrids were not around the fountain as Bernabé had said.

"Where are they?" Nelson shouted nervously.

"I don't know. Maybe they are all busy."

As they were searching for the fauna, a humming sound beckoned them to make their way around the fountain to a small hall that opened into an interior courtyard. The animals were encircling the mango tree that stood in the middle, chanting an enervating bee-sounding verse as they formed a perfect circle around a naked elderly man. Bernabé saw his pony chanting next to the squirrel.

"Furia, Furia." The girl turned her head sideways enough to see who was calling. Bernabé approached her.

"Hush. Can't you see we're conducting a dirge? *Sei cieco*, cowboy?"

"Sure, a dirge. Sure. I've seen many, but I have never bothered to pay too much attention." Bernabé tried to sound worldly.

"It's Mayor Sánchez."

"Mayor Paco J. Sánchez, the hero of San Juan Hill?"

"That's him, right there with the same problem as always. He can't get it hard today, so the giraffe is trying to resuscitate his wiener, breathe some life into it. We're praying for her success. *E una cantata miracolosa!*"

"I don't speak mare yet!"

"A miraculous song. Look it's coming back to life. It's rising from the dead."

As soon as the giraffe noticed the magic effect of the dirge, she sighed and signaled the others to leave them alone. Nelson showed Furia his ticket, and she neighed affirmatively.

"Want to ride, cowboy?"

Bernabé took her by the reins and turned around to see what was impeding the start of the rodeo. It was Nelson tugging at his cousin's shirt.

"Hey, don't forget me. Remember who paid for this. Ask her about the squirrel."

"Your friend the squirrel, is she available for this Gomorrahite who's pulling on my shirt?"

"There's not such a thing as a Gomorrahite, Bernabé," Nelson argued. "Don't you mean a Sodomite?"

"Keep quiet. We are at the delicate stages of negotiations. Don't interrupt."

"Does he have a ticket?"

"He sure does. Show her your ticket, Nelson. Jerk-off, now you have to go to the bubble-gum machine and buy the squirrel some gum. Make sure it's Bazooka. Then offer her some. She goes wild when she smells Bazooka. But save a few for later on. She's very greedy and will try to hide them in different places so she won't have to work as hard during the winter."

Nelson, determined to appear at ease, ambled toward the vending machine. Failing to judge the distance in that obscure primordial setting, he crashed against the paper-mache mounds. That was when he heard a female voice trying to learn the chorus lines to the foreign tune of an inebriated patron.

"And it's no, nay, never.
No, nay, never, no more!
And I'll play the wild Robert.
No nevermore."

A singing monarch butterfly and a ruddy-faced man in an unbuttoned guayabera, making love in the shade of the paper-mache mound; they had been interrupted by the racket.

"Is that you, Sean?" the man asked Nelson as he ran his hands through the butterfly's antennae, getting yellow dust on his fingers. "Leave the Chivas bottle and keep the change."

"His name isn't Sean," the butterfly said. "Our waiter's name is Felix, and that's not him."

"Let's try again, my dear lepidoptera: 'rover' not 'Robert.' Robert is a man's name."

"I am not singing until that man leaves," muttered the sensuous insect.

Bernabé, fearing an eviction from paradise because of the commotion his friend was causing, ran to help Nelson. He apologized to the butterfly and her man. He then went straight to the vending machine and bought fifty-cents worth of chewing gum, telling Furia to give one to the squirrel in Nelson's name. Then he placed the rest in Nelson's pockets.

"My friend's friend, the one with the hair parted in the middle, sends you this present." Furia gave her one Bazooka while pointing to where Nelson was. "He has many more and would like to share them with you."

The squirrel couldn't believe her eyes and, waving her tail energetically while holding the precious morsel in her paws, approached Nelson. She grabbed his hand and led him to the top of the mango tree. There beneath a canopy rested a platform where the squirrel exchanged love for gum. As her ruby lips blew sticky bubbles and her expert mitts undressed a trembling and flaccid Nelson, the sound of a loud neigh and a victorious yahoooo reverberated throughout the eastern side of paradise.

The Last Supper

The shots that killed the sniper were drowned out by bells calling the faithful to prayer. With the last rounds, the soldiers finished flushing out the remaining rebels that had mounted the April Fools' offensive from the hillocks surrounding Xawa. Juan Benson, Don Andrés' gardener, thought he heard something interspersed with the tolling bells. He dismissed it in his mind as the buzzing of bees building a new hive to accommodate their queen. Benson was helping the club's gardener to reshape the shrubs damaged by flying shrapnel during the rebels' hasty retreat. Inside the Ladies' Tennis Club's kitchen, the servants toiled with six crates of California apples, apricots, and pears that had arrived a few hours before at the port of Isabella. They were a gift from Floyd Conway to the new president on the occasion of her installation.

The inaugural dinner for the president of the Ladies' Tennis Club was Xawa's most exclusive affair. This year the privilege of wearing the presidential sash had fallen to Mrs. Fanny Fern. Her husband, Mr. Joseph Fern, was Xawa's most respected sugar baron. He was also the man who had convinced the government to conduct saturation bombing in the nearby hills. He had ensured his wife's election by donating a swimming pool to the club, which had helped sway the critical votes. Fanny, who hailed from New Orleans, had met Joseph during his school days at Tulane. She had been impressed by his suave manners and old-world charm at the debutante balls during Mardi Gras.

This year's election had been close. Three separate ballots were required to choose the new leader. Rivalry between Cuquín Valley and Pituca Josende had split the vote, paving the way for Fanny. Her mandate, according to the bylaws, was to last forty-two months and five days.

The dignitaries from outside Xawa had begun to arrive for the occasion. From the port city of Isabella came Mr. Fern's business associate, Benigno "the Basque" Juánez, and his elderly mother, Belinda Zubitegüi. Rumor had it the Basque was still bottle-fed at night by the decaying matron. Mayor Sánchez was picked up at the marina in Mr. Fern's yacht. He had come from the capital city dressed in blue knickerbockers. The mayor came alone. His mistress had registered at the Telegraph Hotel the night before, and his wife, Claribel, too drunk on a bottle of extra-aged dry Bacardi she had started at breakfast, remained at home. Exactly two weeks after the party, she would kill herself by jumping from the World Line Pier into the shark-infested waters of the bay.

The poet laureate, Lisander Pons, arrived with his fiancee, Vicky Rey. He was to delight the exclusive audience with the fruits of his muses. The acclaimed national contralto Aïda Lopez, was in attendance, as was Helen Valdés-Curl, wife of the muriatic acid tycoon Pete Frey. Helen drove the 444 kilometers alone in her red Cadillac convertible, her long scarf floating in the wind.

Father Santos, Xawa's gift to the clergy and the newly appointed Bishop of St. James in the Orient, arrived for the occasion accompanied by four identical Oriental acolytes named Horse, Snake, Monkey and Cat. They held the train of his silk- and gold-thread embroidered cassock at all times. Bishop Santos would come down in history as the man who saved the guerrilla leader, Faithful Chester, unwittingly becoming the destroyer of his own class. The neophyte bishop was Nelson Guiristain's godfather.

Joining the outsiders was the cream of Xawa's society: Don Andrés Pardo, his daughter Nellie, and her pet pig Rigoletto; his son-in-law Nelson Guiristain; the President and Vice President of the Xawa branch of The Royal Bank of Canada; Mr. Floyd Conway and Mr. Howe, respectively; Loly Espino escorted by her younger brother, Cioci (her husband, Senator Zubizarreta, was away at a political rally for his reelection campaign); Mrs. Cuquín Valley and Mr. Valley; María Rosa, her daughter Macuqui, her husband Dr. Gastón and her mother Mrs. Peña (the emeritus president and founding member of the club); Pituca Josende and her husband, Chief Justice Josende, who still limped from the shot he received during the landing at Dunkirk and the only Xawan ever to receive a Purple Heart. All the above arrived in their carriages: Mr. and Mrs. Rudolph Guiristain were driven to the event in their Mercedes.

While the doormen were busy letting the final deliveries in, a number of curious eyes had gathered around the passion-vine-covered chain-link fence to get a glimpse of the celebrities. Struggling to climb all the way to top of the ceiba tree, a pudgy nineteen-year old was inching his way to a commanding view of the party. His name was Rulfo. Below the ceiba, the servants, under the direction of Delfina, were busy setting up the banquet table to accommodate the one-hundred guests and dignitaries invited to the event. Juan Benson had finished his gardening task and chopped up an old avocado tree to feed the club's fireplace. Fanny had insisted on having the brick fireplace lit. It reminded her of her childhood mansion in the Crescent City. To counterbalance the effects of the heat radiating, from the hearth exacerbated by Xawa's steamy temperatures, four massive blocks of ice would flank the fireplace once it was lit.

The seating arrangements threatened the delicate harmony of the club membership. After negotiations mediated by Father Santos and Floyd Conway, Pituca Josende finally acceded to be seated to Fanny's left. In return she was given a free hand programming the aquatic events in the new pool and would cut the inaugural ribbon. A beaming Cuquín Valley sat to Fanny's right.

"That's not where the forks go," Delfina thundered. "The forks always to the left, the big ones always closer to the plate. No, no, no," she continued, "The napkins must be folded like butterflies in flight. Please don't make the chairs creak so loudly!" She proceeded to scrutinize the recently delivered sacks of oysters. Contemptuously, she announced to the delivery man that his mollusks weren't fresh enough and that his boss's reputation was at stake. Then she turned to her helper and said, "I wonder what you people would have done if you had to prepare banquet tables for one-thousand guests? When Miss Nellie got married, that's what I did. That was really something! This is nothing in comparison. The whole Telegraph Hotel was booked solid with wedding guests. The Prince of Spain came personally to present Nellie with a sapphire choker which any of these women would kill just to hold in their hands for a few seconds."

Then Delfina looked up at Rulfo and yelled, "Get out of that tree. This is not for ruffians to see. Out of there or I'll call the *rurales*." There was not a word from the arboreal sloth-like figure, but what Delfina couldn't see was the stream of orange piss which fell directly into the punch bowl below.

The string of guests began to arrive for the cocktail hour preceding the supper. Fanny Fern, with her plump Teutonic face and the firm stomach that goes with a barren womb, greeted her guests at the club's romanesque entrance. By the time Floyd Conway walked in, her hands were already tired and her lips puckered from the numerous greetings and exchanges.

"Floyd Conway. Always so punctual," Fanny said sarcastically.

"I know I'm a bit late," said Floyd, attired in a light-blue frock coat and breeches the color of clay.

"It doesn't really matter. I was being bad. It's so good to see you. You're one of the first in. You know these people have no sense of time, but don't pick up that nasty habit." Fanny's smile found an echo in Floyd's.

"I am a trifle late, but I'm rather distressed by the news about the Queen Mother."

"Ah?"

"She was bitten by a pet corgi after she tried to stop a fight among the royal canines at Windsor Castle."

"Was it serious?"

"Her Majesty had three stitches on her left hand after the incident. The quarrel involved ten dogs, including two belonging to Princess Margaret. I believe the Lord Chamberlain also was nipped while helping the Princess."

"Well, would you care for some port or sherry to ease your sorrow?"

"I'd rather have some Chivas. It's a mosquito repellant."

"Lazarus, bring Mr. Conway a tall glass of Chivas."

"Yes, Ma'am."

"Floyd, I love your kilt! Who made it? Was it Gloria Olivé, the local seamstress, or Sarah Bosard, the *hautecouturier*?" Fanny seemed genuinely interested in the garment and its maker.

"Oh, no, my dear. They wouldn't know where to start. My sister, Vera, sent it to me."

"You should come visit. I almost forgot to tell you that we have a Rhodesian Ridgeback. It's a beautiful creature."

"I shall come by tomorrow at tea time. But how did you manage to get such a rare specimen? Was it smuggled?"

"Oh, no. A friend of Joseph's brought it as a gift. Excuse me, Floyd. I see someone at the gate." Fanny walked a few paces toward the main doors, and turning her head around, raised her voice to say, "I do hope the Queen Mother's hand heals in a few days."

"I pray to God it does," added a somewhat solemn Floyd Conway.

Fanny stood under the lintel waiting for Helen Valdés, who was detained at the gate. The arriving guests had a grandiose view of the fifty-two horseshoe arches which delineated the perimeter of the great room, the Mozarabic rugs that hung from the marble walls, and above all, the great staircase flooded by the lights of the candelabras and lined with hibiscuses and performing musicians dressed in their terra-cotta colored suits. Helen Valdés was still held back at the entrance, struggling with the uncooperative gate. The latch was somehow stuck and it wouldn't open. It was obvious Helen was becoming desperate. The orchestra sounds wafted out across the garden and she could hear a dulcet flute shining over Aragón's Orchestra's rendition of "The Constitutional Cadet," Helen's favorite song. She was about to miss her favorite dancing tune and cried for help. But no one came to her rescue. Juan Benson, still busy dismembering the tree, was too far from the gate to hear her cries or the beeping of the horn. Fed up with the situation, Helen got out of the car and shook the gates in despair. Finally, the latch gave way and the gates swung open. Helen was in such a rush, she left her car running and scurried as fast as she could, losing one of her high-heel shoes in her flight. As she ran past Fanny and entered through one of the side doors, her long Cordoban-leather skirt rustled slightly; her tanned, freckled shoulders, glossy hair, and diamonds glittered. Not looking directly at any one, Helen advanced to the dance floor, ignoring the gentlemen who stood silently admiring the beauty of her figure, her full shoulders, her bosom, her back. "What an exquisite woman," the fellows said, seeing her.

"It's marvelous to see you, Nellie," Fanny said with fake eagerness and language. "What a lovely blue gown! Your pet is adorable and I love his teal jacket." Nellie didn't pay any attention to Fanny and settled the folds in her dress. She had never liked Fanny because she was a foreigner, and Nellie would have loved to have been one, too.

Fanny's fleshy hands were patting Rigoletto when she realized Don Andrés and Nelson were standing next to Nellie. "Don Andrés, Nelson! I am so sorry. I didn't see you come in." A look of embarrassment came over Fanny's face. "May I take your cane, Don Andrés?"

"It's quite all right, Fanny. You know how attached Nellie is to Rigo. She made us walk behind Rigo in case he spotted a truffle or two."

"Nellie, I hear rumors you're expecting your first? Is it true?" There was a note of sadness in Fanny's voice.

"Yes, it seems that way. Excuse me, I think Rigo has found something interesting in that pot. See how he has straightened his tail, and his snout is directly pointing down?"

"Some port, Nellie? Gentlemen, a bit of sherry?"

Nellie didn't answer. She was already next to the potted tamarind. Don Andrés and Nelson, each carrying a glass of sherry, walked inside where a group of men had congregated under the rotunda.

"If it isn't Don Andrés Pardo and Nelson Guiristain," shouted a perky Welshman. "Your father was looking for you, Nelson. He asked if we had seen you. He said you were supposed to meet him here at seven."

Nelson's face turned pale. "Excuse me, Don Andrés, Mr. Conway. I must find Daddy." He walked out with a clumsy, pained gesture, holding his stomach, his forehead beaded with sweat.

Nelson headed for the club's grounds. He was sure he would find his father at the handball courts, practicing his serve. Inside the club, the conversation continued.

"So, Mr. Conway, what's your opinion of the rebel attack?" asked Don Andrés.

"The usual. Nothing to be alarmed about. I've lived through ten of these insurgencies since I settled in Xawa. I don't worry about them anymore. Besides, these things tend to fizzle out like seltzer water, and if the rebels are ready to face martyrdom, so much the better. I have no respect for

martyrs. It's sheer idiocy. Don't lose any sleep over this. You
know very well, Andrés, that with money, there's nothing one
can't cure. I'm certain last week's bombing has turned the
rebels into mashed *pôme de terre*. Oh, I see Peter Frey coming
in our direction."

"Is he coming alone? I saw his wife getting out of a red
convertible as we drove in."

"They always travel separately to avoid kidnappers.
There are some big concerns, like Gravi Laboratories, that are
pressuring Pete to sell them his new formula for muriatic acid
with Pirey."

"Hi, boys!" Pete Frey greeted the circle, impeccable in the
latest Italian-style suit, though his hair seemed to have been
hastily finger-combed. It was smooth in the front but sticking
out behind like a sea urchin.

"Hello, Pete," the men responded.

"How's business?" Conway hurried to ask.

"Boys, I'm going to make a big request today," he said,
gulping his highball. "I drove four-hundred kilometers to be
away from all that, to have some fun. I don't want to hear
about it. So let's ask the poet to recite for us."

"He usually does it during the after-dinner drinks,"
Benigno the Basque intervened.

"Well, tell him I want to listen to an early recital. Tell him
it's Pete Frey who wants to listen to his muse.

"Lazarus," ordered Don Andrés, "tell Mr. Pons, the man
wearing the leaves around his head, that I must tell him
something."

"Yes, sir."

A few minutes later, the poet laureate acquiesced to
Pete's request, and the circle tightened under the dome.

Lisander cleared his throat with a shot of cognac to feed
the muse.

"I've seen wings come forth
  from firm women's shoulders

seen butterflies fly out
of trash heaps."

The poet made a pause, cracked his bony fingers and continued,

"I come from everywhere
To everywhere I go:
I'm art among the arts
and in the mountains,
I'm a mountain."

And then, with his eyes focused on the dome, in rapture, his lips parted, he took a deep breath before his final verse.

"My poems please the strong
my poems which are sincere and brief
they're as rugged
as the steel used
to forge a sword."

"To forge a sword" was still echoing through the clubhouse when a rather inebriated Pete Frey embraced the poet, impregnating his linen shirt with the stench of winy sweat, and mumbled, "I really love your poems, pal. It's the absolute truth when you say your poems please the strong, and that's why I like them. I'm strong! I'm a sword myself and I'll slice like a piece of Swiss cheese any motherfucker who wants to mess with me." Then Pete looked Lisander straight in the eyes and said, "Buddy, there's something I don't quite understand—that art and mountain stuff."

Lisander, who was obviously pleased, proceeded to explain. "It means that I'm at ease talking to the president of the Royal Bank, for instance, or to my maid."

"No shit, Lisander! I feel just the same." Pete let go of the embrace and, shaking the poet's hand, said, "Next time you're in the capital, give me a call. I'm going to show you the best time of your life. And now I have to take a leak."

The men continued talking about their favorite subjects, women and business, but were careful not to offend Don

Andrés with their crude remarks. Don Andrés cleared his throat every so often to signal his displeasure if the boys got carried away. He was regarded as a man of high moral standards, a true gentleman, a man of dignity.

Lisander partook of the conversation for a few minutes and excused himself, promising Pete more poems at the prescribed time. His face still beamed from the adulations as he walked back to his fiance, Vicky, who waved from the bar. Vicky was carrying on an intense conversation with her friend Loly and her child, prodigy brother Cioci. The group was discussing Cioci's discovery of a presumed extinct amphibian in a cave near the hamlet of Small Corral. Lisander joined the ongoing conversation and took a genuine interest in Cioci's discovery.

"A literary genius," Don Andrés said to Mayor Sánchez, who had joined the group a bit late and had caught the last two lines of the last poem.

"Yes, it's amazing. I've heard him a few times at the Athenaeum. I especially enjoyed one called 'Errant Love.'"

"What's the view in the capital on the uprising we experienced in this region a few weeks ago? I read Faithful Chester's manifesto, *History Will Absorb You*, and I must admit it has distressed me a bit." It seemed to be Don Andrés' opening remark to everyone he spoke with that evening.

"We don't think Faithful Chester, the guerrilla leader, has a chance in Hell. The minute the armed forces coordinate their efforts, he'll be history, running with his tail between his legs. If you excuse me a minute, Don Andrés, I have to telephone my sugar at the Telegraph. Tell the waiter when he comes by I'm low on my libation. I'll be right back."

Outside, Nelson had looked everywhere for his father. He had checked by the handball courts and the croquet lawn and was about to give up his quest after he passed the badminton net when he spotted something shining by the pool.

"Daddy, Daddy," Nelson shouted when he saw his father near the pool. "I've been looking for you everywhere. I thought you'd be at the handball courts. Luckily, something was shining that led me here."

"Don't shout! I am not deaf! Well, it was no star of Bethlehem that brought you here. Probably my gold watch." Rudolph barely glanced at his son, took a final puff from his Havana cigar, and threw it in the pool. "Where were you? I told you at seven. You have this tendency to muddle and spoil." He sounded angry.

"I know, Daddy, but Nellie wasn't feeling well. You know she's pregnant."

"That's no excuse," he said in a gruff voice. "You're a man and she's a woman. It's her job to be pregnant and yours to come on time when I tell you and to carry out in exact detail what I have said. I hate careless people! Did you complete the business consolidations I asked you to do?"

"Yes, sir. Here they are." Nelson took out a long piece of paper filled with official seals and stamps. He waited for his father's praise. There was none. The old man read the paper, told him to file it, and turned around.

"I'll file it tomorrow, Daddy."

"What do you mean, tomorrow? Go to the office right now and file it. And not a word out of you!"

"But, Daddy, the dinner is about to begin and Nellie…"

"I said not a word. You're too fat anyway." At that moment Rudolph Guiristain longed to break something.

"Yes, Daddy!"

The club still hummed like a beehive and a fine mist had started falling outside when there was a sudden stir and all conversation hushed. The crowd rushed sideways and then moved apart to let Fanny walk to the strains of the orchestra, which struck up at once "Pomp and Circumstance." Behind the regal Fanny walked Mrs. Peña, Cuquín Valley and Pituca Josende. The space where Nellie should have walked, but refused, was filled by Helen Valdés-Curl. Fanny walked

slowly, waving to the guests as though trying to prolong the
first moments of her mandate. At Joseph Fern's request, the
musicians changed the tune and played "When The Saints Go
Marching In," a bit of nostalgia from her native land. When
Fanny finally reached the banquet table, her face beaming
with bliss, the orchestra switched melodies again to the Club's
alma mater, lyrics by Mrs. Rudolph Guiristain set to music by
Ernest Lecuona and sung with gusto by the invitees and Aïda
Lopez, whose deep voice overpowered the rest.

The Little Father, as Father Santos was affectionately
called by his friends, stood up and asked the visitors to keep
quiet and bow their heads in sign of respect, if not repentance,
as he gave the invocation:

In spiritu humilitatis, et in animo contrito suscipiamur a
te, Domine: et sic fiat sacrificium nostrum in conspectu tuo
hodie, ut placeat tibi, Domine Deus.

The hungry guests sat down at the U-shaped table after a
resounding "amen," but parted with the blessing, which was
to produce a soothing effect on the friendly souls.

No sooner had the guests settled down to eat after the
Bishop's benediction, when Mrs. Peña offered a toast in honor
of the newly elected President Fanny de Fern. The octogenari-
an raised her glass and, in a thunderous voice that was out of
character, said, "To Fanny, a seed from far away that has
rooted deep in the red clay of Xawa."

"To Fanny, To Fanny, Viva Fanny, To Fanny," echoed the
walls of the large ballroom.

Only Nellie had remained conspicuously silent and had
refused to stand up for the toast. "What's the fuss about her
being a seed from far away? I was practically born overseas
myself, and I don't make a big deal about it," she whispered to
Rigo, who was seated by her feet; Nelson hadn't returned from
his errand.

The waiters bustled, and the room was full of noise and
movement following Delfina's orders to bring in the evening's
courses. The tiny scrolls with the menu in miniature gothic

script were bound with sterling silver rings and placed inside the empty crystal water glasses engraved with the club's crest. As each guest retrieved the menu, his glass was immediately filled with sparkling Amaro mineral water. If anyone could read lips, it would have been easy to decipher the menu. Helen Valdés was reciting it to herself:

Appetizers: Oysters Vieux Carre Fanny
                Alligator Tail Fingers
Soups: Creole Turtle Soup
                Filé Gumbo
Entrees: Venison Churchill
                  with Mulled Wine
                Quail Fricandeau
                  with Chianti Classico
                Crawfish Fanny
                  with Riscal White
                Bison Tongue in Green Mayonnaise
                  with Barolo Red
                Yeux du Pompano aux Fines Herbes
                  with Moroccan Bordelaise
Vegetables: Almond Rice
                Braised Belgium Endive With Walnuts
Desserts: California Apricots, Pears, Apples
                Fidenza Belforti Parmigiano Reggiano

"The oysters are delicious," remarked Pituca as she finished devouring the last dozen in record time, the empty shells scattered around the plate.

"Yes, they are quite good," answered Floyd, though Pituca's statement was meant for Belinda. "I understand its one of Fanny's family recipes. And Mrs. Josende, if I may say so, you do have a healthy appetite."

Pituca felt embarrassed as all eyes focused one her shell-filled plate. "I'm afraid I've a weakness for oysters," she said, although she had the reputation of not letting a single dish pass her way without sacking it completely.

"It seems more like a passion," interjected Loly Espino as the waiters were bringing the soup.

There was absolute silence for a few minutes. Only the
clatter of spoons could be heard as the diners touched and
emptied the bowls.

"When is Nelson returning?" Don Andrés asked his
daughter as he savored the mulled wine.

"I have no idea, Papá! But I don't think Rigo likes this
party. I think he wants to go home."

"Nellie, don't make a scene. We will leave as soon as your
husband returns."

Don Andrés went back to enjoying the wine and tilted his
head to the right to address Rudolph Guiristain. "How much
longer until Nelson returns, Rudolph?"

Guiristain, Sr. laughed out loud. "Ha, ha, ha, it should
take him five minutes, but in Nelson's case probably two
hours, especially after he married into your family." Mrs.
Guiristain pinched him under the table.

Don Andrés pretended not to hear him and added, "I hear
rumors the communists have infiltrated the guerrilla movement..."

"Such a morbid subject war is. You can talk about it
later," Mrs. Guiristain said to be polite, thinking her husband
wasn't going to answer Don Andrés.

A tipsy Rudolph with vacant eyes waited a few more seconds to answer him, as if he was ransacking his brains to find
the proper words.

"You know what I think of the guerrillas." And without
anyone else noticing him but Don Andrés, he grabbed his balls
in defiance and shook them for a while, laughing contemptuously.

Don Andrés, taken by surprise, didn't wait for the garçon
and poured himself another glass of mulled wine, and at a loss
for words said, "The venison is particularly tender, Mr. Guiristain."

"I have an important announcement to make," said
Helen. "I have convinced my husband, Pete, to donate a new
hardwood dancing floor for the club."

There was loud applause.

"On behalf of the Ladies' Tennis Club, and in my capacity as President and as my first official act, we thank you and Peter from the bottom of our hearts."

"I also have an announcement," Mrs. Peña said as she washed down the quail with a flood of Chianti. "The Sacred Heart of Jesus Jesuit School will hold its first sixth-grade swimming meet in our new pool facility."

The next round of applause was about to start when Pituca Josende stood up and yelled in anger.

"I am the only one with the power to authorize any aquatic activity. I was promised that if I..."

Floyd Conway didn't let her finish her statement, shouting, "Silence, please. Silence. This is nothing more than a simple misunderstanding, Mrs. Josende. Do you give your permission to hold the Jesuit swimming meet at the Ladies' Tennis Club?"

Once more all eyes were on Pituca, and feeling the pressure, she responded, "I do." Floyd's quick maneuvering caught Pituca by surprise. "But all further events must be approved by me one month in advance."

"And now, I propose a toast to the new pool." Floyd raised his glass.

"To the new pool," answered the crowd.

The great cornucopia that had provided the banquet lay empty, and the guests busied themselves discreetly repositioning their false teeth or chatting with each other with the serenity and good will that only a full belly can induce.

"Isn't it a lovely clock?" said Vicky to her poet.

"Yes, indeed. But the beauty of that chronometer cannot match my love for thee." Lisander kissed Vicky's hands, leaving green mayonnaise residue on her palms. She blushed and, under Cupid's spell, kept her eyes fixed inquiringly on Lisander's black pupils. She was moved by a spirit and burst

out, "How do I love thee, Lis? Let me count the ways. I love
you when you brush your teeth. I love you when you sleep. I
love you in the shower. I love you at the tennis courts. I love
you when you gargle. But above all, I love how you love me!"

"Did you have a nice ride, Mrs. Frey? Ours was a bit
bumpy," inquired Benigno the Basque, looking at Helen.

"Please don't call me Mrs. Frey. Everybody calls me
Helen," she said as she rearranged her bedouin shawl to cover
half of her face. "My ride was awful but uneventful! The roads
are filled with potholes, but I had some fun running over two
roosters and a pig."

"How's your daughter, María Rosa?" asked Cuquín, turning sharply around. "Is she better from her illness?"

"Macuqui is a little better, but she could be much better if
she were to listen to Dr. Cabrera and take her medicine properly. I told her not to take her clothes off with the windows
open. It was the draft that made her sick."

"I understand perfectly. I know how defiant teenagers can
be. I have four myself."

"And your mom, Cuquín, still living at Miramar?"

"Oh, no. She lives with us. She lost her mind and doesn't
remember anything, not even me. She only remembers the
days of the week in French. You know she lived in Blois as a
child when my grandfather served as consul in that Gallic
city."

"It saddens me to hear it. Loneliness is the only preven-
tion against the outrages of pain."

Cuquín didn't quite understand, but feeling the conversation was getting too personal, she quickly excused herself with
the pretext she had to introduce the night's performers.

"Ladies and gentlemen. I have the honor of presenting
our nation's leading contralto, Aïda Lopez. She will delight us
this evening with her most famous pieces. Immediately following, our poet laureate will enchant us with his latest inspira-
tions."

"Music, maestro." Aïda cleared her throat, and in her husky voice thanked Cuquín Valley, who had introduced her. Aïda was in the middle of one of her favorite renditions, "Martha, Tiny Rose Bud"—at the precise moment when her voice was reaching the crescendo, "...Martha from my garden you're the flower..."—when a thundering noise was heard and some of the chandeliers came crashing to the floor. Then all the lights went off and the confused screams of the guests rang out.

"The guerrillas! It's another attack. It must be Faithful Chester!"

"My leg. You're sitting on my leg."

"Rigoletto, Rigo, where are you, baby?"

"Let the rebels know that I'm the only one who can arrange the aquatic bookings."

"The government will drive them out of here in no time. Be calm. There's no need to worry..."

Aïda kept on singing without the orchestra. She wasn't about to let them spoil her evening. Then she heard a voice ordering her to the floor, and when she ignored it, she was forced down by a blow to her knees. Immediately, the guests heard the sounds of someone being dragged along the ballroom towards one of the side doors. There was silence when Rudolph Guiristain gathered enough courage to stand up and, groping through the room, reached the wall and flipped on the emergency lights. Then a scream was heard.

"Pete! They have taken Pete! My Peteeeeeeeee! I knew it, I knew it," Helen was sobbing deeply and beating her chest.

"Those awful guerrillas. I thought the soldiers had swept them away." Fanny crawled to her side to comfort her.

"It wasn't the guerrillas. I begged him to stay home. They wanted the formula." She sighed in pain, "Oh, Peteeeee!" She cried, holding her red shawl in her hands, lifting it from time to time to wipe the mixture of tears and eyeliner as it crept down her cheeks.

"Someone bring this woman a glass of sherry! Let the orchestra play. Maestro, please. Nothing has happened here. The party must go on," ordered Floyd. "Carry on, carry on."

Nuts and Bolts

"Dammit, Nelson! I told you one anchor plate and three bellows! And what'd you give me? Three tie rods and a Pittman arm!"

"Sorry, Grady. I must have gotten mixed up," Nelson answered contritely as he grabbed the unwanted parts which were being shoved back at him.

"No shit. You get mixed up every time you turn around. Now, get me the parts I asked for and make it snappy. I ain't got the whole day," he said disgustedly, drowning his words in a brownish syrup of tobacco-tainted saliva.

"Three bellows and one anchor plate. *Voilá*."

"What in the hell is 'walla?'" Grady mumbled without turning from his work. "I sure didn't ask for one. You'd better not have gotten the wrong stuff again."

"Oh, no, Grady. Voila is a Gallic word that means 'here you are.'"

"This is America. Speak American when you talk to me."

"There is not such a thing, Grady. You meant to say speak English. Has anyone ever told you, you have the hands of Lecuona, the concert pianist?" Nelson made his observations while looking intensely at Grady's long, dirty fingers.

"Just gimme what I asked for before I get pissed off! What's the matter with you? You queer or something?"

"Could you sign here, please?" Nelson requested, his face paler after Grady's belligerent words.

"Ain't got no time to sign. Go ahead and sign for me."

"I need your last name?"

"Enlow, E-N-L-O-W."

"Oh, that name must be from Aberystwyth in western Wales, like Mr. Conway," Nelson responded cheerily, waiting for an affirmative answer that would ease the tension.

"We're from Georgia. My family ain't from that place. We're from Georgia," said Grady, grabbing the parts as he finished his sentence and turned back to his work. He shook his head and mumbled to himself.

"I don't detest working in this stockroom," Nelson said to the spare parts. "Thanks to Uncle Ben, I've got this job. Bernabé told me exactly how Uncle Ben managed. He gave one of the owner's girlfriends an extra month to retrieve the pearl earrings she had pawned if she lobbied her sugar daddy for my job. Her name is Lori Walters; she is a chronic gambler, Harry Rosser's sex kitten. Rosser is one of the owners of this outfit—Rosser and Dunlap Trucks and Rigs. It beats picking tomatoes."

He kept addressing the greasy parts.

"I am learning fast, and with my system of labeling every one of you, I make few mistakes. Today is an exception, my dear Pittman arm. It has been raining so hard the labels are peeling off from the humidity. I will have to re-glue them when the weather turns a little drier. I must admit there are times, like today, when I feel I should have brought the suitcase with our assets, like I was supposed to do. But I emerge from that delirium as fast as I enter it. I start hearing voices telling me how to hold the baseball bat, how to choose my friends, what career to select, what girls to date, how I make stupid business deals. Then Daddy's voice goes through my mind like an old tape I can't turn off or erase. I see his figure in front of me, projected against the wall, his blond mustache turning up at the ends. When I can't take it and yell, 'No, Daddy. I am not going back,' and I throw a shock absorber against the wall, and his mustache goes limp and he disappears, and my hands begin to shake, but my stomach holds.

"He died last December when he found out I had failed to bring the suitcase with one-third of our assets, as Mr. Conway had recommended and as Daddy had finally agreed. The other two-thirds were confiscated by the government on November third, exactly three months after I made it to the embassy. That day, I was told, his blood pressure rose and he fainted. His friends thought he had had a heart attack, but the old oak was able to take the blow. He was counting on the other third safely producing dividends. Don Andrés, my father-in-law, may he rest in peace, brought Daddy the news that, though I had made it inside the embassy compound, the guards had successfully wrested the suitcase from me as I ran for the gate. He cursed Don Andrés, telling him it was all his fault; that he should never have allowed his son to marry into a family of cuckoos that had made their money when it was possible to tie down a dog with a schnitzel; that he had opposed our marriage from the very beginning. Don Andrés told my wife that as Daddy was about to put his hat on to go see Mr. Conway, he dropped like a bird. It was a massive stroke that killed him."

"I am glad he never knew that it was a wave that took the suitcase and not the militiamen as he was told and as everyone still believes. Daddy would have despised me. I would never have been able to take his scorn. I hadn't expected a wave. It just came. It was the answer to all the prayers I have said since I was a child. I really didn't realize what had happened to the suitcase until I tried to reach for the handle. There was no handle; there was no suitcase. I was waiting for my stomach to start grumbling; ready for its habitual eruption. But it didn't come. I felt free for the first time in my life. And it was a good feeling. Then I took a piece of toilet paper from my pocket and calmly wiped off the salty mist from my glasses. I began walking toward the marketplace. I didn't know exactly why I headed in that direction, but I let myself go. On the way, I stopped a few times to pluck the hibiscus flowers from the hedges that fenced many of the mansions along the boulevard. I sucked on them, and their nectar gave me the strength to walk the distance to the market. The market was almost closed for the afternoon recess when I got there, the stands, almost empty, with very few goods to sell. I found what I was looking for, another cardboard suitcase like the one Delfina had lent me. This one, which didn't have a lock, had to be closed with a piece of rope. I bought as many newspapers as I could find and filled the suitcase. Then I walked back, whistling, to Embassy Row. I was sure of myself as I approached Raleigh, the guard, a tall, thin man from the country. He didn't carry the traditional M-19 rifle issued to all embassy guards, but instead had a machete as his weapon of choice. He must have had acne or smallpox as a child because his face looked like an extinct volcanic chain. I told him I was bringing newspapers for the consul. He eyed me suspiciously and said he hadn't seen me before, but I reminded him many newspapers had been confiscated and that the new administration had hired new personnel. He wasn't convinced, but I stood firm with my story. When he went to consult with his superior, I rushed inside the compound before the guard could stop me. He rushed at me with his machete, cutting through the air as he swung it, preparing to hurl it. The machete reached the door a second before I did and sounded like a gong when it hit the heavy metal doors. That providential knock saved my life. Having heard the crash against the door, the consul opened it the very same moment I was trying to get in. I didn't recover the suitcase. My conscience has always been clear whenever I have said that the guards took the suitcase. You must be tired of listening. I am going to hang you where you belong. I will keep talking to the tie rods.

"The following day I went to the Papal Nuncio's Palace, riding in the Ambassador's silver Jaguar. To fool the guards who had been posted around the embassy, and who were playing this very loud mambo music to force the consul to surrender me, I was to go inside the trunk covered with bags filled with mangoes, pineapples, soursops and cherimoyas. But I had a hunch the ambassador's cook was a government informer. She was overly kind to me. My father taught me to distrust kindness above all. I asked the ambassador to disguise me as his chauffeur and let me drive the car. He agreed. My disguise was simple: the chauffeur's cap with the union jack, my own reddish mustache, and dark sunglasses. A few blocks after we cleared the gate, with the ambassador sitting in the back seat, we were stopped by state security. We were asked to open the trunk. I told them we were carrying fruits to ship to the ambassador's mother in England. He insisted, his rifle pointed at my forehead. I was scared, but my hand held firm as I placed the key inside the keyhole and opened the trunk. After smashing all the fruit with the butt of his rifle, making a genuine tutti-frutti puree, he let us drive on. At Nuncio's I was given a fake passport, and I disguised myself in a Carmelite's cassock with a wooden rosary. That same afternoon, I arrived in Kingston, Jamaica. From there, the Royal Bank, thinking the suitcase was coming in the diplomatic pouch, had arranged for my flight to Montreal via Miami. Once I deplaned in the Magic City, I never returned to the plane.

"My wife, Nellie, Don Andrés and the kids were expected to leave Xawa in a few months after I had become established in Canada. They were supposed to exchange our mansion for exit permits, but Don Andrés decided to burn every single piece of furniture inside Villa Ronda. I guess Daddy had the right idea about Nellie's family. She was finally issued an exit visa exactly one year after I left. When I saw her at the airport, she wasn't the same Nellie I had married. It would have been easier to leave the old Nellie. Her dreams of a graceful life in Mondovi had become an obsession. She screamed for Rigoletto in her dreams. The nightmares diminished after six months, but she remained laconic and taciturn. I have asked her many times how she had managed to leave since the family fortune was frozen in the banks and they didn't have a cent to bribe the immigration officials. Her reply to this date has always been a constant, 'Sergio's father passed away.'

"Today I am working overtime. I volunteered for it. I prefer being among the pipes, nuts, bolts, hexes and coils. I usually go home late, sometimes very late. People think I am an exemplary provider for my family. I hear Reverend Fender has even mentioned me in his sermons. Actually, what I am really trying to do is save some extra money to bring over the only creature on earth capable of fulfilling me. My friend Bernabé is attempting to locate her whereabouts. Marina, the matron of the house I used to frequent, is reestablishing her business in Miami and is gathering her fauna. Bernabé thinks he might be able to get me some news about her.

"I don't want to think what I would do if she were to knock at my door. Such a hold she has on me! That squirrel drives me crazy. Maybe it is the way she uses her paws. Once I spent a whole week up in the tree with her, but she never took her mask off. I had to kiss her through her nylon whiskers. She is the only woman with whom I haven't suffered *post coitam tristitia*, and that is such an extraordinary feeling, I am not willing to give up! I will call Bernabé from Pepe's Bar after work. I can truly say that Bernabé is teaching me to be patient, to wait for the opportunity. He's waiting for Uncle Ben's fortune. I'm waiting for a lost squirrel, who I'm sure is working her way back to me.

"There's Grady again. He's smiling. He must have gotten his paycheck. He isn't really that bad a guy. He's like that with everybody, including his pregnant wife Erin. I see Antonio is coming earlier for the late-night shift. He sabotages my work. He has tried to derail my system for remembering the names of spare parts. He has been switching my labels around. Antonio says he worked as a foreman for Daddy in one of our factories. I don't remember him. I told him I did, but I lied. I guess he's trying to get even with me for whatever grudge he still holds against Daddy."

"Hey, Nelson! This anchor plate is cracked. I need a new one... Shithead, I'm talking to you!"

Naked Dina Reading
by Window

"Can I rest now, white butt?"

"I can't talk and paint at the same time. You paint with the right side of your brain, and if you keep on blabbering, you'll fuck it all up."

"Is that so, moon butt," answered Dina crisply as she wet her fleshy lips.

"Open your legs a bit more and relax. *Ecco*! That's what I needed, a slight scumbling right here." The brush grew wilder as Liazzo tried to cast a shadow where the newspaper rested.

"C'mon, rumpy! I'm tired!"

"Let me do some dry brushing and then you can take a break. But first I've got to see what I'm doing from a distance, for a better perspective. On, yes! I like that soft focus."

"I like it hard!"

"Keep still!"

"It was easier when men gave me jewelry."

"Be still!"

"Can I sing?"

Liazzo nodded.

"Hm, hm, hm."

"Is that singing?"

"I'm clearing my throat, you little pubic hair!"

"Now, you've made me lose my concentration! You know it drives me wild when you say that..."

"Stop it, stop it. The window is open, you beast."

Liazzo kissed Dina all over her naked body, dipping his tongue in the pallet, leaving her breasts burnt with sienna and her buttocks as indigo as the Côte d'Azur. Dina flipped the newspaper to her favorite page, the beauty tips, and pushed the post-impressionist painter to one side.

"I feel like singing now. You go back to your painting."

Breathing heavily, a rainbow-tongued Liazzo stood up and crossed the room to look at his lost perspective.

"...hm, hm, hm, it was three in the afternoon when Lola was murdered, and those who heard her in agony all swear that she was singing: That man was my whole life, that man was my great torment, that man has just killed me and I still would love to kiss him.... Oh, Lola! Oh, my darling, little Lola!..."

"Hush! Let the newspaper float with the wind to make it look more ethereal."

"My crotch is getting cold!"

"Tell it to wait a little bit longer. Tell it it's becoming art, and art is like a growing organism. It needs care and attention, but above all it needs lots of patience. Art, Dina, is like life, it grows out of love."

"Make sure you get my best side. Am I a better subject than Mrs. Peña?"

"The old lady you painted with the bridge and the angels. What's the matter, are you getting old and forgetful?"

There was no answer from Liazzo.

"Oh, rumpy, you're so sensitive. C'mon, a little smile for your chocolate bar. C'mon and warm my pimento, you little pubic hair!"

"Do you make love with words? My imagination is being abandoned by reason. I am becoming an impossible monster!"

The palette landed on Dina's body, splashing the newspaper as the whirling Liazzo spattered hues on the living nude. Dina breathed deeply, controlling the tempo and chewing her bubble gum with slow, sensual contentment.

Soul Train

Nelson waited impatiently for the morning express which was already three hours overdue. He glanced from time to time towards the west where the railroad tracks wound along the river bank. Though he was careful not to look conspicuous, he was moving restlessly, and his white linen suit and wide-brimmed panama hat betrayed his upbringing. It was his first time traveling in third class. Before, he had traveled in Don Andrés' private wagon, which was hooked to the regular train. But the wagon had been confiscated and was being used to haul cane for the nearby mill.

Nellie had bid him farewell an hour before. Tired of waiting, Nelson had urged her to return home. When they kissed goodbye, he noticed her face was beginning to show wear and her figure was growing matronly with the last stages of pregnancy. She wore her petticoat and her red sequined gown. She kept the rays of the early morning sun at bay with her parasol, prompting some in the crowd to comment, "Look at the crazy woman with an umbrella when it isn't even raining." Nelson got more nervous when he heard the remarks. Nellie had Rigoletto on an emerald leash to control his mischievous disposition.

"How much do you want for that pig?" asked a tattered-looking man.

Nellie didn't answer; Nelson rushed to say that the animal was not for sale.

Nelson heard the sounds of a distant whistle and saw the shuffling of feet on the cracked boarding platform. He tightened his grip on the cardboard suitcase he had borrowed from

Delfina. As he approached the tracks, he was gripped by the momentary fear that the potent glare from the engine's headlight would reveal the contents of the suitcase. When he saw the train coming to a halt and the crowd beginning to board, his fears were relieved.

After checking the suitcase, he boarded the 'Tawana.' In true revolutionary spirit, the coal burning locomotive had been christened "Tawana" in honor of an African martyr. The gold lettering on the locomotive, flanked by two red and black flags, glistened. Nelson walked through the cars until he found an almost empty compartment. He crumpled down in a wicker seat. The Tawana blew its whistle, pulled out of the station, and started slowly steaming across the marshes east of the city.

From time to time, Nelson would lift up his head and glance through the window. Outside, the sun blazed upon the tile roofs, and he could still see the great bronze cross atop Xawa's school of the Sacred Heart casting its shadow upon the crowded plaza. In the horizon, the deep blue range of the Sierra Morena rose into the thundering sky.

"It doesn't seem like a scene set for a revolution," Nelson thought aloud, and immediately looked around to see if anyone had heard him. Luckily, the only other passenger, a woman in a red bandana, had gone to the toilet, leaving the compartment impregnated with the odor of sweat. Nelson coughed as he breathed the suffocating atmosphere of the enclosed cubicle.

The Tawana began to run faster and ascend along the edges of deep ravines dotted with royal palms. He welcomed the fresh air. Through the window, Nelson could see giant ferns and hear the splash and ripples of the Deep River as it drew its life from the hills. Soon, having had no sleep, he grew drowsy with the rocking motion of the train. He leaned his head against the window frame and closed his eyes.

A jumble of characters invaded his dreams—his father, a squirrel, truffles, and a pig. Then his head was dangling back-

ward. The Tawana was reaching the most difficult pass in the mountain and began to rattle and whistle as it grew darker. The train came closer to the walls of the pass where the mahogany trees at the summit shut out the sunlight. It felt deep and cool. Nelson was awakened by the train jolting to a stop. He pulled himself together, straightened up, and looked out the window. His neck ached and his mouth was completely dry.

The militiamen guarding the train yelled angrily at the passengers to step out of the cars. As Nelson tried to stand, he fell to the floor; his legs were numb. He frantically beat his legs. When he felt the blood rushing into his muscles, he managed to squeeze through a tunnel made by the passengers as they hoisted their baskets up in the air to save their contents.

"The engineer says we're carrying too much weight. Some of us will have to stay behind if we are to climb this pass," said the irritated guard.

"Where are we?" asked the woman with the red bandana, licking her fingers and holding a greasy drumstick.

"We're on the Sierra Morena Range."

She looked around, noticed the ocean in the distance, and said, "I hate mountains." Then she opened her mouth as if to yawn. Instead she let go of a loud burp.

"I will not stay behind in this wasteland. I have important matters to attend to in St. Christopher and..." Nelson immediately recognized the voice of the hirsute man with deep circles under his eyes. It was Mario, the fake sultan who years before had choreographed the Odalisque Conga. Mario was about to continue his tirade when he was abruptly interrupted by a tall, ragged militiaman. Nelson thought the guard was going to strike Mario with the butt of his M-19. Mario threw up his hands and fell back with such a jerk that he lost his balance and fell to the ground. He scrambled back to an upright position and, cleaning the dust on his pants, shouted, "I'm traveling on business. I have been invited to join the National Ballet."

"Everyone in first class stays behind," roared the captain of the militiamen.

"The revolution says we are equal. Why don't we get rid of some of the baggage so that everybody can stay on the train," shouted Mario.

Nelson thought about his father and the suitcase with the assets and yelled back. "Shut up! First-class exploiter!"

The crowd roared with approval and hissed at the first-class passengers as they got back on board.

"Hey, you? Want to have a wing?" said the bandana woman as she sat down across from Nelson and proceeded to clean her teeth with a blade of grass.

Nelson nodded and held the chicken wing with both indexes and thumbs, but before he had a chance to enjoy the morsel, she added, "You eat funny!"

"Oh, I have tennis elbow," Nelson was quick to respond.

"What's that?"

"It's a sickness that doesn't let you hold anything with just one arm."

"How do you get it?"

"From…from repairing tennis shoes." Nelson sighed in relief.

"You're a cobbler, ah? My father was a cobbler. Here, have the other wing." She tossed it across the narrow aisle.

Nelson was so relieved his true identity wasn't discovered, he swallowed both wings at the same time, ate the bones, and spat out of the window what he couldn't chew.

"I'm gonna see my son. I haven't seen him in three years."

"Oh, is he in a boarding school? I mean…" Nelson grew nervous again.

"Nope, he never liked the navy. He never learned to swim. When he was a boy, my brother grabbed him and threw him right in the middle of the Deep River because he said that was the only way he was going to lose his fear of water."

"Did he?" Nelson relaxed.

"He almost drowned. That's why I still hate my brother so much. Though I know I shouldn't since he was cursed from my mother's womb. He cried in her belly!"

"That's impossible."

"He did, and that's why the whole family feared him. Maybe you've seen him around. He drives a jeep. His name is Rulfo. Anyway, my son is coming from training with the militia," she yawned and fell asleep, never finishing her story.

Nelson took advantage of his friend's tiredness and started to walk very slowly out of the car, heading for another car, away from his inquisitive companion. Nelson found a seat across from the doorless toilet, sat down and buried his face in a smudged newspaper. This was not so much to prevent any type of conversation, but to allow the smell of the newsprint to mask the odors of the ranking, putrid latrine. He hoped the suitcase was still resting in the baggage compartment. He had a sense of guilt for not checking it, but he didn't want to give the slightest indication of apprehension and pretended to be asleep.

It was dawn when the Tawana whistled, signaling the last stop. The station wasn't crowded, and Nelson easily retrieved his valise from the baggage compartment. He clutched the suitcase with such force that his fingertips became stuck in the plastic handle. He walked briskly out of the station and waved at an empty taxi, but it kept on going. There was a taxi strike. Years later it would come out that the KGB had orchestrated for the owners to reduce the taxi-cab drivers' wages. When havoc ensued, the process of nationalizing the industry was achieved in a week's time.

Nelson kept afoot and stopped to ask directions from a man who seemed to be suffering from some kind of persecution complex. The man was elderly, his abundant makeup already filled the wrinkles which furrowed his face. His dark glasses and fake moustache—glue melting onto his sweaty

lips—betrayed his condition as a fugitive from the government. It was obvious he was hunted by the feared G-2 secret
police. By the time the man finished pointing in the direction
of the nearest bus stop, his moustache was dangling on one
side. The man didn't seem to notice it, and Nelson failed to tell
him.

As he sat down in the bus, Nelson felt as he always had,
that he was a vassal to his father. If they lost everything in
Xawa, there would be enough in Montreal. In Quebec his
father would make him work six times as hard to regain their
financial status. He looked out of the window and noticed the
gigantic billboards filled with slogans. All signs in the capital
city pointed to the fact that the new order wasn't about to be
delayed by his father's bravado. He felt sick and vomited out
the window.

"Hey, drunk! It's too windy to be throwing up. Don't you
see you're spraying everybody with your vileness," a woman
yelled.

Nelson apologized and got off at the next top, his white
linen suit soiled with gastric juices, dust, and exhaust fumes.
He was across from Embassy Row. He crossed the street and
started to walk up the lengthy thoroughfare. When he walked
by the Canadian Delegation, a guard feeding the hungry
pigeons smiled at him. He faked an interest in the birds and
approached the man. He clearly read the name on the guard's
shirt pocket, Raleigh. It would have been extremely simple to
gain access to the Canadian Delegation, leave the suitcase,
and from there seek asylum in the British Embassy, half a
block away. But Nelson felt frightened and walked to the
nearby seawall to get his thoughts in order.

He sat on the seawall, facing the ocean, his feet dangling
in the air. He tried to ease thoughts of his angry father calling
him a failure by thinking about Nellie, but the more he tried
to conjure her image the crisper the squirrel woman's sem-
blance grew. Suddenly, he realized he had spent most of his
life in bondage. It all became clear. He placed the suitcase on

the wall and watched it wobble. Nelson lowered it to the beach, scarcely a meter below his feet. The razor-edged coral scratched and cut the surface of the suitcase. He felt calm, determined, his body unable to control him anymore, his stomach at ease. Nelson's mind, cushioned by the foam and the breeze, ebbed with the tide. A small, frolicsome wave, that had been watching from afar, tiptoed to the seawall. It whispered to the bruised suitcase to come and play, to take a plunge. As Nelson's eyes focused on the bobbing rectangular object drifting towards the Gulf Stream, thirty-three years of serfdom came to an end.

Fairview

Mrs. James B. opened the cans of beans and weenies and corn nibblets and then dipped three spoons of lard in the heated skillet. As the lard began to melt, she placed the biscuits in the oven and stirred the gravy. When the melted lard started crackling, she covered her face with a rag and submerged the chicken quarters in the scalding bubble bath. She always covered her face to prevent a stray drop of liquid lard from marring her face.

When she finished cooking, realizing her face was still swollen, she applied an ice pack to the area under her eye. She held the ice against her cheek for a few minutes while she munched on a drumstick with her free hand, sucking the marrow with gusto. When the ice cubes disappeared, she placed the food in the oven then walked to her bedroom, licking her lips on the way. Mrs. James B. opened the second left drawer of her dresser and looked for her makeup kit. Her swollen cheek was red and cold when she applied the bronze-color base to cover the bluish marks under her eye. She wet her lips, using them as a palette to dip her index finger and get rid of the excess makeup. She changed out of her jeans and blouse and put on a house dress, preparing for her husband's return.

Mrs. James B. paced up and down the house as she waited. To ease her fear, she tried to remember her day as Miss Technical Mark. She had appeared on top of a washing machine, clad in an itsy-bitsy red bikini, saying with a big smile—while she raised her left leg towards her shoulder and winked her right eye—"Ingenious innovations in household appliances mean more free time for love."

The telephone rang and Mrs. James B. rushed to answer. "Hello."

"I ain't coming home 'til late."

"Why? Something come up with the baseball team?"

"I said I'm gonna be late. I gotta meeting."

"Then it must be something having to do with sports."

"Don't be so nosy, woman. It ain't got nothing to do with sports. But don't let my supper get cold!"

"But…"

Click.

Mrs. James B. sighed in relief.

The former Captain of the Leon High School football squad usually arrived with a big commotion, burning rubber, honking the horn of his wild Mustang, and cursing his luck. He would slam the screen door and go straight for the icebox, searching for his brew. He would drink a can in a single gulp, crush it with his fist, then throw it against the kitchen wall to signal Mrs. James B. he was ready to eat. Sometimes he would skip dinner, put down a six-pack, slip into his old football jersey, and play with an invisible ball. Mrs. James B.'s job was to stand by his side and cheer him on to make the winning touchdown. Then he would suddenly stop his final play, shout that he was still the most valuable player the sorry squad ever had, and that he had bigger balls than anyone else in the history of Leon High School. Then he would complain she wasn't cheering loud enough, that it was her fault he had hurt his knee and he didn't make the last cut with the Chicago Bears.

"You told me I was getting fat, so I ran as fast as I could and I tripped against one of the hurdles, and it's your fucking fault, you bitch!" he would shout in anger.

Sometimes Mrs. James B. would forget the very first time he beat her up, the day he punctured her womb. She would remind him that she had nothing to do with his knee injury,

and that he didn't make the final selection because Craig
Moody made the impressive throw which convinced the coach-
es to draft him instead. Then all hell would break loose, and
he would chase her around the living room, tackle her, and
beat her up once more, calling her a goddamn liar. Later in
the evening, a contrite captain would kiss her and beg her forgiveness.

This evening it was going to be different; he wasn't coming until late. Mrs. James B. pushed a chest of drawers to one
side and reached behind it, looking for the old photo album
she had constructed from The Pawn Shop pictures. It had a
mother of pearl cover. She opened it up to the page she had
marked with a piece of toilet paper and where she had pasted
the last three pictures she had bought. She had convinced
Stanley to give her one extra picture for all her previous pur-
chases. Fifty-seven black and white pictures depicted her family history. Two recent snapshots of a boy and a girl graced a
new page. She had inscribed on the back: "To Mom, I'm playing some mean football this year. The academy stinks. I can't
wait to eat your biscuits and gravy. Love you, your son, James
B. III." For the second picture she used pink ink and dotted
every "i" with a small black-eyed-susan "Mommy, Seth asked
me to go steady with him. His father is the wealthiest man in
Oglethorpe County. I am wearing my favorite dress so you can
see it in the picture. I love you, your daughter, Missy."

"Nellie ain't goin' to outdo me," she said as she closed the
album and headed for Nellie's place.

Nellie was surprised to see Mrs. James B. striding across
her yard, and to hear the rapid thudding of her shoes as she
came up the five steps to her porch. Mr. James B. must be
away on a game, Nellie thought to herself. Otherwise, he
wouldn't let her visit. Nellie rushed to the door, and before
Mrs. James B. had a chance to yell her traditional "yoohoo,"
the door opened.

"Mrs. James B., what a pleasant surprise! Don't tell me
there is an early shipment at the packing house!"

"I hope I ain't interrupting anything."

"Oh, no. Nelson is working overtime, and the children are playing outside," Nellie reassured her friend.

"I just had to come over. Mama finally sent me our family album and I had to show it to you. She sure took her sweet time. These are mostly pictures of Fairview, the family plantation. You must be careful not to touch them. These were the ones the Yankees didn't get."

"Oh, Mrs. James B.," Nellie said in shock. "Did another bee get you? That side of your face is swollen."

"It wasn't a bee this time. This time a wasp zapped me. They're building a nest by my backdoor. I went out to the clothesline, and on my way back, that nasty little son-of-a-gun got me."

"I will go and get you some Chinese balm. It will make it go down in a few minutes. It's made from powdered truffles. You just make yourself comfortable while I get you the balm."

Mrs. James B. sat down on the couch rehearsing in her mind the narrative of her family history, especially the parts she thought would impress Nellie the most.

"Here you are. A small quantity will make it go away." Nellie dabbed her finger in the small container and spread it over the swollen area.

"Thanks, Nell," Mrs. James B. said with feeling, which took Nellie aback. "This is the album, Nellie. You be careful when you turn the pages. It's very old. Not as old as the city in Mexico I told you about a while back, but old enough."

Smelling of tiger balm, Mrs. James B. began her family saga.

"Be careful, Nellie! Lick your finger. It's easier that way. That's Fairview. It had beautiful French windows, a real Frenchman from France put them up. The flowers tumbling over the verandas are wisteria. There ain't none in this area, but in Fairview they grew as wild as weeds. The trees lining the driveway were cedars, and my great-great-grandfather had the slaves plant them. The Yankees chopped them down to keep warm in the winter and left none for us when they knew we were hungry and just barely alive! Flip the page, Nellie. This is my great-grandmother; her name was Amanda Bailey. She was the tallest woman in the county. Look at her beautiful inky lashes. I wish I had got them, but my sister beat me to it. I got these droopy ones from my father's side of the family. Those ain't relatives. Those are the negro servants. Probably relatives of Naomi, the colored woman that works with us in the packing house. That's why I don't talk to her. I'm sure her relatives helped the Yankees destroy Fairview. Amanda was an expert at dealing with her Negroes. She told them what to do once, and didn't let them get sassy with her. That's my great-grandfather, Amanda's husband. His name was Red."

"Are you related to Red Hodel from the fish market?" Nellie asked.

"Well, Nellie Mae, we ain't white trash. It's a nickname because his hair was red. Red wasn't that cute. He had sort of a funny nose, like a cucumber, but he was as shrewd as a weasel. He could sell you just about anything he wanted."

"Who are the twins?"

"Them two little girls on his lap are my granny and her sister, Sarah. They dressed in the best French fabrics money could buy. The French make a lot of things like windows and doors and fries."

"My father always got our lace from Belgium, from his friend Christian," Nellie added proudly.

"Well, now that I think about it, one of the twins dressed in Belgium fabrics and fine stuff like that."

"And the horse?"

"That fireball belonged to Granny. She rode it every morning and almost fell from it while jumping a hurdle. I'm sure glad she didn't, because if she had, yours truly wouldn't be talking to you right now. Not so fast, Nellie. I took my time when you showed me yours."

"Excuse me. I'm developing poor manners. What's that?"

"That's the barbecue. It was one of the few things the damn Yankees left standing. I reckon they couldn't burn a place that's used for burning. Flip that page right quick!"

"What is it, Mrs. James B.?"

Mrs. James B. started an uncontrollable sobbing and Nellie did her best to calm her down.

"It's the picture of my great-aunt Sarah as a grown woman. She was shot by a Yankee soldier. She had a hearing problem, and when the soldier shouted, 'Freeze,' she didn't hear him, and she got it right in her forehead."

"I understand, Mrs. James B. Believe me, I understand your suffering, your humiliation. Don't you worry, I can assure you, you will be with me at Mondovi."

"She was engaged to be married. Her beau called her 'Sweetheart.' Ain't that sweet?"

"Who's this?"

"That's my great-grandma and Granny. They worked as nurses during the war. My great-grandma shot two Yankees that were abusing her favorite Negro servant; so much for their equality crap. Then great-Granny lost her mind. She thought my grandma's pet rabbit was her husband and prepared what little there was to eat for him. There were days my grandma told me she had to watch the rabbit eat her share. Then great-Granny started having headaches and throwing up, and she believed herself to be pregnant by the rabbit. Grandma was so hungry in the Winter of '65 she took the rabbit, strung him by the neck, made a fire, and had it for supper all by herself. Flip that page before I start crying again."

"That's Granny in the hospital when she got gangrene and the doctor cut off her middle finger. Oh, Nellie, look! That's my great-grandma and her dress. She made it out of a curtain. That's so sad, so sad. When Fairview was sacked the first time, General Sherman stole all of my great-grandma's party dresses to take north to his ugly wife."

"Just like what happened to me. It wasn't a general but a fat commander, though he wasn't a commander then. I can't bear to say his name. He stole all my dresses for his mistresses."

"Did he really?"

"Yes, but I don't wish to discuss it."

"Whatever suits you, honey. That's our hometown before that shithead General set it afire. That was on a Wednesday, and the following day they rode to Fairview and burned it to the ground, stole all our family jewels, even my great-great-grandfather's sword. He fought against you people in Mexico. That's how he got that sword. They were so nasty, those damn soldiers, they threatened to cut off Granny's finger if she didn't give the General her gold thimbles."

"Did she?"

"Let's just say she kept her finger. That one is the last picture of baby Audry. The only picture left. Her mother was a friend of my great-grandma. I think her name was Beverly Norton, but everybody called her Lee because she looked so much like General Lee. Anyway, Lee gave birth three months before the town fell. Baby Audry was stolen by a union soldier whose wife was barren and taken up north." Mrs. James B. began to cry with loud wails.

"Calm down, Mrs. James B. Calm down. I'll make you some coffee."

"I'll be okay, Nellie. Just open the window. I need some fresh air. Forget about the coffee."

"Cry more if you have to. I know how painful memories can create havoc in your mind."

Mrs. James B. took a whiff of fresh air and pretended to calm down.

"What about that trip to Mondovi, Nellie? Do you have a big house there with a hairy, swarthy man like that picture you showed me?"

"It's not a house. It's a palazzo, and our friend Sergio is much nicer looking than the swarthy man. Sergio has the beauty of something unattainable...his eyes are two still lakes in which your soul can attain tranquility. He will take you by the hand and personally escort you throughout the city. He will introduce you to the best of society and tell them about your family's humiliation and misfortune. They will all understand your years of suffering in silence, and in a few days, you will be the talk of Mondovi. But, Mrs. James B., you must not tell anyone about this trip. Not even Mr. James B."

"I cross my heart and swear to die. I won't tell a soul."

Many Tulips Later

Xawa-on-Deep River
"Year of the Heroic Effort"
"Happy Birthday, Baby"

Nellie Pardo
18 NE Avenue Z
Belle Glade, Florida
Estados Unidos

Dearest Baby:

I keep writing, but there's no answer! The last letter you sent to me was on April 16, 1962. I've kept on writing you every 9th of each month to remember your birthday, which is today. I wish you the best because you deserve it. Do you remember when you cried so much because you thought you couldn't have your birthday party because you had the chicken pox?

As I told you in my many letters, Magda doesn't write for me anymore. She moved to St. James in the Orient. She and Lazarus, Juan Benson's son, split up last April. He worked in the chemical plant—the night shift—but one day he came home early and heard his bed talking and found Magda in it with old Waldo. There was a big scene, and you could hear Waldo's hysterical cries for blocks. Then Lazarus broke a bottle of malt by banging it against the bed's headboard, and with the sharp neck, was threatening the old man. The neighbors came and restrained Lazarus. Since Waldo is Rulfo's friend, Magda was blamed for enticing him to commit antisocial behavior; this is what the paper calls it. When you were here we knew it by another name. Anyway, Lazarus forgave her on the condition she had to get rid of all their furniture because it reminded him of her affair. After a week of tossing and turning in bed, trying to come to a decision, she waited until Lazarus was at work and put all the furniture in a cart and left him. People blamed her, but nowadays it's easier to find a man than to find furniture. I know Magda, and I'm sure it wasn't that easy to make up her mind. Besides, I think she was tired of waking up every day at four-thirty in the morning when Lazarus got aroused. Magda told me she could set her alarm clock to his thing. It didn't matter to him if she was sick, not in the mood, or with the monthly visitor. After all this scandal happened, Lazarus started drinking heavily and lost his job. He's now a Jehovah's Witness, which is against the law. My friend Yaya used to have a cat named Jehovah. Good thing they are both dead now, otherwise they'd be in jail.

Lazarus' father, Juan Benson, died on Christmas Eve. Before, it would have been a big problem since everybody would have been ready to party, and partying and mourning don't mix. But we don't celebrate Christmas anymore; it's prohibited by the authorities. That would have been great news for Rigoletto and all the other larders who were the main course of the Christmas Eve dinner.

Juan died of a spider bite. He was messing around in one of those agricultural brigades and couldn't see. I guess they were desperate for people. Oh, yes, I remember why. It was when Hurricane Flora (was it Flora?), anyway, it was one of those hurricanes that dumped a lake of water on this town and the vegetable harvest was all but lost. He couldn't see because he went blind a few years back from messing with poison ivy. He was trying to gather rotten tomatoes. I'm sure it was a black widow. Tomasa is helping me with the letters now. She's no longer with Rulfo. He left her for a much younger woman, almost a child. I call it a favor, but it's not really one since I let her borrow my black patent-leather shoes for her Sunday stroll. (Those were the shoes you told me I could have the day you left.)

I still visit the master's grave. I don't go as often as I'd like. I have to go walking, and my arthritis is getting worse. I wish I could bring him tulips, his favorite flowers, but that's impossible. Though he doesn't really need flowers because he was a living saint, and a saint's tomb always has the smell of fresh cut flowers. How are the children? Nelson, Jr. must be around fourteen, a man. If I saw him walking down the street, I wouldn't recognize him. María-Chiara is ten years old. Tell her that the olive-oil bottle is safe with me. Have you visited with María Rosa? Once she blamed me for your mother's death. I had nothing to do with it. The lady choked on a quail bone. I had told everyone that day after that dark butterfly crashed against the living room lamp, bursting the light bulb, to be careful. I remember everybody laughed at me. María Rosa thought I should have been more careful when I deboned the little bird. It was fate!

Waldo Dieste, of course, is still alive. He's one-hundred years old! The monument to Mario, the sultan, is being re-sculptured. It's going to be called "Toiling Women Revolting Against Oppressor." Each one of the dancers will carry a rifle, aiming it at the sultan. It's just a slight change, so don't be too upset. Your face looks beautiful in stone, but your hair has gotten a little green. That's why I'm always telling you to take care of your hair. I'm afraid it might be an omen. I remember when I took you to that dance. You were the most beautiful of all the dancing girls. You've always walked with such grace. Are you taking care of your skin? Is Nelson putting almonds in your bath water? I wish I could be there with you to take care of all your needs.

I think I told you in one of my letters—in 1966, I think— about Van Der Xawa, the one that painted, not houses, but pictures of people and little blonde girls (in case you don't remember, he painted Mrs. Peña's picture with the bridge). He was arrested for painting dirty pictures. He was living with Dina. Remember her? She's the one whose son died about five years ago and was J.L.S.'s mistress. I hope you know how to read initials because we're prohibited to mention his name. He's a traitor. Consuelo Palomo told me Dina told on the colonel. She told Rulfo that the colonel was stealing from the People's warehouses. That's why he was declared a traitor. Consuelo said she did it because the colonel was going to find out she couldn't have any more children and he wanted one of his own. It seems that Dina was faking her monthly visitor by buying chopped liver at the butcher shop and smearing it on her napkins so the colonel thought she was a whole woman. Then we had the meat rationing and there was no more chopped liver, so rather than letting the colonel know the truth, she accused him to save herself from that painful moment. We always want to forget something, baby, so we create stories. It's less painful that way. I don't remember the painter's first name, but Dina shouted at dinner time: "Liazzo, it's dinner time!" Anyway, baby, he painted her naked in many different ways, like on top of a table with an orange in her mouth, or reading a newspaper on a green rocking chair (except she wasn't really reading since she doesn't know how to read since she was never taught how by the literacy brigade) and also with broken wings in a very dirty pose. All these pictures were shown to the whole town in front of what used to be Ariza's Cafe. Now it's called the People's Cafe. I don't know why, because I hardly see any people going in. Ariza left for Spain in 1966. He was also put on trial for being a friend of Mr. Conway, but the revolutionary government traded him for two Spanish Pegasus buses. I feel sorry for Dina. She has never had luck with men. She was born to be a dime and not a quarter.

I am sure you remember Consuelo. She and her husband, Hilary, adopted one of the twins that were burned; the other one died. The twins, Tula and Tila were going to a children's party at the Casino dressed as Siamese Hawaiian dancers inside a single rope skirt, and there was a lit cigarette on the floor, and they were standing right on it, and when everybody realized what was happening they were on fire. Tila died a few days later, and Tula was in the hospital for two months. After that happened, her mother went mad, and Consuelo, who lived upstairs, went every day to visit the child in the hospital and fell in love with the little scar-faced girl and ended up adopting her when the mother hanged herself in the asylum. I think it was with the sheets, but it could have been with a towel. I'm not too sure about it.

Please, baby. Write me! I'm getting very old now. I hope it isn't because of the pig. I pray for the larder's soul every day, which is like praying for all of us, since he became a part of us. I forgot to tell you that I haven't seen Dina in years. No one has seen her after the dirty pictures were shown in the public square. Maybe she was so ashamed and moved to One Hundred Fires, where she's really from. Remember to be always faithful to Nelson, for a deceiving woman shrinks. I know you'll never yield to temptation, but you're in a strange land, so don't take anything from strangers because it could be a love philtre or something worse that might make you crazy. And remember also to bring happiness to the children, so they can have a good supply of it when they are older. Life eats away happiness! But above all, make sure they don't become so self-sufficient. I hear in that country everybody is so self-sufficient; how can those people be generous to each other when they are so self-sufficient?

With the unchanging love of,

Delfina

P.S.: Rulfo was named commander in chief of the province. He has a younger girl, almost a child. He dumped Tomasa and shot the only female vulcon left. I just got a postcard from Hilda. Tomasa says it's from St. Christopher. Tomasa is getting hairs on her upper lip, but I don't have any. I love you...

Gelati

"Passengers en route to Montreal may deplane but must be back by 4:45. Make sure to take your boarding pass with you."

I left my carry-on bag behind so I wouldn't arouse the suspicion of any of the flight crew. And I was getting quite experienced at leaving bags behind. I helped an elderly lady out of her seat and walked slowly through the aisle, greeting the stewardess as I left.

"Be back by 4:45," she said with an automatic smile.

"Of course," I answered.

My heart was pounding when I stepped out of the airport and a taxi driver offered his services. I started racing down Le Jeune Street, but realizing I looked very conspicuous moving at that pace, I opted to walk fast. I don't know how many miles I had walked when I realized that I was going in circles. I was completely disoriented and fearful when I stopped to ask directions from a man with a fake mustache. His face looked familiar. He was pushing a fruit cart. As I approached him, he ran away, dumping most of his lemons, oranges and mangos on the busy street. Years later I realized he must have thought I was an undercover policeman trying to crack down on vendors without permits. Luckily, I found a public phone and searched in my pockets for the tiny piece of paper with Bernabé's number.

"Hello, Sunrise Apartments," said a raspy voice.

"Yes, is Mr. Guiristain home?" My voice was trembling.

"Mr. who?"

"Mr. Guiristain."

"How do you spell that?"

I was so tense I had forgotten the alphabet in English.

"The name is Guiristain."

"Fuck off."

"Yes?"

Click.

I sat by the curb. My pants were soaked with sweat. The harder I tried to remember the alphabet the more confused I became. The thought of the police searching for me made me spring up and call again.

"Sunrise Apartments."

"Yes, Mr. Guiristain."

Click.

My only hope now was to find the Sunrise Apartments. I looked in the yellow pages and memorized the address. It was exactly seventy-two blocks up the road. I started my trek.

I saw a large faded sun. It dangled from an arch over an entrance, and to the side there was a sign which at some point must have had letters but was now faded. I crossed beneath the arch and found myself inside a dilapidated apartment complex. I felt a sense of relief. I walked around, peeking through the windows in a frantic search for my friend. By the time I had inspected sections A through H, I had seen an elderly couple lying drunk on a linoleum surface, a pimp beating a prostitute, and a lone, naked child playing with his own excrement. Then I heard a loud siren and hid inside a huge trash can. When the sound grew fainter, and I was sure it wasn't for me, I emerged smelling of putridness. I thought about going back to Xawa and surrendering to my Daddy and Nellie. Then I heard the sounds of a very loud radio playing rock-and-roll music. I followed the melody, and saw a man with his back to the window dancing by himself in his underwear. I knew I had found Bernabé. I knocked on the door and he peeked through the screenless window.

"Who is it?" he said as he reached for his glasses resting on top of the radio.

"It's me, cowboy." And before he had a chance to put his glasses on, he knew immediately who I was. There were two people on earth that knew him as 'cowboy,' and the other was an Italian mare named Furia.

"Jerk-off," he screamed, his voice quavering. He opened the door and we embraced and cried as he repeated between sobs, "Things must be awful over there because you sure smell like shit."

"I have to hide. The police will be looking for me. I'm supposed to be on my way to Montreal."

"Relax. No one is going to find you in this rat hole. Besides, you'll ask for asylum tomorrow. They are used to it. Everybody does it."

"This place is awful. How can you live here?"

"It's cheap, and I guess you'll be my roommate again."

"And your wife and the kids?" I changed the conversation. The thought of staying there made me sick.

"Still in Madrid. As soon as I save some money, I'll send for them. I'm not planning to be poor in this country for any length of time."

"At least everybody made it to Spain."

"So how did you escape, because you were under surveillance?"

I explained my ordeal, except the part about the seaborne suitcase. I told him how things were back home, my thoughts about the political situation, and our chances of going back.

"I'm glad you made it," said Bernabé, embracing me again. Then he continued, "I'm working as an ice cream man. I have to dress as a clown."

"As a clown?"

"Yes. Life is hard here, but, don't despair, you can still have some fun on weekends."

To ease my amazement, he went to his room and came out dressed in his clown outfit. We laughed and he offered to hire me as his helper.

Our truck was painted bright green with bright yellow balloons circling the words "Italian Ices, Gelati." We took turns driving it and collecting the money. We played our catchy circus music loudly as we made our way through Coral Gables and Coconut Grove, attracting the gluttonous offspring of the rich. Their mothers or maids smiled as they exchanged their money for our frozen goods, and a winking Bernabé held their hands a second too long as he handed them their change. Many were the nights that, thanks to this technique, we enjoyed the company of the ice cream ladies, as he preferred to call them. He was a good buddy, the best. He never forgot me, always insisting the ice cream ladies bring a friend for me. He called them cones. I only conversed with them. I had no other interest because a few days before, I had found out how much the squirrel meant to me.

On Sunday mornings it was our ritual to take the bus to Palm Beach. We would wear the shortest shorts possible, a V-shaped t-shirt and a pair of thongs. We would parade ourselves up and down the fancy streets—Mar-A-Lago, Vista-Del-Lago, Worth Avenue—searching for rich ladies taking their poodles for a relieving stroll. Our approach was simple. As the dog was crouching next to his favorite telephone pole, Bernabé would walk by and kick the defecating canine from behind. Our hope was the animal would react angrily and bite one of us. After the snap, our lawsuit would ensue. Bernabé often screamed as he kicked the animal, "Rich again, rich again, God omnipotent, we are rich again!"

We tried for a whole year, but were never successful. The dogs would simply start howling in fear. Then Bernabé would pat the dog on the head the moment its unsuspecting owner tried to calm the hysterical little beast.

"There's nothing to fear, Bristol. Don't be afraid of the nice gentleman. He wants to be your friend."

I continued in the ice cream business until I was told by the route manager he didn't need two people working in one truck. Bernabé pleaded with him, but I had to go. Bernabé was furious. He wanted to quit himself, but I calmed him down. Bernabé then told me I didn't have to pay my share of the food and lodging until I found a new job, that it didn't matter how long it took me.

A few days later I was out of a job, but still happy to be free from Daddy's suitcase. It was then I received an unexpected call.

"Is this Mr. Guiristain?" said an unfamiliar voice.

"Nelson or Bernabé?" I sounded puzzled.

"The owner of the Xawa Import Company?"

"Speaking."

"This is Pepe Fernández."

"Pepe?" Now I was confused.

"Pepe. I was one of the truckers for your import company."

"The one with the limp?"

"The very same one. I found out that you were here and without a job, and if you don't mind, I want you to come to Union City to give me a hand with a small business I am starting."

"What sort of enterprise?" I assumed the tone of a boss.

"It's a stuffed-potato stand on the corner of Berger Lane. We will be partners. And you can stay with us until you find your own place. I'll help you with the security deposits. So what do you say?"

I panicked. I didn't want to be a businessman ever again. I didn't want to take that risk, especially if we were to succeed.

"I have to think about it," I said curtly.

"Listen, Nelson. What do you have to lose?"

I resented that he called me by my first name.

"I have to think about it. I don't know how things work in this country."

"We have to start anew somehow. We have all come here naked with one hand in front and one behind. So don't think about it too much. With my will and your brains we'll conquer Berger Lane."

"Thank you for calling, Pepe. I'll be in touch."

I never returned his call.

A week after Pepe's call, I joined a crew of tomato pickers. It was led by Dr. Gastón Robau, one of our leading heart surgeons; Chief Justice Josende; and an array of ex-senators of the Republic, from Senator Alvarez to the last democratically elected senator, Zubizarreta. (He was the incumbent for 31 years and three dictatorships and managed always to be reelected or reappointed by special decree. Many attributed his political luck to the scores of children he had fathered in his district. They all voted for him or were members of the undemocratic regimes that automatically appointed their dad to the powerless congress. They were good to their father because he neither demanded nor expected anything from them, but always made sure his tribe had enough to eat.) An array of ex-entrepreneurs were also part of the tomato-picking crew. They included a number of members of the Association of Beef Producers and the owners of The Vegetarian, the most elite of the epicurean restaurants in St. Christopher.

We worked from sunup to sundown in Homestead. Our foreman was a freckle-faced, wavy-haired tyrant from Alabama named Billy Cloonan, Sr. To antagonize us even more, he always brought his son Billy, Jr. along. He would steal the tomatoes from our baskets and put them in his own. Billy, Sr. worked us like dogs, and our lunch break was at the most fifteen minutes long. He paid us by the basket of unblemished fruits. One day he was so rude to Chief Justice Josende, Surgeon Robau intervened on his behalf.

"Do you realize whom you are addressing so disrespectfully?" the medical doctor said to the grumpy foreman.

Billy Cloonan, Sr. raised his eyebrows and answered, "Yeah, an old fart that can't pick a tomato without scratching it."

"With all due respect, sir, you are addressing Chief Justice Josende, who almost single-handedly wrote our 1940 Constitution, one of the most progressive pieces of jurisprudence in the Western World. It provided for sick pay up to three years upon contracting a disabling illness, two years paid leave for pregnant ladies, a four-day work week, free universal medical services, free elementary, secondary, and higher education, free school lunches, free child care for working mothers, trial by competent judges, the right to strike without the fear of scabs stealing your job, and the right to habeas corpus."

"And who gives a shit. Get back to work. I see you've picked five baskets in ten hours at fifty cents a basket. That ain't much to feed a family, and your old fart friend has only two!"

I lasted for three months in the tomato fields until fate took me to the stockroom. A few days after I started working as a tomato picker, Bernabé came up with the scheme that was going to restore him to opulence. He became a bookworm. He who had always detested reading, who received his baccalaureate because of his perfect 20-20 vision and ability to cheat. I became alarmed when he refused to look for a new crop of ice cream ladies because he said he was too busy reading. I thought Bernabé was going mad. One morning he came in with twenty-two books on the Nazi concentration camps and the plight of the survivors. He took on this task with the same ardor with which he pursued the fauna at Marina's place.

"Once in a blue moon one gets a chance like this!" he blared as he finished the first book.

Holy Radishes

"Aïda, any news from yo' mama back home?" inquired Naomi as she was trying to floss her front teeth with a piece of radish root.

"Oh, yes, I received a letter from her yesterday," answered Aïda with a lofty smile. "Che says of the letters I sent her with the nylon stocking che got only one, the right foot with the flint for the lighter inside. Che wants me to send her right away two left feet in separate envelopes because che is sure the mailman that's stealing everysing might let her have a pair of stockings for her if I send two of everysing."

"Can't she git dem ut de Five and Dime Sto'?" asked Naomi, somewhat surprised.

"Oh, no! There is no nosing over there. Nosing, very bad, very bad!"

"Ah sorry fuh yo' po' mama!"

"But I am happy because che sent me the music chit of the song I sang at Regalia's Cabaret Show in the television when I made my debut. I am very happy because it was the first song I sang for the big public. You know I am a contralto, and I taught María Callas how to make her registry better." As she finished her speech, Aïda let go of a few low thundering notes to impress Naomi.

"Dat's whut ah always say, de lawd will provide. Yo' mama didn't git de stocking but yuh got yo' music."

"How are your childrens doing?"

"The chillun are in school. The truth is dat Gay, Jimmy and Alfonzo are in school. Dey got uh good head lak der mama, but Andrianita, she lak her papa. She said she ain't gonna go no mo' tuh school. An told at girl ah wuz gonna give her uh good beatin'. She yelled back at me dat she wuz gonna merry some boy named Zachariah. Ah ast her who he wuz, and she said he wuz her boyfriend. Ah wuz so mad ah hit her and she yelled again. When ah saw dat Zachariah, ah knew trouble wuz already here. He gave me de same feelin' her papa did, an eardquake. And when ah saw him leanin' tuh feed uh bird he wuz carrin' on is shoulder ah wuz sho mah first baby wuz gone. Dat wuz de same thing her papa did when ah lost mah head fuh him. Ah useter put so many pretty ribbons on Andrianita's head fuh her tuh wear. She looked so pretty! Ah wuz 'spectin tuh make uh nurse outta dat girl. Aïda, yuh better keep an eye on dem radishes and stop yo' singing! Yuh already let go two bad ones, and Jack's gone come fussin' and shorten our break and mah feet are killin' me." A bit of anger crept into her voice.

"My eyes, Naomi, my eyes. I need new glasses." Aïda excused her lack of dexterity.

"Ah don't know whut tuh do, Aïda," Naomi's face grew somber. "Ah got skeered when ah ast her and she told me she got her womanhood three months past!"

"Oh, Naomi, Naomi, you must send her to Spain, right away! Yes, yes, to a convent in Spain before is too late. That's what my mother told her friend, Luz, when che found out my milk sister, Amparo, was kissing Mario through the back iron gates. There's obedience in Spain for parents, and rectitude!"

"Ah guess ah might have to send her dere. How far way iz dat from here?"

"Vicky, do you know what Dina, the new one, told me?" whispered Loly to Vicky a few stools away from Aïda and Naomi. "She said she defected in East Berlin during a medical conference. I don't believe it. I asked if she knew Dr. Sotolongo at the university, and she said she met him once. Any medical student that went through the university had to know Dr. Sotolongo because he taught anatomy. I know because he was my cousin's godfather." Loly kept raising her pitch as she talked to Vicky.

"Hush. Tssst. She's going to hear you."

"No, she is not. See, her stool is empty. She's inside the little office talking to Jack. She spends a lot of time talking to Jack and chewing gum, but she chews gum like a riffraff with her mouth open." There was a touch of rage in her voice, or maybe jealousy. She sounded flustered.

The chatting suddenly came to a halt. There was silence as a new avalanche of produce entered the belt, increasing the tempo. The workers' hands were caught in an allegro frenzy, moving like violins driven by a frantic conductor. When finally the movement came to a moderato, the whispers started again. Loly was the first to break the silence.

"Vicky, did you know that Aïda is divorced?"

"Not so loud, Loly! I can't believe it. Who told you?"

"I heard someone say it at Pepe's Grocery. She got divorced a few months after her son was born."

"She has a son! She never talks about him. But how old is the child?"

"Yes, a son, but he is no child. He's about twenty-five, lives in North Carolina and was adopted by some family there many years ago."

"She doesn't look that old. But it's hard to tell with singers and those types of people because they have plastic surgery. I wouldn't waste money on that. Besides, physical beauty is ephemeral. Time will corrode it. It's like my Lisander says, 'True beauty lies in the soul.'"

"Do you remember when she sang at the Ladies' Tennis?"

"How can I forget that night! Lisander recited with gusto. Have you heard anything about Cuquín or Fanny?"

"Fanny and Joseph Fern were killed trying to leave the island. A government PT boat spotted their yacht 12 miles north of Isabella, and they were machine-gunned."

"Stop! Don't say anymore. I'm getting sick."

"Here, Vicky. Smell my handkerchief. I sprinkle it each morning with 1800 Cologne."

"Thank you, Loly. I must tell Lisander. I'm sure he will write a poem about their tragedy. He was fond of them. You know that if Pituca finds out about Aïda, she won't invite her to the canasta party. I still can't believe it. Divorced!"

"Divorce is a shame. I never divorced Senator Zubiza-rreta. Our marriage was annulled by Father Santos. But Pitu-ca won't have to worry about inviting Aïda. There's no party this week. Her husband is sick."

"Sick?"

"I don't know with what because you know how secretive she is, but I know he's sick because I saw Dr. Cabrera leaving her house with his brown bag. That's where he keeps his instruments. He can't practice here. Before I forget, has Lisander been able to find a job?" (Loly always kept control of their conversations.) "My brother Cioci is working as an acolyte at St. Philip Benezi. He gets paid by the service. Wed-dings are the best because he gets to bring the leftovers home."

"Cioci has been luckier than my Lisander." Vicky inhaled deeply. "But believe me he has tried. I feel for my Lis! Last month he got so depressed because he walked every single day answering the want ads, but no luck, and I got nervous when he started talking about Socrates, not the guy that used to own the curio store across from your uncle in Xawa, but the Greek mathematician who killed himself. I thought Lis was going to do something silly, or as Mrs. James B. would say, that he was coming to the end of his rope. In his desperation he answered an ad about writing lyrics for new songs. I wept when I found out what he was doing. That's so demeaning for a bard of his quality! I told him not to use his real name, that it would give him a bad reputation if people were to find out, especially when we go back home. But he's such a talent that he wrote the first lyrics in less than one hour, and that's very fast since he had to use his bilingual dictionary. The song has to be in English. He mailed it to WMIA and in a few days they sent him a check for thirty dollars. He bought himself a new vest with the money."

"How does it go in case I hear it on the radio? Of course, there is no comparison with his poems," Loly rushed to say.

"I am so embarrassed, but I am going to tell you because we have been friends since I met you at Apostolic Boarding School in our beloved Xawa. But please not a word, not even to your brother Cioci. He wrote it under the name A.D. Jova, a great composer from the Middle Ages. If you listen to it on the radio one of these days, I hope you won't reveal the true identity of A.D. Jova."

"I swear by my grandmother's remains I won't say a word to anyone, not even to Cioci or my sister Mely." Loly kissed her thumb and index to validate her oath.

"Lis called the song 'Coconuts.' It is very poetic," Vicky said as she jiggled her gold bracelet.

> Island rhythms were beating in my head
> Coconuts calling passions fed
> Cool, breezy nights, hot, white lights
> Your body dancin' in time always to be
> always to be mine
> My heart was beating with every caress
> Coconuts whispering as they confess
> True intentions, real emotions
> the night slowly slips away, you're such a,
> such a good lay.
> Coconuts, co co coconuts, co co coconuts,
> Well, I'm coconuts over you, baby.

"Vicky, it's beautiful. I can see the hand of a poet in it. But what is 'good lay?' I don't understand."

"Loly, that is the English contraction for 'lady.' You know like 'did not' is 'didn't' and you drop the o, so 'good lady' is 'good lay' and you drop the d."

"Hey, gals, I wanna hear that song. It has a good beat. Who was singing it?" shouted Mrs. James B.

"Oh, no, no. Don't tell her, Loly!" Vicky covered her mouth.

"I declare, Nellie, your friends are a bunch of sissies! And where's that Mirta. She owes me $2."

"She is not here anymore. She is in the Everglades, training with the freedom fighters. She bought her gun yesterday at The Pawn Shop. Though, it was not the machine gun she wanted," Loly answered for Nellie.

"Are you going to Pituca's house for the canasta party?" Vicky knew there wasn't going to be a party, but she asked Nellie to bring her into the conversation.

"She won't answer you. She ain't here. She's someplace else," Mrs. James B.'s nagging voice hurried to say.

"Guns remind me of the day the Germans destroyed the bridge," Nellie muttered.

"See, she is talking to me," Vicky grinned.

"What bridge are you talking about, sugar?" Mrs. James B. inquired.

"The bridge. The bridge over the Ellero River."

"Didn't I tell you she wasn't with it? I know Nellie like the palm of my hand," Mrs. James B. chuckled. "She's thinking about her country."

"I think about Xawa all day long," remarked Vicky.

"She ain't from there. She's from Mondovi, and that's a fact, so mind your own business."

"Maybe she hasn't gotten over her father's death or the destruction of your zoo. My favorite animal was the Flying García. Which one of you came up with the crazy idea of disguising those street dogs?"

Mrs. James B. misinterpreted Loly's candid observation. "Listen, Lolita, what happened with the zoo is none of your business. It was an act of God. Those were real animals. We imported them from South America. It cost us a bundle to bring them here. So leave it there! Don't push me! If you push me, I'm gonna kick you so hard I'm gonna send you flying to Mexico!"

Loly was going to say something back, but her words got tangled up in her mouth and she ran from her stool and started walking and jumping around the work area to relieve the tension. Mrs. James B. was mad and lit up a cigarette. She played with the smoke, making rings.

"Whut's de matter, Pituca? Yuh ain't saying much today." Naomi pushed her stool closer to Pituca's.

"I have a cold," she answered.

"Das funny, yuh ain't got no sniffles."

"Hey, Naomi." Aïda pressed her index to her lips, signaling her to be quiet, and whispered into her ear, "Yesterday che has to sell all her charms to The Pawn Shop. Her husband is no working. He had a heart attack last week. I am the only one that knows that che sold her jewelry, and now you know it, too. I saw her coming out of the chop and I followed her. I know exactly what che did."

"Ah sho' see dem charms hangin' from her bracelet."

"Those are no the real ones. Che got those from bubblegum machines that gives you charms and gum."

"Das real sad, Aïda. Real sad. We is de same, lak sisters, four chillum and now no hosband. When ah git home tonight, ah gonna cook her some good gizzards. Do you want tuh come tuh?"

"Thank you very much. I will come and sing for you!"

"Come ah six."

"Did you know Pituca is a descendant of Ignatius Earthmound?"

"Is that a fact?" Naomi's curiosity was stronger than her not wanting to appear dumb, and she asked, "Who's dat?"

"The famous patriot."

"Ah!"

Aïda noticed Naomi wanted to say something else and asked her, "You have a problem to tell me?"

"Ah have wanted tuh ast yuh all dey long. What's a milk sister?"

"You could have asked before. A milk sister is a baby that was fed by your mother while she was feeding you. You see, Luz had no milk and my mother had plenty for the two of us." Naomi was going to say something else when the foreman appeared.

"Okay, stop the yakkity," said a short and pudgy figure with a pear-shaped nose and a stubby neck smudged with lipstick as it approached station number five. "Reverend Fender is coming during the lunch break. I want you to pay attention to what he has to say to y'all. Let's show some respect to the man of the cloth. If I hear you were nasty to the reverend, I swear I'm gonna send you to the celery, and you don't know how good you have it here with the radishes until you have to work with the celery. The radishes are the cadillac of the packing bidness. And talking about bidness and to save y'all busybodies some wondering, bidness is good so I have to hire myself a secretary. She's starting this afternoon, and she is gonna count how many bags each station puts out every hour."

There was no need to say who the new secretary was. Jack and Dina had been carrying on inside the cubicle for a while. She was smiling at his side, holding a legal-size pad in her left hand. A pencil rested comfortably in her cleavage.

"That nose gives me the willies, and she is a tramp!" Mrs. James B.'s lips rounded to form the adjective.

"Good afternoon, ladies. Praise the Lord!" said a tall, wiry, thin man in checkered trousers and patent-leather shoes. His ears were covered with clumps of hair which reached outward like sea anemones, adorning his bony face. "I'm sorry I took a bit longer to get here, but I had a man who rushed into my office wanting to be saved. He had been a sinner all his life, but he repented and accepted the only plan for true salvation. Praise the Lord! But when I was on my way over here, I realized I had left these beautiful inspirational cardboard fans which I was bringing here for you to help relieve the heat. It's sure hot today." The reverend took one of the fans and fanned himself. "I will distribute them and some literature at the end of the word. I recognize some familiar faces here. I see Mrs. James B. I know for fact she accepted the Lord as her own personal savior years ago in Bradford-ville."

"Amen, Reverend," shouted Mrs. James B.

"How many of you have prayed to an idol?" There was silence. "I say, how many of you have knelt in front of a statue to pray to it?" The audience was still, and the reverend's face grew puffier and puffier with rage. "Don't be shy. I've been to Tijuana when I was in the army. I seen thousands of you kneeling in front of statues, subjects of the Whore of Babylon! Don't you know that the Lord himself said, 'Thou shall not have other gods before me!!!'" He banged the conveyor belt with such force the machine cranked up by itself, delivering loads of radishes. The reverend seemed oblivious to the incoming produce. The capillaries that covered his face threatened to burst. "I've seen your temples of doom with their many gods. And who do you think made those gods? I'm gonna tell you who. The Pope and his imagination which leads people to eternal fire! Imagination, my dear children, is the crazy woman that lives in the house of the mind. We must destroy that woman! How many of you are planning to return to your Tijuana-like churches?"

"Not I," said Mrs. James B.

There was silence until Loly spoke.

"We are not from Mexico."

"Ah ain't either," Naomi seconded Loly.

"Be more respectful of the reverend," shouted Jack.

"It's okay, Jack. It ain't them talking; it's the devil that's afraid I'm coming to uproot him forever. Hallelujah, hallelu-jah, hallelujah."

The reverend looked up at the ceiling, took a cleansing breath, and thundered, "I want you to listen carefully. I want to take you safely to the promised land, your land."

"What he saying?" asked Pituca to Aïda.

"He is a Protestant priest. He wants us to pray for our homeland. I think Mirta sent him."

"I always say a rosary for it. Look, I keep it inside my pocket. It's my mother's amethyst rosary. One of the few things I managed to bring from Xawa. I hid it in my body, but don't ask me where."

"Hush," said an attentive Mrs. James B.

"I had this revelation last night while I was in deep prayer. There was this train and it had an engine. The engine was dark and colored red and lit by a brimstone lamp. The blood-filled boiler reflect like a mirror, revealing the devil to be the engineer."

"Lawd a' mussy," Naomi cried.

"Idol worshippers and their Pope and his wolfish allies—like the owner of The Pawn Shop who dresses like a lamb, but who's really a hungry cur—all sitting in horror and staring at their train tickets. The train dashed on toward that awful place as the hot wind scorched their hands and faces. Hotter and hotter the air became, as faster and faster the engine roared. Louder and louder their screaming grew, as nearer and nearer to the flames they came. The passengers begged and pleaded in vain for the devil to stop the Hell-Bound Train!"

"Praise the Lord!" Mrs. James B. raised her hands and swung her body like a wind-battered sea oat.

The reverend suppressed a belch in his throat.

"But do y'all know what he did? He laughed and joked at their agony. Do you know what agony means?" Loly raised her hand, but the reverend ignored her. "Agony, it's a word from the Hebrew that means pain, pain, and more pain. And after the devil finished making fun of them, he said, 'You should have never listened to me! I was behind those statues of saints and other idols you worshipped in vain.' Then croaked the devil with an awful yell, 'We're here! We're here. You're in Hell now! You and your Pope in a lake of fire, eternally in flames that will never tire!'"

The reverend walked around the nave, getting his inspiration from the frightened faces of his audience. "Then I awoke and realized what the dream meant. It meant I was to come and preach to my Mexican brethren before they are all drowned in the next flood. For that flood we had a few weeks ago was meant as a warning sign of things to come. He was merciful and only slew the Mexican animals. But it was a signal for the bigger one that is to come. The one to come will rage with full force. Water tumbling down in a never ending sheet. Water will gush, cluttering the sewer holes; waves of sulphur will swell, and sheets of brimstone rain shall lash the rooftops! The skies will crack, and the muddy torrent will follow the sinners anywhere they'd hide." The reverend's voice quivered and then grew harsh. "For all idol worshippers' hairs shall stand up as a flashing neon sign, signaling the raging waters where to find them. That is why I asked Jack Jackson to come and let me preach the Word to y'all, so the sinners can be saved. I want you now to raise your hands and repeat after me: 'Lord, I'm a sinner. I shall not pray to idols so I can be saved from the flood.'"

Naomi and Mrs. James B. quickly raised their arms in fear, while Aïda, confused, but inspired, reached the full potential of her contralto registry to the tune of the Ave María. The rest knelt as Pituca lifted her rosary and began to pray.

"I see the devil is still within some of you," screamed an exasperated Reverend Fender as he walked to where Pituca was kneeling and yanked the rosary beads from her hands and crushed them under the heels of his boots. "It may have been a dream, but the Hell where y'all are headed is real." The reverend's eyes glittered with excitement and he burped.

"Not me, Reverend," shouted back Mrs. James B.

"You must give up all amulets and incantations, for the wages of sin is death. For the railroad of LATER leads into the station of NEVER!" He was shouting at Pituca, waving his finger in front of her face as the baffled woman recoiled in fear, unable to understand what had transpired.

"The wicked shall be turned into Hell! Thank you, Jack. Thank you, ladies. And I want you to go home and think about what I just said. You are sinners on your way to Hell. I want to turn you away from that evil road. Amen, amen, amen. I want you to go and with a hammer, or if you don't have a hammer, with your silverware; it could be a spoon or a knife handle, to smash to pieces all the idols you have at home and come and enjoy some fellowship with us at the First Living Souls and Prayer Temple Church. Amigos, I love you!!"

The reverend approached the ladies and started giving away the cardboard fans to everyone except Nellie, who politely refused since she already had one.

When the reverend left, the workers were still in a daze, but he heard laughter from the cubicle, which was surrounded by a pale-blue shower curtain, placed around it for added privacy, and Dina's tremulous voice saying, "Amen."

Baruc Atá Adonai

"*Baruc ata adonai elohainu*." Bernabé stood in front of the medicine-cabinet mirror and enunciated each word carefully, aspirating the consonants, watching his lips and tongue as he said each word, arching his eyebrows from the effort.

"What's the matter with you? It doesn't make sense to quit your English class at the Betsy Ross Center and start taking Hebrew. Is it because it's demeaning to be a clown all day long? Maybe you'll be happier picking tomatoes. I really fear for your sanity, Bernabé."

"Take it easy, Jerk-off. There's no need to fear. Bernabé is here!"

"I'm worried about you."

"You should worry about your little, furry squirrel. Not me," Bernabé giggled.

"You are so cruel. You know I have been searching for her since I got here." Nelson's eyes watered.

"Did you really do it with her, or were you afraid she would chew your wiener like a pecan?" Bernabé laughed.

"I'm going out for a walk." Nelson sounded wounded.

"C'mon. I was only kidding. Aren't we touchy these days!"

"Nellie and the children are supposed to arrive from Xawa soon, but if I see her before, I swear, I wouldn't know what to do."

"Tell me something, did you ever see her face?"

"I'm leaving!" Nelson opened the screenless screen door.

"Wait. Don't get mad. Listen to this first: *Baruc ata adonai elohainu, melech ha-olam borai, minai b' samin*. Great diction, ah? I'll bet you a cold beer that you don't know what it means?"

"No, I don't," said Nelson.

"It means spices are good for you. I'll give you another chance. Answer me quickly. How many patriarchs? How many matriarchs?"

"I don't know."

"You lost. Go to the Seven Eleven and get me a beer. Make sure it is a Miller High Life because that's exactly where I'm heading, the high life."

"There's one in the refrigerator. I hid it from you under the tomatoes," said Nelson retracing his steps. "Here. Catch."

"It sure tastes good! Better than a Winston! Well, buddy, I'm going to tell you the key to my success. A month ago, I read an ad in The Sun Herald of a man who was seeking his long-lost relatives, survivors from the Nazi camps. He had escaped from Prague before the roundups, but his relatives stayed behind and were deported to Poland. He goes by the name of Stanley Davis here, but he said he was known to his family as Benjamin Stain."

"So?"

"So I did some research on the man, and he owns a pawn shop in Belle Glade, which is a sleepy little hamlet by the Big Lake."

"The Big Lake?"

"Yes, Lake Okeechobee. In Indian it means Big Lake."

"I'm impressed, Bernabé. I never thought you knew how to read. But that town doesn't sound like a hot spot for a bon vivant like you."

"It beats living in this dump. But who's thinking about living there for a long time. That's not the point. The fact is that the old man is loaded. He's looking for a relative, possibly to leave him all his wealth. I'm sure he has a secret compartment somewhere on the floor of his store, and it opens to a stair which leads to an underground cavern where he keeps his dough inside empty beer kegs or milk cans."

"But you are not related to this man," Nelson said defiantly.

"I am. Last week, I changed my name from Guiristain to Stain. Permit me to introduce myself, Barney Stain, at your service. I am a great-nephew, son of Miriam, his sister Esther's youngest daughter. You see, Jerk-off, Miriam made her way to Xawa with her infant son after the Allied victory in Europe. She was one of the few who escaped Sobibor and was given refuge by a local family who took pity on her and her baby. Three days before her escape, she had given birth to a bright-eyed baby. What color are my eyes?"

"Blue."

"I rest my case. So don't say another word, and let me finish. The Nazis allowed her to keep the baby since they were doing experiments with her milk and the baby's nutrient-absorption rate. Anyway, they lived inside a piano until the end of the war. Miriam's family was all dead. She settled in Xawa since she was told it would be easier to enter America from there. Miriam patiently waited her permission to immigrate to the United States. During her days in Xawa, she worked as a nanny for the Guiristain family. Two years later, she contracted yellow fever during a family outing to the Zapata swamps and died, leaving behind her son. The child was later on adopted by the Guiristain family."

"A fascinating lie," Nelson remarked.

"Maybe. But let me show you something," Bernabé said while he rolled up his sleeve and removed the bandage which covered part of the inside of his right forearm. There were a series of bluish numbers tattooed.

"I can't believe what you are doing! It's a hoax. It is preposterous!"

"No, Nelson. It's survival. Miriam was a survivor. Stanley is a survivor. I intend to be one also.

"There was no Miriam!"

"Yes, I'm sure there was. Only the circumstances of her death have been altered. *Ecoutez*! (That's French.) Miriam had been married for a week before her husband, my dad, was detained. She was deported the following day. Papá was good, an honest man who would have adored his wife. His name was Aaron, and he was a concert violinist with the Prague Philharmonic. My heart aches when I talk about them. (Here I take a deep breath and sigh.) Mamá never saw Papá again. She often cried bitterly at bedtime. I think that deep inside she never knew for sure whether she loved a dead man or a living person. She died with the absurd hope of seeing him again. Mamá blamed herself for having gone to Grandma Esther's that evening when Papá was arrested. But the self-reproach was unfounded. What would have changed if she had stayed home?"

"Nothing."

"You see. You're getting into the story. But I won't give Stanley a chance to answer, and I will proceed with my next question. Could she have saved him? Foolishness! And now I begin to speak in a low, soft voice. That night when she returned to an empty, ransacked house, she realized his fate and sensed hers. She buried the only things of value she could find by the guava tree near the kitchen door."

"There are no guava trees in Prague!" Nelson said triumphantly.

"You always come in handy, Jerk-off. What sort of flora would be appropriate?"

"I don't exactly know. Maybe a maple tree."

"So, she buried the only things of value she could find by the maple tree near the kitchen door: the petals of a dry daisy preserved between sheets of toilet paper inside a book of love poems, *Viaggio All' Amore* by Marco "Petrarca" Pietralunga, and musical sheets with annotations for unfinished compositions, their edges charred. By the time she finished the internment in the concentration camp, Mamá's emerald eyes had lost their sparkle and her cheeks sagged; her lower jaw hung open in awe. Don't you think I should get an Oscar for this performance?" Bernabé asked his friend as he smelled his armpits.

"What's next?" said Nelson with the cadence of a self-righteous man.

"I am glad you ask," Bernabé said as he rested his arm on Nelson's shoulder. "First, I'm taking a shower and tomorrow I'm getting circumcised."

"Bernabé, I think you are going mad. Circumcision is dangerous at your age. Besides, who would believe your story?"

"He will. Mark my words, he will."

On Sunday morning, Barney Stain rode the Trailways bus to Belle Glade and met the old man. At first, according to Barney's own account, the old man was hesitant, distant. To use his own term "a hard nut to crack." Bernabé wasn't getting all the family lore right, but his horror stories were so vivid that Benjamin Stain succumbed to his farce, embracing him. He stayed with Uncle Ben that very same night. He called Nelson the following morning, telling him that the living conditions were Spartan, but that he could smell the money buried somewhere underneath the stacks of old picture albums, toasters, mattresses, and percussion instruments.

"Jerk-off, in the still of the night I can sniff the fragrance of those crisp greenbacks waiting for the skillful hand that could deliver them from captivity," remarked Barney Stain to Nelson as he was about to hang up.

The following weekend Nelson left for Belle Glade with Barney's belongings and met Uncle Ben. He was tall, bony, and though scrupulous about personal cleanliness, he looked unwashed. Barney introduced Nelson as an old friend in need of a job.

Et Tu, Delfina?

What's taking you so long, Guida? You always finished first. I guess age is catching up with you too, or maybe loneliness. All your friends gone. Take your time and don't let me rush you. Don't mind me. You know how grouchy I get when the mailman makes that "no" sign with his finger and waves at me from afar. He doesn't bother to come by anymore. See all those marks on that cashew tree? Those were for the hours she hadn't written me. It filled up soon. Now I make my marks on that jacaranda, but keep days. I'm glad you're here with me. I remember the night I found you by the porch. It was the night of the big hurricane, and you were soaked and trembling. I'm so glad you stayed behind.

I don't know what's gonna become of us, Guida. I was going around the square, trying to avoid the crowds, when I heard Rulfo screaming from the podium about how everybody has to cooperate one-hundred percent with the food plan so that shortages would become a thing of the past. Then he shouted that we were falling behind, and that he wasn't going to allow that. There was silence and I thought something had happened, but people started clapping and the platform was filled with noise and excitement as Waldo Dieste started talking. He said, "I'm 107 years old, and I have been eating fish fed with hens' droppings since I was ten." Then Rulfo grabbed the microphone and named him vanguard collector from our district. As Waldo was getting his award, the crowds started chanting the food-plan song: "Our caca fertilizes the corn fields, the corn kernels feed the clucking hens, their droppings energize our finny friends and the people happily eat the fish

fillets." Then a dog started barking, and Rulfo got off the
stand and strangled the animal with his bare hands. He
shouted, "Nothing can stand in the way of the Food Plan, not
even a barking dog." He grabbed the limp canine, walked back
to the stand, and showed it to the crowd. Its tongue was hanging out as it drooled.

I felt like going straight to the plaza and telling that silly
old man, "Waldo, you liar! I know why you're still around. It
was all a mistake. She took Dina's son instead of you." But I
was in a hurry to meet Tomasa to barter the eggs you had
given me. I hate her, but I have to trade with her. Sometimes
you have to trade with the enemy to survive. She's a thief. She
sleeps around with the military and steals from them.

When I finished my business with Tomasa, Rulfo was still
at it, screaming that our scientists, in an effort to make the
blockade of our motherland a boomerang that would hit the
enemy back, were working very hard to put in our skins the
green stuff that makes leaves green. Then we could make our
own food from the sun just like plants do. Then there was
silence, and then the crowd roared with applause. Rulfo didn't
waste any time to add that, when that happens, we must
always keep our eyes wide open, for the enemy would try to
spray us with leaf killer. Each time he jerked around the
stand and banged on it, his paunch moved the opposite way
like a giant wave of blubber rolling backward.

Do you know that Waldo comes every day to write his
name on the tally sheet that must be kept by the toilet? He
keeps track of your last bowel movement and the quantity. He
reports those that aren't regular. They are given a month to
get their excrement together. If they don't improve, they are
declared traitors and paraded in a cart through town. I
haven't had any problems. You see, I have this deal with Liazzo, the painter, the one whose paintings were burned on the
square. We borrow from each other. Yes, ma'am, we borrow
from each other. So when Waldo comes by, we are able to meet
our quota. There's always a way to go around a mountain. Do

you know that what keeps that man so regular is his love for Dina. He's still waiting for her. Liazzo is very grateful to me since I managed to get him a piece of fabric so he could paint. It's the only piece of cloth he has, so he paints a picture of Dina during the night and erases it the following day when he wakes up and starts all over again. He says it keeps her memory alive. He paints her in different positions, and sometimes she doesn't look like a woman, but like a broken toothpick with ice cubes. But he says it's her, and I believe him because he ought to know. She disappeared years ago, after the burnings. And that's exactly what's going to happen to those fish fillets Rulfo is promising. They're going to disappear before they arrive!

Oh, Guida, towards the end, when my Nellie was here, we had also little to eat! The master couldn't get his money out of the bank because it was frozen, and then he was put in jail. I remember Nellie was nursing María-Chiara. She was used to the best.

You should have seen her wedding, Guida. There were at least one-thousand guests and the sky was the brightest it has ever been. She looked so beautiful in her white lace gown! The dress was a gift from Mr. Van Ryckenhem, one of the master's friends. He lived in some faraway country, because the dress came inside this big, yellow box covered with funny-looking stamps. I fixed her long train so she wouldn't trip. Her mother couldn't do it because by that time Nellie was already an orphan. She married Nelson, Mr. Guiristain's oldest son. They were engaged for eight years. He was studying business in the capital. He proposed during one of his trips back here. It happened at the old Tennis Club, under the cover of darkness, the day the moon fought with the sun and the cocks started crowing at mid-morning. He was shy, and those are the most dangerous types. I remember he took her hand, and I cleared my throat to let him know I was close by in case he had anything else in mind. I followed the baby everywhere she went. Virtue,

Guida, is lack of opportunity. And she was such a pretty thing...

They were finally married at seven o'clock in the Jesuit church, now the headquarters of the Ministry of the Interior and the Militant Muliebrity. The staircase to the church was covered with tulips and orchids, and there was this long, red Turkish carpet, a gift of Mrs. Habra, the woman who read the coffee grounds. When I heard the music, I started shaking with emotion. I was holding her pet pig. She insisted the animal serve as ring boy, except he was no boy. The master said no, but then he changed his mind when Nellie refused to get married without her ring boy. Besides, he was afraid Nellie might go mute like when her mother died. I released the animal when the priest gave me the signal. He dashed straight for the altar, carrying the rings in a small pouch which hung from his collar. The ring boy had no way to go but straight since rails had been placed to keep him going in the right direction. The flower girl, who was a real girl and not a flower, trailed behind and arrived five minutes later in step with the music. I remember I had helped the priest take out all the church's gold objects and then polished every single one. It was a day's work. During the wedding mass, all the guests had to squint their eyes because of the glare. Father Santos was a very good friend of the master, and he took out Saint Laura's hipbone especially for Nellie's wedding, placing it right next to the couple's kneeler to provide them with special protection—in what Father Santos called this Valley of Tears. Saint Laura is our very own patron saint. She used to live in Solís Street with her sisters Bertha, Matilde and Celina. I remember seeing her walking up the hills to round up the kids for catechism. I was told she was what is called an evangelizer, which I don't know exactly what it means. The fact that the priest permitted the bone out of its resting place was considered a great privilege, except Father Santos didn't realize that, while he was talking in priests' language, the ring boy was chewing on the holy hip. The sexton saw what was happening, rushed in, and forced the ring boy's mouth open until he coughed up all the bone pieces. Luckily he was able to glue the hipbone back together. But the priest never again lent it out.

But it was the bouquet I made for her that caught everybody's eyes. I had gone the night before to Josefita's, Josende's old widow, the Chief Justice's mother. She had this beautiful garden, and she let me take some of her favorite flowers for the bouquet. I took a few fronds from her feathery asparagus fern and waited for the widow's famous flower-of-the-dance blossom to open. It blossomed every night at nine o'clock. I remember the blooms opened slowly, and Mrs. Josende cut them, and I arranged those beautiful big white flowers in the bouquet. When Nellie saw it the next morning, she was so taken by the bouquet, she thought it had come from Mondovi, a gift from Sergio and Adriano, the master's friends. Mondovi is the place where Nellie wanted to be born. I didn't have the heart to tell her the flowers were from the widow Josende's garden and that I had made the bouquet. But I was so proud when the organ started playing and the petals danced with every step she took.

After the wedding was over, everybody went to Villa Ronda, the master's house. There were one-hundred tables set in the garden. I personally kept an eye on the servants to make sure everything was in its place. There was enough liquor to swim in, and the food, though I personally wouldn't touch it, I heard the guests saying was out of this world. There was quail, buffalo tongues, fungi (not the ones between your toes but the ones rich people eat), fish eggs, wild geese, and five bear hams—a gift from the Spanish prince—and millions of other things that I don't recall now, because if I did, I'd probably throw up. But it was a beautiful wedding, and I kept everything running smoothly. My baby was used to the best, and I promised myself she would never go hungry. I had known hunger in my youth, Guida, but not my Nellie, not if I could help it. She wasn't going to eat boiled roots! There was no way I was going to let my baby go hungry. There was no way!

So I knew the pig was our only hope, and I started calling him saviour, because he was going to deliver us from hunger. I used to get close to his ears when he was asleep and whisper softly, "Saviour, saviour, salvatore." That way he would get the idea. He never opened an eye and I realized my whispers were falling on deaf ears. I tried to reason with him, but he didn't even seem to care. He stayed where he was with his belly up, snoring. The fact that he was so spoiled and that he didn't care if my baby lived or not made me very angry. She had been more than a mother to him. A woman who had given in to every whim that spoiled fat pig had ever had. I cursed him.

Take your time, Guida. Don't rush it. That Wednesday morning when Nellie was getting ready to visit the master in jail, I was sharpening the knife, rubbing it against the sidewalk curb. Someone had stolen my grinding stone. (Later on, I found out it was Tomasa because she tried to sell it back to me. Sometimes a thief loses track of what she steals.) I was trying to open a rusty can of his favorite food. Once I had it opened, I smelled it and had to rush to the faucet to wash out my nostrils. That awful smell has stayed with me ever since. That's why I have to rub garlic cloves under my nose every morning.

I went back to the counter and poured all that junk on his gold plate, the one that has his name engraved in fancy swirling letters. But I heard steps and quickly hid the plate under the sink.

"Delfina, Delfina, where are you when I need you the most?" It was my baby looking for me.

"Yes, baby. I'm here, where I always am, by the stove," I said, trying to act as normal as possible.

"Do you think Daddy would like to see me in this dress or in my lavender?"

"Baby, that's the only dress you have," I reminded her. "The only one I managed to sneak out of the mansion. But don't you worry. For your next visit I'm going to get you the finest lavender dress." I didn't know what I was saying when I promised her I would get her a lavender dress. There wasn't a single store in town with any merchandise, much less a lavender dress. I had to bribe the guards that were posted around the master's mansion to get her that dress.

"But make sure it isn't the silk lavender. I want the taffeta lavender with the pearl neck."

"Yes, baby! Don't you worry about a thing. You make sure you give the master his favorite tidbits and tell him not to worry, that Delfina has everything under control and that we are going to get him out soon."

"What's for dinner? I can't eat those awful sweet potatoes again! If you serve me those again, I swear I will get up from my chair and smash the plate."

"We'll get you something good. I promise, baby." I knew for sure he was our only hope to help us bribe the guards.

She left in her green taffeta dress. I kept an eye on her damsel figure as she tiptoed through the weeds and nettles whistling some foreign song. I kept watching her until she turned right at McFarlane Avenue. I waited a few minutes to make sure she wasn't coming back for her parasol. She had left it in the bathroom. She had the habit of using it on the days she didn't wash her hair to keep her head dry. I remember I rushed inside to rescue the golden plate. It was right where I had left it, but it was covered with tiny hungry ants. I picked them out one by one; if I had washed them off it would have ruined that awful smell that was meant to wake up that greedy rascal. You know, Guida, it has never stopped amazing me how ants, animals, and rich people have the same taste in food. I was bitten several times by those fiery creatures, but it was for a good cause. People are able to make great sacrifices if they are moved by love.

With a clean plate in hand, I started looking for him in his favorite resting places: under the shade of the cashew, in the room across from the sink, by the wash tub. But he was nowhere to be found. I started praying out loud, my voice trembling with fear. "Maybe Tomasa got hold of him": this line had somehow gotten mixed in my Hail Mary. I panicked. I rushed inside the house to get a decent dress on. I was going straight to Tomasa and tell her to leave him alone when I heard him snoring under the shade cast by the shed and the nearby guanabana tree. I sighed in relief while my heart was pounding as hard as when the master pinned me against the staircase rail. When his mouth was crazily searching for mine, I kept my head moving sideways although my heart was already his. I guess the heart can't tell the difference between love and fear.

He was sound asleep, in a deep slumber, his breathing deep and irregular as if he had run hard for a while. His red-dish hair shone with the sun's rays that filtered through the holes in the shed's roof. He looked almost handsome. I walked slowly to calm my nerves and placed the plate by his nose. His breathing was still heavy. I placed the plate right under his nose. He took a deep whiff and his left eye opened slowly. He had long dark lashes. He sniffed some more and rolled over and was fully awake and was hungry as ever. He started eat-ing fast, and I realized I didn't have much time. Nellie could be back any minute and kidnappers sent by Tomasa were surely on his trail.

I had no choice. I went to the kitchen and took the knife which I had used to open the stinky can. I had to protect him, Guida, and save him for us. He didn't notice me when I raised the blade behind his back. He was eagerly munching when I was going to plunge the dagger downward, but somehow the sun shone on the sharp edge, and he turned around, but it was too late. The blade struck. He only managed to mutter three lonely, high-pitched oinks, for I muzzled his mouth with the plate. Mixed with the squeals, I can swear he said, "You too, Delfina?" as a spurt of blood hit my eyes, blinding me for a few seconds. He didn't try to squirm.

Guida, I was a sacrificer, but not a real butcher. It took me a while to cut the head off and hack his limbs. I can swear by the master's bones that I killed him boldly but not angrily. I placed the fat in a sack, the head and guts in another, and the rest I salted for us to eat and to sell. Luckily, Nellie was taking her time coming back. I dragged the sack of fat to Lazarus, one of the militiamen who was guarding the mansion, Juan Benson's son, and gave him three pounds of lard to ransom Nellie's lavender dress and one more pound days later to get his wife to get some news on the master's fate. She told me of the evil plan, but I didn't cry. If I had cried, I could have been accused of being a traitor. I simply said, "He got what he deserved." I cried later, on the way back home, begging the master to forgive me for such horrible words. My tears made one thin streak on Nellie's dress. It was so light she didn't even notice it. But I knew it was there and it made me happy she was going to wear that same dress during her next visit.

When I got home, I closed myself inside the shed and started making sausages, pickling the feet and ears, and salting the rest of the meat. I didn't salt the whole animal, but left a big ham leg for supper and got all the skin prepared to make rind. A few minutes before he was one thing and now he was becoming many things for many people: sausages, hams, ribs, chops...life.

Nellie arrived muddy and breathless. She had been attacked by some gang of kids by the river. I bathed her and sprinkled lemon juice on her hair. Immediately she began looking for him. She looked everywhere, and since she was becoming desperate, I told her I had seen him with a girlfriend. It made her jealous but calmed her fears. Then I told her María-Chiara needed to be fed, so she wouldn't think too much about the larder.

That evening Nellie had an appetite! She was so hungry she even sucked the bone marrow and fought with Nelson Jr.

for the last piece of rind on the plate. She took the big bone to her room to gnaw on it. The money that I made from that larder and the meat I salted kept us going for almost six months, until she left. But she hasn't answered my letters since I told her we ate Rigoletto. I wrote her his death was peaceful, from an overdose of sleeping pills.

I've kept her room just as she left it. I stopped the clock the minute she left with the kids. It was 6:35 a.m. Her pink slippers are still under the right side of her cot, and her little pillow, which she loved to rub between her fingers to fall asleep, is right under the big pillow which she used to cover her face with. She couldn't fall asleep if she saw the tiniest bit of light. I put fresh toothpaste on her toothbrush every single day in case she arrives unexpectedly. She has always been afraid of bad breath. I know the larder's spirit is thirsting for revenge, but my love will be stronger, and she will answer my letters. I just know she will. Have you finished, Guida?

That's a nice egg!

The Pawn Shop

"How many picture albums in that stack?"

"None."

"You're not looking in the right place. Second shelf to your right."

"Oh! Twelve."

Barney and Ben were taking inventory of the shop. The system was tedious, and all the accounting was done with an abacus. Ben had an adding machine, but he preferred the sense of control offered by the beads. They were working on the old picture albums given as collateral for small loans, usually less than ten dollars. There were twelve dusty albums on the shelf: twelve people who had defaulted on their loans; twelve who had gambled with their past and lost it all.

"How should I price the pictures?" asked Barney after placing the albums on the table.

"From which album?" replied a frizzy-haired Ben from the top of the ladder.

"The one with the shiny cover."

"That's called mother-of-pearl, and there are two of them."

"The one with the woman resting her elbow on a veranda."

"Oh, that one. If the subject is dressed like a lady, like the picture you were talking about, or a gentleman with a hat or cane, 5¢ each. Family gatherings, 2¢ each. And family gatherings with the mansion as background, 3¢. I even remember who pawned that album. It was a man from South Carolina named Bailey. It was his grandmother's album. What a shame, what a shame. I'd sell everything in this shop just to have my mother's photo album. It was burned with everything else the night the Fascists were given free rein and roamed free through Prague. I left for America the week after, not because I knew what was coming. I wasn't that smart. I had a cousin in New York who had sent for me to work in his tailor shop."

Barney had busied himself with the pricing of the photos, stopping when a particular picture caught his eye, and had hardly paid any attention to Ben's discourse.

"Who buys these old pictures, Stanley?" asked a curious Barney.

"How many times have I told you, you don't have to call me Stanley anymore? Call me Uncle Ben. Benjamin, that's my real name. It's the name my mother gave me in honor of her great uncle." There was a long pause before Ben spoke again.

"What were you saying?"

"Who buys these old photos?"

"Wandering Mormons who have baptized their long-dead relatives and are looking for their pictures."

"How do they know if it was one of their relatives?"

"That doesn't really matter, Barney. They just want old-looking pictures. This is America. Everything is prefabricated, even the past. You'll learn like I learned."

Barney looked puzzled. "What are Mormons?"

"A religious sect from the Midwest."

"Who else buys these things?"

"Southerners longing to rescue the mythical pre-Civil War days. And now it's time to take a break." Ben breathed deeply, and the beads of sweat collecting in his elbows were as heavy as candle wax.

Ben slowly climbed down from the top of the roller ladder where he had been perched all morning, cleaning and straightening out the old toasters to his right and the crystal to his left. Once on the ground, he opened the cabinet where he stored liquor, and took out a cobweb-covered bottle and two glasses. He poured an exact amount of wine.

"Here, Barney. We've done good work today," Ben said as he grabbed a stool.

The men toasted to life and sat down for their break.

"I want you to go this afternoon to the bank and put these emerald charms in the safe-deposit box." Ben extracted the baby-shaped emeralds from his back pocket and held them in his palm for Barney to see.

"Are you going to keep those, Uncle Ben?" Barney seemed to have taken a genuine interest in the charms.

"I don't know yet. I want to give the lady who pawned them some extra time. She reminded me of my sister Stella."

"I thought you said you didn't trust banks."

"I don't. I keep in that box only special pieces. But none of my wealth."

Barney's eyes grew wider at the last remark.

"Do they belong to Miss Walters? She comes here quite often?"

"No. They belong to somebody else. Miss Walters usually pawns the necklaces and earrings Mr. Rosser gives her. Before I forget, let me give you your pay."

Barney looked carefully to both sides. He was expecting Ben to reveal the whereabouts of his fortune. But the old man took his wallet out, and the open-mouthed billfold revealed five twenty-dollar bills.

"Here you are. Forty for you, and the rest I'm going to mail to your wife and kids overseas. You don't know how lucky you are. When I began to work for my cousin at the tailor shop, I made two dollars a week."

Barney was visibly disappointed. He had been waiting patiently for the moment when the old man would pull on the secret plank and the creaking wood would reveal an underground chamber bursting with bags of doubloons and precious stones, gold and silver ingots, and stacks of bills reaching all the way to the chamber's ceiling. In his mind, he wasn't going to steal it all. His plan was to take part of it. He would empty the bags and fill them halfway with sand and place the doubloons and stones on top. The old man would never find out. At first Barney thought of stealing it all, but he had grown fond of Uncle Ben. Then he would bury everything he stole, wait a while not to arouse any suspicion, dig it out and have fun in Acapulco.

"Thank you, Uncle Ben," he said, his mind still searching the cave.

"Let me pour you some more wine. It's good wine, Barney. Smell the cork."

"Smells good."

"You're just saying that. I know you don't know anything about wines. But, listen, did your mother ever talk to you about her life in the camps?"

Barney got nervous as he usually did when Uncle Ben wanted to know about his mother and her family. He cleared his throat and said, "Grandma Esther had told Mother not to worry about the false rumors of deportation, and to prove her point, she mentioned how my father had been invited to entertain the German officers with his violin. She proceeded to tell Mother the harshness attributed to the Germans was rubbish, nonsense. 'A people that love music can't be all bad.' Those were Grandma's last words to my mother. She made Mother promise not to think negatively and to come first thing in the morning for some whitefish and bagels. By this time, they were not allowed to go into restaurants or coffee houses, and the curfew started at midday. Grandma was the eternal optimist. The following day the Czech police knocked on her door and ordered her to leave her house with what she had on. As she marched out of her neighborhood with Mother at her side, escorted by SS guards, she clung to the idea they were being interned inside Germany to protect them from their fellow Czechs. While she was holding mother's arm, her house was being pillaged by the people who lived near the ghetto, their mouths filled with salmon and bagels. She told mother always to have mercy. Two days later, she died of suffocation in one of the trains headed for Treblinka. They were deported in different freight trains to different camps. There were hundreds of people packed inside each car, its iron doors locked with thick bolts. Mother was glad she didn't have to see her mother's agony.

"My sister Esther loved music. She played the harp like an angel." Uncle Ben heaved and coughed. "We took music classes at the same time, but she was much better. She had the talent for it."

"I love music, too, Uncle Ben! I can play some mean bongos. I guess the talent runs in our family." Barney tapped a conga rhythm on the table.

Both men took sips of wine, and Barney continued, "Mother told me her best friend, Roswitha Stück, who was Jewish but had forged papers and passed herself off as an Aryan, had risked her life by rushing to the queue where Mother was waiting to enter the car and managed to give her a piece of pork shoulder.

"Pork?" intervened Ben. "Then she wasn't such a good friend."

Barney saw his future fortune evaporating in front of his eyes and corrected himself. "Of course. I forgot. It was a chicken leg. Of course, Roswitha wouldn't do a thing like that. Then Roswitha was brutally pushed aside by the German soldiers, but she insisted on remaining near Mother and one of the guard's rifles came down on her heard. She fell to the ground, never to see my mother again."

Uncle Ben was somber and heaved a sigh, covering his face with his hands.

Barney felt sure of himself and continued his story. "That chicken leg kept my mother from starving to death. She hid it in her bosom, taking it out when everybody was asleep to gnaw on it and mitigate the hunger pangs. Many died during the trip to the camp. Do you know what Mother said was the worst part?" Barney loved to accentuate the dramatics each time he realized Uncle Ben was enthralled by his tale.

"What was it?"

"When she felt the urge to relieve herself and realized there was no place to do it. Mamá said she looked around and didn't see a latrine. She swore she wouldn't do it in front of strangers. But Mother had a knack for invention."

"What could she do in that awful situation?" interjected Ben.

"She had a few straws in her pocket, from her wedding reception. She was wearing the same dress. She had noticed before there was a small hole in the corner of the cart where she was squatting. Mamá was really something else. She linked the straws to make a longer one and then she connected it to her *pipi* and in that way she relieved herself and no one knew it. Her apparent restraint gave her the nickname of Miriam the Camel lady, since she seemed to hold her urine longer than anyone else."

"It's amazing how in the midst of tribulation the human spirit finds ways to humor others. Blessed be the name of the Eternal."

"It certainly does. That's why I'm always joking around. I have to. First, I suffered as an infant, and then I suffered my mother's suffering, which she bequeathed to me, and then my own... That's why I laugh so much."

Barney sighed, moved by his own words.

"What about the kapos, Barney? Did Miriam mention anything to you about them?" Uncle Ben asked with genuine interest.

"Oh, yes. The Kapos..." Barney paused, his brain racing full speed to find any information stored in its memory banks.

"Were they good?" Uncle Ben insisted.

"Oh, were they good! And ours particularly was great! That's what Mamá always said since I don't remember anything from that time. But I remember she said it was light-blue." Barney smiled triumphantly.

"Light blue?" Ben said out loud.

"Yes, light blue with a soft top."

"Soft top?"

"Yes, a soft top and it had four doors and such a large trunk, two persons could have easily slept in it. It had the most sophisticated brake system ever developed, and it was fast. My Dad clocked it once sixty miles per hour, certainly the fastest in all Prague."

Ben was puzzled. "Do you mean they wore light-blue uniforms and soft-top helmets?"

"Yes. That's exactly what I meant. I think I have been pricing too many photos and my mind got confused with something else."

"Continue, son. I thought you were having a mental lapse. You could with all you have gone through."

Ben's comforting words relieved Barney's tension and he remembered all he had read in the many books he had checked out of the library during his research for an easy fortune.

"The kapos made Mom strip, and if she didn't do what they ordered they beat her with a bicycle chain. They were very cruel to their own. Mother said once one of them beat her up with a shovel."

"With a shovel?"

"That's what she told me," Barney sounded convincing.

"That's real cruelty. And to their own people! Fear, it's the great stripper of humanity. It makes the prey want to act like the predator so it won't be eaten."

"The kapos were also in charge of food distribution. They gave the others little and hoarded the rest for themselves. Then Mother's luck changed, if you could call it luck. Dr. Mengele, with his ominous monocle, selected mother for the farm. Mother thought she was going to work in the farm inside the camp, but much to her surprise she was placed in a comfortable cell by herself and fed properly. Then three days later she learned she formed part of a human dairy. Dr. Mengele had this strange craving for human milk and routinely selected lactating mothers for his farm. All dairy products consumed by the high-ranking officers of the SS came from Mengele's Dairy. The women were milked twice a day at dawn and at dusk."

"How did your mother manage to escape?"

"One day she found out the fate of the woman who was occupying the cell next to hers. Her milk production had dropped and she was sent to the furnace. It was the fate of all the dairy women. Mother found out through the man who brought her food tray that there was an uprising in the camp, and she told him she wanted to join it and begged him to leave her cell unlocked. Many died trying to escape, but she made it past the barbed wire fence. Until her dying day, Mother's back still showed the deep furrows made by the barbs. She said she got diarrhea from gobbling down whatever seemed edible, roots, leaves, bark. It was winter when she fled Sobibor.

"But how did she reach Xawa? That's the name of the place, right?"

"After the war, she got forged papers from a relief group called Stella Maris. They sneaked her across national borders disguised as a gypsy, and she finally reached Spain. In San Sebastian she begged for food and money in front of the churches or in the train station. Sometimes people took pity on the poor gypsy woman holding her scrawny-looking infant. But sometimes people spat on her and called her slimy gypsy and many other nasty things. Mother told me she was glad when they insulted her, thinking she was really a gypsy. She looked forward to the provocations. Mother said she hated gypsies as much as she hated Germans. The gypsies were in charge of her unit at the camp and had stolen her front tooth's gold cap while she was asleep. When she awoke from the pain, the cap was already gone. Several times they beat on her stomach with a truncheon. She said the pain was so intense she fainted and was forced to crawl back to the barracks through puddles of raw sewage. When she had enough money saved, she went to the port of El Ferrol and asked which one of the merchant ships heading for America was the cheapest. She paid our way, and we slept next to the boilers. When she landed in St. Christopher, the capital city, she knew she wasn't in New York. She complained to the captain in her broken Spanish, but he answered that they were in America. In Spain, America is everything from Alaska to Argentina. She learned the hard way."

"Did she stay in St. Christopher for a long time?"

"Mamá stayed there working as a maid for a few months. It was there that she met Mrs. Guiristain while serving at a reception the lady of the house was giving. Mrs. Guiristain was impressed by my mother's manner and high refinement. She offered her a job, and that's how we ended up in Xawa. But what Mother really wanted was to join her uncle in America. She didn't know exactly where to find her Uncle Benjamin. She thought you lived in Chicago. I think someone is knocking, Uncle Ben."

"You check and see, and as soon as you come back we'll finish this bottle."

Barney gulped his wine and headed for the door.

"Hello, may I help you?" Barney's eyes stopped at two imprisoned buttocks yearning to be free.

"I'm just browsing, thank you. Where's Stanley?"

"He's in the rear, sorting out a few things."

"Ain't seen your face around here before. You talk funny like my friend. You must also be from Mondovi, I reckon."

"No, ma'am. I was born in Europe."

"Is that a fact? Anyhow, how much are those in that pile?" She pointed to the pile of old photos.

"Those run from five cents to three cents apiece."

"I was here last month, and they were a penny each."

"Inflation, ma'am. The past is always more expensive than the present."

"I reckon I'll look some more."

Barney waited, sending piercing looks at Mrs. James B.'s buttocks as she sorted through the pile, took a few and discarded the rest, creating her past at will. When Barney thought she was finished, he approached the customer.

"Anything else, ma'am?"

"Don't be a pest. I hate nosy clerks. I need time. Do you think I could go through these piles in one second? For crying out loud!"

"Excuse me, ma'am. I thought you were through since you came to the counter."

"I was using the counter glass to look at my hair."

Mrs. James B. continued digging in the pile, at times feeling like an archeologist. When she was finished, she had bought enough pictures to have a three-generational family, including a couple of very recent snapshots of two children, a girl and a boy. The boy was dressed as a cadet. The girl, in a hoop skirt and carrying a small parasol, was standing near the front entrance a of a finishing school for young belles.

"Here you are!" She handed Barney her pictures.

"Let's see, ma'am. You have three family gatherings, five pictures of the mansion, eight portraits of a lady and five of a gentleman. Anything else?"

"That'll be all."

"It's $4.50, ma'am."

"Four fifty? Are you sure you ain't gypping me?"

"Ma'am, the register says $4.50," Barney said as he looked at her breasts with desire.

"It's okay. I reckon I got a lot of them." Mrs. James B. eased her stance when she noticed he was looking at her so intensely. She liked it and smiled.

"Come back and see us. You take care now, you hear!"

"I surely will. Tell Stanley he should give a special price to his good customers."

"I will, ma'am. Here's your change."

Barney controlled himself. He didn't want to spoil his future with Uncle Ben by bothering the customers. But as he gave her back her change, he used his old trick of caressing the Mrs.' palm. She pretended not to feel it and hurried out to build herself a past, her breasts bouncing and her hips as inviting as a flashing neon sign. She was murmuring when she left, "It's like Mr. James B. says, you can't beat a pinch-gut!"

Barney didn't hear her, and as he went back to the rear of the store, Uncle Ben had finished pouring two more glasses of wine and had gotten another bottle from the cabinet.

"Keep telling me about Miriam, bless her soul."

La Morte de Floyd

Floyd Conway faced the wall and, once again, began counting the small holes in the coquina that served as refuge to the larvae of Canadian butterflies. The mothers had laid their eggs at the beginning of their tropical sojourn. The monarchs basked in the sun, innocently gorging themselves on the lethal nectar of cashew blossoms. If Conway had looked more attentively, he would have noticed the cells were empty.

It was his third time in front of the wall, and the sky was as bright as it was the day he decided not to continue his voyage to Charleston and stay in Xawa. The soldiers waited for Rulfo's orders and cracked jokes about the length of the commander's penis. One of them looked at Conway and asked him if he wanted a final puff from his cigarette. Floyd shook his head and requested a shot of whiskey. The guard was puzzled and walked to the great room of the dilapidated Ladies' Tennis Club, now a barracks, to ask the commander if he should grant the request. Rulfo laughed loudly and walked back to the wall to deliver his response in person.

"I see you have a final request," the commander said sarcastically. "Whiskey is the drink of the people's exploiters. That beverage is officially banned, erased from our memories forever!" he growled.

"Don't be naive, Rulfo," Conway said to the man facing him whose belly cascaded towards his knees in a torrent of adipose tissue inside his olive fatigues. "Go to the Provincial Military Headquarters and open Colonel J. L. Sanchez's personal bar, the one he stole from Don Andrés, and you'll find the finest whiskey this side of Edinburgh. I think he beat you to it," Conway smiled sardonically.

Rulfo remained silent for a few seconds, playing with his pistol, and then added, "Do you want to play Russian roulette? You'll be the only player, and there are no blanks."

It was now Floyd Conway who didn't respond. Rulfo paced back to the barracks and yelled to the soldiers, "I'll shoot the next one of you who bothers me."

Floyd looked around and saw the Ladies' Tennis Club pool at a distance. It looked more like a giant bowl of minestrone with green and brown floating debris suspended motionless in the putrid broth. He wasn't frightened but impatient. After all, it was his third time facing the firing squad. Conway felt like tending the plants that surrounded the coquina wall. This had once been the club's handball court. Conway had helped choose the oleanders that were knee-high when planted and now towered over the back of the wall. The foliage of the pink poincianas from the Turks and Caicos, one of his gifts to the club, embowered the tile roof of the clubhouse. The ceibas still fanned the tennis courts, now without nets, and the passion vines covered the chain-link fence, though no longer fulfilling their original purpose of obstructing the view from the curious masses.

"For Christ's sake, get it over with," shouted a sweaty Mr. Conway.

"Shut up, gringo. We'll do it when we're ready."

"I am not a gringo. Weren't you taught anything at school?" Conway tried to appear in control, but his voice quavered.

"You speak English, don't you?" sad the corporal.

"Of course I do." There was a brief pause. "We invented it."

"Then you are a gringo and we make gringos clean our asses with their tongues. On your knees, gringo!" Then the corporal turned around and addressed one of his men. "Hey,

Mongo, you have a big ass. Take a crap and let the gringo wipe you off."

Mongo was hesitant. "I don't mean to challenge your order, comrade, but it is considered a national resource and can't be wasted. The food plan, corporal."

Floyd Conway was thankful for the food plan that had saved him from being forced to perform such a debasing task as his last deed on earth. He had been arrested a month before at the Telegraph Hotel, where he made a home in the arms of his perennial butterfly. There had been a knock on the door and he had responded automatically, "Sean, leave the bottle by the door," as was his custom. Conway ignored the persistent knocking, but when he was about to share his nectar with the butterfly, the door was kicked open and five armed men surprised Conway with the hot muzzles of recently fired guns held to his temple. His first reaction was to cover his mate and reassure her that it was some sort of mistake. She was nervous, her antennas were pointing down.

Floyd had insisted to the officer from the secret police that he was a British subject, should be treated as such, be released without delay or hindrance, and be given all lawful aid and protection. He was knocked out by a rifle butt. His bedroom, bathroom and closets were searched. One by one, the men smashed all the China figurines which his sister Vera had sent him over the years from Aberystwyth: the Tower of London, London Bridge, Big Ben, St. Paul, Queen Mary patting the future Queen Elizabeth. When their efforts proved futile, they made the butterfly turn over the sofa bed to examine all the coils. Then, with the sharp blade of the bayonet, the mattress was viscerated. When the search ended, the alcoves were covered with the shiny dust of a fleeing butterfly, who ran gasping across the courtyard, leaving behind, on the top of the chest, her falsies, ash blonde wig and depilatory cream.

"This is a mistake. I demand an apology for bursting into my flat without an invitation," boomed Conway as he came to his senses.

"Shut up and get dressed, or would you prefer to go naked?" The man who addressed Conway was sixteen years old, but his voice sounded rough and hollow. Conway didn't argue and got dressed.

He was interrogated for two days and accused of aiding the enemies of the state by divesting the capital which had been stolen from the people and transferring it abroad. He was going to deny all the allegations when he fell from the stool to the floor. He was blindfolded and had lost his balance. Conway was groping, searching for his stool, when he felt on his buttocks the sharp points of bayonets that urged him to stand up.

"You're gonna tell me where Nelson Guiristain is hiding. We know you opened the bank's vault and gave him the assets," said the slender man with a pencil-thin mustache and a sweet smile that would have softened a Xawa duenna.

"I want a shot of whiskey," answered Conway with the firmest voice he could muster.

"I see you don't want to cooperate, Mr. Conway. It's certainly a pity." The interrogator scratched his upper lip. "The boys are going to have fun with you. I can't do anything for you if you don't cooperate."

Floyd Conway heard the long, horrifying cries of people being tortured and took advantage of a small lull in the cries to try to reflect on his life. But his mind reeled. *My father was a Welsh officer and a gentleman who came to England to better his fortunes. He joined the Royal Navy and was killed during the Crimean War. He was wild and reckless, but he had many noble qualities and was much loved by men, and I am afraid, by women. The Royal Marines had disembarked, and he was occupying a trench which for some hours his company held under heavy fire. When the Turks charged with fixed bayonets, he rose to meet them, but at the same moment the bugle sounded the retreat. The others broke and ran, but Father sprang to the top of the trench and called, "Come back, you cowards. Let's give the Turks one more volley." He fell upon the trench*

with his body stretched along its length. But he wasn't dead,
and when one of the Turks got close he pulled at his scabbard
and let him have it.

A violent slap made him fall again, and for the first time
he felt for Don Andrés when he smelled the sweat, blood and
body wastes that had collected in the cement floor crevices. He
failed to recognize them as his own. Conway was hearing different voices now that they were questioning him and kicking
him and pulling his nails. He fainted, and he was left alone for
a few minutes until the interrogator finished trimming his
mustache and dunked Conway's face in a bucket filled with
ammonia.

"You don't look too good," said the man. "I told you those
boys were gong to ruffle your feathers. Do you want to
smoke?"

"I want a shot of whiskey," Conway said, pausing on each
syllable.

"Of course, but you don't have to pant. First, let me know
where the suitcase is with the Guiristains' valuables. We
know they haven't been transferred out of the country. I'm
your friend. I know you were doing your job as a banker. But
those boys don't believe me when I tell them that you were
doing your duty. If you don't tell me, they are going to get
really upset, and if you refuse to talk...I don't know what they
might do. I might not be able to protect you any longer. Tell
me what I want to know, and I'll personally bring you a bottle
of Chivas and the butterfly. Think about it, Conway. We're
going to find out from you or from somebody else. But if you
tell me first, I can make life easier for you.

"I want a shot of whiskey," Conway muttered.

"I see you're hardheaded, but we can crack you as easily
as a nut. But to show you I bear no grudge against you, I'm
going to let you go to the bathroom so you can refresh yourself.
Maybe a little water on your head will help you remember,
and then I'm going to let you have the evening off." He patted
Conway on the shoulder and helped him get up.

The interrogator led him to the bathroom and Conway sat down on the latrine, his hands tied. He was confused, and a throng of images spun through his mind, stopping at his cousin Abigail. He head someone breathing next to him, and turned in that direction.

"Abigail, from the first moment I saw you, I thought you were the living form of the statuette of the Greek shepherdess who had always stood at the end of Mother's mantelpiece, playing the coquette with the shepherd lad on the other side of the clock. I must confess to you that as a boy that shepherdess was my ideal of feminine loveliness."

Conway was about to reach for Abigail when he heard a sonorous fart which shrouded the memory of his childhood love in a cloud of gas. It was coming from the toothless man sitting next to him. If both hadn't been blindfolded, Conway would have had no trouble recognizing the tall imposing figure of Mayor Sánchez, or Paco John to the free-roaming fauna at Marina's place. Conway turned his face to the source of the fumes.

"I should have never stayed here. Vera was right. We sighted land at seven in the morning, and as the steamer made its way toward shore—the captain being careful to avoid the coral reefs—I ran to the bow and stood alone peering over the rail. Little did I know that before me lay the scene that would entrap me. As the ship threaded the sand bars, I was so excited my throat choked. In front of me, under a flashing sun, I saw the palm-fringed harbor, and, a few kilometers away, a white village of thatched mud houses surrounded by strange rock formations rising out of a steaming swamp. I could hear the chatter of hundreds of playful monkeys over the rustling of the palms. Their barks and cries echoed from every part of the swamp as they sprang from one branch to another, the palms bending like trout rods, then sweeping back into place again with a swishing sound. It was this scenery that prompted me to disembark and commence my trek to the village of

Xawa with my machete in hand, fighting the jungle. In every Briton there is the soul of an explorer waiting to emerge."

Paco John was snoring when Conway finished rambling and lifted himself up from the toilet. He tried in vain to wipe his arse, and like a desperado, banged on the walls with his side to lure one of the guards in to let him out. Conway explained his sanitary plight and the guard, who was new at the job, pitied him, releasing his right hand.

"Do you mind releasing the left instead of the right? I am left-handed," asked a distressed Mr. Conway. Before leaving the rest room, he waved in the direction of his silent neighbor and said, "Take it easy, old chap."

As he walked back to his cell, Conway sensed that the guard was a neophyte and demanded in his most authoritative voice, "Before retiring for the evening, the interrogator said I was entitled to call my wife." The guard was flustered by the request, but acquiesced when Conway persisted.

"Hello, Embassy of the United Kingdom of England, Scotland, Wales and Northern Ireland," the voice at the other end answered.

"Ambassador Gatlings, please."

"I am afraid the Ambassador won't be able to take your call. He has been recalled to London for consultation. He will not return until next week."

"Listen, this is Floyd Conway. I am a personal friend of the Ambassador. I have been unjustly incarcerated. I must speak in a hurry for the guard thinks I am talking to my wife. I need for you or any other embassy official to press my case so I can be released." He lowered his voice for this last sentence. "I'm being tortured."

"We will do our best, Mr. Conway. Do you have your passport number or your birth certificate?"

"I do, but all my papers were destroyed when the flat was searched."

"I am afraid it's going to be more difficult to help you."

Conway mustered all his energy and yelled, losing his usual aplomb, "Listen, you bloody bastard. I need you to get me out of here."

"I am terribly sorry, sir, but if you cannot prove to us you're a British subject, there's nothing we can do for you. You could be lying to us. You could be an American or a spy."

"The ambassador knows me personally."

"I am sorry, sir, but the ambassador would have to corroborate what you're saying, and he is at the Court of St. James at present."

Click.

"Sir, however, you could... I guess he hung up. People get so touchy in the tropics, but we must carry on, carry on."

Conway made a sign to the guard that he was through and was escorted through a maze which led into his cell. There he was tied down to the cot until a mustachioed man awakened him at four in the morning.

"Conway, Conway, wake up! You have had enough time to think about it. We know that you have connections in the Ministry of Interior that are conspiring against the government. We know that you made a call to the British Embassy. Tell me once and for all where that suitcase with the money is and you can go home to your butterfly. This is your last chance!"

"I don't know any of those people. I don't know what you're talking about. I haven't committed any crime. Your men searched my flat from top to bottom and found nothing. I have nothing to do with this rigmarole. I want a shot of whiskey," answered Floyd.

"I see you're taking me for a fool. I can't waste my time with you! Boys, boys, take his clothes off," ordered the interrogator in a harsh tone.

Conway, in his slumber, fought them off the best he could, kicking, scratching, and as a last resource vomiting and urinating to keep his captors at bay. When he felt the tips of their burning cigarettes, he was already sinking into unconsciousness. The interrogator lifted his eyelids to check on his condition and ordered the boys to extinguish all smoking materials and give the prisoner an adrenaline shot to wake him up for the next round.

When the second round began, Conway found himself as part of a larger group. He recognized most of its members: Mr. Ariza, Dr. Gastón Robau, Benigno Juánez and his mother Belinda Zubitegüi, Bishop Santos and Tito Guiristain, Nelson's father's cousin. They were sitting down on the floor in a circle when the routine began, except for Mr. Juánez who squinted off into a corner, tittering in confusion and asking his mother to bring him his bottle of milk. The usual rhetoric proceeded. The agitated chief interrogator asked, narrowing his eyes, his voice sounding hoarse, "Why do you hate the people? Which one of you helped the Valleys to escape? Where have you hidden the people's money? When did you become a CIA terrorist?" The prisoners remained silent except for Belinda.

"We don't know anything. There's no proof against us! We have committed no crime!"

The prisoners heard a hollow sound. Belinda's head had been cracked by one of the guards. Her son Benigno and the other men remained motionless. None made the least gesture in support of Belinda, not even to help her get up. They were afraid of the beatings, wishing she hadn't spoken up.

Before Conway was released a week later, he was made to walk along a long corridor, formed by the passion vine covered chain-link fence and the pink poincianas, while a contingent of the Militant Muliebrity harassed and spat upon him. He failed to recognize in the crowd some familiar screaming faces, those of Tomasa, Magda and Dina Ferro, his eyes temporarily blinded by copious spit.

He was walking in a daze, wandering through the old part of town, searching for the butterfly's nest. From her bathroom window, she had seen him coming and rushed to close the front door. He knocked at the door and begged her to open up. The house remained still and Conway crouched under the window sill and fell asleep, staring in bewilderment at the moon floating above the window's grating. He woke up when a dog lifted his hind leg to let go a warm stream. Conway wasn't sure why he had been let out while the others remained behind. He wasn't sure what he had said to the interrogator, but felt the pain of the range of cigarette burns that ran from the nape of his neck to his funny bone and from his shoulders to his fingertips. Inside the small wooden house, the butterfly leaned against the bathroom window, weeping bitterly. She had been harassed by the police and her body was covered with black and blue marks.

"Nelson Guiristain is an asshole. I shouldn't have confided in a man who can't arm wrestle. What did he do with the bloody suitcase?" Conway pattered as he walked briskly toward the river to avoid the crowds. "He must have given the guard the wrong password. He was supposed to answer negatively when asked if his name was Raleigh. Montreal cabled a while back inquiring about the assets. It read, 'The apples aren't ripe.' I know what I'll do." His eyes lit up. "I must go to Lazarus. He might know something."

Conway changed his direction and, instead of heading for the river, he veered to the right and signaled the bus to stop. He got in and paid the fare with the only capital he had left, five cents. The bus was overcrowded, with people riding on the front and rear bumpers. The effects of the blockade were beginning to be felt, and there were no more spare parts to repair the five regular buses that lay idle in the terminal. He got off on Clara Barton and looked up to find his bearings, but had trouble determining where he was. The big Sherwin Williams sign that served him as his beacon had been removed. He was lost. He asked someone how to get to Joey Varona Street. The man mistook him for an Eastern European, and when Conway thanked him for the directions, he said, "Don't mention it, tovarish."

In reply Conway shot him the bird.

He knocked at the big mahogany door, and thinking no one was home, flung it open. Conway felt relieved to see Lazarus, an armadillo-like man who escorted him to the kitchen, apologizing that Magda and the kids were already asleep. Lazarus lifted the third and fifth tiles under the sink and a ladder came into view. It led to a small basement, a mini-bunker. Conway went in first, holding on to the lichen-covered walls. The flimsy ladder cracked under his weight. On the way down, Conway thought luck was beginning to smile on him. Lazarus was his contact with 'the man' in the Ministry of Interior. 'The man' in the capital city of St. Christopher was the pivotal link who facilitated the money transfers out of the country. Conway's previous plan called to snitch on 'the man' to create a smoke screen for his grand finale of divestment. The government agents would busy themselves capturing 'the man' while he transferred all the assets. He was glad he hadn't snitched on 'the man.'

"Mr. Conway," said Lazarus, "the man wants to know if you have any news of the whereabouts of the suitcase."

"Not at all, Lazarus. It's a big mystery, though I think I might have a lead."

"You do?" Lazarus asked, his eyes anxious and a lock of hair hanging over his forehead.

"Yes, I do."

No sooner had Conway spoken the last word when the pencil-thin mustached interrogator tapped Conway on the shoulder. "Mr. Conway. We meet again. But so soon. I thought you didn't know anything about the suitcase. Obviously, we were wrong. We let you out too early."

"Lazarus, you bloody bastard," Conway said as he gritted his teeth and thought about fighting his way out of that rat hole. The interrogator's luger aimed at his temples convinced him otherwise. "I assume I'll have to follow you."

"I'm afraid so, Mr. Conway."

In the mansion that harbored the secret police headquarters in the once exclusive Oña Heights, he was given the treatment reserved for V.I.P.s. The boys were glad to see him back. They played with him for twenty-three hours, nonstop. When they were through, he was dragged to a tightly sealed solitary confinement cell which seemed more like a cold, airless tomb. It was built to hold one captive. It already housed two. The two men inside didn't seem to notice the new arrival, even when Conway's massive body completely absorbed their five inches of breathing space.

When Conway woke up in the midst of the rancid dampness of the pit, he was wet and naked. He didn't know whether he was covered with blood or with spittle. He couldn't move and was unable to remember how he had arrived. He felt thirsty and asked for a drink. He hadn't realized yet that his neighbors were his only audience.

"Don't drink a thing," said the tall man to his front. "If you drink, you'll go into convulsions."

Conway opened his eyes and told the tall man his voice sounded familiar. The man introduced himself, though they were unable to shake hands.

"I'm Mayor Sánchez."

"I knew it. By Jove, Paco John! We used to down two bottles of Chivas at Marina's in a single gulp while we waited for the girls." Conway tried to turn around and screamed in pain.

"Don't worry, the pain will go away. You used to do the butterfly. She had some mean knockers." Conway had to make an effort to understand the mayor. The tip of his tongue had been burned off and the scar tissue obstructed his speech. "Don't move. Try to relax."

"Who's the other guy?" Conway managed to say.

"He's Benigno Juánez. I think he passed away an hour ago. Can you feel his breathing on your back?"

"No, I can't." There was silence.

"They won't remove him until tomorrow to torture us even further. It's psychological. Let's try to sleep. When you sleep, time seems to shorten. You'll get your memory back.

You're still in shock. They dunked your head in a pail filled with dog shit, vomit, and goat piss."

Conway was beginning to nod when they heard the screeching sound of the iron door and saw a shadow approaching. It was the interrogator.

"Get him out and blindfold him," he ordered the guards. "He's being transferred to military headquarters. Rulfo wants him now. We have no use for him anymore."

It was hard work to take him out. His belly had become wedged against Paco's buttocks and one of the guards had to put used motor oil on Conway's back and front to slide him out. Mayor Sánchez pretended to be asleep.

The men finished their cigarettes and cocked their rifles.

"Well, here's your chance, you bloody bastards," Conway shouted. "Don't shoot me in the back. Shoot me now!"

The men gaped at him in amazement, their lips tightly shut. Their faces were drawn in lines of mockery.

"Go on!" he continued shouting. "Fire a volley. Make this piece of land a place that will be forever England! Make ready," he screamed, and started singing 'Rule Britannia.'"

The men hesitated and then raised their weapons. Conway looked in the muzzles.

"Now then. Firing squad...attention!" They were obeying Conway's orders. "Ready!...Aim...Fire!"

The platoon fired in unison. He heard the first sweep of the bullets passing above his head. They fired again, and his eyes and nostrils were filled with lead and smoke, and his last thought was for his sister Vera and the Mexican prints in her parlor that had inspired him to cross the ocean blue. Then it seemed as though the sunlight on the old Ladies' Tennis Club building and on the reddish earth of its abandoned gardens had been shut off. Conway felt he was dropping into a well of blackness, sinking deeper and deeper.

"Britons, Britons never shall be—!" Conway's cry was never finished.

When Rulfo heard the discharge, he rushed to the wall. But it was too late. The vulcons that roamed free around the club were already pecking Conway's brain.

"You fucking assholes! I wanted to direct this execution myself!"

Conversation

"Pass the salt, Junior."

"Daddy, Daddy, Nelson is kicking me under the table."

"María-Chiara, don't call me 'Daddy!'" Nelson Sr. said harshly. "I don't like it! Call me Papá. And, you! Wipe that smile from your face. Pass me the salt, and stop bothering your sister."

"Mommy, what're we eating?" María-Chiara asked as she heard the sounds of a pepper steak being made to jump into the scalding oil.

"You're so stupid," Nelson Jr. hurried to say. "The same thing we have every day, burned rice and charred pepper steak."

"Why don't you two be quiet for a second and dunk your bread in the olive oil?"

"That's yucko, Daddy!"

"I told you not to call me 'Daddy.'" Nelson, who had never laid a hand on them, jumped from his seat ready to spank María-Chiara, but his hand stopped before he could strike her.

"Oh, Daddy, Daddy, oh, Papá, Papá," cried María-Chiara, shaken and surprised by her father's attitude, promising never to do it again.

"I'm sorry, pumpkin." Nelson said remorsefully. "Papá had too much work today. Here, give Papá a big kiss."

"Hey, Papá, guess what?"

"Huh?"

"Hey, Papá, guess what?" echoed María-Chiara.

"Shut up, showoff," Nelson, Jr. groaned.

"Let her go first. She's your little sister."

"That's not fair."

"I say what's fair and what isn't," Nelson thundered out of character.

"I have a loose tooth," said María-Chiara with excitement.

"Let me feel it, pumpkin." Nelson jerked his head in María-Chiara's direction, leaned over the table, and with his middle finger touched the rocking tooth. "It's almost ripe. I'll pull it out tomorrow afternoon."

"Hurrah, hurrah! I can put it under my pillow for the tooth fairy!"

"Okay, shrimp. It's my turn now. Hey, Papá, guess what?"

"Huh?"

"I made the baseball team!"

"What baseball team?"

"Coach Olsen's baseball team!"

"Ah."

"I'm gonna be playing shortstop! He said I was good. I want to be like Coach Olsen when I grow up. Did you know he made first cut for the L. A. Dodgers? He throws a fastball."

"I don't know what you are talking about, young man, but I know you haven't read the two books I gave you for your birthday. And that was a month ago," Nelson said as he refilled his plate with olive oil.

"I forgot, Papá, but they're on my desk. I'll do it first thing in the morning. I swear!" Nelson Jr. crossed his index finger and thumb and kissed them as he swore.

"You should have started reading those books the minute you unwrapped them! They are masterpieces of Western thought. 'Simple Verses' by one of our friends, the poet laureate, Lisander Pons. He said, 'our wine is bitter but it's our wine.' And Homer—I read 'The Iliad' in the fifth grade in Xawa, at Sacred Heart. I still remember some of the verses":

Anger be known your song, immortal one,
Akhilleus' anger, doomed and ruinous,
that caused the Akhaians loss on bitter loss.

"I promise I will. I swear…"

"Promises, promises, promises," Nelson banged on the table. "I'm tired of empty promises!"

"But, Papá, I just forgot to…"

"Don't be disrespectful to your father. I can't take this lack of respect. I'm going to the bathroom. And not a word out of you!" As Nelson walked to the toilet, he rummaged frantically in his pants' pockets, searching for something special. Engrossed in this search, Nelson kept on walking, bashing his head against the door frame.

"You lost something, Papá?" asked María-Chiara. The squeaky sound of a closing door was her answer as Nellie walked in with the pot of rice and the skillet with the charred pepper steaks awash in grease.

"Where is your father?"

"He went to the bathroom," both answered at the same time.

"María-Chiara, you're such a copycat. You say everything I say."

"Children, behave! God is at the table."

"We're hungry!"

"You will have to wait until he returns. It is poor manners to start without him."

"Who? God?" asked María-Chiara.

"No, no, your father."

Nelson sat in the toilet and turned the shower on with his free hand and pretended to be under it. He took out a piece of bubble gum from his left pocket, put it in his mouth, and began chewing it and blowing bubbles. They were big bubbles that burst, leaving a thin membrane of gum covering his face from his eyebrows to the tip of his nose. While his lips were busy forming bubbles, Nelson's thoughts were lost in Marina's place and the first time he ever saw the squirrel's face. He was mumbling to himself, "I have saved $500 for you, my sweet 'sciurus.' If I only knew where to find you so we could be reunited, be together for life…I would leave them the minute you arrive. Together again, my sweet rodent. I'd live to buy you bubble gum, to make you happy!"

"Nelson, are you okay?" said Nellie as she tapped slightly on the door.

"Yes, dear. I'm almost through!"

"We are waiting for you!"

"I'll be right out as soon as I dry myself."

Nelson popped the last bubble, sat up and put his head underneath the shower. Then he took a towel from the rack and dried his locks. When Nelson came out of the bathroom his head was still wet.

"Hurrah! We can eat now!" María-Chiara shouted.

"It doesn't seem too bad today," said Nelson Jr. as he began to munch on a piece of steak.

"I have told you three-thousand times not to talk with your mouth full. If your grandfather, Don Andrés, were here to see you, he would die of shame."

"Sorry, Papá."

"Is Grandpa dead?" inquired María-Chiara.

Nelson nodded and forked the unsuspecting pepper steak.

"Papá, you smell of bubble gum!" María-Chiara said. "I want some."

Nelson didn't answer.

"I thought you had taken a bath before," Nellie asked.

"I did, but I got hot again."

"I know, sometimes I take three baths a day. There is no breeze in this country."

"The steak is juicier, Nellie," Nelson said, trying to be nice as his teeth sank into the meat.

"I memorized the cooking instructions you gave me. But I am having trouble making coffee again. Mrs. James B. had to help me the other day. Could you write down the directions again, please?"

"I surely will," Nelson said mechanically.

"Pituca's husband is very ill."

"I surely will."

"I said Chief Justice Josende is very ill."

"Sorry. I thought you were asking the same question. I think Bernabé told me something to that respect. He said he's coming Wednesday for dinner."

"Who is coming?"

"Bernabé and his Uncle Ben."

"Why do you have to do this to me? You know I can't cook. You just can't invite people without me knowing about it. You think Tomasa and Delfina are still around!" Nellie sighed.

"You won't have to cook. I'll do the cooking! Besides, you're filling your belly every day thanks to Uncle Ben. So shut up!"

"I can't believe my ears, Nelson Guiristain. You are becoming as vulgar as the peasants with whom you work," she rebuked Nelson, and sighed again.

"Papá, can you tell me that story again?" Nelson Jr. asked to ease the tension.

"What story?" said Nelson annoyed.

"The one about your escape?"

Nelson smiled for the first time and began to retell his tale.

"So I had taken the train to St. Christopher and had walked from the train station to Embassy Road. I was carrying the suitcase with our assets. I approached the gate of the British Embassy and the guard spotted me. I told him I was bringing newspapers for the ambassador. He told me to open the suitcase, but I refused."

"What's refused?" asked María-Chiara.

"Shut up! answered Nelson Jr.

"And when he was about to pry it open, I lifted it unexpectedly and hurled it toward his face. The force of the impact knocked him unconscious. The other guard saw what was going on and rushed to help his friend, but I had already sought the protection of the embassy compound."

"I'll bet you were scared, Papá," said Nelson Jr.

"However, during the run for my life, I couldn't get hold of the suitcase because the guard had started firing in my direction—though it is illegal, according to international law, to fire at a person already inside the embassy gate. Once safe inside the embassy, I heard motorcycles and cars, and I sensed that heavier vehicles must be approaching."

"How come you knew that the tanks were coming?" asked Nelson Jr., completely enthralled with the story.

"Then more guards appeared, squealing tires and shouting obscenities."

"What're obscenities?" demanded María-Chiara.

"Do we have to listen to her? Obscenities are poopoo and weewee. And now hush! Please, Papá."

"Now and then, a bright light flashed through the split between the blinds. The consul tiptoed to the window to get a better grasp of the situation outside. Everywhere there were soldiers and militiamen with rifles. The embassy was completely surrounded. Suddenly, the consul yanked the cord and the blinds opened wide."

"It seems they are coming towards us," he said into the darkness.

"At that moment there was a merciless loud banging on the door, probably with the butt of a rifle. The consul didn't seem to worry. His face remained unaltered."

"Wow!" shouted Nelson, Jr.

"Open the door before I break it down!" a determined voice shouted in anger.

"The consul seemed amused by the threatening voice."

"No, no! Not by the hair on my chinny, chin, chin."

"I know that one, Papá!" María-Chiara said with a big smile.

"Shut up!" replied Nelson Jr.

"Children, please! Remember God is at the table," interjected Nellie.

"I give you two minutes to open this door!" yelled the determined voice.

"You can huff and you can puff but you won't blow this door down! Besides, old chap, the key was lost this morning. I would suggest you go home and take your siesta. It's too early in the afternoon to create such a ruckus."

"Preparing myself for the experience of the forceful entry and my arrest, I waited in absolute silence. I had this vision of the door being broken down and pushed off its hinges against the wall. In my mind, I saw the big hall mirror, the one with Queen Victoria crowning its frame flanked by two carved servants, a Hindu and a Bantu. The mirror was shattered. I saw the corridor filled with armed men, their boots grinding the pieces of the shattered glass into a fine dust."

"I left my fantasy and heard the door about to break down. For the first time, I feared for my freedom."

"Did they break it down?" Nelson Jr. wiped his sweaty palms with the napkin.

"We heard the screeching sounds of a vehicle coming to a sudden stop. And there was silence. A man dressed in a gray suit with an olive, leather coat that reached to his ankles and a panama hat with a lowered brim got out of an unmarked car. The captain, who had been threatening us, shouted at the man in gray. The man in gray slapped him. His armed comrades remained motionless. There wasn't a single sound. The man in gray left in the unmarked car. Immediately, the seige of the embassy was lifted. The consul turned to me and said, "They are such excitable people. What would you care to drink, some local rum or a good Drambuie?"

"Is the man in gray one of Mr. Conway's infiltrators?" I asked the consul.

"Rum or Drambuie?" was the answer to my question.

"By all means, Drambuie," I responded.

"Wow, Papá! Do you think you can tell this story to my friends?" said Nelson Jr.

"Maybe one of these days," answered Nelson, and smiled once more.

"Mommy, what're we having for dessert?" asked María-Chiara.

"Mom, when are you gonna put my things in the drawers?" Nelson Jr. asked, coming out of the spell his father had cast. "It's sort of hard to dig for my T-shirts in the suitcase."

"The servants will place them in the right drawers when we return to Xawa." Nellie's voice sounded determined.

"But why can't you put the in the drawers like all normal people do?"

"When the day comes, we won't have to do any sorting."

Nelson Jr., realizing he'd be digging for his T-shirts for a long time, changed the subject.

"Mom, how well do you know Mrs. J. B. Olsen?"

"She is a friend. We work together at the packing house. She lives in the corner house."

"I know all that. But are you really close friends?"

"We work together at the packing house," Nellie reiterated, and seeing her peeling hands, started to cry.

"I have just remembered my father's hands, so delicate, so smooth. He used to go for a manicure at Tuto's Beauty Care at least twice a week. He would have cried if he could see my hands, so I am crying for him."

"I'm sorry about your hands, Mom, but how well do you know her?"

"She gives me a ride to work. She's my friend like Sergio was my father's friend from Mondovi. She is not like Pituca, Loly, Vicky and the rest. They pretended to have what they didn't. I know them from Xawa, and they didn't have as much as they say they did. Mrs. James B.'s family lost it all during the Civil War. She has endured immense hardship like we are now, but there's still some class in her. Class is like matter; it can never be destroyed."

"Great! Then do you think you can talk to her so she can speak to Coach Olsen? Because I don't want to play shortstop. I'd rather play first base. But don't tell her I told you to tell him. Tell her it's something you thought about yourself. Have you seen Coach Olsen bat? He's the greatest!"

"Papá, guess what?" María-Chiara got into the conversation.

Nelson jerked his head in the opposite direction. He didn't answer.

"Mom, I want a pair of rose-colored shoes." María-Chiara turned to her mother while playing with her food.

"How many times have I told you no rose shoes in this house? Any other color but rose!"

"Why not? Rose is my favorite color in the world," insisted María-Chiara.

"Because I say so and that's it."

"Mom, you and Papá are getting so grouchy lately," Nelson Jr. said.

"Shut up, shut up, shut up. I'm sick and tired of all of you."

Nelson banged once more on the table, and María-Chiara's favorite glass went crashing to the floor. He then brought his arm up to squint at his watch, and María-Chiara cried in terror.

Nelson rushed to the front porch yelling, "Don't wait up for me tonight. I'm going back to work, to do overtime," he said with a firm voice.

Nellie rushed after him.

"Please, Nelson, you can't leave!" She strained her voice, trying to shout. "I told you there's a big radish shipment coming early and Mrs. James B. is coming to pick me up."

"When do you have to leave?" he yelled angrily from the car.

"By three or four in the morning."

"I'll be back before that."

Nellie heard the car screeching out of the driveway.

She used the rag hanging from her waist to wipe her face, and went back to the table.

"Guess what, Mom."

"What is it this time, María-Chiara?"

"Do you want to hear something? I'm gonna tell you anyway. There were two brothers, Pete and Repeat. Pete was eleven and Repeat was twelve. Who's the oldest?"

"Repeat."

"There were two brothers…"

"Shut up, María-Chiara. I swear, you're so stupid!" Nelson Jr. left his seat and muzzled María-Chiara's mouth with his palm. She bit him.

"Ouch!"

Nellie intervened, forcing Nelson, Jr. back to the table.

"Mom, he's kicking me again."

"I am so glad my father didn't have to see you two savages. You will learn some manners when we leave for Mondovi."

"I ain't going nowhere, Mom. I made the team!"

"You don't say 'ain't.' You're talking like a peasant. And you are going!"

"I'm not going either!" said María-Chiara while still thinking about Pete and Repeat.

"Don't talk back to your mother. Both of you are going, and that is it. We will live with Sergio and Adriano until we find suitable quarters and your father finds a job as Sergio's business comptroller."

"Papá has a job here!" shouted Nelson Jr.

"It is not the same. There, he would recover his social position. He will be somebody again. People will tip their hats to greet him in the morning. I will be back where I was meant to be born. I will be Nellie again."

"Is that near Xawa where Delfina lives?"

"María-Chiara! Who told you about Delfina? Don't just stand there, answer me!"

"He did." Her accusing index pointed to her brother.

"Don't you ever mention that name in this house. As far as we are concerned, that woman is dead!" Nellie started sobbing. "I am so sorry, Rigoletto. I should have stayed home that day. Papá was really okay. I could have saved you from Delfina, that assassin!"

"Mom, could we go out and play?" asked the children, somewhat frightened of their mother's reaction.

"Go and do whatever you want to do. I am tired of it all, too. Rigo, Rigo. I didn't forsake you!"

The Call

"Barney?"

"He's busy taking inventory. He can't come to the phone. I'll give him the message."

"Mr. Stain, this is Nelson."

"Well, hello, Nelson. Barney is on the roller ladder. I usually do it, but my back is killing me today. I hurt it years ago in Chicago. I was lifting a heavy cutting table and that's how it all started. I'll tell him you called."

"Mr. Stain, I must talk to him. It's urgent! He left a message for me at work and Barney doesn't do that unless it's real important."

"I'll holler at him, but don't keep him long. He hasn't finished and he wastes a lot of time. When I was his age, I would finish a whole suit in three days. I worked at a tailor shop. And I also worked during the night at a sandwich shop. You people are spoiled nowadays. I came from Prague without a penny and I got no handouts. I made it on my own. Barney, Barney, you have a phone call. It's Nelson. Make it quick. There's plenty of work to do! Are you still working on the toasters?"

Barney climbed down slowly, step by step, taking his time and puffing his Marlboro.

"Hello."

"Barney, it's Nelson. You left a message at work. Anything important?"

"Jerk-off. I was going to go by your house and give you the good news in person, but this damn old man wouldn't let me leave. He said I have to be through with this fucking inventory by this afternoon."

"But what is it, Barney? You know I don't have much patience."

"I saw her."

"You saw who?"

"I saw her, your squirrel, the bubble-gum maniac."

"Are you sure it was her? Don't kid with me that way." Nelson's voice sounded strained. "Where did you see her?"

"Calm yourself! I was selecting some beers at Pepe's Grocery. You know how I love to drink different brands. I had this bottle of St. Pauli in my hands when I saw this woman buying a box of Bazooka. She opened it right in the store, and her hands were shaking as she grabbed a handful of gum, got rid of the wrapping paper in a fraction of a second, and gorged herself with the Bazooka. C'mon, man, who would do a thing like that unless she was the squirrel?"

"But Barney, anybody can buy a box of bubble gum," Nelson sounded disappointed.

"Yeah, but can anybody blow a triple bubble?"

"It's the squirrel, Barney! I can't believe it. It is! But where and when can I see her? I've saved $500 for us. I was going to use it to find her, to hire a detective, Interpol... Did you follow her home? Did you introduce yourself?"

"No, I didn't."

"Barney, you idiot!"

"Nelson, cool it! I asked around who she was and where she lived, but no one knew exactly. A woman said she was new in town. Then Pepe came to the rescue and told me she had come recently in a boat and was working at the packing house. How does that grab you for a sleuth job?"

"Oh, my God! She's working where Nellie works!" Nelson sounded frightened.

"Isn't love a many splendored thing?" Barney said

"Did she look okay?"

"I guess you can say she looks okay. Her boobs were a bit droopy. But you be the judge. You should know better than I."

"I wouldn't, Nelson. She insisted on keeping her costume on each time we did it. She said it excited her more."

"So how did you do it?"

"It had a zipper. She opened the zipper."

"That's really amazing. How come you never told me that?"

"There was no need for you to know. You would have made fun of it."

"Did you ever get your wiener caught in the zipper? That hurts!"

"No, Barney, I didn't. But I don't know what to say to her, what to do, what to tell her, how to love her like she deserves. She's such a delicate creature."

"Big guy, if you go to Pepe's Grocery you're bound to see her sooner or later. The way she pops that bubble gum, she'll be back in two days. Stand guard by the cash register where Pepe keeps the bubble gum and stuff like that."

"I can't. That's too late. I need to see her sooner than that, before I lose it completely. You don't know how tense I am. I know what I'll do. Nellie has to work tonight, and Mrs. James B. is supposed to pick her up. She thinks I am working overtime, so I am not going back right away, so she won't get suspicious. Then when I get home I'll offer to drive her to work."

"Get off that phone and back to the job…"

"Hey, Nelson, the old man is nagging me again with his fucking inventory. I'll go by your house tomorrow to let you know what happened."

"Thanks for the great news. I love you, you son of a bitch."

"Hi, baby." Nelson came in the kitchen and kissed Nellie, who was panicky planning the next day's menu.

"What are you doing here so soon? I thought you were doing overtime."

"Let me put María-Chiara to bed, and I'll come back. There wasn't much overtime and they sent us home earlier. But here, Nellie, this is for you." He handed her a small white paper harboring a chocolate eclair.

Nellie was surprised with the eclair and amazed he was willing to put the kids to bed. It was the first time he had done it. She was going to bite the eclair but decided to put it in the refrigerator and enjoy it tomorrow when she didn't have to work.

"They are sleeping like two logs," Nelson said.

"They are faking, Nelson. They do it to me all the time. They always chat until late."

"Since I don't have to work, call Mrs. James B. and tell her she won't have to pick you up tonight. I'm going to drive you to work. I want to be near you tonight."

"But, Nelson, who's going to take care of the kids while you are gone. We just can't leave them alone."

"Nothing will happen. They'll be asleep. They won't even know I'm gone."

"No, no, Nelson."

"What do you mean, no! I am driving you to work and that's it!"

"No, you are not! Once in my life I was irresponsible and left my Rigo alone and I never saw him again. I'm not going to do it to the children!"

"That's insane, Nellie. You left him alone because Don Andrés was in jail. You had to, like I have to drive you to work."

"No, you are not!"

"Okay, have it your way! But I'm not staying here."

"Where are you going? You can't leave."

Nelson slammed the door so hard it fell from its hinges, got in his Falcon again, and flew up the street, leaving behind a cloud of dust. He was thinking out loud as he rode towards the packing house.

"I'll tell her I've always been in love with her and hand her the $500 as a sign of my never ending desire. I'll rent her an apartment nearby. I'll bring her lunch to work and massage her tired legs. I'll cook for her. I'll be her love slave. I'll pre-chew her bubble gum so her jaws won't get fatigued. I'll descend into the ocean depths to find the suitcase with the money and build her a palace that will rival the Taj Mahal."

Nelson found himself in front of the packing-house gate and was going to get out of his car when he heard the night watchman yelling in his direction.

"Hey, the packing house is closed. We're fixing to unload now. If you ain't got no business here, beat it or I'll shoot you for trespassing."

The night watchman meant business, so Nelson took heed and backed up towards the front nave of the packing house where he veered to the right, heading back to town. He was angry at the world but especially at Nellie, who had stymied his original plan.

"I'll write her the wrong cooking instructions," Nelson thought out loud again. "I'll write: 'Step number one: open the valve all the way and light the match.' She will surely blow up with the gas stove all the way to her stupid Mondovi. I'll unpack the suitcases. And then I'll write her a letter as if I were Delfina telling her something about her silly pig."

Nelson smiled at his last belligerent thought and felt as free as the day he left the suitcase go its own way. When he returned to the house, Mrs. James B. was pulling into the driveway to pick up Nellie. He parked the car behind Mrs. James B. and walked inside whistling.

"Howdy, Nelson."

"How do you do, Mrs. James B.?"

"I'm doing just fine. Were you meandering around town?"

"I was working overtime."

"At least you ain't got to deal with radishes. But I ain't working there for the rest of my life. Tell your wife to hurry up. Tell her there ain't no bugs like last time. She's afraid of bugs. I'll bet you you didn't know that."

"Nellie, baby, Mrs. James B. is here," Nelson said in his sweetest voice.

"Don't call me that name!"

"Mrs. James B. says she's tiring of waiting."

"I was about to walk to her house, risking my life if her husband had seen me, to tell her I couldn't go to work because you weren't back."

"But I'm back and she's here."

"Please don't leave the children alone."

"I promise I won't." Nelson kissed her on the cheek.

"I am going to have the eclair for dessert." Nellie showed him the white bag.

No sooner had Mrs. James B.'s car disappeared behind the tall Australian pines than Nelson scoured their bedroom, searching for an envelope with one of Delfina's letters. He was about to give up when, tucked away or maybe lost inside the lining of their suitcase, he found an envelope containing one of Delfina's first letters. The envelope had the familiar stamp with the dove and peace design. He carefully altered the postmark and eagerly wrote Nellie a letter as if it was coming from Delfina, though in care of himself since he knew she wouldn't read it and would throw it in the garbage can if it was addressed to her.

Canasta

Pituca was looking through her kitchen window watching the ripe mangoes as they swung with the breeze when she felt the sharp edge of the peanut can she was trying to open dissect her thumb. She cursed her luck, washed her wound under the faucet, and proceeded to straighten up her living room. The guests for the canasta party were about to arrive.

Her husband, ex-Chief Justice Josende, had been particularly chirpy that morning before leaving for camp. He had been given the honor of commanding the assault brigade that was to recapture the replica of the Ladies' Tennis Club. It had been a controversial issue, but Colonel Mirta Vergara had chosen the Chief Justice for his leadership abilities. Pituca was proud of the fact and planned to mention it during the game. He ate more than usual during breakfast, and when he complained of heartburn, Pituca told him to take a glass of water with two spoonfuls of bicarbonate.

After much soul-searching, Pituca called and invited Aïda. Pituca prayed to God she wasn't committing a mortal sin by inviting a divorcee to her house. She had such a beautiful voice, and today was a special day, and, after all, she was the last person to sing at the Ladies' Tennis Club during the last supper. There was another guest at the party, a very special guest. But it was to be a surprise for her friends, so her name was kept secret until her triumphant debut. The special guest was rehearsing her appearance. She was to conceal herself in the bathtub behind the shower curtain until Pituca gave the signal. She had arrived the night before all the way from Philadelphia.

"Until later, my sweet jasmine," said Chief Justice Josende, as he walked to the door with his usual limp.

"Did you get the colas?"

"Yes, I did. I put them in the freezer, so don't forget to get them out in about an hour. Otherwise they'll burst."

"Please, pull up your pants."

"I'm losing weight with the training."

The chief prepared to leave and checked to see that he wasn't forgetting any of his military gear for the big assault.

"Remember, the doctor said you should take it easy!" The commander did not hear his wife's words. He was already marching through the streets whistling "Over There, Over There."

Pituca sat on a folding chair and took a couple of puffs from a cigarette. She always took two lingering puffs. It wasn't ladylike to smoke the whole cigarette. She never smoked in front of her husband, out of respect. She sat up and looked for her last piece of jewelry, a charmless bracelet. She couldn't find it in its usual place, and, in fact, would never find it. The Chief Justice had pawned it the week before the fire devoured The Pawn Shop in order to buy his army fatigues and binoculars. She heard someone struggling with the mute doorbell and rushed to open up.

"Hi, Pitu." The greeting was followed by two kisses which landed nowhere.

"Hi, Loly. I'm so glad you could make it. You weren't at work yesterday."

"I know. I took Mely to the health clinic. She was running a high fever."

"Nothing serious, I hope!"

"Oh, no. It was a slight catarrh."

"What's of your half brother, Quinn?"

"He left for the seminary yesterday."

"It's such a blessing having a priest in the family. No doubt, Quinn will follow in Father Santos' footsteps. He led an exemplary life. I don't understand why the Holy See is taking so long in declaring him a martyr. Our Father Santos will be Xawa's first saint and martyr. I hear a car. Could you get the door while I look for my bracelet?"

Loly opened the door to see a number of women descend from an old beat-up station wagon. Once the preliminary kissing was over, they sat down to some serious canasta.

"Are we playing for a price?" asked Loly.

"Yes, we are!" answered Pituca. "Two S & H Green Stamp books."

"Just what I need to make the ten books I need for an early American lamp."

"Do you remember the last supper we had at the Club?"

"How could I forget the day I lost my Pete? Today is the fifth anniversary of his disappearance," said a somber Helen Valdés-Curl from inside her black shawl. "He was a man for all seasons. I know deep in my soul that he was tortured, but he never revealed the formula for Pirey. That awful day I will curse with my last dying breath. It's a day that will live in infamy." She collapsed back into the chair.

"Maybe he's alive," Pituca intervened.

"No, he's not. He didn't know the formula by heart. He made me memorize it to protect the company. I am the only person on earth who knows the formula, but Pirey has become obsolete. There are more potent bleaches in the market. He died in vain. All heroes die in vain if they could have lived longer."

"I remember it all happened during Fanny's installation party, bless her soul," said Loly. "Fanny died an apostle of freedom, fleeing tyranny, massacred in her yacht. When we go back to Xawa, we should change the name of the club to honor her memory. The Fanny de Fern Ladies' Tennis Club."

"And Martí Street should become the Fanny Memorial Boulevard, lined by her favorite tree, the myrtle," added Aïda, who hardly knew Fanny but had heard about her at the packing house.

"Cheer up, girls, next year we will be back in Xawa, and these days will be nothing but the specter of a bad dream."

"What was Floyd Conway's remedy for mosquitoes? Anyone remember?"

"I remember. A bottle of Chivas."

"Who was the first freely elected president of our beloved Tennis Club?"

"My grandma, Mrs. Peña!" shouted Macuqui, who was there not to play but to work on her homework.

"Who remembers the name of Nellie's pet?"

No one could remember.

"Maybe that was too hard. What about what the Aragón Orchestra was playing during the ceremonies?"

Helen stood up, "'The Constitutional Cadet,' my favorite song."

"And one last question to retrieve the past which will be our future on a not very distant day. What was the fish course served during the dinner?"

"Yeux du Pompano aux Fines Herbes," shouted Macuqui again.

"Isn't Victoria coming?" asked Loly, somewhat concerned and putting a temporary stop to the question-and-answer contest.

"She said she would. But she is acting a little strange lately."

"That's because Lisander is in Miami. He's trying to validate his law degree."

"It must be tough for her. They are inseparable."

"Who dealt last time?"

"Pituca did," said Loly.

"Then it's Helen's turn."

"Who was Xawa's richest man?" Aïda tried to revive the game.

"Joseph Fern."

"No, he wasn't. It was Mr. Valley," Pituca answered categorically.

"Who cares anymore!" said Helen Valdés.

"I heard Ariza is in Madrid working for the subway."

"That's awful. That was my favorite cafe in Xawa. My father always conducted his business meetings there," said Aïda.

"I didn't know your father was a businessman," said Pituca. "What did he own?"

Aïda didn't want to respond and changed the subject. She had said it many times at Pepe's Grocery and had come to believe it. She had forgotten that these people were really from Xawa.

"I haven't seen Nellie and Mrs. James B. for over a week."

"Maybe they're working on a new zoo."

"She's always been so...so flighty."

"Just like Don Andrés," remarked Pituca.

"There's someone at the door."

"It's Victoria."

Vicky slouched on the empty chair, her eyes red. "We were wondering if you were coming or not. Deal her a hand, Helen."

"What's the matter, Vicky?" asked Loly.

"Nothing!"

"Don't lie to me. It's written all over your face."

Vicky began to cry with such pathos that all the players began to sob.

"What's the matter? You can tell us."

"It's Lisander. It's Lisander," she said while covering her face with her hands.

"Did he have an accident?"

"Worse than that. I lied to you. He wasn't validating his degree in Miami. He has a band, and he is the lead singer and plays the electric guitar. He is been touring the state, and I saw him on Channel 10 last night. He wears his hair slicked back, uses a red sequined vest with no shirt underneath and tight blue velvet pants, and...and...and he wrote me he's in love with one of the Shirelles."

"Is he that well-known?"

"You know that song, 'Coconuts?' He wrote it."

There was silence in the room.

"He tried to be a poet, but nobody reads anymore. He couldn't find a job anywhere. He applied for a position with the OAS, but to no avail. We have three kids to feed, and what I make isn't enough. I love him and I will drink with pleasure from this bitter chalice. If he wishes to return, he knows he will find in my soul generous forgiveness, eternal love. God wished it, and so it was... I love him forever."

"The creep doesn't deserve your love. Besides, a poet of such magnitude should have known better than to descend into the abyss of vulgarity. I know I will never sing again. But I refuse to cheapen my talents like he has done."

"Hush, Aïda. Vicky is in distress."

"I'm sorry, Vicky. I just got carried away."

"Bring Victoria some sherry," said Helen. "It's the only solace for loneliness. Floyd Conway saved my life with a drink."

"We only have cherry cola," said Pituca. "It might have the same effect."

"Vicky, you aren't staying home alone. Bring the children and stay with Mely and me. As a matter of fact, you can move in if you want to."

"Thank you, Loly," said Vicky between sips of cherry cola.

"Let's keep playing, ladies. Who stole the joker I had?" prompted Aïda.

"There she goes again. You didn't have a joker; it was a three of hearts. Haven't you played this game before?"

"Well, excuuuse mee! I thought I had a joker."

"Ladies, may I please have your attention. I have an important announcement to make. I have a very special guest who has come from far away to be with us today."

Pituca tapped the cola bottle with a fork, but no one appeared. She tapped it hard and still no one came. Pituca left the room and went into the bathroom, where the mystery guest was hiding, and found her snoring, napping in the tub.

"Wake up, wake up." She shook her.

"Oh, I must have fallen asleep! I was following their conversation until they started talking about Fanny Street. You know that street shouldn't be named after Fanny! I got so incensed, I fell asleep. Anyway, it was such a long trip."

"Hurry, They're waiting for you!"

When she arrived and made her triumphal entrance, the old members of the Ladies' Tennis Club were so moved by her presence that they stood up and sang their old alma mater. Then the crowd chanted, "Cuquín! Cuquín! Cuquín!"

"I'm so touched," she said, and scratched the itching boils that plagued her skin. The membership crowded around her, like girls in a beauty pageant, and covered her face with kisses, leaving lipstick marks of different shades on her cheek.

"When did you come? We thought Rulfo had killed you!"

"It was awful, but we managed to escape."

"Let me bring you a drink," said a diligent Pituca.

"Rudy and I knew we were under surveillance when we heard about Don Andrés' death and the incarceration of Floyd Conway. Rudy came up to me one night and whispered into my ear, 'Belle, Belle,'—he always called me that—'we must leave immediately. Rulfo's men are on their way, and their orders are to shoot us on sight.' I remember I put on my dress, and we left in a hurry. There was no moon, so we escaped through the woods behind our home. We hid in the swamps east of the Deep River, and for months we ate nothing but roots and worms. At first, I refused to eat, but I was so hungry by the end of the first week that I devoured those creatures with gusto. I began to call them vermicelli, washing them down with a sip of muddy water. That's why my skin is filled with boils. The doctors say its a chronic condition I got from eating the vermicelli." Cuquín's beautiful alabaster skin had indeed wrinkled and become parched.

"How did you escape?" asked Aïda.

"A peasant friend of the family, Juan Benson, who used to be a farm hand for Don Andrés, sneaked us out under the cover of darkness past the coral reef, and from there a fisherman took us to Cay Salt from where we hoped to enter America. But it wasn't easy. We were taken to Nassau by the British marines, and from there transferred to a ferry that took us to Liverpool where our case was debated and our status decided. We tried in vain to get in touch with Mr. Conway's sister, but we couldn't remember the name of their home town. By then, we had no money, and Rudy began to work illegally in a coal mine. It proved too rough for him, and he died six months later. Thanks to Sister Michael Joseph, who took an interest in my ordeal, I'm where I am. I live in a convent in Philadelphia, where I have taken my first vows in gratitude for my deliverance. When I overheard in my dreams that someone proposed changing Martí Street to Fanny Street, I had to come to beg you to reconsider and change it to Rudy Valley Street. He deserves it more, and he was a native son of our beloved Xawa. Fanny de Fern stole the election from me and everyone here knows it."

"I still think Fanny deserves that street," said Loly. She was also instrumental in the acquisition of those fine tapestries in the Great Room…not to mention the swimming pool."

"That must be Loly. She's always been a brown-noser of the Fern family. But let me tell you something, they are gone and we are here. That street belongs to Rudy. Who do you think brought the sewage system to Xawa if it wasn't Rudy Valley? No wonder we suffered so much. You're a bunch of ingrates!"

"Please, ladies, please. Let's have a toast to the memory of Father Santos. We all agree that he was one of Xawa's best."

"To Father Santos, to Father Santos."

"No one is leaving until we finish this hand," said Aïda. "I have waited since Xawa to be invited to one of these card games, and I only need one card to win."

"Too bad, Aïda," said Loly. "Canasta! I win the two S & H books!"

Meanwhile, the troops had gathered in front of the cardboard reproduction of the Ladies' Tennis Club. Only a ditch separated the troops from their objective. Colonel Mirta Vergara was using her binoculars to calculate the risk factors involved in the attack when she saw a lonely figure charging towards the ditch, disappearing into it, and then struggling to climb out of it. The other guards followed his example while Mirta kept calling them names and commanding them to return to their positions. It was too late. They were following the lead of Chief Justice Josende, who had suddenly fallen down during the charge and was found by the rest of the platoon face up, staring directly into the sun. He had no pulse.

The Apocrypha

Nelson Guiristain
18 NE Ave Z
Belle Glade, Florida

Xawa
February 19

Nelson, please give this letter to Nellie.

Dearest Baby:

I hope that if you get this letter it will find you in good health. Oh, baby, I must confess something to you even though I know you don't want to hear from me. But I am getting up in years, and I can't carry this burden to the afterlife.

I didn't kill Rigoletto. What I told you was a lie because he was actually lost that day and I thought Tomasa had gotten hold of the animal and made bacon out of him.

Baby, Rigo is alive! Ariza, the owner of Ariza's Cafe, was hiding him in his house, and when he left for Spain, he took Rigo with him. He had promised Don Andrés he would look after you and your pet. It was hard to look after you then because of the political situation, so he did the next best thing.

Ariza knew Don Andrés had a close friend in that town you were supposed to be born in—Sergio, I think that was his name—and sent him there because in Spain it's too dry to keep an animal that only eats truffles.

I never told you the truth because I knew you didn't have a way to go and see him. But he's happy over there, digging for his truffles and socializing with pigs of his own class.

I had to tell you for my conscience couldn't bear the burden anymore.

I love you,
Delfina

Nelson folded the letter and placed it inside the envelope, which he had made from one of Pepe's Grocery bags to add authenticity to his plan. He walked nimbly to the mailbox, in case Nellie were to arrive unexpectedly, and deposited the letter. On the way back to the house, he felt somewhat guilty and said to himself, "After all, she wrote me a white lie when we were courting!"

The letter would arrive sandwiched in with the regular mail.

Silence

Angelina's coffin rested on the mahogany table that had been adorned with lilies and cloves. Lit by two Easter candles, her fleshy lips seemed to have been forced to smile by the embalmer. Her appearance had the expression of weariness, not the calmness which is expected on the faces of the dead, the face of someone who had left something undone. Parted in the middle, Angelina's hair cast a shadow on the aquamarine scarf that was tied around her throat. Her milky complexion was turning sable. Resting on her chest, her hands clenched an emerald crucifix.

Father Santos prayed in a crushed voice at the foot of the casket as the evening breeze from the sea, scented by the cloves, steadily consumed the candles.

Angelina had died unexpectedly. That morning she had taken Nellie with her to the shoemaker for a new pair of boots and to pick up four leather suitcases which had been bruised during their last European sojourn. Angelina was planning a trip to San Miguel Spa where she would take the medicinal waters to cure a bladder infection while Don Andrés was away on a business trip.

She had told the chauffeur to stop by the bakery to quiet the cranky and hungry Nellie with her favorite treat.

"Mamá, I'm so hungry!"

"Didn't Agripina serve you breakfast?"

"Mamá, that was a million years ago. Can we stop at Falla's and get something?"

"We can't stop. I have to see about the packing of the suit-cases. Do you want to help me?" said Angelina, signaling the chauffeur to stop at the bakery.

"Mamá, I'm starved."

"Look at that belly. There's enough there to feed a king-dom," Angelina said, laughing, and touched Nellie's tummy.

"Mom, you're tickling me," Nellie giggled.

"We're here, ma'am," said the chauffeur.

"Oh, Mamá, I swear by the Holy Mother's mother that you're the greatest mamá in the whole wide world."

"Do you know what you can have...guess?" said Angelina as they were getting out of the Mercedes.

"A guanabana milkshake?"

"No."

"I give up!"

"A midnight sandwich."

"Oh, Mamá, that's my favorite thing in the universe. I love you! But with lots of mustard."

"Yes, with mountains of mustard."

As Angelina got out of the car, she instructed the chauf-feur to pick up the trophy she had ordered from Evora's Book-store for the evening's canasta party. That very moment when Angelina spoke to the chauffeur and the pampered Nellie appeased her hunger by sinking her teeth into the midnight sandwich, Delfina, who was starching the sheets, had the pre-monition that something was going to happen before dusk. A giant tatagua, a nocturnal butterfly, had entered the house in broad daylight, crashing against the living room chandelier. The butterfly burned instantly and the light bulb crackled and went dead upon impact.

Nellie remained close to the casket, gazing at her mother. The tears trickled slowly down her cheeks and dropped on her mother's scarf. When the lid covered her mother's face forever and Delfina, Agripina and Felicia, the three maids, hurried to soften the coffin's coldness with a shroud of white orchids, Nellie didn't look but stared at the wall. Don Andrés walked very slowly and placed a band with big violet letters across the shroud. It read: "Exemplary mother. Devoted wife."

It had come so suddenly, Delfina thought as she looked the other way from a cross-eyed Don Andrés who tried to keep an eye on the coffin and the other on her hips. Delfina was nervous. That morning after she finished sweeping the shattered pieces of glass and the charred insect, she readied to clean Don Andrés' upstairs suite. He rushed from nowhere and pinned her against the staircase rail and burrowed his dart-like tongue deep in her mouth. He laughed as Delfina ran downstairs, tripped against the bucket, and rushed out of the house to cry by the cashew tree.

"What's wrong, dear? I just saw Delfina dashing out. Was she crying?" Angelina asked Don Andrés.

"Who knows, my dear. I do not attempt to understand the simple folk," he said as he took Angelina by the arm and led her into the house. Before he opened the door, she instructed the chauffeur not to place the suitcases in the attic.

The other maids hadn't noticed what had happened because they were in the kitchen preparing supper. It was going to be something unique, Angelina's favorite dish, quails in tamarind sauce.

When Delfina entered the house through the back door, her eyes were swollen and tears rolled down her cheeks. Her heart was pounding.

"Those are the eyes of love," said Agripina as she crushed the garlic cloves.

"I ate a cashew and rubbed my eyes..." she said, letting go of a long, quivering sob.

"I eat cashews, too," Felicia said, and grinned.

"Here, Delfina. Take them the first course," Agripina said with a faint smile, and patted her on the back. "Go."

The dishes were piping hot when Delfina rolled the cart into the dining room. Don Andrés sat at one end of the table, Angelina at the other end. The fussing Nellie sat next to her mother where Angelina could keep an eye on the child as Agripina fed her.

"Nellie, eat your sweet potatoes."

"I hate sweet potatoes!"

"Patizaña, the wicked witch, is going to come and get you if you don't eat." Angelina reached for the spoon. "Open wide. This is a charming prince that was turned into a spoon so he could search for the sweet-potato princess in the dark cave."

Edilia's place was set as usual, her favorite wine glass, the plates with her initials, the soft silk napkin. She had died of consumption three years before. Don Andrés insisted that she be served.

"This is the very essence of juicy," were Angelina's last words.

She had turned around to answer one of Nellie's never ending questions while gnawing on a tiny, but meaty, quail wishbone. Then, she got up from the table and seemed to look imploringly and questioningly at her husband as she tried to inhale some air. Angelina placed her hands on her throat and could only feel the beat of her heart. She collapsed. Her mouth twisted and her face became distorted. Nellie, frightened, started to cry. The wishbone had stuck in Angelina's throat. Don Andrés, at the other end of the table, glanced over his glasses and rang the serving bell as hard as he could to get the servants' attention. Don Andrés simply did not understand.

The three maids did their best to revive her with bay-leaf tea, ammonia and cow's urine, but Angelina remained motionless on the floor.

When Dr. Cabrera and Father Santos arrived, her alabaster hands had turned gray and the light had gone from her green eyes.

"My child, God is coming to visit you. Do you want to receive Him?" Father Santos had whispered into her ear as Dr. Cabrera said she had no pulse.

Don Andrés seemed embarrassed by his wife's choice to exit life and by Nellie's wailing. He slapped her. Delfina, who had seen the master hit the girl, rushed back to the kitchen and, startled, said to Agripina, "Everything is so sad!" Delfina choked.

"If someone has to die, it might as well be one of them and not one of us!" the old maid answered.

Delfina's mind reeled back by Father Santos' 'Amen' after finishing the last joyful mystery of the holy rosary. Don Andrés' mother, Valentina, tugged on her white apron; her knee had locked by the cramp that numbed her left leg during the mystery. The old woman, dressed in black with a mourning comb in her hair, her head covered by a gold mantilla, shouted an impetuous 'coño' that brought the prostrate, mild-mannered congregation to attention. The foul word was quickly attributed to the uncouth servant. Don Andrés' mother made Delfina apologize to the full circle of murmuring mourners, of which the aged matriarch was the epicenter.

The rhythm of the candles crackling, of mourners sneezing from the incense, of nostrils clearing, and sobs framed the whisperings of the pious.

"She smoked too much. I never knew she had such a big nose. Everyone in her family has a beaked nose. She loved him like no other woman on earth has ever loved. Did you see Mrs. Peña? So rich, her shoes so dirty. The only thing he gave her was pain. Fanny, the American, is chewing gum. No manners! What do you expect? She is what she is! Angelina hardly had any eyelashes. Fanny's face is like a man's. Most American women have virile faces. She never really loved him. Who? Fanny? No, Angelina. Her lashes were too straight, no curl. I'm really proud of mine. Look. She was too jealous. He was too demanding. I think Cuquín is having an affair. Angelina had to bathe with her dress on. She was showing her age. Did you see the lines on her forehead? They didn't live together, and that's why they were so friendly with each other."

During the time that Delfina served as a support for the wasted Pardo matriarch, her thoughts led her to what her mother had told her years earlier: "People can be happy only in pairs." Then she met Don Andrés' wandering eyes and didn't look the other way.

The bowls of black-bean soup signaled the religious ceremony was coming to a close. The coffin was being placed in the horse-drawn hearse for Angelina's last adieu to the streets of Xawa. It was three o'clock when the funeral procession left Villa Ronda and stopped briefly at the Jesuit chapel of the Sacred Heart for one last sprinkling of holy water. Then it proceeded down Martí Street towards the cemetery. Everything in the street appeared sad. The cyclists were sad, the chicken vendors were sad, the stray dogs were sad. The large warehouses, the government buildings, and the public schools had closed for the funeral. The only office that had remained open was the telegraph, where three important wires were received: one from the Prince of Spain, one from the President of the Republic, and one from Sergio Bruno in Mondovi.

For two years Nellie had not uttered a word. The playful, talkative child seemed frozen inside her developing body. She would spend hours and hours rocking herself in the middle of the room where her mother's coffin once sat, or stare at the blank walls. The only noise was her grandmother screaming. "She is useless. Her father should send her to an institution."

Then Delfina would rush upstairs to cover Nellie's ears and cuddle her in her arms.

The child wouldn't eat by herself. Only Delfina had the patience to feed her. All the while Nellie spat her food. Then Delfina would carry her to her room and show her pictures of flowers, animals, and brightly colored bugs. She pretended to read the captions under the pictures. Delfina did not know how to read.

Don Andrés hadn't followed his mother's advice. Instead he took Nellie to numerous specialists in St. Christopher. They had tried all the known cures, including visits to the zoo where Nellie was placed inside the cage of a sedated tiger. But she wasn't impressed by the feline, and wouldn't give the specialists any clues as to the whereabouts of her mind. At Father Santos' suggestion, she was sent every morning to the convent of the cloistered sisters. Maybe being with people sworn to silence could elicit some response from Nellie, they thought. One morning after feeding Nellie a media noche sandwich, Delfina gave her a box with the old family pictures which Don Andrés had left lying on top of his desk. Delfina was showing Nellie the photos when the adolescent smiled and said, "He's cute." Delfina turned the picture in her direction and there was Angelina as a young, smiling teenager posing with a piglet on her father's ranch.

Speedy

The men gathered in the fairgrounds, where the first zoological attraction of the Glades had stood. It was pitch-dark, and they recognized each other by their scents. Their secret meeting was about to commence when heavy raindrops began to pelt the conclave. Lightning flashed at a distance, confirming nature's wrath.

"This place is jinxed," said the man who smelled of fish. "I told y'all I didn't want to meet here. If we stay where we are, we're gonna drown like all them animals did awhile back."

"There are no jinxes, no hexes. To say those words is blasphemy. Satan is never idle, brother," a hoarse whisper refuted the fish-vendor's argument.

"We better move this gathering someplace else, 'cause jinx or no jinx, it's pouring already," said the man with the baseball cap who smelled of jockstraps. "Besides, I'm hungry, and the little lady has dinner waiting for me."

There was silence in the group. Only the scents of fish, jockstraps, bleach, chewing tobacco, and candle wax could be perceived. The man who smelled of candle wax finally spoke.

"Let's all go to my house of worship. But we must enter through the back door and cause no commotion."

The raindrops had turned into hail as the men covered their heads with their hands and blindly jumped into the pickup bed. The man with the baseball cap had concealed four beers under his old number 24 football jersey and, taking advantage of the bowlegged reverend's slow pace, opened the bottles. The men quickly chuggalugged the brew before the reverend had a chance to reprimand them. As they were leaving, a man in a white Ford approached, and the reverend waved for him to follow.

They entered as quietly as possible, though the fish vendor tripped and fell on top of one of the pews. The reverend's church had different levels assigned arbitrarily to the faithful by the reverend's assessment of what progress their souls were making. The highest level was fifteen feet from the ground and five feet below the pulpit. The other three levels descended progressively until they reached the ground floor, which he called the realm of the tempted souls.

"Let there be light," the reverend's voice thundered through the temple as he turned on the switch. The faces of the men shone in the light. All except for the last man to enter, who wore a mask. He was the first to speak.

"At the request of the reverend, I come to speak to y'all. The reverend and myself, we go back a ways. We were buddies in Korea." He smiled, and his teeth were yellow-stained and diminutive like those of a dwarf hamster. His eyes protruded through the slits of the mask, and his eyelids were three sizes bigger than those of a normal primate.

"I want to thank you, Speedy, from the depths of my soul, for you heard our cry and came right quick. Speedy, this community needs a man like you. The Lord already sent us a flood, and I'm afraid a great plague will follow."

"A man of the cloth is always eager to help another man of the cloth, even if they are different cloths."

Speedy shook the reverend's hand, and the men noticed he was missing his thumbs. And his indexes had compensated by becoming overdeveloped at the tips, looking more like big toes than fingers. His right cheek was covered with blotches which formed rings around a chain of extinct acne craters.

"So what's going on, Reverend?" asked a tobacco chewing man. "What's all the fuss? I ain't got much time to waste. I got a woman and three younguns to feed at home."

"I shall let Speedy speak his mind."

"Thank you, Reverend. I'm sure y'all have noticed lots of strangers are moving in, right?"

"Right," answered the group in unison.

"These people ain't only moving in, but they're taking jobs away from us folks."

"They sure are!" answered the baseball man.

"If we want to keep earning our daily bread, we ain't got no option but to get rid of them."

There was silence.

"Sometimes you have to get mean. Sometimes you have to get right nasty. Think what would have happened to us if we had been nice to the Indians. We would have been scalped, right? And that's why the reverend has asked for my guidance. Believe me, that man has tried. He is just trying to prevent the great plague."

"Could you get to the jist of the matter? I've got to get home."

"Let him go home," shouted the baseball man. "What can you expect of a man who's pussy-whipped and has three strikes and no balls? I don't trust a man who only makes girls."

The grease man stood up and left the ground pew and spat a syrupy tobacco wad on the floor. At the door he stopped and glared back. "Have a good one!" he said, and walked away.

"Many deserted Cheesas in his darkest hour. The same has happened here. Who else is gonna betray the Lord's plan?" The reverend paused and looked at the men below. "I see no one leaving this temple, Speedy."

Speedy spoke in a soft whistling voice, and as he did, his right eye twitched. "I was talking to you about the Indians, and the reverend tells me the Indians are coming back."

"We ain't got no Indians here, Speedy, except in Big Cypress Swamp," the fish vendor said with authority.

"Yes, we do. I see them working at the packing houses; I see them opening grocery stores. Soon they'll overrun this town, and we'll be worshipping statues, right, Reverend?"

"Amen, amen, amen. Believe me, brethren, I've tried and tried numerous times, and Jack can vouch for me. I have been door to door, warning them their idol worshipping was leading them to hell. I even went as far as to go to the packing house and preach the good news, and Jack Jackson can tell y'all if I speak the truth or not. I had this battle raging within me until a small voice told me that the Philistines have to be destroyed. The Bible says, 'The slaying of the impure brings greater glory to God.'" The reverend belched at the end of his discourse.

"Do we hafta go that far?" the bleach man and the fish vendor asked at the same time.

"The reverend is trying to preserve his flock, and he's willing to cast out the wolves, but I say unto you, before you cast out the wolves, you must strike down the leader of the pack."

"I know who that is!" the baseball man shouted. "That's my neighbor."

"You speak too fast. You don't think," Speedy scolded him. "Let us use our minds. Who brought the first of them people here?"

"I don't know. I reckon it was the...well, I don't really recall," Jack said, somewhat puzzled.

"I'm gonna tell you who. It was the owner of The Pawn Shop. Satan incarnate. He's the leader of the gang. So let me ask you, brother, what happens when a branch is sick?"

"It must be clipped," answered the reverend.

"That, my friend, is your answer. That Pawn Shop harbors the sick branch. Once that branch is cut, its leaves will dry out. Tonight, at twenty-six past midnight, we're gonna ride by that place and apply some heat to it to make the hermit crab leave its shell."

"What's he saying?" inquired Red, who was hard of hearing.

"He wants us to do something to Stanley's business."

"Is that just to scare him off?" yelled Red to Speedy.

"We'll begin there."

The men swore alliance to the Korean War veteran as he took out from his pocket four Lone Ranger masks and five sets of Indian headdresses from a paper bag. He called the reverend to the pulpit and proceeded to take his shirt off and paint the reverend's torso with army-surplus camouflage paint. He suggested the rest do likewise to each other. They removed their shirts, exposing the same saggy, hairless, bluish-white skin. When they were finished painting each other, Speedy spoke.

"Now I'm gonna go to my vehicle and I'll be right back."

The men were puzzled but excited. When Speedy came back, he had in his hands five bows and arrows.

"We need some wick to tie to the tips of the arrows and then dip them in kerosene. Reverend, do you have any wicks we could use?"

"I don't exactly have any wicks, but I know what we can use."

The reverend opened the woman's bathroom and brought back a few napkins from the dispenser.

"Everybody listen carefully. Tie these real good with these pieces of copper wire to the flint, and, like Speedy said, dip them into that kerosene container."

Speedy inspected each arrow to make sure the incendiary rag was securely fastened.

"Good, boys. Y'all did a fine job. Once we are within striking distance of The Pawn Shop, we're all gonna fire at the same time from different angles. Reverend, we need a prayer."

"Let us bow our heads for the invocation. We ask for the success of our mission as once was commanded to the Israelites: 'Avenge the Israelite People on the Midianites, and they took to the field and slew every male, then they seized as booty their beasts, herds and all their wealth and destroyed by fire all the towns in which they were settled.' I want you to dwell on the word 'fire' which is precisely the same element Speedy wants us to use to purify our town, and..."

Speedy interrupted, "Reverend, it's inspiring, but I must teach the braves the battle cry. Okay, boys, as we surround our target, I want y'all to cry out, 'Remember Chekaika.'"

"Who in the fuck is Chekaika?" inquired the fish vendor.

"He's the sleepy warrior, the Indian who tried to scalp my grandma when she was sixteen. Bless her soul." Speedy sighed as he shed a lonely tear for his departed relative.

"Then why cry out the Indian's name?" asked the vendor.

"There's no time to lose. I'll explain it later."

"Can we do this tomorrow? I'm kind of tired, and I have a load of oysters coming in at the crack of dawn. Frankly, Speedy, I ain't got much time to spare tonight."

"That ain't no problem, buddy. We'll all chip in and give you a hand after our mission is over. We'll get them oysters inside your fish market real fast. We'll even shuck them for you!"

"Reverend, I need to use your phone. I've to call the little lady and tell her I'll be late for supper."

"Go right ahead, coach. It's in the kitchen, second door to your left."

When the coach had finished talking to his missus, Speedy shouted, "Okay, boys. Let's do it. We're fish-belly white and proud of it!"

The braves made a circle, put their hands together and shouted, "Wahooooo! Remember Chekaika!" Speedy smiled with evil pleasure.

When the attack began, Stanley and Barney were sound asleep. The night had settled quietly over Belle Glade. They had had a nice meal of cabbage soup, roasted lamb, potatoes, apricots, and a bottle of wine. It had been a good day, and the boss was happy. Stanley had retired a little earlier than Barney. He slept on a cot, not because he couldn't afford a bed but because it was a legacy of his days in Prague when the family slept on cots in the basement in case the shouting crowds outside got carried away.

Barney slept in a tattered bed inside a small enclosure which served as his room. The ceiling was too low, and he knocked his head each time he entered or left. The rest of the living space consisted of an open room furnished with two old chairs and a drab reddish table to one corner. It was covered with stacks of dusty notes. At the foot of the table stood Stanley's cot. He planned to make an addition to the building to accommodate Barney's wife and kids.

Barney had fallen asleep that night with dreams of finding the old man's treasures; the old man had fallen asleep right away.

The first incendiary napkins zoomed through the sky and, landing on the grassy knoll in front of the shop, quickly drowned in a sea of wet grass blades. The second flaming arrow, fired by Speedy himself, landed on the roof, its fuel supply cut short by an uncooperative napkin which sprayed its contents en route, falling as a cool dew on the flower pots below. The third projectile made its impact through one of the front window panes, penetrating deep into enemy territory, spewing fire.

"Way to go, Coach," Red Hodel shouted in the still of the night as he let go of his missile, which arched over the targeted shop, overshooting its target.

"Shut up," shouted Speedy back, reprimanding the fish merchant.

The flames began to dance around the wooden shelves and displays, devouring the old tennis rackets, the scratched maple butcher block, and the picture albums containing the old antebellum houses which had withstood Sherman's onslaught but were now being consumed one by one. When the smoke began filtering through Stanley's room, he awoke feeling ill-humored. He looked across his room towards Bernabé and yelled in anger.

"Barney, how many times do I have to tell you you can't smoke inside the place! I had a bad lung when I was a child..." He wasn't able to finish his sentence. Realizing what was happening, he crawled to Barney's bed, opened the window to let in some fresh air, took a deep breath and awoke his nephew from the slumber of death. As Stanley inhaled, he saw a tribe of Indian warriors fleeing into the night, crying, "Remember Chekaika."

"Barney, Barney, fire, fire! The Indians have gone mad! They have attacked us!"

Barney awoke coughing, and smashed the window with one of the old chairs. Both men tumbled out of the sizzling chamber. Once out, Barney took the garden hose, forced open the front door, and started spraying the growing inferno. Stanley yelled and cried for help. Soon the townsfolk were passing down buckets of water from the fire hydrant to the shop's entrance. In the night, no one noticed the four conspicuously absent Native Americans. The communal effort was heroic, and in the end they were able to quench the fire as the roof caved in, but weren't successful in preventing the flames from silently jumping into the fish market.

Stanley saw the end of his livelihood. Only the metal store sign survived the holocaust. Barney, whose axons, deep in his brain, began firing evil thoughts about the old man's hidden treasure, was diverted from comforting his uncle and rushed toward the smoldering debris. He was lifting a charred beam when Stanley tapped him, and he jumped.

"Don't scare me like that, Uncle Ben."

"Sorry, son," he said after a pause, as though speaking to himself. "I need to give you a hand lifting that pile." He pointed to a mound of burning rubble.

"I'll get a shovel, Uncle Ben. I'll be right back." Barney felt relieved. For a moment he had thought Stanley had read his mind. He came back breathing heavily with shovel in hand.

"Start shoveling where I tell you," Stanley instructed.

"Where?"

"Right there."

Barney shoveled with gusto, cleaning up the pile, revealing underneath the stained floor.

"Right there," Stanley said. "Right there, push the right end of that plank."

"It doesn't budge, Uncle Ben."

"Push it with your shovel."

Barney followed his command and the plank shot up into the air.

"Now it'll be easier to slide the others."

Barney's dream was coming true. The treasure was about to be opened.

"I have something really important buried down there. I'm glad I kept it there, otherwise I wouldn't have anything left."

Barney's sinister axons fired another signal within his brain, and as he was about to hit the old man with the shovel and rush down and fill his pockets with precious stones, Uncle Ben turned around, foiling his attempt, and told him to pull out another plank. Barney did, revealing a small ladder which led into the underground chamber.

"Go ahead," said Uncle Ben. "I'll be right after you."

Barney shivered as he took the first step into fortune.

"Hey, grab my hand. I can't jump that far," Uncle Ben said. The last plank was one or two feet from the ground. Barney grabbed the old man with one arm and eased him down. By now, Barney was willing to convince his uncle to share the wealth half and half.

"I'm going to show you my most cherished possession."

There was a small black trunk in the corner, and Barney's eyes shone with greed as the old trunk opened its mouth and Uncle Ben extracted a brown envelope. There was nothing else inside except an old picture.

"This is my biggest treasure. If it had burned, everything would have become meaningless, all would have been lost."

He opened the envelope ceremoniously and took out a large picture.

"This is my mom, Barney, your great-aunt Esther. It's the only thing of value I took when I left Prague."

"Where's the rest?"

"What rest?"

"The rest of the treasure."

"This is my treasure," Uncle Ben said as he pressed his mother's picture against his heart.

Barney couldn't believe it. He had worked all those months in vain; the numbers tattoo, the painful circumcision...and now the old man had nothing left but an old yellow picture of his mother. He thought about leaving the pawnbroker right there and kicking the ladder up behind him so he would be buried in his chamber.

"Barney, we have work to do. We're still alive. We're going to rebuild the store. No fire has ever really driven us away." A sullen, determined look was on his face.

"Uncle Ben, I have something to tell you. I am not your nephew like you think. I lied to you. My real name is Bernabé Guiristain. I read your ad in the paper and fabricated this whole myth about being your long-lost relative. My mother wasn't Miriam. My mother's name was Elvira Echandy and my dad's Tito Guiristain. He died when the *Andrea Doria* sank. He was headed for the Mediterranean with his mistress. She saved my mother's life. But we lost it all after he died. You see these numbers; they are fake. I had them tattooed."

Uncle Ben turned around, looked him straight in the eye, and said, "Stop the nonsense. Of course you are my nephew. Here, hold your great-aunt's picture and push me up to that first plank. I'll wait for you on the surface."

Ubi Sunt?

When Barney banged at Nelson's door, he was covered with soot, sweat and dirt. Nelson peered through the window but didn't recognize his friend. When Barney yelled, "Jerk-off, open up," Nelson opened the door, but it didn't occur to him to ask why he was so dirty and smudged. Nelson, sick with love, thought his friend had been sweeping a chimney, seen the squirrel at a distance, and rushed to tell him.

"Nelson, Nelson, the place burned down! There isn't anything left!"

"Did you see her? Where? C'mon, Barney. You know I don't like suspense!"

"There's only one wall left, and Uncle Ben is crying and praying by it."

"What was she wearing? I'm willing to give her anything she wants."

"There's no treasure, Nelson, no treasure. I have plowed in the sea. I don't know what to do now. I'm tired, penniless, and jobless. The old man is broke. I can't take care of him."

"I'm ready to tell Nellie to move out of the house with the children so the squirrel and I can be together. I have become a bathroom dweller. It's the only place I can be at peace with my thoughts and think about her the way she deserves.

"I told him the truth down in the cave. I forgot to tell you there was a cellar of sorts, but there were no gold ingots, no precious stones, no silver bars. There was only this yellowish picture of his mother. Can you imagine all my work for a stupid picture of an old lady with frame glasses and a wrinkled, square face?"

"I've been to Pepe's Grocery every single day this week. But I know squirrels are elusive and unpredictable. Maybe if I line the way from here to the grocery with bubble gum she will follow the trail, and I'll be able to contemplate my love at last. Though I don't know if I could bear to see her face again. I might die from so much pent-up love."

"What should I do, Jerk-off? I need your advice. My mind is clouded up by the smoke. I don't really have any connection with the old man. I'm not his nephew. You know it. I have a friend in New Jersey, and I could leave first thing in the morning. I might need a couple of twenties from you."

"When you saw her, did you see her eyelashes? I would recognize those eyelashes anywhere in the world. Are her eyes still amber with two tiny dots in the middle of the pupils? I adore those eyes."

"I can't take care of that old man. He's gone crazy. He thinks we can rebuild the business. I want no part of it."

"I placed that letter in the mailbox. Nellie will get it today and give it to me since I am the addressee. I'll read it with amazement and tell Nellie it's from Delfina. She'll say she knows it's from Delfina and refuse to hear it, but I'll read it aloud anyway. Nellie will go crazy when she hears the part about Rigoletto being alive. Then, when she's gone from my life forever, I'll be able to caress that furry forest creature once more."

"I know what I'll do. I'll join the freedom fighters by the lake."

"Barney, I'm a freedom fighter. I've been fighting for my freedom all my life, not those ridiculous men..."

"There's one woman, too," Barney corrected his friend.

"Those silly men playing war: Chief Justice Josende, Senator Zubizarreta, Dr. Robau... I make love, not war."

"Can you lend me forty dollars?"

"I would if I could, but if I give you forty, I'll only have $460 for her, and that's not enough. She needs the full $500. Sorry, Barney, but I can't. Maybe if you lead me to her, there could be a reward, because it would be part of her dowry. But not otherwise."

Barney left silently, wearily, looking at the floor. He walked slowly, bending down every few steps to grab a few pebbles and throw them against Nelson's house. He passed by the lake and saw a woman in fatigues leading a group of five elderly gentlemen storming barracks made out of cardboard. It had written on it in big letters BARRACKS and in parentheses, "Soon to be again the 'Ladies' Tennis Club.'" The troops shouted angrily as they charged against the fortification, slashing it with their machetes. The woman let go a couple of rounds from her machine gun to mark the success of the attack. He reconsidered the idea of joining the forces for pay, to become a mercenary, make some money and head for Jersey. But as he watched, he quickly became disillusioned with the platoon and its agenda.

When he returned to where The Pawn Shop had stood, Uncle Ben was still busy trying to clean the debris. He looked at Barney with bleary eyes.

"That's too heavy for you to lift, Uncle Ben. Let me do it. You have a bad back."

The old man let go of the searing metal beam, sat on a piece of the crumbled wall, put his elbows on his knees, propped his head on his hands, and observed Barney as he continued with the cleaning chores.

A Tulip for the Parted

Nellie Pardo de Guiristain
18 NE Ave Z
Belle Glade, Florida

Dear Mrs. Pardo de Guiristain:

Delfina instructed me to notify you in the event of her death. She made her last mark in the cashew tree, where she kept a record of the days since your departure, and quietly passed away two days ago.

She died on the cot you used as a bed while you lived at her place. Delfina had become very attached to it in her last days. I think that in her mind, you and the cot had become one. She washed it every day with soapy water and used a funny-shaped sponge to scrub it. She would then pour Royal Violets perfume over its surface and adorn the legs with puffy, purple bows. She died caressing its legs and singing a lullaby to the pallet.

I buried her yesterday next to Don Andrés as I knew she would have wanted but was too shy to even contemplate the idea. I hope you don't mind. There were only two other people at her funeral. Perhaps you remember them, Waldo, the old man, and Tomasa. Waldo is the official state funeral director for this region. Tomasa, from what I gathered, came out of guilt. She placed a small bunch of poinciana flowers in the pine coffin and said, "Don't worry about it, the old wretch shouted your name each time I touched him." It doesn't make sense to me, but those were her words. Then she proceeded to tell the corpse she had cheated her many times in their bartering deals. Tomasa went on to say she did it because she was hungry and there were more mouths to feed at her house than at Delfina's. By the end of the parliament, she seemed genuinely contrite.

I truly miss Delfina. She was a good friend. I guess I have forgotten to introduce myself. My name is Emile Van Der Xawa, though most of my friends call me Liazzo. Perhaps you might recall that I painted Mrs. Peña's portrait with the descending bridge. Unfortunately, it was put to the torch a few years ago by a then obscure character who rapidly ascended the revolutionary ladder in this region propelled by collective bitterness. I recall having seen you promenading up and down Oña Heights with your pet.

Delfina and I contemplated the idea of fleeing Xawa in a canoe. I remember I cut a tall mahogany tree Delfina had selected. She knew quite a bit about trees since as a child she helped her father make charcoal for sale as cooking fuel. While I was carving the trunk, an all-encompassing thought enveloped my senses. I realized I was about to leave behind my chocolate doll, my lost pentimento, my Dina.

I couldn't convince Delfina to abandon our project so I squealed to the authorities and told them I had discovered, by chance, the hiding place of a traitor who was trying to leave. The following day the mahogany thicket was razed to the ground and the canoe turned into splinters. Delfina wept when she saw the destruction and I cried with her. Her tears gave me hope of finding Dina.

I don't exactly need your permission, but I'm going to take the legs off the cot and use the canvas to paint my last tribute to my lost love. I am denied any access to canvases since the day I was accused of being a pornographer and my paintings publicly burned at the town square by the Militant Muliebrity. I was rehabilitated by spending four years of hard work at the nearby quarries. However, I am restricted to paint only billboards, exhorting the people to produce more and eat less. But I must confess that when I dot the "i", I draw two tiny dots inside two bigger dots. She had two tiny dots right in the middle of her pupils. The "l" I draw like her legs, slender but firm, and, if you'll forgive me, the "w" like her buttocks and the "m" like her breasts. I am willing to risk my life to paint her as I saw her last, naked, pretending to be reading a newspaper, chewing gum and making bubbles.

Someday, she'll come to me. Someday we'll meet again. That's why if it takes forever, I'll wait for her in Xawa.

I have overextended my notice and your patience, but I have no one to whom I can convey my thoughts. I hope the censors don't get to this letter, not because I care so much about what happens to me, but because I must immortalize her on canvas.

My regrets for being the harbinger of bad news.

With warmest regards,
Emile Van Der Xawa

I Saw Her Again Last Night

It was fate that made me check the day's mail as I was carrying it back to the house to hand it to Nellie. I had previously placed the letter I had written in the mailbox to make its delivery more authentic. So it came mixed with the Spiegel catalog, the Winn-Dixie flyer with Thursday's specials, and our first Sears' credit card. I was happy to have the credit card, thinking I could use it to lavish my love with presents and tokens of my affection. I then noticed two envelopes with the same stamp, the dove with the word "peace" in many tongues. For a few seconds, I was confused. I couldn't tell the real letter from Delfina from the apocryphal which I had written. I panicked, and for the first time since I was freed by the frolicking wave in St. Christopher's Bay, my stomach began to grumble. I calmed myself and inspected each envelope, and in the process sniffed the Elmer's Glue I had used to seal mine. I removed the real letter and placed it in my back pocket. My plan was on schedule.

"Honey, you got a letter from Xawa, but it's in care of me. Isn't that strange? Maybe it's something important."

"Do as you please with it. I am not reading it," she answered curtly.

"I'll open it for curiosity's sake." I pretended not to give it much attention and perused the Spiegel's catalog first, then I used the kitchen knife as a letter opener. I read the first paragraph and yelled as surprised as one could when there's no mystery.

As soon as I began to read that letter out loud, Nellie told me to stop, but I continued, knowing very well she would jump for joy as soon as I read the part about Rigoletto being alive.

"What did you say?" her voice rose to a scream.

"Baby, I think Rigo is alive. He's alive, Baby! He is alive!" I sputtered and faked a few tears of joy. She embraced me with such passion that for a second or two I thought I could forget my squirrel and start anew with her. But her kisses were as cold as rain.

"To think I was so harsh with Delfina." Nellie sounded genuinely contrite. "I must get her picture and put it back in its place on the kitchen wall."

"You tore it to pieces, Baby," I reminded her.

"I will write her and ask her for another one. But before, I must work more and save money to go and see Rigoletto. He probably thinks I'm such an ingrate!" she sobbed.

I was at the crossroads of my life. I had the choice of giving the money to the squirrel so she could find an apartment nearby or giving it to Nellie so she could go Mondovi. I thought so hard my temples were about to burst. There was no playful wave to make the choice for me this time. I thought about running to see Barney for advice, but he was too busy with Uncle Ben's smoldering ruins. I told Nellie I had to go to the bathroom, and on the commode I found wisdom. The answer was revealed to me. I opened the medicine cabinet and from inside the dark bottle of expectorant syrup, floating in a plastic tube, I extracted five hundred dollars. Once Nellie was gone, I planned to beseech the squirrel to move in with me. I would tell her I was a widower, and if the kids were a nuisance, I'd send them away to live in a foster home or give them up for adoption or something. Nellie was in ecstasy when I placed the $500 in her palm.

"Baby, something told me deep inside Rigo wasn't part of the underworld. I have been doing so much overtime waiting for this moment to arrive. You go ahead first and then ask Sergio for our passages. I'm sure he will."

"Oh, no. Oh, Nelson, I love you!"

"There is no time to lose. There's even a blue moon tonight. The moon of lovers, and I know how much you care for Rigo. You must hurry. I would love to be with you and Rigo, but there's only enough for one of us and it should be you."

"But how do I get there?"

"It's easy. You'll take the Trailways bus to the Port of Jacksonville and from there arrange passage on a freighter to Mondovi. Ask the sailors if they know the way to Mondovi."

Nellie began to order me around, and I followed her instructions like a faithful servant. She then went to her room and unpacked the suitcase with the faded stickers which had served as our chest of drawers ever since she arrived from Xawa. For the first time in years I was able to place my clothes in the drawers. She laid on our bed the only garment she allowed herself to take on her trip, her blue, mothball-smelling, wrinkled, taffeta dress. I offered to iron it.

While I was ironing the dress, I heard her moving about the bathroom, splashing her body with rose water. She slipped out of the bathroom and looked for the green balm Naomi had recommended to ease the pain in her hands. The constant sorting of the produce at the packing house was beginning to twist them out of shape.

She carried herself differently once she wore the dress and her hair was braided. She walked to the children's room and tenderly kissed María-Chiara and Nelson Jr. and left the door ajar. To my surprise, she left a pot of coffee ready for me to drink, and as a souvenir or good luck charm, she took the magnet that held in place my daily culinary instructions. I kissed her on the forehead, and she made me promise never to leave the children alone at night. She said she would send for us as soon as she arrived in Mondovi. Then I went back to bed, and until I heard the door bang closed, I pretended to be snoring contentedly.

I saw her trampling toward Mrs. James B.'s place and quickly put on my pants, checked the kids to make sure they were asleep, and left them a note on the refrigerator door secured with a piece of scotch tape. It said we were both working overtime. I know that squirrels are nocturnal and this was my big chance. Before I left, I performed my own bathroom ritual. I gargled with Listerine, shaved, and splashed cologne all over my face and torso. Then I combed my hair to wear it just as I had when I first met her. I was ready to climb up the ramparts that kept true bliss from my life.

I crept out stealthily to avoid being seen by Nellie from Mrs. James B.'s living room. I headed for Pepe's Grocery to see my love at last. I took the long way around. As I walked, my mind dwelt on famous sweethearts of antiquity: Romeo and Juliette; the lovers from Teruel, Dante and Beatrice; Florambel and Graselinda; Don Juan and Doña Inés; Floyd Conway and the Butterfly. I wanted to be a poet to sing of my love for her, and inspired by theirs, I conceived my first and only poem without Barney's help.

> Of course, that my luck disdain
> my mad desires to please,
> nor will I ever obtain
> what others get with ease
> since I demand what no mortal
> could ever receive.

I was engrossed in the second verse when a group of assorted bugs, wheeling and circling around the newly installed flashing sign, signaled that I was getting closer to my destiny. When I opened the door to Pepe's, my thoughts grew silent and reticent. I heard noises and the sounds of the jukebox playing, "I Saw Her Again Last Night." Pepe was wiping the meat counter with a powerful spray, and there was the regular domino crowd gathered around the small table by the plantains. A whiff of the cleanser brought me back to reality.

"What brings you here at this hour?" asked Pepe.

"Overtime!" I said defensively.

"You should work less and play more. Your father never enjoyed life," said Pepe as he continued cleaning the counter.

"Yeah, but he had a bundle of money," shouted Captain Manny, one of the domino players in the back, as he rubbed his index against his thumb.

"Yes, he did." I cursed them in my mind for spoiling this moment with my father's presence.

"It's hard to believe that old man Guiristain didn't have money stashed away in some New York bank," replied Antonio, the man who worked at Rosser & Dunlap.

"No, he didn't," I said hoarsely.

"You should have become my partner in the stuffed-potatoes business!" said Pepe from the counter. "But you never returned my call. Was it pride that kept you from calling back because I worked for you people back in Xawa?"

I didn't respond.

"Well, why talk about the past! The future is what matters. Did you see my flashing sign?"

"It'll be good for the store. You can see it for blocks," I said, and Pepe smiled complacently.

"Sit down! Make room for this gentleman," said Jacinto, the bald player, as he grabbed an empty stool and offered it to me. "You don't cheat like Pepe does at the cash register?" He laughed, and Pepe frowned at Jacinto.

"I can't play today. Maybe some other night," I said, looking towards the front door.

"What's the matter? Do you think you're better than us because you had money in Xawa?" said Antonio as he stared at Nelson.

"Of course not," I said, and slid onto a stool to play.

"Pepe, bring this man a cold Dog's Head. Don't worry. It's on me," said Clavo, the clandestine doctor. "Who's shuffling the bones?"

"It's your turn," Jacinto said as I rapidly filled my mug with Dog's Head. I enjoyed every single bubble, but kept eyeing the door.

"The one with the highest spinner sets," shouted Captain Manny, who was hard of hearing.

"Okay, but you don't have to break my eardrums," screamed Jacinto at Manny's left ear before turning around to ask the rest of us who had the highest spinner.

"I believe I do," I said somewhat timidly since it was the second time I had played dominoes. We had always played cards at the Tennis Club.

"Well, Nelson, Pepe says you had quite a time leaving our suffering land," said Captain Manny as he set his double nine.

"I suppose I did." I tried to sound as humble as possible.

"I understand you very well. I myself had a tough time with that good-for-nothing, bloodsucking vampire, son of a bitch, Rulfo."

"We've heard your story at last twenty times," interrupted Domingo. "Let this man tell us his."

I couldn't resist the temptation and began narrating my heroic saga.

"You are going to find out why we came penniless to this country."

"Pepe, bring this man another beer!"

"I had taken the Tawanda to St. Christopher. There I was supposed to take the suitcase with our assets to the British Embassy. I told the guard the password Mr. Conway had said would change the guard's attitude."

"Is that Mr. Conway, the Englishman who hung around Ariza's Cafe?" asked Clavo.

"Yes, he used to frequent that establishment. The password was 'Dieu et mon droit!' Though now I think he meant to tell me to use it with the Royal Marines who protected the embassy compound. I repeated those words many times to the guard, but my open sesame didn't seem to have the right effect on him. On the contrary, he remained perplexed. I was quite puzzled myself and decided to change plans and tried to bribe the guard with chiclets, by then a very scarce commodity, but he refused. I tried again and insisted, 'Chiclets for your children,' I said. But he remained oblivious to my overtures and continued to refuse. Then I told him I was from the Ministry of the Interior and that we were investigating crooked guards. He didn't buy my story."

"Shit, I bet you were scared," said Jacinto.

"Yes, I was especially when he asked me for my badge and told me to open the suitcase I was carrying. I pretended I was following his orders, but instead, I knocked him down to the ground with a judo throw. The guard remained motionless and everything was very still for a fraction of a second. Taking advantage of the situation, I ran as fast as I could towards the embassy door, but suddenly I saw the other guard blocking the entrance and drawing his gun from the holster. I jumped the fence and ran as fast as I could towards the ocean front while the bullets kept grazing different points of my body. I felt my whole being trying to escape the hunter, but my energy was fading. I trudged on and reached the seawall and plunged deep like a cliff diver. I went underwater for as long as I was able, my lungs ready to burst from the pressure. I remember the waves were big, and when I resurfaced the guards failed to see me. They mistook my bobbing head for one of the many buoys which dotted the bottleneck harbor."

"I don't have a seven or a five. I pass."

"Shut up, Jacinto. Let the man finish his story."

"The guards were shooting at random while I did a butterfly stroke northward. The tide was crawling away from land, and I was riding the waves like a flying fish, kicking for my life. I was about two-thirds of a mile from shore when I saw an ominous red hull. I panicked, and my mouth opened, and a wave crashed inside, filling my belly with saltwater, seaweed, and tiny crustaceans. I thought my end was near at the hands of angry Neptune or the government's PT boat. Someone yelled, 'Hey, you out there.' 'Yes,' I shouted with fear. Then they threw a rope just as I was about to drown. I reached for it. As I was being hauled up over the gunnel, my eyes caught sight of the ship's emblem, the sign of the resistance, a green worm holding a flag in one hand and an M-19 in the other. They were counterrevolutionaries mining the bay's entrance on a boat camouflaged to look like a shrimper. It was a sabotage mission from the Magic City. 'I'm safe,' I said to myself. I was naked and was offered a shot of rum and a pair of trunks. I thanked them and introduced myself as best as I could under the circumstances. I was trying to catch my breath. I remember the captain grinned and said I could call him Catfish. He was hesitant about his name, and immediately I knew it was not real. I realized he was a she. We shook hands smiling as the outboards roared, signaling our flight to freedom."

"That was quite an ordeal. That's why I hate those shitheads so much! The only thing they understand is bullets, bullets and more bullets!" Captain Manny said as he took his handkerchief out of his left pocket to wipe the sweat drops from his forehead.

I had finished my story to the ohs and uhhs of my audience when the door opened and I heard her snazzy voice.

"Give me two boxes of bubble gum," she demanded.

"Bazooka, right?"

"Yes, hunk."

I didn't look at first, but I knew Pepe was melting like a square of butter in an overheated pan. I turned around, fearful of being blinded by her beauty, and saw her winking at Pepe while trying to retrieve cash from her tight pockets. I excused myself from the domino players, pretending I was going to the rest room so I could contemplate her face for the first time. I wanted to look at her eyes to see if it was really her, but I walked too close to the stack of canned tomato sauce. Then I heard the avalanche of cans which made her look my way. I froze when I saw two tiny little dots in her pupils, dots that shone like tiny beacons of love in the cinnamon sea of her complexion. I stood there, watching her in awe, and she seemed to enjoy my adulation. Right there, I wanted to shout my love for her, remind her of our canopy of love at Marina's place. I wanted to scream that I would worship her and become her vestal guardian, that I would wash her with oils and caress her forever, but as I was about to tumble forward I saw an arm encircling the unmasked squirrel. It was the tattooed arm of the packing-house foreman. At that moment, I hated Nellie for not telling me my love had gotten tired of waiting for me, not because she loved me less, but out of loneliness. I felt like going to the bus station to scold Nellie for hiding the truth from me.

She was being handled by that man in such an uncaring way that I was experiencing the pains of hell. Still I didn't want to hit this man. I wanted to know where had he fallen in love with her? Where was he from? How did he spend his free time? I wanted to know everything about this thief who had stolen a part of my life. Before they left, I looked at her, begging for a sign that she had recognized me. She winked, and I knew she had. She was making me suffer to purify my love for her. For she well knows that to deprive me of her presence is to rob me of those eyes with which I see, of the sun that enlightens me, and the food that sustains me. A man without a love is like a tree without leaves, a building without mortar, or a shadow without a body to project it.

To console my loneliness, I have become an avid domino player, though I despise the game. I have built an altar of love in the utility room. It's my secret. We all have secret, unnameable wants, and now you know what mine is. What's yours? I'll let you take a peek at mine:

There is a medium-sized reproduction of a squirrel dressed in a red cape. It has a small crown on its head and holds a pecan in its hands. A silver plate by her feet is filled with bubble gum.

A work of art, isn't it? It's only a matter of time before we're together again. When she knows my love for her is decanted, she'll come to me. In the meantime, I am working overtime and sending her anonymous letters with fifty-dollar bills. They aren't really letters but notes. I sign: "Forever yours, you know who!"

I see her now once a week. I know exactly when she goes to Pepe's to replenish her gum supply, and I'm there playing dominoes and listening to the men's never ending stories of days gone by. I don't care for the bad old days because the good new days are just around the corner. The squirrel and I have exchanged a couple of words, and she continues to wink at me when she leaves. The other day I noticed she had chapped lips and I offered her my Chapstick. She let the stick roll slowly over her lips and then thanked me. I placed it in her shrine, though I was tempted to use it and kiss her this secondhand way. I knew she was testing the cleanliness of my thoughts.

Dans L'Apres Midi

The stars had faded with the dawn, and gray light had begun filtering through a small stained-glass window which portrayed an unblemished lamb surrounded by a crown of thorns. Nellie sat on a hard bench, varnish peeling from the wood, and waited, impatiently tapping her foot. Her stomach churned, growling loudly, and, embarrassed, she tried to appease it with a piece of bacon Delfina had put in her left pocket. She had arrived at three in the morning to beat the crowds and be first in line. The immigration office, housed in what had been the sacristy of the Chapel of the Sacred Heart of the Jesuit school, opened early. Across from Nellie sat a woman in a long black veil that covered her face. Nellie felt the woman watching her, but whenever she turned to look at her, the woman glanced away, as if afraid to be recognized by Nellie.

Nellie kicked the empty bench in front of her, knocking it over. Three times she had been to the old confessional which now served as a service window, and three times she had been sent to the end of the line. The officer had found errors in Nellie's application. First, it was the omission of her middle name. Nellie had written her initial instead of her name because her middle name was too provincial for her taste and she abhorred it.

"Comrade, you must write out your complete middle name. That's what the instructions at the top of the page tell you to do. Go back and erase the initial and write your complete middle name." She pointed to the line with the tip of her pencil.

"Must I write it?" Nellie asked in a defiant tone, looking at the officer irritably.

"Yes, like everybody else. There're no more privileges here. We're all the same." She peered keenly into Nellie's face.

"What about if I drop my middle name altogether?" Nellie tried to coax her.

"To the end of the line. I don't have much patience with parasites. You're lucky the revolution has gone easy with you worms. If it was up to me, I'd have shot each one of you a long time ago!" the woman shouted, her color rising.

Nellie didn't pay much attention to the officer and started to make the corrections while leaning against the wall next to the window.

"To the back of the line, I said." This time the officer gave Nellie a sharper look.

"I don't know how to deal with trash," Nellie muttered in an appalled whisper as she was about to walk back to the end of the line.

"Wait a minute. Wait a minute. I remember you, you parasite! Don't you remember me?"

Nellie shook her head.

"Of course you don't. How could you, right? But I do. I sure do. It was many years ago at the Port of Isabella. I was walking barefoot on the reef. It was low tide, and I was searching for mussels to sell to the oyster house so we could have something to eat that evening. My mother had no money to buy me shoes, but I had to walk on the reef, and it was slippery."

"You obviously have mistaken me for somebody else. I have never heard anything so silly." Vexed by having to listen to her words, Nellie had interrupted.

"Didn't you have a feather hat?"

"Yes, I did," she said with a surprised smirk. "It was one of my favorite hats, a gift from my first nanny. She was French and her name was Florinde. My second nanny was from England," Nellie said proudly.

"Then it's you. You had a pair of rose boots you were carrying while you walked on the beach. You didn't want them anymore and you were about to throw them in the trash can. I remember I ran across the reef to ask you if I could have the boots. You said 'no' and ran in the other direction and tossed them into the sea."

"I hated those rose boots! They were a gift from my grandmother Valentina. She had no taste! You should be thankful I saved you from those awful bluchers."

The officer opened the door of the old confessional and showed Nellie the foot that bore a scar which covered its entire sole, from big toe to heel.

"That day I slipped, and the sharp edge of the reef opened my foot like a hot knife going through a stick of butter. I had no shoes." She limped back to the window.

"Next," the officer said dryly.

Nellie didn't move.

"Next, I said. To the end of the line!"

The second time her application was refused because she had omitted her mother's maiden name. The last time Nellie stood by the window, the limping officer scolded her for failing to separate her surname from her Christian names with a comma. Nellie had just inserted the missing comma and was heading back to the window when the line was closed for lunch.

Nellie's new number was thirty-four. The officer called number thirty-three, the veiled woman's number. Nellie saw the officer didn't bother to read the woman's application, but insisted the Cadillac convertible she was leaving had to be in excellent condition. Then Nellie heard the banging sound of the official seal stamped on the woman's application, and the officer closed the confessional's shutters.

As Nellie and the veiled woman crossed each other, the latter produced from her wrappings a minuscule, grubby piece of paper which she slipped into Nellie's hand. Nellie clutched it and quickly read its contents.

"Nellie, there's something going on. Be careful! A friend who used to drive a red convertible. Please swallow after reading!"

Nellie was chewing on the piece of paper when the door opened and the room was awash in an explosion of light. She looked down to cover her eyes from the glare, not noticing the advancing figure of a heavyset man. She heard the door close behind him and the clicking of the padlock.

"Well, if it isn't Miss Nellie Pardo, or should I call you Mrs. Guiristain? We meet again," the intruder giggled excitedly. Nellie recognized his horn-like voice.

"Let me out or I'll scream. The *rurales* should have shot you."

"There's no need to get personal, baby."

"Don't call me 'baby!'"

"Isn't that the name your dog calls you? I meant to say Delfina."

"I have to go home. I have things to do. Get out of my way!"

"There's no rush. There's no one around. It's past noon. It's lunch time."

Nellie tried to push her captor aside as he grabbed her roughly by her wrist and pulled her to him.

"Let go of me!" Nellie yelled, and bit his hand. He released his grip and sucked on the droplets of blood, only to grab her again. She struggled, but he only laughed.

"I have something for you." He reached in his back pocket, took out three passports, and showed them to Nellie. He read the names written on the first page in bold letters. "Nellie Caridad Pardo Dubrocq, Nelson Andrés Guiristain Pardo, María-Chiara Guiristain Pardo. I wonder who these people are? Do you know them by any chance?"

"You had them all along. May I have my documents?"

"Only if you're real nice, and this time I don't want any stuffed olives or dried fruits. But I could settle for some fresh tuna." He wet his index with saliva and touched Nellie's neck. She recoiled.

"You haven't had a man for a while, right?"

Nellie remained silent.

"Let's see, Nelson disappeared a few months ago. Maybe he tried to escape by sea and drowned, or maybe the sharks had him for lunch. You must hunger for love." He unbuttoned his shirt, revealing a smooth adipose chest with two stringy hairs on each nipple. "It's hot in here," he said, fanning his torso with his open palm. "Get comfortable. That blouse is too heavy, but let me help you so you won't ruin your nails."

"Delfina is waiting for me outside and will be getting worried. If you don't let me go, she's going to come and get me." Nellie was losing her aplomb.

"Don't be frightened, baby," he said as he got closer. "To fear love is to fear life. I know what's on your mind, and the only way to get rid of temptation is to yield to it."

Nellie rushed to the door and yanked in an futile attempt to pry it open.

"Don't you want these passports?" he said matter-of-factly.

"Yes," Nellie answered unwillingly.

"Here." He extended his hand in her direction. Nellie approached and he grabbed her, planting a sloppy kiss on her ear. "I love stolen kisses. C'mon and sit on my lap and I'll give you your passports and tell you exactly how Don Andrés died. I'll tell you anyway. Your father had a peaceful death. I personally saw to it. He was taken to the dungeon downstairs and the crabs came with the high tide and feasted on his eyes. I think he was still alive when we dumped him there. It's hard to tell sometimes."

Nellie felt afraid for the first time and remembered her father's advice of never fearing fear. She was trembling.

"You must be cold, baby. Let me warm you up." He unloosened his belt, but his pants held tight to his distended belly. He pulled them down, showing his olive-green underwear. "Would you care for a drink? Perhaps a glass of port from the cellars of the Ladies' Tennis Club to calm you a bit? I saved a few bottles for you the day the masses repossessed the club in the name of its rightful owners, the people. They got carried away and burned a few things. I knew someday we were destined to meet again, so I saved the wine for you," he said, laughing.

"Were you the one who kept sending me to the back of the line each time I got to the window?" Nellie mustered her courage to sound in control, but with her last words her voice reached a squeak and crackled.

"Oh, no. I had nothing to do with that. She hated you on her own. It was fate that brought us together. Take your clothes off!" He began to caress her hair. "You know something, baby, I don't like your hair up. Undo it for me. I love it long when it touches your back. Like the day you came to see your father in jail. Oh, no. I remember it was long but not braided."

Rulfo grabbed her by her hair, and as she tried to break free from his hold, her dress tore and her Belgian-lace bra ripped, her breasts bouncing free. He forced her down to the floor and bit her neck until she bled. She trembled from anger, pain and fear, and then felt the cool air on her skin and the warmth of an amorphous surface enveloping her.

"Kisses are the small change of love. Give me the big bills, baby!"

Nellie turned pale and stared as if she were frozen. She was rigid except for the movement of her breasts going up and down with her altered breathing.

"Don't you look at me like that!" he growled as a gust of rage shook him.

He didn't see sorrow in her eyes. Not even hatred. He was nothing in her eyes.

"I'll kill you if you don't stop looking at me like that!"

Those were the last words Nellie remembered him saying as the room began to spin and Mondovi careened into her mind. Each postcard Don Andrés had received from his Italian friend, Sergio Bruno, which Nellie now kept inside an old Habanos box, helped to numb her senses, delivering her from her plight. The Piedmont village came to life in her mind with its Belvedere Tower, the new trolley station, The Three Lemons Hotel and the Theater on the Piazza with Eleonore Dusé center stage, her open mouth suspended in time forever. She felt someone embracing her, possibly Sergio, but she couldn't tell because he had approached from behind and covered her eyes. It felt so real she could feel his heavy breathing against her neck on that cold autumn day.

She felt her body rocked back and forth as her mouth recited Sergio's last postcard to her father.

> *When you cable, I always feel a strong emotion that's hard to explain.*

"Yeah, baby. Give it to me!"

> *Perhaps because you're a true friend or perhaps because an immense ocean is between us.*

"I said, give it to me. Talk dirty to me. I know you love it!"

> *Dear Andrés, I'm going through difficult times and emerging from the depth of sorrow. My dear father passed away.*

"Say it. Say take me, take me" he screamed. Her absent look was making him jealous. "Scream! I want you to yell and scream! At least cry. I want you to cry!"

There was a loud scream, then a sigh of relief and Nellie felt the weight of a collapsing mass. She was sure it was Sergio's sorrow.

> *I've found myself old and alone.*
>
> > *Un abraccio,*
> > *Sergio*

Her mind was ready to play back the Belvedere-Tower scene when she was slapped, and then the door closed behind the departing trespasser. Three passports landed on her bruised body as Nellie's lips finished reciting Sergio's last card to Don Andrés. Then she heard him say, "You're gonna beg for my love one day!"

All was calm, all was still, and a fine mist seemed to be falling in the room. She lay silently in the quietness, staring into nothingness, her hands clenching the passports, her mind drifting on air.

Do You Know the Way
to Mondovi?

The night was so still it was possible to hear heavy dew-drops falling from the ficuses when Nellie mustered her courage and cut across her backyard to the Olsen's. She rehearsed her excuses just in case Mr. James B. opened the door, interspersing her lines with prayers that it wouldn't happen. It didn't. The coach wasn't home that night. He had gone with Speedy, Jack, the reverend and a few others to the Big Cypress reservation with the excuse of avenging the fire that consumed two of the town's most prominent stores, The Pawn Shop and Red's Fish Market. Speedy had used Stanley's allegation that he had seen Indians fleeing from the scene of the fire as the perfect excuse to avenge the opprobrium his grandmother had endured sixty-two years earlier at the hands of Chekaika, the sleepy warrior. Nellie knocked on Mrs. James B.'s door, and at the very same instant, on the other side of the Big Lake, Speedy and his caravan of pickup trucks had entered the reservation. They had exchanged their Indian attire for Davy Crockett hats, and went looking for the chief.

Mrs. James B. had placed her unmentionable secret in a yellow glass and put it in the bottom drawer of her night-stand. She heard the leaves rustling and then a slight, almost inaudible knock. She quickly put on her robe and had her hand on the knob when she realized her teeth were bathing comfortably in the glass. She rushed back to her room and put them in.

"Nellie, have you gone squirrel food? If Mr. James B. catches you here, your body will have as many holes as a sieve. But you lucked out. He ain't here."

Nellie, recklessly euphoric, told her friend her news, "Rigoletto is alive!"

"I thought your Papá had passed away a few years back," Mrs. James B. responded.

Nellie refreshed Mrs. James B.'s memory, and told her Rigo was alive and well and hunting for truffles in Mondovi by the foothills of the Alps. Mrs. James B. couldn't understand why a grown woman would get so bent out of shape over a pig, but she kept her feelings to herself.

"Nellie, I'm glad your pig is alive, but it's getting late and I have to be by the Big Lake at the crack of dawn. The reverend is baptizing some folks that just accepted the Lord, including Jack's girlfriend. You know, the one who works with us at the packing house? Anyway, I don't care if she did accept Him as her personal savior. To me, she still looks cheap."

"Mrs. James B., you don't understand. Tonight at twelve I'm leaving for Mondovi, and I would like for you to accompany me. I know how much your family was humiliated by Sherman and how you have continued to bear that burden."

"I swan, Nellie. I don't know what to say."

"There you can be what you were meant to be."

Mrs. James B. felt uneasy with Nellie's pig and travel talk and darted to the kitchen to make some coffee so she could think clearly. Nellie noticed that her face was swollen.

"Mrs. James B., do you know there aren't any bees or wasps in Mondovi?"

"Is that a fact?"

"My father always said the only thing that could bother a mortal in Mondovi were the snowflakes in winter."

Nellie was still standing in the Florida room when Mrs. James B. spoke.

"Well, Nellie, when is it that you are leaving?"

"Tonight at midnight."

"If you see me at your door by a quarter 'til twelve, then you know I'm going. Here, take some coffee home for yourself.

"Thank you, Mrs. James B."

"You're welcome, honey. How far did you say that place is?"

"It's a little bit farther than California, but in the other direction."

Mrs. James B. heard a car approaching and asked Nellie to rush out.

When Nellie left, Mrs. James B. paced up and down the house, looking for an answer. She went to the kitchen and checked on the Jamestown chicken boiling in the kettle for the coach's dinner. This time he hadn't called, and she didn't know exactly how much time she had to make up her mind. Then she thought about her children, James B. and Missy, and how much they would miss her when they came home for their summer recess. Mrs. James B. was almost in tears when she realized she didn't really have any children.

"What the hell, if I don't like it I can always come back. If he really misses me, he'll fetch me," she said aloud to herself.

She put on a pair of tight jeans and high heels and placed her makeup kit and three blouses in a small, brown grocery bag.

Nellie, clad in her taffeta gown, had passed the second stop sign from her house when she heard someone yell.

"Wait up, Nellie."

Nellie hugged her friend, and for the first time they walked side by side.

"I made us some sandwiches for the trip. I stole a breast from the chicken I made for Mr. James B. He can have the rest. I thought about taking my car, but it's got hardly no gas. Are we walking to Mondovi?"

"I didn't bring much cash with me."

"That will not pose a problem. Nelson gave me five-hundred dollars. He has been saving for this day without my knowledge. He sensed this would happen. I am glad I consented to our engagement on the night of the eclipse."

"Hey, Nellie, I have an idea. To save us some money, let's walk to the truck stop and hitch a ride with one of my friends. We're bound to see someone I know there."

"Well, I don't know. Nelson said to take the bus."

"Listen, with the money you save, you could buy something nice for your pet."

"That's a very good suggestion. I guess there will be no harm in stopping there."

"At the next yield sign we'll turn left."

"Aren't your kids coming?"

"I left them with Nelson, and I have sent for Delfina. He said I needed some time alone with Rigo. I'll send for them as soon as I get settled."

"Not so fast, Nellie. I'm on my heels."

"Our encounter will be so filled with emotion."

"I always wanted to go overseas."

"How many more blocks, Mrs. James B.?"

"Three more blocks. We turn right on Avenue B."

"Howdy, boys. Which one of you nice-looking men is gonna give us a ride to Jax?"

"I'll take you to hell if you ask me," answered a man with a large, overflowing belly.

Before Mrs. James B. had a chance to reply, Nellie grabbed her by the blouse and whispered in her ear.

"Not with the obese man. Please, not with him."

"Why not?"

"I'll tell you at another time, but please, not with the obese man."

"Okay, but hush." She quickly addressed the man. "It ain't just for me. My friend is coming also."

The bellyman hesitated, and the thin man that sat across the room, the one with the big mermaid tattoo, took advantage of his indecision and shouted, "I'll give you ladies a ride, both of you."

"It's a deal," Mrs. James B. yelled back.

The thin man walked to where the two women were and began to talk.

"And what takes you two to Jax?"

"My granny is sick, and I'm going up to take care of her, and my friend is gonna give me a hand. Granny is a big heavy woman, too big for me to handle by myself."

"Well, gals, let me finish eating my eggs and we all can hop in my rig." Then he added, "Do you wanna see her dance?" pointing to the mermaid and flexing the only elevation in his entire body, his pecs. The sea creature began moving her hips.

"Ain't he a riot?" said Mrs. James B.

Mermaidman walked to the cash register, paid his bill, and headed for the door followed by the hitchhikers. It was beginning to soot when the door to the trucker's joint closed behind them.

"Damn soot! I hate them sugar mills. I've just finished cleaning the windshield!"

Mermaidman got inside the truck, opened the door and, seeing that it was too high for the gals to leap up, got off the truck, went around, and gave Mrs. James B. a push from behind. Nellie insisted on not being pushed and was hoisted by her hands once the other two were inside the truck. The truck began to back up slowly and headed up Main Street and then turned left at the only traffic light on route to Highway 441.

"How old did you say your mama was?" asked the teamster.

"It's not my mama. It's my grandma. She'll be seventy-one a week from tomorrow."

"My mama passed on a year ago."

"That's a shame."

"Your friend doesn't talk much."

"She has a speech problem. She's almost deaf. Her mother had a rough labor, but I've learned to do deaf people's language. Do you wanna see?"

"Sure. I ain't never seen it done before."

Mrs. James B. started doing her repertoire of made-up signs and talked very slowly to Nellie when the mermaidman told her to hush.

"Hey, shut up a minute, y'all. It's may favorite song." The rhythms of "Coconuts" drenched the cabin and Mermaidman turned his head to face Mrs. James B. as he rocked with the song and puckered his lips each time the song reached his favorite line.

"I'm coconuts over you, baby." He repeated the refrain as he looked at Mrs. James B. with bovine lust.

"Do you know where I heard that song first?" asked Mrs. James B. to distract his attention.

"Where, babe?"

"At the packing house. One of the gals was humming it a few months back. I wonder where she heard it?"

Silence had set in and Nellie looked up to the sky, her head hanging out of the window, studying the constellations and thinking that one of them should be named in honor of her Rigo. And with such happy thoughts she fell sleep while a heavy fog wet her cheeks. It was hard to drive, and Mermaidman wrestled with the wheel, keeping the rig away from the treacherous, soft shoulders. Then there was a loud shout which awoke Nellie from her sidereal slumber.

"Okay, toothpick, that did it. Stop this truck. We want out right here."

Mermaidman laughed and paid no attention to the screaming Mrs. James B. She was fuming, and in her rage pushed her muscular legs with all her might against the gas pedal, forcing Mermaidman's fragile foot to floor the accelerator. The rig sputtered and moved forward at an uncontrollable speed.

"Are you out of your mind? Let go of the cincher, you bitch!"

"If you don't let us out, I swear I'll crash this truck against that tree over yonder."

Mermaidman became frightened by her determination and slowly pressed the brakes with his left foot, begging Mrs. James B. to set his right foot free.

"No tricks, or I'll crash the whole darn thing." She released the pressure she was exerting on his foot and the truck came to a halt. The women jumped out of the cabin near a sign that said, "Mosquito Lagoon next left."

"I hope the 'noseenms' eat you alive, you mouldy sluts!" Those were Mermaidman's parting words.

"What happened?" said Nellie, puzzled by what had transpired, smoothing out the creases in her dress.

"That booger! He got carried away during the fog. He put his hand on my lap about an hour ago and I said to myself I could put up with it as long as he took us to Jacksonville. But after that second big bump, his hand moved down, and he pissed me off. I'll be cow-kicked if I was gonna let that piss-head touch me. If he wants to touch, he can handle his jingle berries! I told you we should have gotten the ride with the fat guy. Why don't you like fat people?"

"I did not say I did not like fat people, Mrs. James B. I don't like people with big bellies. That's all."

"You talk to Pituca in the packing house. She sure has a big gut!"

"She is a woman. It's different."

"So you don't like men with big, fat bellies?"

"That is correct."

"Why?"

"Just because... Isn't there anything you don't like, Mrs. James B.?"

"I hate football!"

"I thought you loved being a cheerleader?"

"Don't get me wrong, sugar. I loved being a cheerleader. It's the players I don't like."

"Why?" Nellie was puzzled.

"Just because…" Mrs. James B. hesitated and said, "Just because they get a beer belly when they quit playing."

"I understand, Mrs. James B. But there are no fat men in Mondovi and no one knows anything about football or baseball."

"Don't call me Mrs. James B. anymore, sugar. My name is Wavene.

Nellie remained silent, and after a while asked how they were going to get to their destination. Mrs. James B. was confident and told her not to worry, that they would hitch a ride with someone.

"We ain't that far away, just a couple of hours south. I ain't gonna give up now. You said there were no bugs over there either, right?"

"My father never mentioned them. I am sure if there are any, they don't bother people. Is Mr. James B. coming to join you? He could come together with Nelson and the children."

"I ain't counting on it. He's never been fond of strange people."

"What about Missy and James B. III?"

"You can lend me some money over there, and I can come and fetch them after their schooling is over. I know Missy is gonna love it over there. She's getting all A's in her school, and James B. III is the perfect gentleman. I think that's why I'm coming with you. That place sounds better for their raising."

They kept talking and signaling with their hands to the approaching vehicles that they needed a ride. They were talking about spending the rest of the night under a big live oak when a scooter stopped a few feet behind them and roared.

"Hey, ladies, need a ride?" said a soft, whistling voice.

"We sure do," answered Mrs. James B.

"You two ladies shouldn't be out this late round these parts. Too many Indians on the loose. How far are you going?" As he spoke Mrs. James B. noticed his tiny teeth and his deformed index fingers.

"Up to Jax to see my sick granny. This is my friend. She's helping me, but she can't speak much. She's kind of deaf mute." Nellie showed her disapproval by pinching her on the rear. Mrs. James B. yelled ouch and pretended it was a mosquito.

"I myself am going to Savannah. Is your grandma real sick?"

"She sure is. She's throwing up cats and dogs."

"How's that possible?" asked Nellie.

"I thought you said she couldn't speak."

"That's all she knows how to say and she says it all the time." Mrs. James B. looked at Nellie and opened her eyes as wide as possible for Nellie to take the hint. She did.

"How's that possible, how's that possible, how's that possible."

"You see. We got her going," smiled Mrs. James B.

"The same thing happened to my grandma."

"She says 'how's that possible' all the time?"

"No, no, I meant that she threw up a lot before she passed on. She had the black vomit. Maybe your grandma has it, too. I'll drive you all the way to her door."

"That's mighty fine on your part. She lives by the docks."

"I took care of my grandma till she gave up the ghost. She was a big woman. It took seven of us to move her every time she went to the potty."

"My granny is pretty big, too, but not that big. It just takes two of us."

"She was strong all the way around. She raised me and my six brothers and sisters. She could throw some mean shoes if we was horsing around." The scooterman looked for something inside his backpack and offered it to Mrs. James B. "You care for some moon pies?"

"I can trust a man who eats moon pies. Them things are my very favorite." She smiled as she bit into the moon.

"Here, give one to your friend." He handed Mrs. James B. another pie. "You should try to please your grandma all you can. You just can't tell how much longer she's gonna be around. That's what I did with my grandma. She made me promise I would do something to this Indian who had been real nasty to her when she was sixteen. That's why my pop didn't have a pop. I was true to my word and he ain't no more. Okay, sweeties, let's go. Your friend can ride in the sidecar, and you can hold on to me on the hog."

"What's in the sack?" asked Mrs. James B. as she sat in the saddle and looked down.

"It's a gourd. Do you want to feel it?"

"It sure is hard and heavy for a gourd! It'll make a nice house for some birds."

"That's exactly how I'm gonna use it. Get a big ole pole and anchor the gourd and hoist in Grandma's backyard. My sister Beulah is living there now."

The sun's glare began to blind the motorcycle riders as they approached the waterfront.

"Which dock?" asked the man.

"The main dock," shouted Mrs. James B. as she held her hair in place with one hand and grasped his waist with the other. Nellie was wide awake, trying to swat with her open palms the flies that had gathered on the sack with the oozing gourd.

Mrs. James B. pointed to a group of houses across the main dock, and the scooter veered to the right toward the houses. The scooterman insisted on accompanying them to the door of the blue house with the bright yellow roof, but Mrs. James B. dissuaded him. She told him how peculiar her grandmother was about strangers and that she didn't want to upset her. They waved to the man from the porch and pretended to open the door with an imaginary key. Luckily, the house had been condemned years ago. When the scooterman disappeared behind the grain elevators, Mrs. James B. grew nervous.

"Are you sure there ain't no football players over there?"

"There are none, Wavene. We don't even have that word in our language!"

"What do them people eat?"

"Food, of course," Nellie said matter-of-factly.

"No, you know what I mean. I mean if they eat regular food like fried chicken, hamburgers, corn dawgs and stuff like that."

"Oh, no! We eat truffles, prosciutto e melone, and pasta. But people aren't fat. There are no fat people in Mondovi! And you can't remember what you don't want to remember!"

"I guess I'll be doing my own cooking. I ain't eating none of that stuff!"

"Do you know what's the first thing I'll do when I land in Mondovi?"

"What?"

"I'll kiss Rigo!"

"How do you know he's gonna be waiting for you?"

"I just know he is."

"I swear, Nellie, you're giving me the heebie-jeebies. Do I have to kiss your pig, too?"

"Don't call him a pig! And I doubt that he'll let you kiss him. He's very choosy!"

"Believe me, I don't want to kiss him neither! So what do we do now, lollipop?"

"Is all very simple, Wavene," said Nellie. "We ask which ship is heading for Mondovi and pay our passage."

"Is that all? That easy?"

"Sure. We don't need a round-trip ticket. We are not coming back." Nellie sounded determined, and Mrs. James B. lost her fear.

"I need a cup of coffee, sugar!"

They walked up and down the docks asking the same questions and getting the same negative answers or simply a shrug. Mrs. James B.'s confidence was beginning to waver when a sailor told them about a ship that was about to dock.

They waited by the shore. Nellie washed the ends of her dress with salt water and sand; the gourd had stained it some. Mrs. James B. puffed on a cigarette. At mid-afternoon, they saw a column of smoke on the horizon. A few hours later the Albenga made several unsuccessful attempts at docking. When it finally succeeded, sailors waved and whistled at them from the bow.

"They have recognized us," said Nellie. "Maybe Nelson cabled Sergio and Sergio informed the ship about us."

"They sure know we are coming. That's a rowdy bunch."

They got closer and Mrs. James B. asked them if they were heading back to Mondovi. The sailors didn't seem to understand and Nellie tried speaking their language for the first time in her life. She was excited to be able to speak to the people she always regarded as her countrymen.

"*Quando ritornano a Mondovi?*"

The sailors signaled them to come on board, and the two ladies started their ascent up the rope ladder. Nellie made sure her dress wasn't caught by the wind to make her look unladylike.

"*Quando partono per Mondovi?*" She posed her question again as she was a few feet from the deck.

The whistling grew into a wild hissing sound as Mrs. James B.'s tight jeans came into view.

"I think I'm gonna like that Mondovi," Mrs. James B. shouted at Nellie.

Nellie turned her face to the ocean, grasping the railing, and said to the wind, "I smell the Ellero River already."